Touchstone

Touchstone

BY LILLIAN JANET

Rinehart & Company, Inc.

New York   Toronto

3471

CONTENTS

PART ONE

Agnes

1850

CHAPTER I

ANDY HART leaned against the hotel railing and squinted into the bright July sun. His slight, wiry body was relaxed, and his pipe, which had gone out, was slack between his teeth. The sun was pleasantly hot through the red flannel of his miner's shirt, and he leaned even closer against the railing, feeling the heat of the wood where the sun had been beating on it a moment before.

Before him, Portsmouth Square shifted and teemed with the numberless human misfits that constituted San Francisco in 1850. Native Californians, of Spanish descent, strolled by in their bright serapes, a certain aloofness betraying their pride in the land, their knowledge of a prior claim upon it. Indians roamed half naked, and Chinese in their coarse blue linen smocks, wide trousers and straw hats trudged with endless weariness, baskets of fish and vegetables suspended from poles over their shoulders. There were Hindus in turbans and flowing outer garments, and here and there a heavily bearded Russian. The French-Canadian was distinguishable by his rapid flow of words and the quick gestures of his dark, supple body. There were a few Negroes. Not many women could be seen—only an occasional satin-clad harlot advertising her calling and finding a ready clientele among the men, the majority of whom wore mining outfits identical with Andy's. Once in a while another type of woman passed by—a stocky, red-faced, hardhanded woman, clad in a gray linsey-woolsey dress that reached just below her calves. Sometimes she wore under it a pair of men's trousers, and stout, heavy shoes. Under her poke bonnet was the sunburned, determined face of the pioneer wife, who had shared the hardships of the trip west with her man. She was still rare in San Francisco in the summer of 1850.

Portsmouth Square itself was alive with the riot of noise and color that characterized the city's gambling district, and its appearance on this hot summer afternoon was but a prelude of what it would become after dark. Not for a single hour of the day was it

3

idle, and even now, as the sun beat down and invited an after-dinner nap or a quiet walk on the outskirts of town, the shouts of dealers and the rattle of roulette wheels could be heard coming through the open doors of the gilded gambling palaces and "hells" up and down the street. Their plate-glass windows shot back the sun's reflections, and the light glanced off their hastily and crudely painted signs.

Outside, in the street, several dealers had set up open-air games of faro and monte, to lure the fresh-air lovers and coax out those who were already inside. The dealer snapped and shuffled the cards with grandiose gestures, and his casekeeper rattled the buttons on their steel rods to attract the attention of passers-by.

"Ready for the first turn, gents!" the dealer shouted. "Place your bets for the first turn! A completely new deal starting over here. Examine the cards yourself, gents! Every corner squared! Place your bets!"

Andy shook his head and smiled as he watched men stop and draw out their bags of gold dust. They never learned.

The street before him was unpaved and dusty, for the first winter rain was yet to come. Horses, mules and oxen raised clouds of dust as they galloped or plodded through the streets. It settled in a thick coating on the little stalls where sweetmeats and yellow-backed novels were out for sale.

Andy was older than most men in San Francisco that year, for men came west young. He wore spectacles. His arms were folded loosely in front of him, giving him a look of complete relaxation and rounding out the impression of an indifferent bystander.

Then, suddenly, his whole attitude changed.

His teeth gripped his pipe, bringing it up to a position at rigid right angles with his face. His lazy squint became a wide, interested stare which no longer heeded the afternoon sun, and he pushed the broad brim of his felt hat back from his forehead as though it impeded his vision.

Coming down the crudely nailed board walk which skirted the dusty street were a man and a young girl, both staggering slightly under the burden of an assortment of purchases which they had apparently just made.

The man was unusually tall; well over six feet, with a thick mat of red hair, the crown of which protruded from under a pushed-back felt hat. He was wearing the red flannel shirt and knee boots of the miner, but every item of apparel had about it a gloss of unworn newness, as well as thick creases that marked the folds in which it had lain in its box at the store. The boots too shone, unsullied by the dust of the street, and the man stepped carefully in them as though to safeguard their finish. Slung across his shoulders was a heavy pack roll such as prospectors were accustomed to take with them to the northern mines. One brawny hand firmly clutched a pick and shovel and the other carried an assortment of buckets, tins and screens, which clashed together with every step and made him resemble a hawker beating his wares.

Andy judged him to be perhaps forty, although his face was youthful. He was handsome, with the strong, earthy features of a farmer or blacksmith. Andy cocked his head slightly, speculating momentarily, as he always did, on what a man's profession had been before he came west. The eyes were gray, set wide apart, and with a frank ingenuousness about them. The nose was slightly up-tilted at the end, and the mouth under a sweeping reddish mustache was wide and full. A good face, Andy decided, pleasant and guile-less. It was slightly freckled and now it seemed to redden, deepening its already ruddy cast, as though in half-pleased embarrassment over the attention the clattering pans were drawing.

The girl walking beside him could not have been more than thirteen, and her resemblance to the man was so striking that a number of passers-by stopped and stared as the two made their slow way. She was tall, somewhat gangling with the awkwardness of her age, and had the same dark-red hair. It was long, and hung untidily about the shoulders of her gray dress. She was carrying a dark suit over her arm, obviously the one the man had discarded after pur-chasing his new attire, and now and again she brushed a stray fleck of dust from it and readjusted its folds carefully.

Over her other arm she carried a basket which apparently con-tained provisions for the trek northward, and from time to time she would set it down, shifting her burdens from one arm to the other. On her head she wore a wide-brimmed felt hat like the man's, and frequently she was obliged to reach up awkwardly with the hand that held the suit and push it back as it started to slide forward over her eyes. Andy smiled at the sight. Her features were like the man's only on a diminutive scale; wide gray eyes, slightly turned-up nose, freckles, and a broad, pleasant mouth. She looked up at her father and they giggled a little self-consciously at each other.

They reached the front of the hotel, and Andy drew back slightly in deference to the amount of space taken up by their assorted purchases.

"Better stop here for a minute and rest, lovey," the man said. "We've still got a good walk ahead of us."

"I'm not tired."

"You will be, never fear. Climb up there on the step and sit for a spell."

"All right."

She climbed up to the second step, balancing the heavy basket against the suit on the other arm, when suddenly, without warning, the oversized hat which had been balancing tipsily on her head slid forward and completely obliterated her vision. The man burst out laughing, the buckets and pans at his side rattling an accompaniment, and the girl joined in, her wide mouth and teeth the only visible features. As she shook with laughter, however, she began to lose her balance, and with a shriek she started to topple from the step.

The pick, shovel, buckets, and tins went flying and clattering about the walk as her father put out both arms to stop her, but Andy had already jumped forward and caught her. With a quick motion he also managed to retrieve the basket of salt pork, flour and black-eyed peas that was lurching past his ear.

"There now!" he said kindly, settling her firmly on the bottom step and handing her the basket. "No damage done."

She pushed back the hat, red and embarrassed.

"Thank you. I'm terribly clumsy."

The man stepped forward and gripped his hand with a quick instinctive warmth that Andy liked.

"That was mighty kind of you, sir. We're much obliged. You all right, sweetheart?"

The girl nodded shamefacedly.

Andy nodded toward the scattered mining equipment.

"Better retrieve your possessions, sir, before someone else decides he can use them."

The man turned, and with Andy's help picked up the things. He settled them in a neat pile and then sank down on the step beside the girl, wiping his perspiring forehead with a red bandanna.

He extended his hand again.

"My name's John Delaney, sir. We're most grateful to you."

Andy took the hand.

"I'm Andy Hart. Isn't the day a bit warm to be doing so much shopping?"

"I want to get started as soon as possible." Delaney replaced the bandanna and nodded toward the girl. "This is my daughter, Treese."

Andy shook her hand gravely. "Delighted, Miss Treese."

The girl peered up at him shyly and murmured something.

"How far do you figure on going?"

Delaney removed his hat and rubbed his head.

"Figured on heading for Marysville and then striking out east from there."

"Over toward Rough-and-Ready, Grass Valley way?"

"That's how the map reads. Know anything about the diggings up there?"

Andy shrugged and resumed his easy stance against the hotel. "Same as every place, I suppose. Depends on the luck."

Delaney took in his attire with a glance.

"You prospecting yourself?"

Andy shook his head, smiling. "I only dress like this for comfort. The law's my business."

"You're a lawyer?" There was admiration in Delaney's tone.

Andy nodded. "I was west before the first strike. Came out because I liked it here. Got sick of the East. They can't take advancement beyond a certain point; it stumps them. They'd rather die of dry rot. But it's different out here."

"I know," Delaney cut in eagerly. "I can feel it already. It's a whole new world out here."

"Hope it stays that way. That's the one thing the West has to offer, in spite of fleas and frostbite and sunburn and the dysentery. There's an undercurrent here you can't miss. Peculiar kind of equality, you might say. You never dare spit on your neighbor because tomorrow he might strike it rich and be a millionaire." Andy took out a match and struck it against the railing.

Delaney leaned forward, anxious to continue the conversation.

"You live in San Francisco?"

Andy puffed diligently for a moment, then shook his head as he flicked the match away.

"Sacramento City! I've been there from the start. Went to Sutter's Fort back early in 'forty-eight—did a little trading, but mostly took it easy. Then, after the gold strike, when everybody began to flock out here, I kinda drifted back into the law, such as it was. Not much of any law here then. But people had to have their claims untangled and their boundaries settled—I got to be a jack of all trades." He laughed a little contemptuously. "Like to see any of those fancy stiff-front lawyers back in Philadelphia rule on whether a man's justified in trading his woman for a brace of pack mules."

"You've had to?" Delaney marveled.

"More than once. Generally I ruled in favor of it, providing the man with the mules didn't think he was getting the short end of the deal."

Delaney shook his head in wonderment and the girl Treese stared up at Andy wide-eyed. The latter drew in deeply on his pipe for a moment. Then he inquired, "Bring your whole family with you?"

"All but my oldest," Delaney answered proudly. "Got a boy sixteen still back east going to school. Stays with his grandfather. My wife's set on having him a professional man. She wants him to come out here later and read law with my brother King."

Andy frowned and studied Delaney for a moment.

"You're not King Delaney's brother!"

"Yep."

"Well, I'll be damned! Beg pardon, miss. Why in thunder didn't you say so?"

"You know him?" Delaney beamed.

"Know him! Used to know him before I ever laid eyes on California. Used to be acquainted with his wife's family back in Philadelphia. That's how I came to know King. I was a young squirt at the time. Remember well when he got married."

"You don't say!"

"Why sure! He came west a little ahead of me, and then when I got out here I looked him up. We had some good times together, just the two of us, before his wife and daughter moved out to join him."

"We're staying at my uncle's house," Treese informed him.

"Are you now! Well, if that isn't—well, say, listen—I'll walk along with you then and help you with your load."

"Why, that's real good of you," Delaney said. Together, they picked up the mining equipment, and Treese, coming down from her seat on the step, walked a little behind him as they started up the street. They left Portsmouth Square and threaded their way through congested streets, into the scattered residential district of shacks and tents.

"Say you brought a wife with you?" Andy inquired.

"Wife and two more little girls; they're four and six."

Andy whistled through his teeth. "Mining camps are rough on women and children."

"Oh, they won't go with me. I'm leaving them here with King. I want to get the lay of the land first, then decide where we'll settle and all."

"You don't figure on making your home in San Francisco?"

Delaney shook his head thoughtfully. "I don't think so. I'd like to get someplace handier to the mines."

"Ever thought about Sacramento City?"

"No . . ." Delaney shook his head again slowly. "I don't know much about the country here. Figured on looking around some first."

"Good idea. Get the feel of the place. Sacramento's a good town, though. As wild as most but no worse. And a nice little spot, although of course I'm moved by sectional loyalty. You have to discount that. But it's handy to the mines, right on the river there, and it's going to grow, you watch."

"I'm mighty obliged for the suggestion," Delaney said cordially. "I imagine a place like that would suit Mrs. Delaney—" Andy noticed the care, the shade of deference with which he mentioned her. "A woman likes a community that's growing, that's going to amount to something. They like nice things, you know, and a proper place for a family."

"Naturally." Andy inclined his head slightly.

"Although I must say she's got more pluck than most," Delaney went on proudly. "Coming west was her idea. Kept talking about it and wouldn't put it out of her head."

"You come overland?"

"No, by clipper. Down the coast and then through the Isthmus."

"Don't say. That's a hard trip. Don't know but what it's easier to go around the Horn even, than through that damned isthmus."

"Yes, it was rough," Delaney admitted reminiscently. "The two little ones had a touch of fever and there wasn't proper food. But we made it, thank the good Lord, and now we're all set to make a new life for ourselves out here."

Andy could not help but be touched by his obvious sincerity. "You—uh—in business back east?" he inquired, cautiously probing into his favorite subject.

"Well, not exactly." Delaney's tone became a bit sheepish. "My father-in-law—that's the one my boy's with now—he had a dry goods and haberdashery place and I worked with him. I wasn't much of a hand at selling, though, so they put me in the office but, tarnation, I couldn't make those figures add up!" He laughed with an almost boyish abashment, and Andy, remembering his first surmise of a farmer or blacksmith, warmed toward him sympathetically.

"New England, eh?"

"Boston."

"That so! I spent some time in Boston. I suppose it's still the same."

"Oh, Boston doesn't change."

"No, I guess not." Andy's tone was sarcastic. "It's pretty much like Philadelphia. That's why I came west."

"Must have taken pluck, though, back in those days," Delaney said admiringly. Unconsciously he had fallen into the habit, so common in the West, of referring to anything besides the immediate present as "the past" or "those days." "Although my brother King was west early, come to think of it. But of course with him it was somewhat different. He had a business in trading."

"Your brother's a man of many talents."

"Oh, yes, he's been around a good bit." Again the shade of pride crept into Delaney's voice, the same little note of deference he had used in referring to Mrs. Delaney. "We never were much alike. Seems as though King was always thinking of schemes for getting ahead and all. He's done well out here, too. He's very smart."

"He's all of that!" There was a touch of dry humor in Andy's tone.

"When he wrote a letter telling us about California and all, that's when Mrs. Delaney began to get so interested. He made it sound like such a great place. And I'm glad now that we came. This place suits me somehow. I just feel everything's going to work out fine for us here."

"I hope it will." Andy was half surprised at the sincerity of his own words. Somehow he actually did wish the best for this tall, awkward man with his heavy red hands and quick-coloring face.

"Of course, King didn't make his money in mining," Delaney went on.

"Well, no. King isn't exactly the type for that." Andy smiled. "Real estate was what he got into. When the first gold strike came, everybody cleared out of town here—could have shot a cannon from one end of this street to the other without hitting a soul. King bought up a good deal of land cheap then and held onto it. Then of course since most of them didn't find any gold they began to drift back and he made a good profit on the land."

Delaney shook his head in admiration. "That's like King, to think up a scheme like that. I wouldn't have thought of it in the first place. If I did, I probably wouldn't of dared take the chance."

"You belittle yourself," Andy countered. "It's a risk to come west at all."

"Well, that's different." His self-effacing manner made him appear to be trying to withdraw within himself. "And anyway, Mrs. Delaney was the one who—" He stopped short as they drew up in front of an unpainted two-story frame house. "Well, here we are!

Come in, sir, and make the acquaintance of my wife. I don't believe King's in right now—but come in anyway."

The three went inside.

King Delaney's was one of the first two-story houses in San Francisco and, surrounded as it was by the shacks, tents and cabins that comprised the city's other dwellings, it had a look of almost formidable prosperity. That look was a true reflection of its occupants, for King Delaney was already one of the richest men in San Francisco, and his house, which in the four months of its existence had escaped two destructive fires, was typical of the "firstness" of King's way of living. He was the first man in the city to build such elaborate accommodations and then to send for his family and have them arrive in style from the East. He was practically the only man in town to employ a household servant, also brought from the East. San Franciscans, even those who had never soiled their hands with menial work before, were now obliged to scrub their own clothing and black their boots. The King Delaneys were the first family to issue invitations for social functions at their home, and it was well known that men with whom King might fraternize on Montgomery Street were not invited to his home for fear their company might be too rough for his wife and daughter.

Inside, the house was furnished simply, almost austerely. King had already begun thinking about building a larger home, and the temporary nature of the present one was emphasized by the sparseness of furniture and luxuries. Only a small part of the household goods had been shipped west.

Nevertheless, in spite of its bare simplicity, there was an indefinable elegance about Margaret Delaney's home, the same kind of aloof elegance that had hovered about Margaret herself when she arrived with her daughter Elizabeth, the first established "ladies" to make their home in San Francisco. It spoke from the polished floors, the delicate cups in which tea was served every afternoon, the refinement and symmetry of each piece of furniture. Here was no taint of the ponderous Empire period whose influence had already been felt in the East, and to which even the most reputable designers had succumbed in deference to popular demand. No ponderous, claw-footed chairs, no heavy-postered beds marred the restrained beauty of the house, a restraint so at variance with the life that went on around it. It was, in the welter of noise and confusion, of greed and passion and violence, a strangely nostalgic reminder of all that was finest and best, and that had been left behind.

Andy, a frequent visitor, never failed to notice this upon entering, and it came over him again with a surge of something that was almost sentimentality as he entered with the man and girl, and felt the first cool breath of Margaret Delaney's home, breathed deeply of its moist, dim air, so revivifying after the dry, dust-choked outdoors. A faint odor of sandalwood from the little carved boxes that held yarn and sewing permeated the air, and Andy felt himself slowly relaxing as he always did here.

"If you'll make yourself comfortable," Delaney said, "I'll find my wife. They're probably all upstairs—" He stopped short.

Andy looked up the stairs, caught his breath sharply with a little whistle of surprise. During their conversation he had drawn for himself a mental picture of the decisive Mrs. Delaney who had promoted their trip west, who had had the fortitude to endure a trip through the tortuous Isthmus with three children, who had plans to make her son a lawyer. A determined woman, he judged. Short, perhaps, a bit on the chunky side, with firm square shoulders and a way of setting her feet down when she walked so that you knew she meant business. Red-faced, perhaps, like Delaney, but with an uncompromising jaw. The real Pioneer Type.

Now, glancing at Delaney, at the slight glow that started up in his eyes, softening their gray and seeming almost to distend the pupils slightly, he knew that the woman approaching was Mrs. Delaney. But the mental revisions he was obliged to make were almost overwhelming.

CHAPTER II

AGNES DELANEY was coming down the steps toward them, a little girl clinging to each hand. The children were glowing and fresh from their naps, and they negotiated the steps laboriously, their breath coming in pants, their pink tongues stuck out with the effort. The woman's gait was steady; even, Andy observed, a trifle sensuous, not coming in short choppy steps from the knees as did most women's, but swinging easily from her hips, giving her the appearance of grace and relaxation. She was not tall, nor was her figure slim, but Andy's expert eye was quick to catch its inviting curves under the tight bodice of her foulard silk dress with its velvet-ribboned flounces and low, rounded neck. The skin that showed at her throat and plumply rounded shoulders was exquisitely white, and there were small gold earrings in her pierced ears. Her hair was dark, almost black. Even in the dimness of the hall it seemed to catch hidden lights and to shimmer as it drew back from its center part.

Irrelevantly, Andy noted that she did not wear the customary lace cap of the married woman. Her head tilted back slightly as though from the weight of the hair that was braided and coiled at the base of her neck, and the effect was to make her even more striking. She had a wide, white forehead, dark eyes and a short, straight nose. Her mouth was full and moist and dipped in at the corners to give it a provocative look. Andy made rapid mental calculations. With a son sixteen, she must be at least thirty-four. She did not look over twenty-five.

At the bottom of the step, the two little girls caught sight of Delaney and ran to him, shrieking with delight. Their exuberance did not ruffle their mother's serenity in the least. It was as if the red-gold beauty of their curls and their round, childish faces were only intended as further attributes to her own beauty, superfluous but pleasant adjuncts to her own complete womanliness.

Eagerly they seized the buckets and pans he had set down in the hall and began banging on them. Their ruffled white pantalettes flashed from under their calico dresses and white cotton aprons, and the flush of recent sleep deepened in their cheeks in the excitement of their new discovery. They began talking together rapidly in thin, lisping voices. Delaney knelt down and began to quiet them gently.

"Now, Florabelle, quiet. Listen, Violet. Hush, darlings. In a minute you can play. In a minute Papa will show you the nice things. Quiet, now." He patted and soothed them into a partial quiet, then rose and took his wife gently by the arm. Andy saw that her eyes had already scanned Delaney's new attire, looked past her husband to the motley assortment of pans and shovels, and had taken in Treese, who stood motionless behind him in the oversized hat. He sensed a slight hardening in her expression and saw her dark eyes come to thin points of displeasure, but she said nothing and her mouth still curved in its suggestion of a smile.

"Agnes dear, we've made a new friend," Delaney said cordially. "May I present Mr. Hart. My wife, sir."

There was such enormous pride in his manner that Andy could not help bowing low simply out of consideration for him.

"Mr. Hart's home is in Sacramento City, Agnes."

"We're most pleased to make your acquaintance, Mr. Hart," Agnes Delaney said. Her voice was like the rest of her, well modulated and smooth, but it lacked warmth, and it did not betray her feelings, which Andy judged were at the moment balancing between distaste and doubt.

"It's a pleasure, ma'am."

She turned away from him, and Andy experienced the strange, chilling sensation of feeling an outsider. It was a rare feeling in California, and in some vague way he resented it.

"You've been shopping, Delaney?" she asked her husband.

Andy started inwardly at her form of address. So she called him Delaney. Almost as if she were a man speaking to another man! And she wasn't pleased about that mining stuff he'd bought.

"Yes, just a few things."

"More than a few, by the looks of it. And that hat on Treese! Was that necessary? Take it off, Treese, for heaven's sake."

Andy watched the girl reach up slowly and take the hat from her head. The leather band of it had creased a little ridge across her forehead, and her hair curled slightly from the perspiration that had started out. Slowly, she turned the hat in her hands. Then she traced around the brim with one forefinger. Her expression was faraway, as though she had heard her mother's command with an inner ear and was obeying from force of long habit.

The discomfort that had stolen over Andy grew into a confusion of embarrassment. He took a step backward toward the door.

"Well, I'll be running along, if you folks don't mind. Got some things to attend to . . ."

Delaney turned to him a little self-consciously. "It was real nice getting acquainted with you, Mr. Hart. I wish you'd stay till King gets home."

"No, thanks, another time. I'd better hustle now. It's been a pleasure, ma'am—Miss Treese—"

He bowed slightly toward Agnes and smiled at Treese.

The girl smiled back, as though suddenly brought to a consciousness of the present. Agnes Delaney did not speak.

Andy hurried out the door.

Agnes looked at her husband angrily.

"Now will you please tell me what on earth all this means?"

Delaney started to speak, but she interrupted him and looked at Treese. "Go upstairs, Treese, and get dressed. You look a sight, and we'll be having tea any minute."

Without a word, the girl started upstairs. She looked singularly bedraggled and ungraceful in her soiled gray dress, dusty shoes and wrinkled black stockings, the cumbersome felt hat dangling from one hand.

"Well?" Agnes gestured impatiently in the direction of the heap of mining equipment over which the two little girls, Florabelle and Violet, were still scrambling.

"Agnes, why didn't you ask Mr. Hart to stay? He was very kind—"

"Oh, shut up!" Her mouth curled contemptuously. "What about all this?" The two little girls stopped playing and stared, their mouths slightly open.

"Why, it's my equipment, Agnes. I want to get started right off. Wasted too much time here already. Why, there won't be enough gold left—"

"Wasted time! We've only been here three weeks and you talk of wasting time! So you go out and spend probably every last cent we've got in the world on a lot of fool trash."

"It's not fool trash, dear," Delaney said patiently, dreading her anger, but noting unconsciously how much it heightened her beauty. "It's all necessary at the mines. If I'm going to do any prospecting I'll need every bit of it."

"Prospecting! Oh, this is wretched!" The color mounted in Agnes's cheeks. "Couldn't you have waited? Couldn't you have asked King's advice?"

"Well, with all due respect to King, dear, he's hardly an authority on the mines. You know he never did have much to do with them."

"And I suppose *you* have! I suppose *you* know all about them! *You* can just start right out and locate a million-dollar claim for yourself!"

"Well, no, nothing like that. But I've bought a couple of good maps—"

"Oh, this is unbelievable!" Her breast was moving rapidly with anger. "And just how much did you have to pay for this trash?"

Delaney hedged. "Whatever it cost, it was worth it. Agnes, I can't go prospecting—"

"I know—never mind. But I also know the outrageous prices these conniving merchants charge. If you got all this for less than two hundred dollars, I'll be surprised."

Delaney, who had spent precisely two hundred and ten dollars for his supplies, did not reply.

"I see," Agnes said scornfully. "So I'm right. And that leaves us one hundred and fifty dollars. With one hundred and fifty dollars I'm supposed to keep body and soul together to say nothing of feeding three children until you get back from God knows where. And with eggs three dollars apiece!"

"You'll be here with King, Agnes. King will take good care of you."

"Charity! Now I'm to take charity from King and Margaret while you chase off with your shovels and pans."

Delaney looked bewildered. "But, dear, I can't understand your attitude. I thought all along that was what we came west for. To look for gold. What else is there to do?"

"Your brother found plenty of other ways to make money."

"I'm not like King, Agnes."

"You don't need to tell me!"

"All the way out here, when I talked about looking for gold, you never objected or said you had any other plans—"

"Well, maybe I didn't. But it was only because I thought when we got here you'd see all the possibilities. I thought you'd put yourself in King's hands and let him advise you. But no, you have to go off and do this! And who knows, you might get yourself killed up there in that wilderness—" Her voice broke and she sat down hard on a bench in the hallway.

Delaney, suddenly construing her anger as concern for his welfare, went and sat beside her, putting an arm across her shoulders.

"Agnes—darling, you're worried about me—is that it?"

She raised her head and stared at him. There was no trace of tears. Her expression was one of utter astonishment. She drew a deep breath.

"Oh, Lord!" she screamed. "Take your hands off me!"

Delaney drew his hand back as though it had been burned. Slowly he got up from the bench and leaned against the banister. He could feel a familiar sense of frustration coming over him, a consciousness of his own ineptness such as always came over him at one of these encounters with Agnes. Never, as far back as he could remember, had he been quite able to please her. He had tried hard, and in so many ways.

Now there was this new thing—her strange objection to his going out and looking for gold. It was completely beyond his comprehension. Everyone came to California for gold, unless they were like King, enterprising and able to find an easier way; or like Andy Hart, without any particular craving for money.

He turned to her. She was still sitting on the bench staring angrily ahead of her. Color showed behind the pale translucence of her skin and her eyes were fixed at a point past him. He glanced at the pile of mining equipment. The pick and shovel were propped at a crazy angle against the stairs and the pans and pails sprawled in an untidy heap. What was he to do? He longed to go to her, to

explain this feeling, this strange conviction he had, that were ⌐
give up the idea of going to the mines he would be giving up his la
claim to individuality. What was it Andy Hart had said? A peculiar
kind of equality. "You never dare spit on your neighbor, because
tomorrow he might strike it rich and be a millionaire."

That was what he wanted. To be, just for a time, a part of that
feeling; to be even the minutest part of the moving, shifting mass
that was the West, not a transplanted dry goods clerk setting up
shop in a different town. He swallowed hard.

"I must go, Agnes. If I don't make out, then—I'll do what you
want. But I have to have a try at it first."

She did not raise her eyes to him. Instead, she said indifferently,
"Do as you like." There was a cool detachment in her tone, as
though she was addressing a complete stranger, and Delaney felt a
constriction deep inside him. For a moment he felt that if he could
go to her and hold her close against him and kiss her, feel her
respond to him, hear her say she loved him, if he could feel the
touch of her warm skin under his, nothing else in the world would
matter; not gold, or the mines, or even the West. If in this moment
she would be yielding and completely his, then he would never
leave.

But even as he watched her, there was a firmness in the set of
her white shoulders, an unwavering, poised look about her. Delaney's own shoulders sagged.

Elsa, Margaret's German housekeeper, appeared in the parlor
doorway to announce tea. Her round, stolid face was expressionless,
but her pale eyes glanced from husband to wife knowingly. Elsa
did not like Agnes Delaney, and Agnes, who instinctively distrusted
servants, returned Elsa's regard in kind.

"Tea's set," she announced. "I'll see if Mrs. Delaney's up from
her nap."

She disappeared up the stairs, her broad hips giving a rhythmic
swing to her skirts. Watching the housekeeper's wide posterior
swing from view at the top of the stairs, Agnes rose and, without a
word to Delaney, went into the parlor. After a moment he followed
her.

The parlor, boasting the one carpet in the house, had more of
a hint of luxury about it than the other rooms. Against one wall
was a sofa, and at right angles to it stood a plain, high-backed
chair in which Margaret habitually sat, and in front of which the
tea table was arranged. Agnes went to the sofa and sat down,
staring at the tea tray with an insouciant disdain of him that made
Delaney wince inwardly.

Against the dark brocade of the sofa, the full whiteness of her flesh stood out in relief, nowhere betraying evidence of angularity or sharpness. There were no jutting bones in her neck, at the base of her throat, only a little, youthful hollow in which her pulse vibrated rhythmically. It seemed almost as though there were no bone structure about her—as though all was the resilient, strong flesh that showed on the surface. Only in the straightness of her posture was there an indication of an inner framework, taut and strong, on which was superimposed the lush, womanly exterior.

"Good afternoon, everyone." Margaret Delaney entered the room, followed by Elsa. "Hello, Agnes. Hello, John. King's not back yet?" Elsa held the high-backed chair for Margaret.

"We won't wait for him. He should be in before long. Save some of those cakes for Mr. Delaney, Elsa."

She poured tea for them and settled back as Delaney took a seat next to Agnes on the sofa.

Margaret Delaney was fifty, a tall, strong woman, big-boned and gray-haired, but with an ease of movement and inbred sense of grace that gave her an appearance of delicacy out of keeping with her size. She had an aquiline nose and a firm mouth, blue eyes that glanced and darted as alertly as Agnes's but held in their depths a compassion foreign to the younger woman. Her hands, broad and capable like the rest of her, were nevertheless white and soft, their strength and agility seemingly inherent rather than acquired. She was wearing an afternoon dress of expensive black silk, fashionably but conservatively cut, its sole relief a bit of point lace caught at the throat by a diamond and ruby brooch. Her dainty lace cap rested with an inflexible dignity on the back of her head, and her hair, arranged in small puffs over her ears, was caught back in a tight bun. There was little variation in any of Margaret Delaney's costumes, and Agnes, who was inclined to consider her dowdy and old-fashioned, was all the same quite aware of the price of the black silk per yard and of the perfect styling and fit of all her dresses. Vaguely, she resented it, and made frequent mental notes on how she would spend the same amount of money if she possessed it.

It was indeed a far cry from the staid old Philadelphia home that Margaret had left to this sun-baked, jerry-built city on the bay. Still, for all that she was misplaced, an anachronism in the swiftly moving scene around her, there was about her a timelessness that defied definition.

The daughter of Jared Stafford, a wealthy Philadelphia shipper, Margaret had been reared with a strict sobriety that shunned worldliness like the plague. In another woman such treatment might have had a desiccating effect, might have choked off womanly warmth abortively and produced a chilly frustration and resentment toward humanity in general. In Margaret Stafford it produced a remarkably opposite effect. It was almost as if she were able to glean the best and reject what was least desirable in her life, to escape narrowness and bigotry through the sheer power of her will.

During her adolescence Margaret acquired a fondness for reading and study. She was not pretty and there were no swarms of beaux clamoring about her and begging favors, but there was already a quiet dignity in her bearing. Without being fluffy or feminine she was every inch a woman in understanding and compassion. The other girls sensed it, and although they liked her they withdrew from her somewhat, as they would have from an older person. Old Jared, a widower, was not eager to have his daughter married and out of his house, and he did not push her and urge her as an anxious mother might have done, a circumstance which proved fortunate for Margaret. For while heaping an attractive dowry on her and shoving her into marriage might have made her terrified and permanently shy, allowing her to live her life with a minimum of interference gave her room in which to expand her mind and personality. She became her father's hostess and household manager, and while her frugality amazed and delighted him, he was nevertheless vaguely aware of a certain brightening about the quiet old mansion, a touch of light airiness and indefinable beauty that her ministrations brought with them.

When she was twenty, old Jared drew a deep breath and plunged into something which set all Philadelphia on its ear. He sold out his shipping business, retired on an income that was rumored to be fabulous, and forthwith took his daughter on a year's tour of Europe. The truth was that Jared was not as unmindful as he seemed of the prize he possessed. Stubborn and shortsighted as he was, he was yet able to discern Margaret's worth. He fully realized that here was no ordinary flibbertigibbet of a girl but a woman already grown, with depth and the capacity to expand and absorb whatever might be put within her reach. He was determined that she should have it.

So it was that a year later Margaret returned with her father from Europe, a tall, erect young woman with a purposeful bearing, and a quiet, educated speech, completely a lady and almost as completely unmarriageable. Old Jared did not mind. He had not taken his daughter abroad to put frills and curlicues on her and throw her to some worthless young man. He was proud and satisfied with her as she was. And if Margaret herself minded, she never showed it.

Shortly after his return to America, Jared entered politics and was elected to Congress. Margaret thereupon became his constant companion and confidante, his official hostess when he was at the capital. It was in Washington that she became acquainted with Judge Hamilton Riggs, a widower fifteen years older than she. When she was thirty, she married him.

Often Margaret looked back on those years of her first marriage as the most tranquil and satisfying of her life. She kept her home both in Philadelphia and in Washington to suit the needs of her husband and her father and she enjoyed the pleasant, confidential way in which they included her in their most secret discussions, took her into their confidence and asked her advice. They respected her judgment, and Hamilton Riggs adored her. He was the most devoted of husbands, and his pride and elation were almost without bounds when, five years after their marriage, a daughter, Elizabeth, was born to them. This seemed to be the final touch in completing Margaret's being, in rounding out her personality with warmth and love and devotion. Then, when the baby was two years old, Judge Riggs died, and within a year old Jared too was gone.

She removed all her possessions to the Philadelphia house, closed off one wing, and continued to live there, maintaining the familiar schedule of housekeeping, shopping and attention to charities. And if there was a hollowness about every action now, she refused to permit herself to succumb to it.

It was during this time that she became better acquainted with the young lawyer King Delaney. She had known him before, slightly. She knew that he had made a considerable fortune speculating somewhere in the Midwest, and had then pocketed it and come east to make himself a lawyer. Judge Riggs had spoken of him as a young man with a future, and he had been entertained often at their home.

After a conventional period of mourning, he came to pay his respects, and Margaret found herself almost unaccountably glad to see him. He was undeniably handsome, and he laughed easily. There was none of Judge Riggs's staid gravity about him. His eyes twinkled with quiet laughter, and he had a way of holding the reins in his slim, strong hands when they went out driving with Elizabeth on a Sunday afternoon that made Margaret's heart give a quick little turn. She was not prudish enough to be scandalized at the thought of falling in love, but she was considerably surprised. She was almost forty.

When he did ask her to become his wife, she accepted without debate, and with no deception to herself.

She knew, for one thing, that King would make a good father. She had seen him with little Elizabeth and knew there was no affectation in his love for her. They were genuinely fond of each other. It was that fondness that helped her decide in favor of the marriage. She knew what King wanted in a wife: a home, respectability, a dignity which she surmised, rightly, that he had never known, some part of the permanence that went with this old Philadelphia house. And, of course, there was the Stafford money. But recognition of these facts was no deterrent to Margaret. Rather, she admired him for being purposeful, and she could sense that King was not a man to ask favors. For whatever she could bring to him, he would return full value in devotion and affection.

She had not been mistaken. By any standards, their marriage had been a successful one. King had kept his part of the unspoken bargain admirably, and she had been happy for the first time in her life with a kind of girlish happiness, a lightheartedness that she seemed to have missed as a young person, and for which she was now making up.

Then King, growing restless, gave up his law practice and went west. It was characteristic of Margaret that she had understood from the first how impossible it was for King to lead a static existence. He had fought his way up from the first, and she was quite well aware that with him the struggle was more important than the goal. He needed what she had to give him; but it was not enough. Margaret had missed him with an almost painful longing until he had built a house and sent for her. When she arrived, the happiness and pride she saw in his face nearly atoned for the long months of loneliness, and for the first time she was able to believe that in his own way he did love her. She was fifty now, and knowing that she could not continue to satisfy him physically as could a younger and more vigorous woman, she was happy in the knowledge that his love for her was built on different ground, and that time could not destroy, but only solidify it. As the years went by, she reasoned, a man became more, rather than less attached to his home, and in this lay her strength.

From the first day she arrived in San Francisco, it seemed that she was right. King was determined to have everything that was best for his wife and daughter, and to make their home the one

center of refinement and grace in the lawless community. Margaret
never asked him whether he had other women. She was quite sure
he did, and she did not wish to put him to the discomfort of lying
to save her feelings. She knew that he was most discreet and would
do nothing that might hurt either her or Elizabeth. If there was a
secret hurt deep inside her she never let it show; she was too sensible
to let it make her miserable for long. She had had more than one
woman's share of happiness in her lifetime, she reasoned. To com-
plain now would be outrageously ungrateful. So it was that she
adapted herself to life in this raw, new world without ever feeling
that she quite "belonged," and even developed an attitude of tolerance toward the unknown women her husband associated with.
They were honest women, in their own way, Margaret told herself,
and if they were tainted with worldly vices, at least they did not
bear the stigma of hypocrisy. Sometimes she would go nearly a day
without thinking of it.

She had not been able to develop the same tolerance toward
Agnes.

Now, looking across the tea table at her sister-in-law, at the
provocative dip of her head on her slender neck, at the almost
intentionally seductive curve of her breast in its low-cut bodice, it
was not difficult for Margaret to understand how a man could be
swept out of his senses by such a woman. It was only hard for her
to believe that it had happened to King.

Neither she nor King had met Agnes until John Delaney
brought her west three weeks ago. Philadelphia and Boston were a
long distance apart, and King had never shown an inclination to
call on his brother. Margaret, who had never had a family outside
of Jared, had been slow to understand this lack of familiarity between two brothers who, it seemed to her, should have taken a
delight in each other. But when she mentioned it to King, he had
passed it off lightly or made some trifling mention of John's moving
in a "different social circle."

When they had at last met in San Francisco, Margaret had
understood what he meant, and because her love for King was so
all-encompassing she forgave him. But from the first moment of
their meeting she liked John; he was, it seemed to her, as childlike
and incapable as King was brusque and efficient. He had the same
charm and tenderness toward his family and these very qualities
made her warm toward him. Agnes she had read at a glance; a
grasping woman, a woman who wanted more than life had been
able to give her, but who, she suspected, would never be quite

satisfied, no matter what the future brought. A voluptuous woman too, Margaret saw, one to whom the pleasures of the flesh were an open book, and who had long since tired of the simple undeviating honesty of her husband. She had felt a little chill around her heart as she caught the first look between King and Agnes. It was a look of almost immediate understanding, of mutual interest, and of surface-hidden desire. She had overlooked it until three nights ago, when she knew for a certainty that what she had feared was indeed a fact.

She was sitting in front of the mirror in her bedroom brushing her hair when King came in. There was nothing out of the ordinary in his manner or appearance, save for a slight flush in his cheeks that gave him a strangely youthful appearance. Margaret looked up and smiled at him.

"The church meeting was late, wasn't it?"

"Oh, not especially. It's so warm tonight. After I picked Agnes up, she wanted to drive a bit to cool off before we came home. Haven't you been stifling here, dear?"

"I didn't mind. Come and sit down."

He went to her and drew up a little stool, sitting down just behind her and starting to braid her hair into a thick plait. Margaret felt a pleasant little ripple of surprise. He had not braided her hair for her in years. She let her head rest back slightly, relaxing under the gentle pulling of the strands. It always made her feel comfortable and sleepy. She remembered other years when they had sat thus and then had gone to bed—

"Margaret." His voice, thoughtful and tentative, broke in on her memories.

"What, dear?"

"Margaret, I was thinking. It might be nice to send for materials pretty soon now and get started building the big house. Would you like that?"

"Why, I don't know, King." There was a puzzled note in her voice. "This house is quite nice. I didn't know that there was any hurry about the new one."

"Well, I only meant—so that you could send for all your nice things, and make a real home of it. Maybe then you'd feel more at home out here." He bent his head even lower over the plait and she frowned a little as she tried to comprehend his meaning.

"It's up to you, dear," she said slowly. "Whatever you say. Will you tear this place down, then? It seems such a shame. The house is really quite good."

"Oh, no, I hadn't thought to tear it down. The lot is plenty large enough for two, and with room to spare. I had an idea we could leave this standing, and then—"

"Then what?"

He finished the plait and dropped it. He pulled the little stool around so that he faced her, and took one of her hands in both of his, looking down at it, away from her.

"Margaret, I was wondering if you wouldn't want to invite Agnes and John to come and live here, when we move into the big house. You know as well as I do that John probably will never find any gold up north to amount to anything. When he comes back they'll need a place to live. I could perhaps find John something to do with me, but there'll be this perfectly good house, with no one to live in it."

"Why, I think that's very generous of you, King," Margaret said warmly. "It's very dear and good of you to think of them. But shouldn't you wait and see first what happens? John might find gold, you know . . ."

"He won't! I know he won't!" King said with sudden vehemence. "And I should think you'd be as interested as I am in seeing that they're provided for. You used to say I didn't pay enough attention to John when we were back east, when I didn't go to see him."

"But I am interested, dear!" she said hastily. "I only meant— well, San Francisco isn't the West. Maybe there's some other place John will want to settle . . ."

"Some other place! You mean away from San Francisco?"

He looked up in sudden anxiety. In an instant she had taken in the boyish flush in his cheeks, the looseness of his slightly parted lips, the bright feverishness of his light eyes.

"Why, yes—why not?" She could feel herself struggling to keep her voice calm; she could feel everything within her fighting to throw back the wave of sickening anger that had swept over her.

"Oh, I don't know—well, of course we can talk about it when the time comes . . ." His voice trailed off indefinitely as though he was seeking a way in which to end the conversation.

She rose slowly, drawing her wrapper around her with dignity. "Yes, let's wait," she said coldly.

She had known then, and the knowledge was a painful, aching thing inside her. But she had said nothing, and would say nothing until it became clear what course events were to take. Only there was Elizabeth to be considered.

At fifteen, Elizabeth was already a woman in many ways, quick to perceive, and unbelievably shrewd when it came to other women.

She might not be able to understand the full implication of the situation, but it certainly would not be long before she realized that something was not as it should be. Even now she had taken a dislike to Agnes, and for no other reason, apparently, than an intuitive one. Margaret, who had always encouraged intellectual freedom in her daughter, sensed that Elizabeth resented Agnes's attitude toward Treese, that she was bitterly conscious of Treese's painful shyness and embarrassment. The older girl did everything she could to draw Treese out and bring her into the conversation, inevitably arousing Agnes's disapproval and creating a situation that smoldered with uncomfortable undertones.

Where Margaret was prudent enough to realize that Treese was often better left alone, Elizabeth, with all the impulsiveness of her years, would let nothing stand in the way of the change she fancied she could bring about in her young cousin. It was her newest and dearest cause, and she threw herself into the crusade with the determination of a zealot. One day it would be a new hair style for the girl, another day a bright sash. Each time Treese seemed more painfully shy and withdrawn than the last, but Elizabeth, undaunted, went at it with new fervor. And with each new attempt Treese emerged more confused than before, even though she had acquired a love for Elizabeth that was half real affection and half breathless admiration.

It seemed that nothing was impossible to this lovely yellow-haired girl who was like a picture from one of Treese's storybooks. At the dinner table she was regarded as an equal, and each new escapade which she came home to relate with delightful candor was received with smiles and mild disapprobation instead of with slaps and reproaches. It was beyond Treese's comprehension how anyone could be bold with such a pleasant, captivating boldness. Her mother had always told her that boldness was unbecoming in a girl; in Elizabeth it seemed the pleasantest of faults.

CHAPTER III

THERE WAS the sound of the front door banging open and shut. The three who were sitting at tea in the parlor looked up. Treese, who had entered a moment before, lifted her head expectantly. A slender blonde girl in a blue silk dress came running in quite out of breath, and a man followed behind her.

"Mother darling, wait till you hear what happened to us right on Montgomery Street! Hello, Treese; hello, Aunt Agnes, Uncle

John. Oh, Uncle John, you should have been with us! It was absolutely the most thrilling thing that ever happened to me! Is there any tea left, Mother?"

Margaret smiled indulgently at her daughter.

"There's plenty of tea left. And sit down before you blow apart. Now whatever can this exciting news be?"

Elizabeth Delaney plumped herself down on the sofa next to Agnes. The latter, whose private opinion was that her niece was ill-bred and boisterous, drew her skirts in a trifle around her. She could not understand Margaret's patience with the girl, and in the privacy of their bedroom had more than once informed Delaney that she considered her far too adult for fifteen years.

"Well, it was simply unbelievable!" Elizabeth exclaimed, taking the cup of tea her mother offered her. "There we were driving down Montgomery Street as proper as you please, simply on an afternoon's outing, and all of a sudden we hear gunfire and shouts—"

"King!" Margaret looked at him reprovingly.

"On my word of honor, dear," he said earnestly, "she begged me to go along. And you know what she is when her mind's made up!"

"Oh, Father, let me tell it!" Elizabeth begged. Her bright blue eyes were sparkling with eagerness over the story she had to relate and her lips were red and mobile with excitement. The wide blue satin bow at the back of her head quivered as if in anticipation and the curls that fell over her shoulders bobbed and danced in time with the darting movements of her head.

Delaney watched her admiringly. What a grown woman she was, in her fashionable dress with her girlish figure showing it off admirably! The blue silk dress opened in front to show a white chemisette, and from under its long wide sleeves peeped matching undersleeves. The rustle of the stiffly starched petticoats whispered under the full silk skirt and she wore a small gold locket on a fine chain. Her kid slippers had a small bow at the instep; her white stockings covered a glimpse of shapely ankle. He supposed it was too old for a girl fifteen, as Agnes said. But she looked so grown and beautiful, somehow, beside his little Treese. He'd like to speak to Agnes about getting some new clothes for Treese. She was only two years younger than Elizabeth, and the calicos which the two little girls wore were too young for her. Of course, Agnes had had a hard time managing, what with the long trip west and all, but he'd be locating a claim soon and then there'd be plenty of money for pretty things. Yes, he'd certainly speak to her. Just as soon as he had a little something to offer.

"Well, you've no idea!" Elizabeth sat back on the sofa with her cup of tea, evidently intent, now that she had the floor, on making the suspense last as long as possible. "There we were out buggy-riding as innocent as you please when we hear these bursts of gunfire, and before we know it Montgomery Street is simply swarming with men, all of them bellowing like mad, until we simply had to stop the horses!"

"Was someone hurt?" Treese inquired, suddenly too curious to keep silent.

"Oh, Treese darling, you've no idea! If you'd only been with us! So Father made me stay in the buggy, although you can imagine how I felt! Simply bursting with excitement, and I did so want to get out and see for myself! Well, and before he even got back to tell me what had happened I could hear everyone shouting, 'He's dead—he's a goner sure!' "

Agnes gasped and covered her mouth with her handkerchief.

"Exactly, Aunt Agnes! So then I just couldn't stand any more. I jumped down and tore after Father—"

"Elizabeth!" It was Margaret's turn to exclaim.

"Well, and when I found him, what do you think it was! Steve Mallott! Steve Mallott and this other man had got in a fight over some woman and this man had taken a shot at Mr. Mallott. He just managed to draw his gun in time to save himself before the man fired again. Killed him dead as a stone, right there in the middle of Montgomery Street! Did you ever hear of anything so exciting?"

Treese was sitting forward on her chair, her mouth slightly open with amazement, staring admiringly at Elizabeth. She was for once unaware of Agnes's disapproval.

"Who's Steve Mallott?" she inquired.

Elizabeth made a little swooning motion backward on the sofa.

"You mean you've been in San Francisco three weeks and never heard of Steve Mallott? Why, he's simply the handsomest, wickedest river gambler on the Sacramento, that's all! I simply adore him!"

Agnes pursed her lips coldly, but Margaret threw back her head and laughed in one of her rare displays of amusement.

"Elizabeth, you'll be the death of me! You know perfectly well if Steve Mallott came closer to you than three feet you'd turn and run like a rabbit!"

"Mother, I would not! Ask Father if I didn't stand right there near enough to reach out and touch him today! Ask him!"

Margaret dipped her head inquiringly in her husband's direction. He shook his head sadly.

"Your daughter was quite unabashed, madam."

"Well, anyway, listen then! That's only the beginning of the story! Right away the men there began to divide into two factions, those who were for Mr. Mallott and those who were for the man who was shot. What was his name, Father? Marvin, Martin, something like that. Anyway he was quite disreputable and deserved everything he got!"

"Oh, my dear, now!" Margaret sighed.

"Well, he drew first, Mother. That's an unwritten law! Ask Father. A man has a right to defend his own life, hasn't he? Well, so the men who were against Steve Mallott started to grab him and somebody went for a rope, and my heart was simply bleeding for him, because I was afraid they were going to string him up right there, and he's simply the handsomest man west of St. Louis! Treese, I must point him out to you some day. Then all at once we could see somebody shoving through the crowd trying to stop the men, and who do you suppose it was? Andy Hart! You know what good friends he and Mallott are. Every time Andy comes to town, he looks him up and they hang around together down there on Portsmouth Square and go out together with those women—"

"Elizabeth!"

"Well, all right, Mother, but I don't see anything wrong with saying out loud what everyone knows already! Anyway, you can imagine what fast friends they would be, getting drunk together all those times— Oh, all right, Mother dear! So there was Andy pushing back the crowd, trying to get them to let go of Mr. Mallott, and then he caught sight of Father, and he shouted at the top of his lungs, 'There's the man can save him! Come on in on the side of justice for once, King!' Just like that he shouted, and I was so proud of Father I could have burst right into little pieces! Although I don't know why he said it that way—'for once.' So before I knew what was happening Father turned to me and said, real mad and excited, like he gets, you know, 'Get back in the buggy, sweetheart, looks like I've got a case!' And then he tore off to help Andy. Well, of course I didn't get back in the buggy. You couldn't have dragged me away from there with a team of wild horses!

"So you can probably guess the rest. They held court right there in the middle of Montgomery Street, and Father was simply eloquent! I never heard anything like it. And of course he got Steve Mallott off. The jury didn't even talk it over; they just all roared at once, 'Not guilty!'" Elizabeth cupped her hands and shouted to demonstrate. Agnes winced.

"And then Andy came over and shook hands with Father, and so did Steve Mallott, and I sort of edged my way in, hoping someone would introduce me, but no one did. I was so furious I could have cried! And then Andy hollered out, 'Come on, now, we're passing the hat to collect a fee. Mr. Delaney doesn't work for nothing!' And he did just that very thing. Everybody had to contribute, even the men who had been on the other side. If they didn't want to, Andy got out his gun and poked it at them. You should have seen the hatful of money Father came away with! I made him take me into the very first store and buy me this sash. Look!"

She got up and pirouetted to the center of the room to display the wide satin sash tied in an enormous bow.

Agnes looked up at King, and for the first time she smiled; the slow, suggestive smile that made the corners of her mouth dip in.

"It sounds as though you're very persuasive, King."

Margaret looked quickly at her husband and saw the flush of color that mounted in his face. He avoided her glance.

"Oh, there's no one like Father!" Elizabeth said affectionately, running over to him and hugging him impulsively. He detached her gently and she ran over to Treese. "Treese darling, do come up to my room with me. I want to tell you all about it, and about this wonderful Steve Mallott! You'll excuse her, won't you, Mother?"

"Of course, dear. Run along with Elizabeth."

The two girls left, Elizabeth bounding out with a half-running, half-dancing step, Treese following shyly after.

Margaret settled back in her chair and sighed with something like relief.

"That girl will be the death of me!"

Agnes arched her fine black eyebrows, and inquired, "Doesn't it worry you, Margaret, to have her flying around the city like that? This isn't Philadelphia, you know. I should think it would be dangerous."

"It is, of course. But Elizabeth's not easily disciplined. If I let her go with King, at least she's not out alone."

Agnes shrugged her shoulders slightly with a gesture that implied complete disapproval and indicated that on no account would she permit *her* daughter to behave so. Then she turned to King.

"John wants to leave for the mines tomorrow, King. Had you heard?"

Margaret gave a little start. No one had mentioned John's leaving tomorrow . . .

"No, I hadn't heard. Do you think that's wise, John?"

"Well, I—"

"He simply won't hear of anything else," Agnes interrupted smoothly. "And you know how these Delaneys are once they make up their mind to something!"

King Delaney turned his head away again slightly with the gesture that Margaret thought was half annoyance. Agnes certainly wasn't subtle enough for him, whatever else she might have that attracted him.

"Going up by boat?" King inquired.

"I thought to, yes. Up towards Marysville and then striking out from there. How's it sound to you?"

King shook his head and laughed a little. "Don't consult me on prospecting, John. It's a closed book to me."

King Delaney was forty-five; a slightly older and somehow slightly smaller edition of Delaney himself, although actually he was as tall. There was none of the raw power about him that characterized Delaney, however. He had an easy grace that made him appear less bulky and less unsure of himself. His features were finer and less highly colored, his hair more sandy than red; all in all, a more subdued Delaney, his words and gestures planned, his actions and expressions not easily read. His blue eyes were not quick to change and reveal his emotions, as Delaney's were. Instead they darted from one person or object to another, probing, analyzing, catching the slightest innuendo but seldom giving any impression except that of complete indifference.

Watching him, Agnes Delaney could see all the more patent signs of prosperity and success that lingered around him, showing themselves in the fine precise cut of his frock coat, the trim tailoring of his fawn-colored trousers that tapered into shiny leather boots. His hair, brushed straight back from the temples, came just to the top of his collar and was dressed with fragrant macassar oil. His sideburns and mustache were full, but fastidiously trimmed. His high brushed beaver, fawn-colored to match his trousers, rested in his lap, and he traced its gracefully rolled brim with one finger. His wrapped cravat and embroidered waistcoat almost hid the white bosom of his shirt; the expensive hand-pleated tucks were just visible, and two pearl studs gleamed in them.

She glanced at Delaney, who was watching her, the delicate teacup balanced in his heavy hand like a butterfly on a rock. How red and ugly his hair looked today! How the freckles stood out on his face, making him look like a gawky country boy. And that

ridiculous miner's outfit. Yes, let him go and good riddance. She
had been a fool to make a scene over it in the first place. She should
have known he'd be no help to her in getting ahead and making a
place for them here in the West. Making a place where Keith could
come and find a career.

No, she was not angry that Delaney was going; she was relieved.
She realized now the futility of her last hope for him, the hope that
in California he would miraculously become an enterprising and
ambitious person. She would have to make plans of her own now.
This was a new country, the West. It wasn't like Boston, where
you got tagged as a dry goods merchant's daughter and stayed that
until the day you died. How she had hated it! Well, it was different
here. Out here no one knew what you had been, and they cared
less. Antecedents were of far less importance than a strong constitution and a head for business.

Margaret had always had everything. Never had to fight and
know what it was to take second place. The scorn inside Agnes
became triumph. Well, she might have her fine house and silk
dresses, but she couldn't hang onto her husband, that was certain.
And before very long she might not be the first lady in San Francisco, either. Money was essential, of course. You had to have money.
Rule Delaney out on that score, too. He'd always been a fool where
business was concerned and he certainly wasn't going to change
just because his surroundings had. There was no use crying over it
now. If she hadn't married so infernally young, and if she'd had
sense enough to look beyond a pair of square shoulders and flat
slim hips, she might not be in this fix today. Take King, for instance.
He had physical appeal, plenty of it, and a head on his shoulders.
He was too good for a woman like that. Never given him any children. Even that girl Elizabeth wasn't his own.

She felt a surge of pride at her own fine, healthy children. Not
pride in them as individuals, for Agnes seldom considered anyone
for his intrinsic value but only as a useful or superfluous adjunct to
her own prearranged schemes. She had known a perverse pride,
however, since their arrival in San Francisco, at seeing the envious
look on King's face when he watched the children. It had given
Agnes an unaccustomed thrill to watch the tenderness and envy
grow as he played with little Violet and Florabelle and told long,
colorful stories of his career in California to the wide-eyed Treese.
Agnes, who had seldom considered her children, with the exception
of Keith, as anything but minor annoyances, was all at once proud
of them and of her part in their being.

They were darlings, of course; Florabelle and Violet especially, rosy and beautiful and irresistible. Treese, even, was a good child, obedient and quiet, and handy with the little ones. She was incurably homely, of course, with all of Delaney's characteristics—red hair, tall gawky frame, freckles. Agnes always took care to shove her into the background when they met strangers. But actually she was a dear child, in her own way. Agnes had never quite found a common ground on which to meet her eldest daughter.

With Keith, of course, it was another matter. At the thought of her son, a warm glow seemed to start from deep inside her, suffusing and spreading until it filled every nerve and muscle and brought color to her cheeks. For as surely as Treese was Delaney's child, so Keith belonged to Agnes. Tall, slim and well formed, with dark hair and darker eyes, he was the image of Agnes. It seemed that no tiniest part of his conception could have been Delaney's. From the tips of his white fingers to his long, supple legs; from the crown of his thick hair to his toes, he was all Agnes. Still boyishly slim, there was none of her soft voluptuousness about him, but his features had all the delicate perfection of hers, magnified and made virile by his masculinity. At sixteen, he was broad-shouldered, with a thin tapering waist and an easy, graceful gait. They were not an hour out of Boston Harbor before Agnes regretted leaving him behind, but her resolution was unshakable. He would be a professional man. He would have a calling. By the time he had finished his studies at college and was ready to join them in California, she would have prepared the way for him, so that he could step into a social and professional circle.

Only, she must have money. She simply must. Without it, all her plans for Keith would come to nothing. And it might be cruel to say so, but Treese—well, the poor child would certainly never catch a husband without it.

She looked up brightly at King.

"John's bought himself quite an assortment of equipment, King. Did you see it in the hall?"

King smiled. "You've got enough there to dig up the whole Mother Lode, Jack. I wish you luck."

Delaney blushed self-consciously.

"I was going to say," Agnes went on smoothly, "we might need some help in getting him to the boat. Would it be too much of an imposition to ask you to take us?"

In her chair at the tea table Margaret sat up a shade straighter, her spine stiffening, her hands closing firmly about the arms. She did not look at her husband.

King, glancing at her, hesitated.

"Why, of course I'll make some arrangement, Agnes. Although I may not be able to take you myself. Tomorrow's a pretty big day for me. But I'll see that there's a carriage ready for you."

"Nonsense, King!" Delaney put in heartily. "You'll do no such thing. Agnes dear, we've imposed far too much already. Don't give it another thought, King; we'll get there in fine shape. As a matter of fact, no one needs to see me to the boat at all. We'll say our good-byes right here."

"Oh—John!" There was a shade of hurt in Agnes's voice that made Delaney look at her with sudden tenderness, reproaching himself. What a stupid clout he was. Of course she would want to see him off. What was he thinking of, to talk to her like that? He reached over and took one of her hands, tenderly. She gave him a quick, blank smile and then looked past him to King, who looked down at first, seeking to avoid her eyes, but then raised his head slowly. The vacuous smile she had put on for Delaney changed imperceptibly, disappeared except for a slight suggestion about the corners of her mouth. One eyebrow rose slightly and her dark eyes glistened with what was unmistakably triumph.

Margaret Delaney looked slowly from her husband, handsome and poised in the armchair, to his brother; awkward, red-faced and red-handed, trusting and childishly possessive, next to Agnes; and then to Agnes herself, outwardly inscrutable but to Margaret all at once transparent as a schoolgirl. And now Margaret was not smiling.

CHAPTER IV

JOHN DELANEY left the next day on a river steamer bound for Sacramento and thence north to Marysville, looking a little ludicrous with his heavy blanket roll, pick and shovel strapped to his back, with his buckets and pans dangling noisily from his belt, but with urgency and fire in his usually quiet eyes. The two little girls, Florabelle and Violet, clung tearfully to him at the wharf, screamed at him not to leave them, and were finally drawn away struggling and weeping by Treese. Her own eyes, so like Delaney's, were filled with tears, but they gleamed and sparkled with the same proud purpose. She looked up at him and he smiled at her.

"That's my good girl," he said, patting her cheek. "That's my brave girl."

Sobs choked in her throat and she could not answer, but she yearned toward his touch like a little animal and her eyes never wavered from his face. He turned to Agnes. There seemed to be no particular bitterness in her attitude. Indeed, it was almost as if her mind were elsewhere. When he leaned forward to kiss her, she even offered her lips instead of putting her cheek forward, and a little blush of pleasure suffused his honest features.

"You'll take good care of yourself?" he asked hesitantly, more to cover his own embarrassment and confusion than because of actual concern. There was an almost formidable self-sufficiency about Agnes.

"Of course. You're not to worry. But do get a letter back to us when you can."

"I will," he promised emphatically, pleased and confused at her unnatural solicitude over his welfare. "The very first mail. But it may take time. Things are slow, you know, up that way."

"Well . . ." They both hesitated. There seemed nothing more to say. Agnes, in fact, seemed almost preoccupied, as though her mind was elsewhere. Her eyes traveled restlessly past him, out over the water where the steamers joggled on the current.

"Well, I'd best get aboard. No use going to all this trouble and then get left at the dock," he stammered. He knelt down to the three little girls and embraced them all.

"Good-bye, my darlings." Small, sweaty hands pressed his face and salty tears spilled over his new red shirt. He rose quickly. "Good-bye, Agnes dear."

"Good-bye. Take care!" she called after him as he strode up the gangplank. At the top he turned and waved to them, and they waved back. Then Agnes said briskly, "Well, come along, children. The carriage won't wait forever."

Little Florabelle, still weeping and red-faced, refused to budge, so Treese picked her up bodily and carried her, while Violet ran ahead and held her mother's hand. Agnes walked steadily and with purpose, pausing a trifle impatiently when Violet's steps slowed, but not paying any particular attention to the child. Her attention was fixed on the street as they returned to the waiting carriage, and she took care to avoid holes and torn boards.

It was late afternoon as they drove back through the dusty, crowded streets toward King's house. He had not accompanied them, but he had sent a carriage, and Delaney had spent most of the ride to the water front exclaiming over his brother's generosity.

Now, as they drove back toward the house, Agnes's thoughts were moving rapidly ahead of her. The wails of the children, still inconsolable over Delaney's departure, seemed to come to her distantly, and she took no notice of the quiet tears that coursed down Treese's dusty cheeks.

At the house she instructed Treese to take the children inside and see that they had their naps before dinner. She might be late. She was going to take a little drive. No, there was nothing the matter. Only take them inside and hurry!

She watched the three figures disappear into the house, Treese's long, rangy one, the two little girls' short, stubby ones, with their quick irregular steps. Then she leaned forward and gave the driver a curt instruction.

They drove on, past the huddled tents and shacks, the open fires where suppers were already cooking, over rutted streets and by quiet groves of trees that furnished incongruous contrast to the chaotically populated sectors. When they reached the top of a hill overlooking the city and the bay, she directed the driver to let her out.

"Soon be gettin' dark, ma'am. Are you sure you want to get off here?"

"Do as I say!" There was a curt impatience in Agnes's voice, a decisiveness to her step as she alighted from the carriage.

When the carriage had made the turn and was starting back down the hill, she watched its progress, standing under a huge old oak tree and noting how crazily the wheels followed the ruts of the road, making the whole carriage bob like a drunken man. When it was out of sight, her gaze became distant, not focused on anything near at hand, but spreading out to include the whole of San Francisco, which sprawled beneath her. Early evening was coming on, and the shadows, as they lengthened, began to cast long patches of darkness across the road, and to diffuse and change the scene below. A little breeze sprang up; the leaves overhead began to sway and murmur. Agnes tapped her foot impatiently.

In a few minutes she caught sight of a buggy starting up the incline toward her. She caught her breath and pressed her hands against her breast as though to still something within her. She caught her lower lip in her teeth and her breath began to come more rapidly.

When the buggy reached the top of the hill it stopped. King reached down to help her and she got in. For a moment they sat, side by side in the half darkness. Then, with one quick motion, he put his arm around her and drew her to him, kissing her hard, so that her head tipped back against his shoulder.

When he took his lips away, he whispered, close to her face, "Did he leave?"

"Yes, he's gone." Her voice was so low he had to bend close to hear her.

"Everything's all right, then?"

"Yes, but what about dinner? Won't they be expecting us?"

"They'll think you're sad about his leaving. The children will say you've gone for a drive."

"What about you?"

"I don't know—I don't care. Agnes, don't talk about anything now but us."

He kissed her again, and she clung close to him, holding the lapels of his black frock coat. When he released her she put her face close to the ruffles of his shirt front.

"King, what did she say the other night?"

"Who?"

"Margaret. What did she say when you asked her about the house?"

"Nothing. She wouldn't say one way or the other."

"She doesn't like me."

"Darling, of course she does. The idea was new to her, that's all."

"No, she doesn't like me."

"Stop saying that. And you mustn't act like you did yesterday afternoon, or everyone will know."

She raised her head indignantly. "What did I do?"

"You know, looking at me like that and saying those things."

"What things?"

"Well, I can't just tell. But you know what I mean. We've got to be more careful. Margaret's not easily fooled."

"I don't like it when you talk about us that way, King. You make it sound so—sordid, and funny somehow."

He pulled her close against him so that his cheek was against her temple and he could feel the smoothness of her hair where it was brushed back.

"Don't talk any more. That isn't what we came here for anyway, is it?"

"No. But I like you to tell me things. You don't tell me anything, and I don't know how matters stand—"

"But there's nothing I can tell you!" King's tone was exasperated. "You know everything I do."

"No, I don't. How would I know what you and she talk about when you're alone at night in your room?"

"Oh, Agnes, don't say it that way."

"Well, it's the truth, isn't it? After all, you sleep in the same bed—"

"You know there isn't anything."

"There is. You just say that."

"But she is my wife, Agnes!"

"There! You see?"

"But, darling, that's different! That has nothing to do with us. You know how much I love you, Agnes."

"You do?" She put her face up to his, not touching his lips, but putting her mouth against his cheek.

"Oh, of course I do. Agnes, don't torment me so!"

He seized her roughly and tried to kiss her, but she kept turning her lips away from him and laughing.

"Agnes, for heaven's sake!" he exploded finally, thrusting her from him.

She laughed softly then and leaned against him, her head against his chest, one hand moving slowly over his silk lapel.

"Darling, don't be angry with me," she whispered. She lifted her face so that her mouth was next to his. Her eyes were half shut and her lips slightly parted.

"Oh, Agnes—" He closed his mouth over hers with a fierce hunger, pushing back her cloak with one hand, and pressing her back so that it arched toward him. Then he took his lips away, still holding her tightly and breathing hard. He looked into her eyes, scanned her face as though to remember every feature forever.

All during the summer of 1850, Delaney was away at the mines and Agnes and her three children continued to make their home with Margaret and King. Once, in early August, Delaney returned, but only for a flying trip. He had not struck anything yet, but things looked good up toward Rough-and-Ready. It was all a matter of locating a good claim, and then beating the other fellow to it. He had seen some of them going away from the diggings with more gold than they could carry on their backs. No, he wasn't going to give up now, something would break for him any day now. It was all a matter of luck and keeping at it, of course. His miner's shirt had acquired a dusty, worn look that made him an "old-timer" in the eyes of the citizenry, and he talked easily of the "diggin's" and of equipment. He left again, loaded with fresh supplies and new determination, and life settled into its regular routine once more at the Delaney house.

There was no cessation of interest on Agnes's part in the prospect of a new house for King and Margaret, and by midsummer it was quite apparent to Margaret that the motivation in the matter had come from Agnes. Agnes, whose position in the West was a shaky one at best if she was to rely on Delaney's fortune at the mines, had already set about establishing security for herself by the first means at hand.

King contracted to have plans drawn for the house, explaining to Margaret that they would be useful no matter when they planned to build. During the evenings, at Agnes's suggestion, he would get them out and spread them on the dining-room table, and together they would pore over them, pointing with pencils and jotting down columns of figures on separate scraps of paper. Agnes's dark gleaming head would move close to King's, catching the rays of lamplight, and her bosom would press close against the edge of the table as she leaned over the plans, swelling and showing startlingly white against the dark of the mahogany. When Margaret entered the room, King would jump up and take her by the arm, steering her to the table and showing her the newest idea for full-length windows in the ballroom or a glass-enclosed conservatory. He would explain in detail their estimates on the work and what materials they had in mind and show her copies of orders already sent out: plate glass, window frames, doors and door hinges, bricks and lumber, iron grating—all had been ordered and were being sent by ship around the Horn.

"By October maybe, or November at the latest, we should be ready to start," he would say, smiling cheerfully as though in an effort to instill some enthusiasm for the project into Margaret. "Perhaps next month we can start digging the foundation and you can show me how you want the grounds laid out. Now look! What do you think of this?"

And he would lean over the table, pointing with his pencil to some new feature, enumerating its virtues and explaining how it was the latest thing in the East. Invariably, Margaret would listen without replying, an expression of peculiar resolution on her quiet face, and when he would demand an opinion point-blank she would answer, "Do as you like, King. It really makes very little difference to me."

The first indication that there might be more behind Margaret's docility than Agnes had admitted came one evening when the three of them, together with Elizabeth and Treese, were sitting in the parlor. King was seated with his newspaper, ostensibly absorbed in it, but his eyes kept straying over the top of it to where Agnes sat beside a lamp, going through some brochures sent out by an eastern furniture manufacturer. She was scanning each page avidly, sometimes letting out a little exclamation, then moistening the tip of her finger and turning the page. Sometimes her forehead would draw together as she speculated meditatively, and from time to time she would cock her head slightly on one side as though to examine some illustration to better advantage.

In her customary high-backed chair, Margaret sat with a pile of fancywork she had been completing, and near her on two low chairs sat the girls conversing in low tones.

At last Agnes's enthusiasm grew too great to be contained in silence.

"Look!" she cried. "Isn't this simply the most fashionable bedroom furniture you ever saw? What do you think, Margaret, would fourteen-foot posters fit in the bedrooms upstairs? They're the very newest thing back east. See there? Fourteen-foot posters each five inches square, with carved angels mounted on the top and crimson velvet hangings."

Margaret, whose thoughts went momentarily to her own sparsely furnished bedroom with its slender-postered bed, dark polished floor and almost monastic bareness, smiled a ghost of a smile.

"Well, it's a fourteen-foot ceiling," she replied.

"Only fourteen!" Agnes's face took on a dissatisfied pout. "Then the angels wouldn't fit. I can't tell from this, though, whether the posters are fourteen feet tall without the angels or with them. Listen, what would you think? 'An advance display in our New York City workshops of the latest commodious accommodations for milady's bedchamber. A spacious bed, six feet square, hewn out of solid walnut, with crimson velvet hangings to keep out lights or drafts, and elegant hand-hewn posters five inches square, fashioned from solid walnut and rising to an imposing height of fourteen feet, topped by delicately wrought angels in attitudes of repose.' Now, what would you think?"

King cleared his throat loudly with embarrassment and Margaret, raising her eyebrows slightly, looked at him. Then she turned back to her fancywork and continued manipulating the needle with its fine thread in and out of the delicate fabric.

"I'm sure I couldn't say, Agnes," she said thoughtfully. There was a pause during which the click of the needle against her thimble sounded in the quiet room as the girls momentarily stopped their conversation. "But wouldn't that sort of thing be rather expensive?"

A quick flush of anger rose in Agnes's face as she looked up at Margaret. "What do you mean?" she asked. Her voice was tight with restrained emotion and her dark eyes flashed.

Margaret's voice was smooth and unruffled.

"I only meant, mightn't it be better to wait and see what sort of luck John has at the mines before you make too many plans?"

Agnes stared at her. The quick anger that had risen in her face began slowly to be replaced by sullenness, and her mouth, usually so moist and full of color, whitened and drew into the suggestion of a scowl. For a moment she stared unwaveringly at Margaret. Then she returned to the brochures, but her hands as they clutched the pamphlets had gone white at the knuckles.

Margaret continued to work calmly, but after a moment she glanced at the two girls sitting beside her. They were sitting quite still, Treese with an expression of confused discomfort, as though she realized the conversation had taken on disquieting undertones which she could not fathom, Elizabeth with a strangely penetrating look about her, staring straight at her aunt.

September was hot and dusty. There was more talk about the admission of California to the Union, and every newspaper carried speculation on whether it would go through and how soon the news would come. The first ground was dug for the new Delaney mansion, and King began to look each day for the ships that would bring building supplies from New England. There were a few hastily scrawled notes from Delaney, all bursting with anticipatory excitement and the conviction that tomorrow or the next day, or next week surely, he would strike it rich.

In September, too, the city was ravaged by another disastrous fire, which gutted the town and ate away tents and shacks like so much tinder. A small force of men was quickly organized to throw water on the Delaney house, which in its isolated position was already comparatively safe, and it escaped damage while the rest of the town was being leveled.

But as quickly as they had been cut down by fire, the people rose once more, laughing, indomitable, building new homes on the ashes of the old. New arrivals continued to pour in, thousands upon thousands arriving by sea alone. The very breath of life in the city on the bay was bold, undaunted, untiring. Lights blazed twenty-four hours a day and the harbor was a choked forest of masts.

Toward the middle of October Andy Hart came to San Francisco again, declaring his avowed intention of not stirring from the city until news of the admission, which was momentarily expected, arrived from the East.

"They'll tear this town up by the roots and then put it back together again!" he declared to King. "And I'm not going to be sitting in the hinterlands while all hell's breaking loose here."

King laughed tolerantly. "I thought you came west to escape the advance of civilization—lead the hermit's life."

Andy frowned and considered for a moment. "Well, so I did." He rubbed one hand over the scratchy stubble of his untrimmed beard. "But that doesn't stop me from watching the rest of 'em make damned fools of themselves."

"Stop lying. If you weren't in on the ground floor of everything that happened you wouldn't be able to sleep nights."

"Well, the hell with that. Invite me to supper, will you, so I can flirt with your pretty daughter!"

Andy was invited, and showed his deference toward San Francisco's first family by clipping his beard and mustache and by discarding his miner's garb momentarily for a loose-fitting, ungainly store-bought suit of black broadcloth.

Margaret was dressed in her customary black silk, but she had put on her best cap of Brussels lace in honor of Andy's visit, and was wearing a diamond and pearl brooch and one of her best diamond rings.

As they sat talking there were footsteps on the stairs. "That's Aunt Agnes," Elizabeth said, jumping up. "Shall I go and tell—"

She stopped, the sentence dangling in mid-air, as Agnes entered the parlor.

She was wearing a new dinner dress of chameleon silk, blue and silver, with a wide full skirt standing out stiffly from a narrow waist. The tight, long-pointed bodice accentuated the roundness of her bosom, and the long tight sleeves outlined her plump arms. Her hair was drawn back from a center part, framing her white forehead. She wore a little Marie Stuart cap of matching chameleon, under whose brim were rosettes of pale-blue satin ribbon.

For a moment no one spoke. Then Elizabeth ran to her.

"Aunt Agnes! If you don't look beautiful! That's the loveliest dress I ever saw in all my life. Whenever did you have it made? And to think you never told us! Why, I saw that material in Larraby's window myself only last month. My heavens, it was fifteen dollars a yard or I would have got it myself!"

She stopped, and a look of puzzlement came over her face. The room was silent. Standing with his back to the fireplace, King Delaney looked all at once white and strained. His mouth was drawn in until his lips were as colorless as the rest of his face, and his hands were clenched into fists at his sides. In her chair, Margaret was stiff and unmoving. She had looked away from Agnes and was concentrating on tracing with her thumb and forefinger the tiny edging of lace on her lawn handkerchief. Treese was staring at her mother with open-mouthed admiration and Andy Hart, still in the center of the room, was lounging casually, his weight on one leg, looking at her with an appraising eye. There was none of the alert respect in his attitude that he displayed toward Margaret.

Slowly, Margaret's head lifted. Her face was ashen. She did not look at Agnes or at anyone else in the room, but stared straight ahead.

"Tell Elsa we're ready for dinner, Elizabeth," she said quietly. Her voice reached into every corner of the room.

The following afternoon Andy presented himself at the house with an invitation for all the ladies to go riding with him. Agnes was napping, and Margaret laughingly declared that at her age riding through San Francisco came under the heading of a distinct hazard, but she gave permission for Treese and Elizabeth and the two little girls to go. Florabelle and Violet squealed with delight at being allowed to stay up all afternoon, but Treese was hesitant.

"I don't know if we should, Aunt Margaret," she said doubtfully. "Mamma isn't up, and maybe she might not like it."

The two little girls began to wail and Elizabeth addressed her chidingly.

"Silly! Mother wouldn't say we could go if it wasn't all right. Come on now. I'll give you one of my dresses to wear. Would you like that? And just think! We might even see Steve Mallott. You'd like that, wouldn't you?"

Treese's eyes shone. "Oh, yes, I'd love that! Oh, Aunt Margaret, do you think it would be all right?"

"Of course. Only see that you keep them away from danger, Andy!"

"They'll be safe with me, Miss Margaret."

"All right, then." Margaret shooed them from the room. "Hurry along and get your things on."

Elizabeth's attempt to outfit Treese resulted in failure. The flounced, beribboned afternoon dress she insisted on lending her hung dismally over Treese's flat hips and draped in large wrinkles over her chest. Elizabeth pulled at the front of it and Treese shrank back horrified.

"If we could just stuff something in there. No, I guess it wouldn't do any good. Well, look, Treese, you'd better wear your own after all."

Treese, somewhat relieved, put on her own best dress, a flowered silk made over from one of Agnes's. The skirt reached to just below her calves and was tied with a satin ribbon about her waist. She put on her coarse straw bonnet whose unbecoming pink trim gave her own reddish complexion an even more violent hue, and they were ready to start.

Elizabeth, cool and grown-up in her walking dress of blue forget-me-nots on fawn-colored silk, surveyed her cousin doubtfully. "Well, it'll do for this time, dear." She poked at the two flounces of her skirt to make them stand out and tied the ribbons of her blue silk bonnet. "Come on, now. Let's not make Andy wait any more."

They tiptoed downstairs, Treese feeling guiltily conspiratorial, and Andy escorted them with a flourish to the carriage, putting the two little girls up in front with him and seating the two "ladies" in the rear. He flourished the whip over the horse's head and they were off.

Ever afterward, Treese was to remember that afternoon drive as one of the most exciting adventures of her life, for it seemed there was no smallest nook or alley which Andy did not show them, no tiniest part of the great sprawling city of San Francisco that they overlooked.

Long Wharf, with its crowded shops, cursing sailors and watery thoroughfare, seemed nevertheless resplendent to Treese. As they passed through, cargoes of teas, silks, and shawls were passed hand to hand and deposited in warehouses while hackney carriages driving at full speed went careening past. Ships that had been beached served as homes or places of business for many, and everywhere they looked was movement and hustling activity as men hurried up and down the steep street that led into the city from the water front.

The buggy lurched as they started up the steep incline to the city proper; the western side of Montgomery Street lay several feet higher than the eastern. Boxes and bales were piled everywhere, for merchants lacked warehouse facilities. Many times Andy was obliged to rein in the horse and wait several minutes for a clear passageway.

Miners' implements were stacked outside dingy little shops and gold dust gleamed darkly in jewelers' windows. Incongruously set in these surroundings they saw a little inn with a pink door and a green roof, bright with flower boxes and English to its very foundation, with a plump, bright-eyed little lady going her rounds with a watering can.

Up and up they climbed; up and up the city rose abruptly. And while they held handkerchiefs over their noses and mouths to keep out the choking dust, Andy described the winter months: how the fog rolled in like a great cloud off the bay, swirling around the torches in the streets and making a man near blind. At Clay and

Kearny streets he stopped the carriage and described the great quag-
mire that had lain there the previous winter, and how whole teams
of horses and sometimes even a drunken man had been swallowed
up in it.

In the enclosure of Portsmouth Square they saw young men
dressed in flowing capes and black hats in spite of the heat. Tattered
uniforms showed underneath. Men had worn the uniforms west to
give themselves a jaunty military air and now adopted the dress of
the native Californian: serapes, spurs and decorated saddles. Bright
carriages lined with rich silk flew past drawn by smart pairs of
horses, and here and there a path was cleared for a "lady," whose
delicacy and sometimes, it seemed, intentional frailty set her aside
from the others. Once in a while one or two young women with
painted cheeks and dressed in men's clothes came galloping by on
spirited horses. Miners in red or blue flannel shirts, felt hats and
silk hats, tall boots, and trousers supported by wide leather belts in
which were thrust pistols or knives, or both, flaunted by. Swaggering
gamblers shouted the attractions of their particular offering and
wore clusters of feathers or a squirrel's tail in their hats to proclaim
their calling.

There were Chinese women, some of them delicate and doll-like,
some bold with a peculiarly brazen and expressionless boldness.
Inside the plate-glass windows of the gambling palaces women
smiled and turned the wheel or dealt the cards. Music from fiddles
and pianos came through the open doorways. The notorious Bella
Union was crowded even this early in the day, and spreading out
and beyond the Square trailed the myriad theaters that had gone
up overnight. Actors, musicians, showboat people from the Missis-
sippi roamed the streets, distinguishable by the florid style of their
dress, even in this day of exaggerated costumes, and by their faintly
disdainful carriage.

It was late afternoon before they returned to the house, dusty
and disheveled. Elizabeth was exclaiming loudly over her displeasure at not having seen Steve Mallott and indicated in no
uncertain terms that Andy had probably arranged it so.

"Jealous, that's what you are! Simply eaten up with jealousy!"

Andy laughed and made the horse fast to the post in front of the
house before helping the girls down.

"Now how should I know where Steve Mallott is? For all I
know he's probably on a steamer somewhere between here and
Sacramento, cheating honest passengers out of their hard-won
gold."

"He's no such thing!" Elizabeth declared indignantly, allowing herself to be swung to the ground. "And even if he were, I'd still think he's the most wonderful man in California!"

Florabelle and Violet were lifted down, tired but excited, and then Treese. The two little ones ran ahead to the house and Elizabeth and Treese skipped after. Andy watched until they were inside, then climbed back into the carriage and picked up the reins.

Inside the hallway Elizabeth called, "Mother! Mother, are you up? Wait till you hear where we went!"

There was a slight rustling sound inside the parlor and Agnes appeared suddenly in the archway, white-faced and stern, her hands tight together in front of her.

"Where have you been, Treese?" she asked. Her voice was low and even, incredibly cold.

"Mamma, wait till you hear where we went, and all the wonderful things we saw!" Treese was breathless with eagerness to tell her mother everything at once. "Down by the water, and we saw all the ships, and then up that steep, steep hill, and Andy showed us Portsmouth Square, and we saw the Bella Union—"

"Who took you out?"

"Andy—Mr. Hart. He showed us the most wonderful places, Mamma . . ." Treese's voice tapered off, became hesitant. "We had the most wonderful afternoon, Mamma—"

"Take the children and see that they're cleaned up. And look at your Sunday dress. You've quite ruined it. Next time I hope you'll ask my permission before doing such a thing. Do you realize the children missed their naps? They'll be all out of sorts tomorrow."

"Aunt Agnes, I'm afraid I tempted Treese," Elizabeth put in. "I did so want her to go, and Mother said it would be all right."

"Please, Elizabeth!" Agnes turned away from her. "I'm only concerned with Treese. What you do is your own affair, apparently. But Treese must obey me. Next time, Treese, you'll be good enough to ask me before you go rushing off with someone like that."

"But, Aunt Agnes, Andy is an old friend!" Elizabeth protested. "And Mother did give her permission."

Agnes wheeled on her. "I don't care what your mother gave! And you'll please not interfere, Elizabeth!"

Treese cringed away, moving toward the stairway and herding the two little girls toward her, but Elizabeth seemed to grow more erect, to square her slender shoulders slightly. Her voice, when she spoke, had a curious, womanlike quality that seemed out of keeping with Elizabeth's usual effusive gaiety. There was a dignity about it that matched Agnes's anger and stood like a stone wall against it.

"This is still my mother's house, Aunt Agnes."

Treese watched fearfully as Elizabeth turned, sweeping past her and the little girls and mounting the stairs with quick, sure steps.

In her bedroom at the top of the stairs Margaret Delaney was dressing for dinner. She had finished arranging her hair, disheveled from her afternoon nap, and was ready to remove her wrapper and put on her dress when there was a knock at the door. She went and opened it.

"Elizabeth darling! Was your ride pleasant?"

She stopped and looked for a moment at her daughter, at the defiant tilt of her head, the red that had mounted to her cheeks, the angry glistening in her eyes.

"What is it?" she asked quietly.

All at once the rigid will power that seemed to hold the girl in escaped in a flood and her shoulders drooped, her eyes overflowed with tears and her lower lip began to tremble. She came inside and shut the door after her, leaning against it with her arms behind her.

"Mother, how long is she going to stay?" The words were thick with sobs.

The hand that held Margaret's wrapper together tightened suddenly and a tremor passed through her frame. She put an arm around her daughter and led her to the edge of the bed, sitting down beside her.

"How long is who going to stay, dear?"

"Aunt Agnes. How long is she going to live here with us?"

"Don't you want her to stay with us?"

"I hate her! You'd think this was her house, not yours. I hate her!"

Margaret looked past her daughter, through the window and down to the road, where a buggy was just disappearing from sight, moving bumpily and awkwardly, the driver seated high in front.

"Well, I don't know, dear. I'm not sure." She spoke softly, but there was a quiet conviction in her tone that belied the words. "I just couldn't say."

At eleven o'clock that night Margaret was undressed and sitting up in bed, her hands motionless in front of her on the white counterpane, their own paleness making them scarcely distinguishable from it. Her gray hair in its thick plaits fell across her shoulders. The bare, cool room was immaculately tidy, all her clothing hung away out of sight. The only note of disorder was her slippers, which toed out slightly at the side of the bed where she had stepped out of them.

She looked up as the door opened and King came in.

"Not asleep yet?" He smiled pleasantly at her.

"No."

"Well, I was just going over the plans a bit with Agnes." He walked across the room and began to undress. Glancing at him, Margaret noticed how handsome he looked with his cravat loosened and his hair mussed slightly. He sat down on a chair and leaned over to pull off his boots.

"You know, on that right wing where we were planning for the extra bedrooms? In case we can't get all the lumber we need right away, there's no reason why that has to hold up our building. Agnes suggested that we might go ahead with the main part of the house and add that extra wing as soon as we can get it. It's a remarkably good idea, I think. Hadn't occurred to me. So if we do that, there's no reason why we shouldn't be started by November. Everything's to be exactly the way you want it, Margaret. I want you to oversee the whole thing."

"I won't be here in November, King," Margaret said quietly.

King dropped his right boot to the floor and looked up slowly.

"What do you mean—won't be here?" He was frowning a perplexed frown, staring at her as though at a stranger.

"Elizabeth and I are going east for a few months."

"Going east!" He was still staring at her in disbelief. "But that's a hard trip just for a few months, Margaret. You remember how you hated it coming out. And you've hardly got here!"

"Nevertheless, we're going. We'll leave just as soon as you can arrange passage for us."

"But I don't see why! Do you dislike it here that much?"

"No. I don't dislike it. But I want to take Elizabeth away. We may stay a few months, maybe longer."

"Longer!"

She looked at him with a directness that startled him.

"We'll stay away as long as it takes you, King."

For the first time, he looked away from her. With thoughtful precision he pulled off his other boot. Then he went to the foot of the bed and sat down on it. With one hand he twisted the heavy watch chain that hung across his vest. His eyes were fixed on the floor a few feet away from the bed, and they were thoughtful.

"I guess I know what you mean, Margaret. I suspected all along that you knew. I hope you'll believe I never meant to hurt you. It was something that seemed to be stronger than I was."

"I'm not thinking of myself right now. I don't want Elizabeth to know. She's fond of you, King."

"Elizabeth!" He looked surprised.

"She's begun to resent Agnes already. She doesn't know, of course." Margaret chose her words thoughtfully. "She doesn't know what all the implications are, but she's not stupid. In some ways she's remarkably adult."

Margaret's pale hands traced the edge of the counterpane. She spoke without emotion, as though she were trying to transfer the logic of her reasoning to him. King studied her thoughtfully, almost with a touch of admiration. How different she was from Agnes! She was all he had ever wanted to make of his life, all the finest and best that an Irish immigrant's son could hope for. And yet Agnes was everything he desired, stirring his blood and making him feel a strange rebirth of vigor. She was like him, almost of his flesh, it seemed.

He stirred suddenly, leaned over and closed his hand over Margaret's.

"Don't go, Margaret," he said kindly. "You won't have to go, you and Elizabeth."

Margaret looked at her husband. There was an honesty in his eyes that she knew she could trust. He was not trying to deceive her now. Only he had not promised to give Agnes up. Had she really expected that he would? Perhaps not. She only knew that in this moment, even though he had asked her to stay, she was more hurt than ever.

CHAPTER V

"RIGHT THIS WAY, ladies and gents!" the man on the dock shouted. "Only thirty dollars a person and no charge for the babes in arms. The *Congress* will take you up the river, the beautiful Sacramento. Could you ask any more than to sail the beautiful Sacramento in a steamer like the *Congress*? I should say not! And with gold bringin' sixteen dollars an ounce, and waitin' to be shoveled up the minute you step off the gangplank! Come on, folks, buy your fares now and take the *Congress*! No pushing or shoving, plenty of room for all!" He paused to mop his forehead and run a pudgy red finger around the inside of his collar already damp with perspiration. He was stout and balding, and his green coat pulled into creases under the armpits.

A rival ship's agent, standing a few yards down the dock from him, cut in sharply. "Don't listen to the lyin' shyster, folks! The *Madeline* has as sound a hull as you'll find anywhere on the river. Ask this agent for the *Congress* about his. No, never mind! I can tell you! She's as rotten as a soft potato, and there's so much bilge in the hold already the flour's soggy! Only twenty-five dollars buys you passage on the *Madeline,* and she'll take you everywhere the *Congress* will and get you there in one piece! No charge for kiddies under four! Right here! Buy your passage on the *Madeline* for the fabulous gold fields of Californy!" The *Madeline's* agent, taller and leaner than his rival and with a sly, penetrating look, glanced triumphantly down the dock. The little stout man glowered and drew a deep breath.

"You can be sure, folks, when the price is lowered, that you're bein' offered a fool's bargain. Take it, if you want, and the risk is your own. But for the sake of the family men who have loved ones at home to think about, I'll break a precedent and offer the inducement of a twenty-dollar fare. Simply to save innocent lives. Twenty dollars, folks. It's a giveaway. Never again will the *Congress* be able to repeat an offer like this."

With ear-splitting suddenness a brass band blared forth from the deck of the *Madeline,* which was moored to the dock, playing lively martial music that made the bystanders drift toward it. The agent for the *Congress* shouted louder, and his face became an apoplectic, purply red. But the music of the band grew louder and his shouts became soundless, until he was like an angry puppet, going through gyrations that had no connection with the activity about him. One by one the onlookers filed past him and began buying fares on the *Madeline.* The agent for the *Congress* dropped his hands in defeat, and his lips curled into obscenities directed at the person of the rival agent. He took out his handkerchief again and wiped his forehead.

The two steamers were moored to the dock, and between them rose majestically the 320-foot side-wheeler, *New World,* which would carry the news of California's admission to Sacramento. The oceangoing steamer *Oregon* had brought the news earlier in the day from the East, and the city by the bay had been wild all day with inebrious joy.

It was October 18, and Agnes Delaney and her three daughters were leaving for Sacramento City on the *New World.*

Sacramento had not been King's idea!

"I'll buy you another house here in San Francisco," he had pleaded the night after his talk with Margaret. "You don't have to go away. And it'll be even better. You'll be by yourself. I can see you often."

Agnes's eyes narrowed angrily at him.

"I don't need to be bought off! And I don't want another

house. I want this house!" It was late at night, and they were alone in the parlor. A single lamp burned low on the table near them. Agnes was standing against the mantel, her hands rigid at her sides, her mouth turned down with bitterness.

"I know how all this happened! Don't think I don't know. It was Elizabeth that started everything. Not even your own daughter and you let her run your life. What does it matter to her if I live here? She's going into her fine new house!"

King took a deep, patient breath.

"It's not Elizabeth, Agnes. It's Margaret. She knows. Known all along, I suppose. She's too much of a lady to make a scene over it, and I'm not going to have her hurt. This won't change anything between us. And Margaret quite understands my relationship with her. She's a very broad-minded woman."

Agnes turned so that her back was to him. He went over to her and turned her around by the shoulders. Indignation, anger and hurt pride were in her face, but her body was firm and inflexible. The soft womanliness had vanished, leaving in its place something taut and icy.

"Agnes, please don't carry on like this. Say you'll do this for me." He tried to embrace her, but something steely and unresisting in her repulsed him. When she answered, her voice was sibilant, almost menacing in its low intensity.

"I'll not stay here! I won't stay in the same town with your precious wife and that girl and be treated like a poor relation!"

"Where will you go?"

"Sacramento City!"

He was sure she had said the first name that came to her mind. He smiled half cajolingly, half pityingly.

"How will you live?"

"I'll manage."

He sighed and walked away from her. At the other end of the room he turned to face her.

"Do you really mean this?"

"I said it, didn't I?"

He shook his head and gave a little laugh. He was not as displeased as she had intended. Sacramento was not a bad place for her. Only a day away. He could tell she was irked over his indifference. Mustn't overplay it, though. Dammit, he did want her.

"Real estate is good now in Sacramento," he said thoughtfully. "You ought to be able to make some good investments, if I advance you a little money. Then, by the time John returns, you'll have a nice start."

"Real estate!" Agnes could not conceal her surprise. She had planned to have this culminate in tears, remorse, forgiveness, repudiation of Margaret, reiteration of his love for her. "Real estate!"

"It's a very good investment," he went on smoothly. "Suppose I give you fifteen hundred in gold to start with. Inside a few days you should show a thousand per cent profit, if you're smart."

Agnes was intrigued in spite of herself.

"A thousand per cent!"

"They're making that much on lots there, so Andy tells me."

"A thousand per cent!" Agnes walked slowly away from the fireplace and sat down. Her eyes had lost their narrow resentment and had widened until they showed large and dark in her face. She stared distantly, deep in thought, and as King watched he could see her hands move slightly in her lap as she counted on her fingers.

Now, standing at the railing of the *New World* in her second-best rose silk dress and bonnet, she was the picture of composure, her white arm resting on the rail, her slender fingers tapping with aloofness on the pearl handle of her parasol; but her eyes traveled quickly over the docks, missing nothing. She was aware of all that went on around her, and for all her air of studied ennui, she was as alert and impatient as the children.

Treese, who stood close to her mother, was wearing her best flowered calico and her straw bonnet. Her handkerchief was already wadded into a damp ball in her agitation.

"Will we leave soon?" she inquired eagerly.

"Yes, soon now. Watch the children, Treese, while I go below and see to our things in the cabin."

"Are we going on the boat?" Violet inquired seriously, looking up.

"Yes, any minute now. You must be good and hold Treese's hand so you don't fall into the dirty water."

"This boat is biggest," the four-year-old Florabelle announced.

"Hold my hand, Florabelle," Treese ordered, as Agnes left the deck. She took a firm stance, her feet solidly planted, wide apart, to withstand the pulling and tugging of the two little girls, each of whom was bent on striking out in an opposite direction.

"Is this how you mind Papa?" she chided, jerking Florabelle backward and getting a firm grip on Violet's wrist. "First thing you know, one of you will be over the side, and then what? The boat would leave without you, that's what. Don't you remember what Papa said about being good? I'd just like to know what he'd say to this kind of carrying on!"

Slowly the tugging subsided, but with a heartrending slow certainty Florabelle's lower lip began to curve out and under, and large tears squeezed from the tight corners of her eyes, trickling down her cheeks toward the corners of her mouth.

"Wanta see," she whimpered.

Treese's heart turned over inside her. She let go of Violet and knelt to embrace Florabelle. "In just a few minutes, darling. When Mamma comes back up we'll walk all around the boat and see everything. But you mustn't fall overboard and spoil your pretty dress and get left behind. Come on, now. We'll go and look down at the docks."

She walked to the railing with Florabelle, seizing Violet on the way and holding them both fast. It was crowded near the rail and they had to stand back slightly. Treese arranged empty crates for the two little ones to stand on and held each girl firmly around the waist.

Standing about on the wharf was an assorted crowd of onlookers. Most of them were men, and the majority of them wore the traditional miners' outfits. The old-timers could be distinguished from the new arrivals by the dusty, worn appearance of their clothes, a patina of wear that gave them a peculiar distinction.

Treese felt a tug at her arm and looked down. Florabelle had turned away from the incongruous spectacle and was staring at the bow of the ship. One dirty finger was in the corner of her mouth, and her eyes were wide with wonder. Treese followed her gaze.

Standing several feet away from them, leaning against the ship's railing, was a young man. His face was ordinary, pleasant enough, although rather lean, and with the suggestion of a line in each cheek. He had a flowing mustache and full sideburns. His hair grew back from a wide forehead at each temple, heightening the square, angular appearance of his face, and his mouth was full, with the upper lip drawn tight over his teeth in a half-grimace as he squinted against the sun. His body was slim and wiry, and the hand that rested on the railing was lean and sinewy. Short, dark hairs that caught the sunlight lay back against his wrist. There was a suppleness, an impression of suppressed movement and energy about him that was noticeable. It was not this, however, which had caught Florabelle's eye and arrested Treese's attention.

From head to foot, he was dressed in the most bizarre costume Treese had ever seen. Even for the flamboyant opulence of San Francisco, it was extreme.

While she and the little girls watched, he donned with a flourish the black felt slouch hat he had been holding in one hand. This, together with his black broadcloth coat and trousers, completed the basic elements of his costume, but there all restraint halted. Under his open coat he wore a white shirt and gaudy cravat. The shirt, frilled and ruffled into a thousand billowing folds, gleamed with an enormous diamond stickpin, and was framed with a hand-painted vest of such magnificence that Treese gasped when she saw it. It was ornamented from top to bottom by a row of gold and pearl buttons, and adorned with life-size painted fleurs-de-lis. His black boots were polished to a dazzling brilliance, and on his fingers were several rings from which gold and diamonds flashed. From his watch, which rested in the pocket of his vest, extended an enormous gold chain which ran up and about his neck, circling it twice like a necklace.

"Funny man," Florabelle murmured. Treese shook her warningly, but the young man did not seem to have heard.

While the three girls stared in a paralysis of fascination, there suddenly appeared from behind him two young women, both expensively but flashily dressed. Both had brassy-colored hair and unnaturally red cheeks, and they were running as though from someone. Treese heard one of them cry.

"Honey, we can go on the boat, can't we? He says you're going to put us off. Tell us we can stay."

The young man, paying no attention to them, looked over their heads at another man who was approaching. Treese gave a little gasp as she recognized the second man as Andy Hart.

"I told 'em they'd have to leave," Andy said. "You try and get 'em off the damned boat!"

The man turned to the girls. "You heard what Andy said. You'll come ashore with me."

"You mean you aren't going to Sacramento?" one of them asked.

He shook his head. "I only came aboard to see Andy off."

The girls began to pout.

"I don't see why we have to leave. We want to go to Sacramento."

"If Andy doesn't want you, then you'll stay here."

The girls flounced indignantly.

"Oh, is that so! Well, I'd just like to know what makes you think you can tell us where to go and where not to go!"

"If I have to pay your passage, I can tell you! Now quit bothering us and get off the boat. Christ Almighty! Last night was last night! It's past. Over. Now get off!"

"We won't move an inch!" the first girl declared, stamping her foot.

The young man looked again at Andy Hart. The latter lifted his shoulders in a gesture of helplessness. Then, with a swiftness that would have been amazing if it had not been for the dormant energy Treese had suspected in him, the young man seized each girl by the waist, lifting them both like sacks of flour and hurling them over the side of the steamer and into the water below.

Entirely forgetting her charges, Treese ran to the railing and leaned over to have a better view. The two girls had emerged from the water, struggling and shrieking, their curls plastered flat against their heads. Between gasps for breath they let loose a storm of profanity against the two men who stood above them laughing, and then, exhausted, they went under again.

Treese marveled at their command of such language and wondered who they were. She had never heard girls talk so before, and although she had not completely understood the conversation they had had with the two men, she was sure that gentlemen never addressed ladies in such a fashion. She returned to Florabelle and Violet, who were shrieking with delight at this new game, and continued to watch the spectacle from there.

The men on the dock were immediately galvanized into action as the two young women hit the water. There was a cracking sound as a pistol shot was fired to note the excitement, and a roar went up as the men crowded to the edge. One of the miners, very drunk, shouted his intention of rescuing them.

"Outa my way!" he roared, plunging into the water. His gallantry was the signal for similar action on the part of several others, and soon the water was crowded with flailing arms, so that the heads of the two girls were scarcely visible among the swarm of rescuers. Broken sentences floated up from the churning water.

"I got 'er!"

"Hold still, sweetheart, I'll save you!"

"Don't fret, honey!"

A rope was thrown over the side of the dock, and after a tremendous amount of grunting and panting, the girls were hauled up.

The young man on deck adjusted the gold chain about his neck. When the position of the cravat and shirt ruffles suited him, he extended his hand to Andy. "Well, I guess I'll be going. Remember what I told you about keeping your eye out for me for a place in Sacramento."

"You'll never settle down. You like riding the river too well."

"No, I mean it. Keep an eye out, will you?"

Andy shrugged. "I'll do it. Only don't let me break my neck looking for a place and then you turn it down."

"I won't. You don't need to worry. Let me know."

"All right."

"You coming again soon?"

"Not for a spell. I'm not as young as you, you know. Wears me out, chasing after women like those." Andy motioned with his head toward the dock.

The young man pushed him. "Like hell!" He swung easily away from the railing and started toward the gangplank.

"So long, Andy! Don't forget what I said!"

"You bet! And take it easy on the suckers!"

Treese watched him swagger down the gangplank and disappear into the crowd. Andy Hart turned away and for the first time caught sight of them. His face broke into a broad smile and he hurried toward them.

"Why, if it ain't Miss Treese and the charming little ones! Don't tell me we're going to share this boat ride?"

"We're going to Sacramento," Violet announced.

"For a trip?"

"We're going to live there," Treese said shyly. "Are you on your way home?"

"Yep. Got what I came for—or rather, I stayed for the celebration, and now I'm going." He frowned thoughtfully. "How long have you ladies been standing there?"

"A long time, Mr. Hart," Treese said.

"We saw those girls get throwed in the water," Florabelle said.

"Well, now, I must say you ladies are getting an early education in the ways of the West," Andy observed, settling back against a post and lighting his pipe. The sun glinted off his spectacles and cast reflections on their surface so that it was difficult at times to see the expression of his eyes, but Treese had a warm, pleasant suspicion that they were laughing.

"And where is your fine hat, Miss Treese?" he inquired.

Treese looked down sheepishly. "Oh, it's—it's a little big. It doesn't stay on too well."

"Doesn't stay on, eh?" Andy considered for a moment. "And just the right kind of hat for a trip like this, too. Why don't you fetch it up here? Maybe I can fix it up for you."

Treese's mouth fell open. "Oh, would you, Mr. Hart?"

"Run along. I'll keep an eye on these two while you get it."

By the time Treese came bounding back on deck, hat in hand

and quite out of breath, all three were seated on the deck, with Andy, fully warmed up to the business of amusing his small charges, flourishing cards with an amazing dexterity and keeping up a running line of chatter not unlike that of a barker at a medicine show. All three sat cross-legged, Violet and Florabelle with wide, amazed eyes and open mouths, Andy with his hat pushed back from his forehead, his spectacles glistening in the sunlight, beads of perspiration standing out on his forehead.

All three looked up as she approached. Immediately Violet and Florabelle scrambled to their feet, seized her and pulled her down beside them.

"I guess we'll be going pretty quick now, won't we, Mr. Hart?" Treese inquired.

"Any minute now."

Treese glanced about her and Andy watched her out of the corner of his eye. In spite of the girl's plainness there was an eager curiosity about her that in moments like this made her almost attractive. When she was deep in thought, her gray eyes acquired a depth that made them darken, and it was easy to forget her too prominent coloring, her oversized hands, the thinness of her awkward body. There was something touching in the grown-up way she handled the children. It was obvious she was accustomed to caring for them, and her adult approach to them was out of keeping but somehow moving, in comparison with her own youthful naïveté. She seemed accustomed to responsibility; ingrown, somehow. Andy noticed that she seldom laughed. Now her eyes seemed faraway, as though she was not concentrating on the immediate excitement around her, but on thoughts of her own. Suddenly she spoke.

"Mr. Hart, who was that man with you?"

Andy lifted her hat to the light and began the delicate process of threading the rawhide through.

"Name's Steve Mallott."

Treese gasped. "Elizabeth's Mr. Mallott?"

"As much Elizabeth's as he is anybody's," he chuckled.

"But those clothes!"

"Those clothes are, you might say, the mark of his profession. He's a river gambler. Makes his living gambling on boats like this one. Works up and down the Sacramento."

A little speculative line creased Treese's forehead. "Does he cheat?"

Andy stopped short in the knot he was tying. He considered the question for a moment, his thin, scholarly face thoughtful, his shining spectacles covering what was in his eyes.

"Well, now, that's hard to say," he said slowly. "I never heard that anybody caught him cheating." He seemed satisfied with the answer. He completed the chin strap and held the hat out to her. She did not take it immediately. She was looking past him, distantly, to the wharf where the steamer was still moored, and there was a note of speculation in her gray eyes.

"But you don't think it was right, do you, treating ladies like that?"

Andy took out his handkerchief and mopped his forehead.

"Well, now, there's a very fine line of distinction there. Matter of fact, I'm not just sure that you'd call them ladies."

"Papa always takes his hat off when he meets ladies," Violet said.

"What do you mean, not ladies?" Treese inquired.

"Well, now . . ." Andy's reply was drowned in the roar of the engines, as they started pumping deep within the ship. The great side wheels lashed at the water and the big steamer began to shove away from the dock.

"We're moving!" Violet shrieked.

The two little girls scrambled to their feet and ran for the railing. In a flash Treese was after them, dragging them back.

"I wanna see!" Florabelle wailed.

Andy got up and lifted them so they could see the progress of the steamer. The men on the docks were waving and growing smaller as the *New World* drew away, and the shore line of San Francisco grew smaller and more vague. The buildings diminished and ran together, and a kind of green and blue and purple indefiniteness settled over it. The size of the ship seemed to grow, until it was enormous, a whole city, a whole world. They were leaving behind them the bay, the Pacific, the last water link with the East. They were headed inland, up the mysterious and wonderful Sacramento, into depths of a land that promised riches or disillusionment, poverty or opulence, into a wild, beautiful new land whose beauty was unseen now by the multitudes who came to scrabble in its centuries-old, luxuriant earth for gold. Infinitesimal as they seemed among the thousands who had come west, fighting, suffering, searching; mingled as they were and lost in identity, they remained individuals, and to each of them the West was, at this moment, not the kaleidoscopic, crowded, ever-shifting scene it had first appeared to them in San Francisco. It was a promise held out to them as individuals, a promise whose fabric was the strength and beauty and driving earnestness that had compelled each of them westward.

Forged in the mundane desire for gold, it had acquired, through suffering and endurance, a kind of undeniable grandeur.

CHAPTER VI

KING DELANEY, who had had apprehensions about sending even so intrepid a woman as Agnes alone up the Sacramento with three children, had personally commissioned the steamer's captain to watch out for them, and to be responsible for seeing that they were established at the City Hotel before leaving them. The captain, impressed with their importance by the fact that they were to be cabin passengers and that King had paid him one hundred dollars for carrying out the request, did everything possible to make the trip comfortable for them, and as a crowning touch invited them to have supper at his table. By nightfall the deck was already crowded.

In the captain's quarters, Agnes, Treese, Florabelle and Violet were seated at the dining table, together with two other cabin passengers, a minister and his wife, who, by virtue of their established respectability, had also been invited.

The minister, Reverend Mr. Sloane, was a thin, gaunt man, unusually tall, with sparse dark hair and a protruding jaw which gave his mild appearance a touch of peculiar belligerence. Mrs. Sloane was short and was characterized by a sort of gelatinous plumpness which gave her a flabby, unsolid appearance. Her straw-colored hair was drawn straight back from her face and rigidly knotted at the back of her head, except for a few shorter hairs which stuck out wispily at the sides of her face. Her skin was a pasty white, with the exception of her nose, which was perpetually red, as though from weeping. Yet she wore an ingratiating smile. Her attire was an uncompromising black.

Treese, watching her, could not help making a mental comparison between Mrs. Sloane and her mother.

Agnes was still wearing her rose silk, but she had freshened her toilet since coming aboard, and her immaculate freshness was like a breath of cool, sweet air among the dusty crowded passengers. Her dark hair, drawn back smoothly from its center part, smelled faintly of verbena, and the edge of a lace handkerchief protruded slightly from the bosom of her dress. She smiled readily, praising the captain into paroxysms of blushes over his ship and showing an avid interest, which Treese completely failed to comprehend, in the Sloanes' plans for bringing Christian order and decency into the mining camps north of Marysville.

When they were introduced, the Sloanes shook Treese's hand gravely, Reverend Sloane with his cold, dry hand, Mrs. Sloane with her moist flabby one; said they were glad to meet her and that she was a fine brave girl, and a big girl too—wasn't that nice—and that she was no doubt a great help to her mamma. Promptly forgetting Treese, they turned their attention to Violet and Florabelle. Mrs. Sloane was enchanted with them both, particularly with the four-year-old Florabelle, whose blonde innocence never failed to attract admirers, and even Reverend Sloane unbent enough to allow her to sit on his knee for a short time before the soup was served. His knee was bony, and Florabelle, not particularly at ease with him, soon scrambled down and ran to Treese, burying her head in her sister's lap. Mrs. Sloane was enchanted at the "sweet, modest little darling," and insisted on being seated next to Florabelle at supper, a prospect for which the latter showed a noticeable lack of enthusiasm.

Agnes, proud as always when her children were being admired and complimented, went to some pains to discuss with Reverend Sloane the problem of bringing Christianity to the West and blushed with becoming modesty when he informed her that the problem of Christianizing California would never be entirely solved until more God-fearing family women like herself came out to make decent, respectable homes for their men.

By midnight they were only two and a half hours out of Sacramento. Florabelle and Violet had fallen asleep and Treese, without undressing, had lain down on the cabin's other bunk. She did not sleep, but kept her eyes wide open, listening to the rhythmic chug of the engines and the churning of the wheels, hearing the faint motions Agnes made as she moved about the room preparing for the landing. Once Treese sat up and looked at her.

Agnes was sitting at a small stationary table with a little satchel open in front of her. She had opened it and was busily counting the bags of gold dust and the ingots that were inside it. Treese thought she had never seen such an accumulation of wealth before in her life, and her eyes grew wide. Then, slowly, as though sensing that she was being watched, Agnes turned to her. There was craftiness in the look, almost, it seemed, a touch of guilt, but Treese realized only that it made her ill at ease, as though she had been caught peering somewhere she had no business to be.

"Well, what are you looking at?" Agnes demanded.

Treese swallowed. "Nothing."

Almost immediately Agnes's expression softened. She got up and came over to Treese, patting her cheek. "Get a little sleep now, Treese. We'll be getting off soon."

Treese settled back in the bunk, but she could not sleep. Tenderness was rare, coming from Agnes. She could still feel the place on her cheek where her mother's hand had touched it, smooth and exquisitely cool.

Florabelle and Violet grumbled sleepily when they were awakened and dressed, and Treese petted and talked with them to distract their attention while she drew on their clothes. She was so excited herself at the prospect of actually seeing the fabulous Sacramento City that she could scarcely find the buttonholes and tie the ribbons.

"Just think, we're really here now. Our new home! This is where we're going to live, Florabelle! Listen, Violet, as soon as you get your bonnet on, Mamma will take us up on deck and we can see Sacramento. Won't that be exciting? Do hurry, now, and put your arm through here, Florabelle! Look now—there! Oh, how sweet you both look!"

"Where are we going to stay?" Violet inquired.

"In a hotel. In a real hotel! The captain is going to take us ashore himself and see us there."

"Do we have to pay?" Florabelle inquired.

"Yes, of course. Now come on. We'll go up on deck."

Agnes bustled over to them. "Are they ready, Treese? All right, fine. Now, do we have everything? No, we can leave the bags. The captain has promised to help us with them. All right, then, come on!"

Agnes herself was excited, and Treese could see it in the blush of color that suffused her cheeks, the way her warm lips were half parted, the glow and sparkle that made her dark eyes dance. In her rose silk dress with her dark cloak thrown over it and her little bonnet, she looked scarcely older than Treese. Treese seized the children by the hand and followed her mother on deck.

The large crate was still on the deck of the ship, and she lifted them up so they could sit on it and see over the railing. Violet screamed with excitement and kicked her feet against the boards. Florabelle followed her example.

"Hush, now!" Treese remonstrated. "Now, be good and look."

The deck was already crowded with eager passengers, all shoving and pushing for a place at the railing as the ship nosed in and was made fast at the Embarcadero, a strip of land separating the river from Front Street, where the city proper began. The Embarcadero, where ships docked and where all the loading and unload-

ing went on during the day, was but dimly lit now by the light of
torches on Front Street, but Treese could form a vague, imaginative
picture of what it must be like during daylight. She could see the
outlines of piles of crates and barrels and bales, and could see the
silhouettes of some other ships drawn up beside the *New World*.

All Sacramento had turned out to welcome the steamer. Not
only because she was one of the finest on the river, but because it
was known ahead of time that the *New World* was carrying the
news of California's admission to the Union. And as Treese and
Agnes and the little girls watched, they saw a man hang far over
the railing of the ship and bellow in a thunderous voice that echoed
and re-echoed up and down the Embarcadero.

"She's admitted!"

Immediately a cannon mounted on the levee was fired several
times. Treese and the girls put their fingers in their ears to still
the roar. In this position they watched a man mount his horse and
gallop at breakneck speed through the dimly lit streets, waving his
hat. They removed their fingers from their ears and his excited
shouts reached them.

"She's admitted! She's admitted! California's admitted!"

Spurred into action by the signal for which it had been waiting,
Sacramento suddenly was transformed from a sleepy city of tents
and flimsy frame buildings into a panorama of light and noise.
Bonfires were built in the streets and torches blazed up and down
the length of the Embarcadero. Lights shone from swinging saloon
doors, and against the fires figures moved and danced and gyrated
like puppets on strings in an orgy of celebration. They danced, they
sang frenzied, tuneless songs, they embraced each other with hysterical abandon. Sacramento lunged into the fierce fire called
patriotism.

Agnes, leaning against the railing, felt a surge of excitement. An
excitement that was mingled with a kind of unreasoning terror at
the thought that in a few minutes she would be on shore, in the
middle of the shouting mob, and that the *New World* would leave
and she would be alone. Alone in Sacramento! A place so far from
Boston in spirit and heritage that it might have been China. And
yet coupled with this sinking fright was a kind of primitive exulta-
tion. Even as she asked herself whether she had done right to insist
on coming west, and to undertake this trip inland; even as she
wondered what would become of them in a land without law,
where horse stealing was punishable by death and murder too commonplace even to make for interesting table conversation, still she
felt a warm current of confidence, starting from deep inside her

and spreading warmly through her whole body. If it was lawless, then laws would have to be made. If there was no social order, then society would need leaders. If these people were restless and brawling and without restraint, so much the better. For here no one need worry about family or background or what came before. All that was important was what was to come. All that mattered was the future. And somehow in that moment Agnes was convinced that this Sacramento City, which had already in its short life suffered the ravages of fire, flood and riot, this city of tents and saloons, rough shacks and rougher men, had a future.

"Welcome to our city," said a voice behind them.

They turned to see Andy Hart, bowing slightly and extracting from his waistcoat a large gold watch. He opened it and examined it. "Two-thirty on the nose. Fine time we made. May I be of assistance to you, madam?"

Agnes drew herself in. "Thank you, Mr. Hart. The captain is taking care of us and escorting us to the hotel."

Andy bowed again, and Treese thought there was the shadow of a smile on his face. "As you say, Mrs. Delaney. Let me wish you good fortune, then, and a speedy reunion with your husband. We'll meet again soon, I trust?"

Agnes inclined her head slightly but did not look at him.

"Good-bye, ladies," Andy said, turning to them.

Treese felt slightly embarrassed and ill at ease. She was sorry to see him leave, and was torn between Agnes's animosity and her own desire to tell him how much she liked him.

"Good-bye, Mr. Hart," she said shyly. Agnes threw her a warning look.

Florabelle, completely oblivious of these undercurrents, seized his coattails.

"Stay!" she pleaded. "I like you!"

Andy grinned and detached himself gently. "Be a good girl now. We're most ready to go ashore."

"You must come and visit us," Violet said expansively.

"Well, now, you bet I'll do that." Andy grinned and looked toward Agnes, who had turned her back. Treese caught his eye and something warm and understanding passed between them. Then the gangplank was lowered and the passengers began to pour off. He moved away and was lost in the crowd.

The captain edged his way toward them, holding two of their valises. Agnes had a firm grasp on the satchel containing the gold.

"All ready!" the captain roared over the noise. "I got somebody to carry the trunk to the hotel. We better get started!"

Agnes turned briskly, her eyes alight with excitement. "You hold onto Florabelle, Treese. I'll take Violet. Don't let go her hand. Ready, now?"

With the captain serving as a battering ram, they made their way to the gangplank, half pushing, half shoving their way down to the dock.

"This way!" the captain shouted. "Don't mind if the men stare. Women and children are a pretty rare sight." As if to bear out his words, a dirty-shirted man reached down to caress Florabelle's curls. He was rewarded with a disarming smile before Treese noticed and jerked her away. The strangeness of the night and the wild town frightened her.

"Make way! Make way!" someone yelled. "Woman and children!" Instantly there was a scuffle as the men began to vie with each other for the honor of clearing a path and holding a torch to light their way. Treese felt self-conscious as she walked along holding more tightly to Florabelle's hand.

"Where's everybody going?" the little one asked.

"They live here."

"All of them?"

"Yes. Hurry along now."

"Outa the way! Can't you see it's a lady?" There was a sound of a blow and one of their phalanx of protectors was rendered unconscious.

They were momentarily halted by the press of the crowd and Treese looked around her, hoping for a glimpse of Andy Hart. Back of them the *New World* loomed tall and impressive. Its decks were almost emptied now, except for a few members of the crew. It looked strangely deserted. She watched as a handful of the last passengers made their way down the gangplank and onto the Embarcadero. There was more shouting and they started to move again.

There was a commotion next to them and they turned. A man had fallen to the ground and several persons were bending over him. Treese recognized Andy, who had knelt quickly and was holding the man's head.

"Just a drunk, ma'am. Don't get excited," the captain reassured Agnes. Agnes drew in her skirts with distaste. "Come along, Treese!"

Treese paused for a moment. She saw Andy raise his head and noticed that there was a grave expression on his face. There was no laughter behind his spectacles now, and Treese even fancied that he had grown pale.

"Where's Dr. Spaulding?" he asked hoarsely. "Somebody get Dr. Spaulding."

CHAPTER VII

FOR SCENES of sheer terror, Treese was never to forget the month that followed their arrival in Sacramento on the *New World*.

The man who had collapsed on the dock died almost immediately, stricken with cholera. Six more were dead on the following day, and the daily mortality rate rose swiftly until it passed the hundred mark. The same ship that had brought the joyous news of California's admission to the Union had brought with it a scourge even more terrible than the fires and floods which had already ravaged and gutted the town during its brief existence. Fear descended like a great heavy hand over the city, and roads were choked with men trying to get away only to fall by the wayside, themselves stricken. Agnes, too, tried to get away, but the futility of any such attempt soon made itself evident. There were no wagons to be had, and it was impossible to travel far on foot. In the stricken city, parents deserted children and children their parents, so frantic had become the fight for self-preservation. Screams of the afflicted and of their loved ones who could only stand by helpless filled the air night and day. The city's seventeen doctors worked tirelessly to check the epidemic, to give relief, but the toll rose relentlessly, and daily the disease claimed its victims. Priests and ministers joined in the effort to save lives and many of these, together with doctors, were among the fallen. Funerals became so commonplace they were scarcely attended, and long trenches were dug in the City Cemetery to receive the bodies.

All during the early days of the epidemic Agnes was conscious of a feeling not so much of terror as of indignation. It was unbelievable that anything so disastrous should have accompanied her arrival in Sacramento; it was still more unthinkable that she should find herself shut up in a hotel with fifteen hundred dollars in gold in the little leather satchel under her bed and yet be unable to make use of it. After her first futile effort to escape the city she resigned herself to the idea of remaining there, and devoted all her energies toward keeping apart from the general contamination. She had all meals served in their hotel room until even that service was discontinued by the management, whose ranks had been decimated by the plague. Then she was obliged to go abroad herself and find food, a task she performed not so much with fear as with intense annoy-

ance, for it could truthfully be said that not once did it occur to
Agnes that she or the girls might become ill. She was too basically
healthy, like a strong, sensuous animal, to admit that she might be
a prey to the scourge that struck down others. She had never known
illness; even her pregnancies had been but minor inconveniences,
and childbirth had been a momentary pain.

Her main motive in avoiding the suffering that was everywhere
evident was simply to keep her frame of mind on as even a plane as
possible. She felt keenly that the success she was determined to
make in Sacramento hinged almost entirely on her own level-
headedness. It was the one thing she had been able to maintain, all
through the hardships of the long trip west. It was the one thing,
she admitted, that had enabled her to seal a bargain with King
which a sillier and more emotional woman might have cluttered up
with entanglements and promises. She was not going to lose it at
this stage of the game, and she deliberately avoided as far as possible
all contact with what might tend to terrify or distract her.

She was not entirely insensible to the suffering about her; it
was simply that she saw her obligations in a narrow path whose
confines were herself and her children. Beyond that, she would not
stray in thought or action lest that straying produce some deviation
from her avowed purpose.

When the epidemic was eight days old, she began to be concerned over her finances. King had lent her fifteen hundred dollars
and Delaney had left something over a hundred. She had already
used more than a hundred and fifty for the hotel room and for
food, which was being held by speculators for fabulous sums, and
she began to be genuinely concerned over how long it would be
before the cholera subsided. She had planned on retaining at least a
thousand for whatever business deal she might be able to transact
as King had instructed her to do.

The fact that she was unable to cast about for a suitable investment also was irking to her. No one would discuss business of any
sort and, indeed, most of the town's enterprises had been shut
down either by death or by the fear of it. The streets were deserted
except for the stricken, who fell by the score in paroxysms of vomit-
ing and fever. Day by day her temper grew shorter and Treese was
hard put to keep the children amused within the four walls of the
hotel room, and to keep them out of the way of Agnes's irascibility.
They clamored to be allowed out of doors and when she refused
they put up such a protest that she was obliged to invent new games
which would keep them occupied. They were, by turns, Injuns,
river captains, merchants with bolts of bright material to be sold.

They were grand ladies, dressed in Agnes's gowns, which she some-what reluctantly permitted to be used as an aid in keeping them quiet. They pretended to be sick and Treese acted as doctor. They put on impromptu tableaux. They imitated every animal they had encountered in their limited experience. And yet even then, by three or four in the afternoon they were tired and flushed, bored with the little room, tired of their games, their tempers were short and they wept at the slightest provocation.

Treese was a miracle of patience at these times. She tried never to reveal the fear that was in her own heart. For while Agnes felt only an irritation, an aloofness from the terror that was all around them, Treese felt its presence keenly. She was every moment aware of the stifling breath of the dying about them and the cries of the sick penetrated to their hotel room even through the children's cries and laughter, cutting like a cold blade against her heart. Her hands would grow cold and wet with fear and she would tremble violently and hold the children tight against her until they cried out impatiently.

Before dawn on the 29th of October she was awakened by whimpering moans from Florabelle and found her violently nauseated. By noon Violet was ill and all during the day and night Treese and Agnes remained by their bed, placing cold cloths on their hot foreheads and comforting them as best they could. They took turns searching the streets fruitlessly for a doctor. Time seemed to dissolve as they worked tirelessly, fought with desperation to hold it back. All their efforts were to no avail and before midnight, before either of them was quite able to comprehend and absorb the crush of events, both Florabelle and Violet were dead. They died quietly, with only a slight whimpering protest, small hands raised against the inexorable blackness.

When it was over, Agnes threw herself across the bed with a harsh sob and wept, clinging to their small bodies and emitting dry strangling sounds. It was nearly a quarter of an hour before she raised herself and saw that Treese had sunk to the floor in a heap.

"Treese." Her voice was tremulous, fearful. "Treese!" It rose until it was almost a scream. She knelt down quickly and weakly tried to pull the inert form up from the floor. She could feel that the girl's body was hot with fever. With her last ounce of energy she dragged Treese to the other bed, loosened her clothing and covered her. Slowly she rose and leaned against the wall. She could feel the strength leave her legs until she could scarcely hold herself erect. Her clothing was drenched with perspiration and clung to her. Her hair had come loose from its pins and combs and was straggling down her back.

"What am I going to do?" she sobbed to the room which was all at once lifeless and suffocating, full of the sight and smell and sense of death. "God! What am I going to do?"

Andy leaned down and with considerable effort lifted his boots. The exertion caused him to fall back. He lay there for a few minutes before he sat up and began pulling them on. It felt strange after ten days. His hands fumbled. The fingers were stiff and swollen with recent fever. The strain of trying to pull on the heavy boots was almost pain. Perspiration began to dot his forehead and he cursed weakly at the boots. "God damn!"

He finished the job laboriously and rose, steadying himself with both hands against the small table near his cot. He had been among the early victims of the cholera and had not left his office since. Dr. Spaulding stopped as often as he could and brought some food. It was as much attention as anyone was getting.

His legs buckled under him and he sank back on the cot. Feebly, he reached out for the whisky bottle that was on the stand and brought it to his lips, taking long grateful gulps of it. It trickled out of the corners of his mouth and down his beard and neck. He opened his eyes a trifle wider and passed the back of his hand across his forehead. His shirt was wet with perspiration, and the smell of stale sweat, together with the stink of excrement and vomit, made him frown and turn restlessly on the pillow in an attempt to escape it. He turned back in irritation; it was everywhere. He looked toward the windows. All of them closed. He raised himself slightly on his elbows, then sank back with a thud. He raised the hand that held the whisky bottle and summoning all the depleted reserve of his strength, sent it crashing through the window nearest the cot. He lay back again and breathed hungrily of the damp autumn air that rushed into the bare little office. He'd have to get out of here. He'd have to start getting around. Maybe tomorrow. Right now he was so hellishly tired. He'd have to look up the Delaneys. That fellow Delaney was all right. And somebody'd have to see about those three young'uns . . .

When Andy arrived at the hotel the next day, pale and wasted, Treese was still fevered but she had sunk into a fitful sleep of delirium. While he waited outside at the curb, firmly grasping the halter of the tired but priceless rawboned nag he had confiscated, Agnes put on her black dress, pinned her hair up with hands that trembled and tied on her black bonnet. The color was completely drained from her usually glowing face and the slight exertion of dressing made a clammy perspiration start out upon her body.

She went downstairs and joined him wordlessly. She took the halter from his hand and grasped the gun he handed her, standing watch over the precious horse and wagon while he went inside. In a few moments he returned carrying a small blanket-wrapped bundle. He was breathing heavily under the burden. His eyes were wide with the effort, strained and bloodshot. He deposited it in the wagon and went back inside to return with a second bundle. He placed it beside the first one and swayed weakly, catching at the wagon for support. He then drew himself erect, pulling his shoulders back and moving his head slightly from side to side, his chin up as though to catch his breath. Agnes gave him back the gun and stepped up to the high front seat without help. He climbed up after her and picked up the reins.

They rode in silence to the cemetery and Agnes watched him gently lay the bodies of the little girls in one of the fresh long trenches dug earlier in the day. There were no coffins. The cemetery was deserted momentarily except for them, and the earth as he shoveled it over the small bodies made little plunking sounds. She closed her eyes and prayed that their souls might be commended to the ever-loving and eternal care of their Creator. It was an automatic gesture. She had not the slightest imaginative theory as to the fate of their souls at that moment. The brown earth that heaped into a growing mound over their physical remains seemed to her inescapable and imprisoning.

When it was done they got back into the wagon and drove north along Tenth Street. At J Street Andy pulled on the reins and the horse came to a patient halt.

"I'll have to leave you off here, Mrs. Delaney. I promised the doc I'd put this wagon to use." He nodded toward a blanket-covered mound on the curb. Agnes shuddered and climbed down.

"Thank you, Mr. Hart," she said without emotion. She felt no real gratitude toward him and no resentment. It could have been anyone with a wagon. The wagon was the important thing. Strange, how values had a way of changing. In San Francisco she had looked longingly at the satin-lined carriages and desperately wanted one. Now the dirtiest, rough-boarded rig was a godsend. Anything to cart away the dead or help the living escape. Only there was no escape now. There was Treese lying in the hotel room; food must be found, and fresh water. Agnes circled around the pile of bodies that Andy had started to place in the wagon. She did not look at them. She did not look back as she proceeded down J Street. The

horse market at Eighth was deserted. It was the first time she had
seen it without its customary crowd of swappers and buyers. The
stalls were open and desolate; even the mules were gone. Stolen
probably, she thought. She heard men's voices coming distantly.
There were two of them and they were quarreling about a
horse.

"Git off, Pa!" It was a young man's voice, low and menacing.

"Go t' hell. I seen the nag first." Heels hit against flanks and
there was the sound of scuffling hoofs. Then a shot split the motionless air and there was a heavy thud, followed by a moment of
silence. The horse started up again and galloped off, its hoofbeats
diminishing in volume. Agnes turned for the first time and looked.
There was an old man lying quite still just inside one of the far
stalls. She looked away quickly, keeping her eyes rigidly front. She
walked on hurriedly through the deserted streets. At Fourth Street
she stopped and leaned against a closed saloon. One of its swinging doors had been torn off its hinge and hung crazily.

Agnes could feel fatigue and hunger and weakness surging up
and engulfing her. Her knees were utterly without strength. She
would rest a minute. She was so tired.

For the first time in her life, Agnes Delaney knew the knifings
of a remorse so acute that it was actual physical pain. Even as she
told herself that the thing was all of Delaney's doing, and that if
he had stayed with them and protected them Florabelle and Violet
would still be alive, even as she sought in a thousand excuses to
vindicate herself, still her conscience knew no surcease. She had
neglected them; she had been indifferent to their well-being. She
had been too sure of their immunity. Perhaps she had not taken
adequate precautions to protect them. They were only babies and
she should have been more attentive to them. She should have
watched closely and looked for some sign, some symptom. Maybe
then she could have—but no, how could she have known? When
grown, healthy men were falling in the streets at this very minute,
how could one tell if a baby was ill? Laughing and playing right
up to the last and never giving a sign—

She thought of Treese and her footsteps quickened as she
goaded her already depleted strength into taking her back to the
hotel. Treese was already sick; she must hurry back and see what
could be done for her. She must save her, no matter what. If
Delaney should come back! In the tangle of her own tortured
thoughts, it did not occur to Agnes that this was the first time in
her life she had feared Delaney's disapprobation. In this moment
all that had gone before—King, the business she had anticipated,

the fortune she had hoped to earn—everything that was not connected with the agony of the immediate present, had become cheap and insignificant and shoddy. She could not even think of it without a stab of remorse and a quick wave of self-reproach. All that kept recurring, burning itself into her wounded, weakened consciousness was the thought of redeeming herself in some way. She must make up for it! She would never let Delaney think she had been careless or negligent with the children. He would have to understand. She would make him understand. For she had loved them too! Maybe not in the foolish, sentimental way he had. But in her own way. They were hers and she had been so proud of them! He would have to believe and understand.

She dragged herself up the steps to the hotel room and to the side of Treese's bed. The girl had awakened and was moaning quietly, tossing from side to side and throwing back the covers. Agnes covered her and sank down beside her, burying her face in the counterpane.

All that night, without stopping even for food, Agnes watched over her, bring her fresh water which she had bullied from a vendor earlier, smoothing back her hair, talking to her in a voice that, had Treese been able to hear it, would have been scarcely recognizable as Agnes's. She lit a lamp and kept it turned down low, across the room from the bed so that its light would not shine on Treese. She brought a chair to the bedside and sat in it, rocking gently back and forth from time to time in her nerve-racked anxiety, twisting her skirt in her hands. Just before dawn she dozed off fitfully only to waken with a start as the first light came through the window. Anxiously, she leaned forward and put her hand on Treese's forehead. It seemed a little cooler. Agnes sank back in the chair and drew an exhausted breath. For the first time she remembered Keith and wept with a kind of hysterical thankfulness.

If Agnes had been a woman more given to examining motives and determining cause and effect in any given circumstance she might better have comprehended the meaning of what happened during the next few days, might even have understood its significance in the light of what was to follow. If she had been less inclined to live only for the moment, and had been able to see reasons behind what she did, she might have been able to understand the mental state in which she found herself. As it was, she found herself obeying impulses and going through motions utterly foreign to her without ever being exactly sure why she was doing so. It was as though there were a constant pressing pain upon her conscience which she had to relieve and for which relief could only be found in a penitence of self-denial. She was never away from Treese's bedside for more than a few moments. All during the early part of November, while Treese was recuperating, she remained beside her, comforting her, bringing her as much fresh food as she could find no matter what price she had to pay. She put aside her own grief over Florabelle and Violet in an attempt to comfort Treese over their death, to assure her that Delaney would soon be back and they would be together again, that their love for one another was strong enough to sustain them even through this.

At such times, when Agnes would hold her hand and sit beside the bed talking earnestly and anxiously to her, Treese would stare with frank and wide-eyed surprise at her mother, aroused from the lethargy of her own misery by the sheer novelty of it. She could not believe that this was Mamma, always so beautiful and distant and unapproachable, who now sat, looking pale and thin, almost disheveled, and comforted her with an earnestness that sometimes was near entreaty. As she began to grow accustomed to it, she would lie back and listen, answering Agnes in monosyllables and half sentences, assuring her mother again and again that it would all come right in the end. As soon as Delaney returned they would set about finding a house where they could be happy and forget all that had gone before. It would almost seem then that their devotion to each other was limitless and that nothing was so important to either of them as comforting the other and making the burden of mental anguish lighter.

To Treese this devotion, this desperate desire to enter into a secret and special place in her mother's affection was intensely real and actual. Plunged into loneliness and grief, without any of the human companionship and warmth she had known in Florabelle and Violet's love, she was more than ever eager to feel close to someone. And to have Agnes ready to offer it to her, to be miraculously admitted to what had always been closed to her before seemed too wonderful to believe. Again and again, weak and heartbroken as she was, she felt a thrill at the thought of Agnes's nearness and found comfort for her grief in thinking she had found in some measure the love that had been taken from her. It did not occur to her that the motivation behind Agnes's attitude was any different from that behind her own.

All during the hectic days when the epidemic rose to its crashing climax, when the streets outside were littered with dead and dying, and while Treese, deathly pale and gaunt, lay in the bare hotel room slowly gaining back her strength ounce by ounce, Agnes never swerved from her course of penitent devotion. If anyone had

asked her the cause for her sudden humility, she would have had an
answer ready immediately. She was alone in a strange and terrifying city of dead men. She had lost her two babies, her darlings; she
had snatched back from death's door her other child. She must keep
this last thread of her little family intact. Nothing must happen
now when she had suffered so much already. She must give Treese
every comfort and love, for they were two alone in an unfriendly
world. They must give each other strength to go on. And yet not in
the welter of platitudes that would have sprung to her mind would
Agnes have included the real cause.

Since the day when she half walked, half ran back to the hotel
from the cemetery in a fever of remorse, she had not called by
name the feeling that never left her for a moment. And if she had
ever asked herself the reason for her state of mind, she would have
been quite satisfied with the trite explanations that had such a ring
of logic to them. Because it was a thing which had never happened
to her before, it was quite beyond her grasp to realize that for the
first time she was afraid of Delaney and of what he would do to her.
Why hadn't she stayed in San Francisco and taken what King
offered her? There was something terrifying in the thought of
Delaney's huge frame with its latent fury and strength roused to
an anger that stemmed from deep within him, from a hurt that
struck deep at the core of him. Remembering his childlike delight
when the children were born, Agnes went cold with a panicky fear
when she thought of his return. And because Treese was so like
Delaney, because there was so much about her that seemed to be
Delaney himself, it seemed to Agnes that in offering an excess of
devotion to Treese she was somehow atoning to Delaney. They
were alike, Treese and Delaney. If she could make Treese forgive
her and love her, then Delaney would too.

What she had not counted on was Andy Hart's sending for
Delaney and his return from the mines at a time when she had not
yet prepared herself to face him.

It was the second week in November that Treese was allowed
for the first time to sit in a chair near the window where she could
look out at the river. Agnes wrapped her warmly in a quilt and
then sat beside her reading from a book. For perhaps two hours
Treese listened, her head tilted slightly toward Agnes but her eyes
intent on the scene outdoors. She had lost pounds during her illness,
and her skin, which had a pale sallow cast, seemed to be stretched
tight over her cheekbones, giving the shadowed places underneath
a ghostly sunken appearance.

Agnes, who had given little or no attention to her appearance since the death of Florabelle and Violet, was in black, and her own pallor matched Treese's. Her hair seemed to have lost its luster. It was carelessly knotted at the back of her neck and a few stray hairs escaped the pins and combs, giving it a drab, lifeless look. Her plump hands were thinner and bonier and there were little lines of black under the neglected oval nails.

"There, now," she said, closing the book. "That's enough for the first time. You'd better get back in bed."

"Oh, but I like it here!" Treese protested. Her gray eyes were enormous in her emaciated face.

"Plenty of time for it later on." Agnes's tone was brisk and authoritative and Treese permitted herself to be helped to the bed. Agnes covered her and went back to the window, to the chair Treese had vacated. For several minutes she rocked back and forth quietly, looking out over Front Street and the Embarcadero to the river with unseeing eyes. Absently, she patted a straggling hair into place. Her whole body seemed to sag, its muscles too lifeless and inert to support it. Her shoulders, usually firm and resolute, were rounded slightly, and in her lap her fingers toyed restlessly with the fringe on her shawl like the fingers of an old woman. For the first time in her life Agnes was completely at a loss.

Somehow she must reach Delaney. He must be told what had happened. But how could she tell him? Of course, it might be weeks before he could send word back of his whereabouts and before she would be able to reach him. In the meantime she would have to collect her wits. There was barely a thousand dollars left in the satchel. When that was gone, what would become of them? How could she go begging to King for more money? And look at her! She was acutely aware of her drab, flaccid appearance. What had she to offer King now with all the spirit, indeed, the very soul, gone out of her? Then how would they live? And Delaney! She could not bring herself to face the accusation she knew would be in his eyes.

She got up and went to her trunk, bringing from it the leather-bound Bible she had received as a wedding present and in which were noted the births of her four children and the deaths of two of them. She sat once more by the window and this time she opened the Bible and began to read silently from it. She had heard that people derived comfort from the Scriptures in times of spiritual trial. She had never read it before, except in snatches at church, and the words seemed strange and stilted to her. Some of the passages she could not comprehend at once. She read through them several times until the letters ran together and her eyes ached.

> "This know also, that in the last days perilous times shall come. For men shall be lovers of their own selves, covetous, boasters, proud, blasphemers, disobedient to parents, unthankful, unholy, Without natural affection, truce-breakers, false accusers, incontinent, fierce, despisers of those that are good, Traitors, heady, highminded, lovers of pleasures more than lovers of God; Having a form of godliness, but denying the power thereof: from such turn away. For of this sort are they which creep into houses, and lead captive silly women laden with sins, led away with divers lusts . . ."

Agnes glanced out the window at the dingy water-front scene and looked back quickly, shuddering. She flipped the pages back to the Old Testament.

> "The Lord is my shepherd."

Well, now, this was better. She never could understand Paul anyway. She had read the Twenty-third Psalm before and it went off easily and quickly.

> "Yea, though I walk through the valley of the shadow . . ."

Her eyes were wet with a quick flow of tears so that the words blurred. She wiped them and went on. That was all very well, but it was too familiar, too easy for comfort. There should be something less pat in the solace she sought.

> "I will lift up mine eyes unto the hills, from whence cometh my help. My help cometh from the Lord, which made heaven and earth . . ."

This was more like it. Maybe the Lord would be with her and watch over her in the face of Delaney's wrath.

> "He will not suffer thy foot to be moved: He that keepeth thee will not slumber. Behold, He that keepeth Israel shall neither slumber nor sleep . . ."

She tried to imagine what Israel was like. It seemed a world away from Sacramento.

> "The Lord is thy keeper: the Lord is thy shade upon thy right hand. The sun shall not smite thee by day, nor the moon by night. The Lord shall preserve thee from all evil: He shall preserve thy soul. The Lord shall preserve thy going out and thy coming in from this time forth, and even for evermore."

Agnes sat back in her chair and stopped rocking. She contemplated the words she had read, and a flow of warm sentimentality engulfed her. What a good and wonderful thing the Bible was. How perfectly it met every trial and comforted every sick and wandering soul! She pressed it against her breast and closed her eyes tight in an ecstasy of self-redemption. How vain and foolish she had been ever to neglect it in favor of more worldly pursuits. She would read it every day hereafter; every day it would remind her of the folly and impermanence of mundane affairs. It would remind her of the good, the eternal right.

She was not aware that anyone had entered until her eyes fell on the doorway. Delaney was standing there watching her. With a little cry she got up, sending the Bible tumbling to the floor, and ran to him. He caught her to him, holding her close and kissing her until she began to feel weak. Even in her terror over what she must tell him Agnes noted with a strange sense of novelty that it was the first time in years that she had enjoyed being kissed by Delaney. She pressed close to him, wanting it to last a little longer, but he pushed her away to look at her.

"You're thin, Agnes. Oh, darling, but thank God you're all right!" He was slimmer than when he had left for the mines, and his hair, somewhat longer, curled over his collar to give him a youthful appearance. He was unkempt and his reddish mustache was scraggly and untrimmed, but his gray eyes were bright with happiness as he looked at her. He caught her to him again and rocked slightly to and fro, holding her close. "I heard about the epidemic up north. Everybody was running up there, trying to get away from it. Only I thought you were in San Francisco until Andy Hart got word to me. I've been so worried about you!"

He looked at her again, his eyes wide with tenderness. "Agnes— you're all right?"

"Yes. *I'm* all right."

He caught the inflection of the pronoun and his face clouded. He looked around the room quickly and caught sight of Treese asleep in bed.

He stood rooted to the spot. "Treese—?"

"She's all right," Agnes said quickly. "She was sick with the cholera. But she'll be all right. She's just sleeping."

He seemed to be holding his breath as he looked slowly around the room at the other empty bed. It was a long time before he looked back at Agnes and when he did his face was white. His voice was low, but there was a strained quality about it when he spoke.

"Where are the children, Agnes?"

"They've—they're—" She stopped, her throat constricted with fright as he towered over her.

"Where are they?" His voice was still low. She could feel the intensity behind it, the fear, the apprehension, the desperate hope.

"We did everything we could, Delaney! It wasn't my fault. People were dying in the streets! I did everything I could for them. I never let them leave the hotel. I went and got food for them and cared for them. I didn't let them see anybody. It wasn't my fault, Delaney! I did the best I could!" She seized his shirt in her hands and twisted it, pleading for his understanding. "Delaney, I tried. I did the best I knew how for them! I nursed Treese back. I saved her—"

He reached up and took both her hands from his shirt front where they clung. He put her from him and went to the empty bed, dropping down on the edge of it and burying his face in his hands.

She put one hand to her throat and stared at him. Her heart was pounding inside her and her hand was cold. Her lips felt dry, incapable of moving. She took a step toward him and hesitated.

"Delaney—"

With a great effort he raised his head and looked at her. His face was ashen now and deep lines seemed to have appeared out of nowhere. The eyes that a moment before had been full of light and warmth and passion were dead and expressionless. His mouth was white, an almost indistinguishable line.

"Agnes, can you ever forgive me?" The words carried a deep-flowing strain of anguish, a remorse and self-flagellation that reflected what she herself had been suffering. He was all at once haggard and worn, years older than when he had stood in the doorway looking at her. She stared at him.

If he had wept or railed at her, beaten her even, she would not have been surprised. She had expected violence. She was not prepared for humility. Collecting her senses and trying to force herself into some sort of presence of mind, she walked away from him, back to the window. She pressed her forehead against the cool glass and looked beyond the noisy street, the littered Embarcadero, beyond the quiet-flowing river, out and out into infinity until the horizon blurred and ran together and sky became indistinguishable from water. She must think. This was a time to think, not be emotional. Her foot touched the Bible. She stooped over mechanically and picked it up, putting it on the little table.

For a long time the silence of the room remained between them. Each was alone in a separate little sphere of thought and emotional reaction. Delaney did not move from the bed, and Agnes, without looking at him, could see the abject curve of his strong back, the despair with which his great hands covered his face.

She became conscious of a new feeling. A lightness, almost a relief stole over her, freeing the limbs that had before felt heavy and dull. It was as though a body from which her mind had become alienated was returning to itself. She felt a new buoyancy, a springiness, as if there were no weight or impediment in her whole being, only nerve and breath and strength. She stood quiet, experiencing the metamorphosis, feeling it take place within her. She knew she was free again.

The grief she had known over Florabelle and Violet was now a thing she could look at and recognize. She could examine it and see it and know it for what it was. It was no longer a searing thing within her. Her passionate concern for Treese was in the same way separated from her immediate consciousness. It was there, to be sure, but it was no longer compelling and hurting. The battle with her conscience that she had expected to wage until the last day of her life had unexpectedly been won for her through the intercession of Delaney. What physical battles she would have to wage to win a place for herself in this raw new land she could face. Agnes was flooded with relief.

There was a little cry from the bed as Treese awoke and caught sight of Delaney. Agnes turned to see him run to her and hug her hysterically. Then both of them were crying and talking at once, their two bright heads close together.

Agnes watched them. Funny how they always knew what to say to each other. It was almost as if they spoke from each other rather than from themselves, as if they anticipated each thought before it was spoken. They agreed without knowing what the other had said, because their thoughts were so interwoven. She observed them with a curious detachment, a certain aloofness. They really were very much alike.

CHAPTER VIII

IT WAS A GRAY, rainy day late in November. Front Street, from one end of the Embarcadero to the other, was mud; gray, sluggish, immovable mud. Planks had been thrown across at corners to form crossings, but almost as rapidly as they were put down they sank out of sight and new ones had to be procured. Horses strained and struggled to pull heavily loaded freight wagons, and the small, patient mules used to carry loads north to the mining camps sank in almost up to their bellies.

Agnes Delaney stepped briskly but with care along the rough board walk that skirted the street. Her black shawl was pulled close about her and her skirt was raised slightly to avoid the mud. Her black bonnet was tied in a smart bow under her chin. All trace of the lethargy that had overcome her earlier in the month had disappeared. Her firm, smooth cheeks were touched with color, and her hair, pulled back tidily, was beginning to curl slightly with the dampness. She walked firmly and with purpose. At the corner of Front and K she stopped. In front of her the street presented an impasse, lying in great inert morasses which closed over wheel tracks almost as quickly as they were imprinted in it and sank once more into sluggish quietude. Men floundered across it to the Embarcadero, muddied to their thighs, and the most recent board crossing was already invisible.

Agnes looked about her and tapped her foot impatiently on the walk. Directly across, she could see her destination, a tent pitched on one of the reasonably dry spots of the Embarcadero. Over the flap of its entrance was a rough board sign:

WILLIAM P. LEAMER

Freighter

and

Undertaker

She frowned impatiently and looked about her. A man in a soiled mining outfit was standing near, lounging against the front of a building and watching her with mingled deference and curiosity. Agnes did not hesitate.

"I wonder if you'd mind—" she began.

The man leaped to instant attention.

"I would have offered, ma'am, only—"

"It's quite all right."

He lifted her bodily and started across. Agnes, her attention still fixed on the tent opposite, did not look up at him. She was distantly aware of the strength in his arms, however, and when he put her down she felt for an instant a tremor so familiar that she gave it scarcely a second thought.

"I'd be happy to pay you," she murmured.

"Oh, no!" She noticed now that he was young, not much over twenty. "We don't see many ladies, ma'am."

"It was most kind of you." She started toward the tent, already forgetting him.

William Leamer straightened from his desk, a board set across two crates, as she entered. He was a small, unctuous man with a cringing manner, as though the desire to please was the motivating factor in his life. His head was balding and shiny, and Agnes took note of the little ridges of black under his fingernails, the pressed-in dirt that followed the lines in his hand. She shuddered a little.

He rose hastily, fumbling behind him and producing a black formal coat which he drew on. His eyes took in her black attire. He pressed his hands together in the manner of a sympathetic clergyman.

"There's something I can do for you? Perhaps a permanent resting place and dignified services for one near and dear? How few of us escaped the scourge. How few indeed!" He shook his head sadly.

With a businesslike finality Agnes sat down on an upturned barrel opposite him.

"I've come on business," she stated bluntly.

Mr. Leamer frowned. He was accustomed to dealing with women only on matters of funeral arrangements, but that would hardly come under the heading of business.

"I'm not sure that I—" he began, breaking off questioningly.

"Freighting business," Agnes explained, enunciating clearly.

Mr. Leamer sank back behind his desk, staring at her with mounting interest and not overlooking the faint curve of her figure that showed from under the wrap.

"It's Mrs. Delaney, isn't it?" he inquired. "I've already made the acquaintance of your husband. Allow me to express my sympathy in your recent bereavement. But how few, how few indeed, escaped the terrible scourge."

Agnes moved slightly with impatience. "What I came to see you about, Mr. Leamer, concerns your business in freighting."

He brightened. "You're moving some things out here? Well, fine. From Boston, isn't it? You can depend on my wagons, madam. They're the sturdiest in California. And my drivers—absolutely dependable! Absolutely! Temperate men, all of them."

Agnes's patience was giving out. "That was not exactly what I had in mind," she snapped. "I have in my charge a consignment of goods for which you'll find a ready market in the mining camps. I'm willing to sell it to you for twenty thousand dollars."

"Twenty—twenty—" Mr. Leamer paused, wide-eyed and staring.

"Ten barrels of tea!" she went on briskly. "At three hundred dollars a barrel; sixty barrels of flour! You can get forty a barrel for that. There's a fourth of your investment already."

Mr. Leamer ran a hand across his forehead as though to clear his brain.

"But I don't understand. Those things are hard to come by. Where did you—"

"Twenty barrels of salt pork and several crates of eggs!"

He calculated rapidly. "Pork will bring as much as flour, and as for the eggs . . ." He breathed in with a little whistling sound and Agnes held her breath. She would not tell him about the whisky yet.

He narrowed his eyes and looked sideways at her. "It's all in good condition? There's nothing—"

Agnes drew herself up primly. "I've taken the shipload on consignment from my husband's brother, Mr. King Delaney of San Francisco, whose reputation I'm sure you're acquainted with."

Mr. Leamer warmed as if by magic. "Mr. Delaney! Well! Well, now, let's examine this thing. Of course you know it's a risky business. I might never be able to get it to the mines."

Agnes's mouth curved in the suggestion of a smile. "With the sturdiest wagons in California, Mr. Leamer? And drivers who are absolutely temperate?"

He cleared his throat noisily. "What I meant was, twenty thousand seems like quite an asking price."

She rose as if to leave. "Naturally, if you're not interested, there are other freight agents. And a thousand bottles of whisky aren't easy to come by. I imagine they would bring at least thirty dollars a quart."

Mr. Leamer leaped up and took her arm. "Now, now, Mrs. Delaney! Nothing in haste, I always say! Shall we consider this proposition further?"

Agnes allowed herself to be led back to the barrel.

"I only meant," he began, rubbing his hands together and then putting them behind him, under the tails of his undertaking coat, "to raise twenty thousand on such short notice might be something of a feat. However, it seems to me there might be a way profitable to both of us." He walked up and down the small enclosure of the tent. "Say, for example, you were to let me have the consignment of goods without a cash payment."

Agnes gasped indignantly and he held up his hand.

"Suppose I were to take it north and sell it, then split the money with you. I daresay you'd come up with more than your twenty thousand and I'd be repaid for my trouble as well."

Agnes's mind was moving rapidly. She was not adept in business matters, and she had come into Leamer's little tent with her heart in her mouth, following the instructions in King's letter. This would be taking a chance, and she had a vague premonition King would not approve, were he to find out. But if he didn't find out . . .

"There's a piano," she said thoughtfully. "I imagine a piano would bring quite a sum."

"Ten thousand easy!"

She was quiet for another minute. "And if there's any loss?"

He lifted his shoulders slightly. "Shared by us both, too. But you stand to gain in the long run."

Agnes's mind flew ahead of her again. More than twenty thousand! How much more? Even twenty thousand was more than she had dreamed of. Enough to bring Keith to California, enough to build a fine house.

"And I suppose this transaction need not be our last, Mr. Leamer?"

"Precisely my idea, Mrs. Delaney."

Of course King wouldn't go on sending her goods without getting paid for them. She couldn't expect many more such gifts no matter how much he loved her. But with an arrangement like this, she might, as Leamer said, gain in the long run. Only, if anything happened to it, if anything went wrong on this first deal, what would King say then? She drew her breath in, squaring her shoulders.

"I'd like this in writing, Mr. Leamer."

His small, anxious face broke into a smile. He swung around and seated himself, taking out paper and pen. He held the latter poised for an instant, then looked up at her craftily.

"If this is not to be our last transaction, Mrs. Delaney, it might be a good idea to draw up papers of, shall we say, partnership?"

Agnes sat a little straighter and replied with dignity, "We can draw up separate papers for each consignment, Mr. Leamer."

His smile faded until it was faintly contemptuous. "As you say."

He busied himself with his pen for several minutes, then handed the paper to her. She read it carefully, framing the words with her lips and studying them until a little line was formed between her eyebrows.

"Does it satisfy you?"

"It seems quite in order."

He handed her the pen and she wrote carefully, with effort, in round, childlike letters: "John Francis Delaney, Esq., by Mrs. Agnes Delaney, his wife."

Leamer looked from the signature to Agnes, lifting his eyebrows knowingly. Agnes returned the look, but steadily, almost coldly. Rebuffed, he looked away again, taking the paper from her and examining it once more.

She rose and fixed her bonnet firmly on her head.

"You may send your wagons any time, Mr. Leamer. It's the *Portland* and it's at the Embarcadero right now."

"Good day, Mrs. Delaney."

He got up quickly and hurried to the tent flap. She swept out without speaking again.

Outside, a fresh board walk had been thrown across the intersection and she hurried across it. Maybe she was taking a risk. But how would King ever know? She didn't like that Leamer, either. Could see right through that scheming head of his. And it wasn't all business there, either. Well, she knew how to handle men like that.

Twenty thousand dollars. Twenty thousand! Why, with twenty thousand dollars—and he said it wouldn't be the last. She'd have to figure some way to get around King. Well, she'd be willing to pay him something. She could bargain with him, on the one hand, and with Leamer, on the other. And when she didn't need Leamer any longer, he would be left by the wayside. She smiled a little. And to think she'd been afraid when she went in there! Why, there was nothing to it.

She began making mental pictures of what she would do with the twenty thousand or more when she collected it. A person with that much money needed a place to keep it. There was a nice little iron safe in that shipload of goods; King said so in his letter. She hadn't mentioned it to Leamer, so he'd never know. She'd send a wagon down for it right now, before his men got there.

She hurried down the street toward the hotel. She'd have to begin thinking about getting them a house. A person with twenty thousand dollars didn't just live hand-to-mouth in any old hotel room. Yes, a house would definitely be the next thing.

By the end of 1852, Agnes Delaney had gone through two floods and an intervening fire. She had seen the new house she had bought burned to the ground and had watched the floodwaters seep in to soak and destroy carpets and furniture. She had experienced losses in wagon trains and in real cash, but she was worth a quarter of a million dollars.

Sacramento was prospering and Agnes with it. New industries were opening up and respectability was making a feeble attempt to creep into the city. Crimes were still looked upon with an air of acceptance; murder was inevitable. But slowly the course of things was beginning to change. The year 1852 saw a city of strange inconsistencies. The mud was still deep on Front Street, but there were more skirts trailing in it, and the skirts were of finest silk.

During the ten years since its founding by Captain Sutter in 1839 it had lived an industrious, peaceful existence at the confluence of the Sacramento and American rivers, knowing little of greed or excitement or vice. It had prospered, but with such quiet inconspicuousness that few outside its inhabitants knew of its being.

Now, overnight, everything was changed. It was the "jumping-off" place to the mines. Supplies were centered there, and to the men who had spent months of voluntary seclusion gathering a fortune, it offered release; a semblance, however crude, of civilization.

Sacramento was rapidly beginning to resemble a well-laid-out eastern city. The Embarcadero, still serving as a landing place for steamers, ran between the river and Front Street. Running north and south, parallel to the river, the streets were consecutively numbered—Front, Second, Third, Fourth, and so on, as the city expanded. Intersecting these, the streets bore letters of the alphabet, with J Street the principal thoroughfare of the growing town. There was no time to think up names.

Buildings seemed to rise out of the ground overnight. There was the Snyderian House at Front and I streets, on the shore of Sutter's Lake. It rose to a tremendous height of four stories and boasted bathing rooms for gentlemen. The Orleans Hotel was raised in twenty days, its original structure having been brought around the Horn aboard a clipper ship, each piece of timber cut and numbered at an eastern mill. These and other hotels were quick to spring up and rival the City Hotel with its frame three-story structure and ornate balcony (from which many old-timers remembered dropping champagne bottles on the night of its grand opening).

Hackney coaches cruised for fares along Front Street, and for two dollars a man might be transported from the levee to Seventh Street, or to Fourteenth Street, twice the distance, for only an additional dollar.

Agnes's association with William Leamer, which she had not considered prudent to reveal to King, had proved profitable, and shipments of goods which King managed to procure for her were resold at the mines at almost unbelievable prices. After the first shipment she had insisted on paying King, more to keep him from investigating her activities too closely than out of a sense of fairness. Delaney made repeated and unsuccessful trips to the mines, and during these absences King invariably found some matter which called him to Sacramento. Agnes, whose luck never ceased to amaze her, congratulated herself more than once on her astute handling of the situation, but she was sensible enough to give immediate attention to any advice King might bring with him. It was largely for this reason that she found herself engaged in real estate ventures, for lots in Sacramento brought almost as much as in San Francisco and rents were proportionately high. She collected in Delaney's name a thousand dollars a month each for the rental of two saloons on J Street. And now, as she brushed her hair at bedtime, she would contemplate the possibility of turning some other project to advantage in augmenting her growing fortune. The tragedy of losing Florabelle and Violet had taken on a dreamlike quality and there were times when she could not quite remember how they looked. But as they receded from her mind, thoughts of Keith came more frequently. Before long now he would be coming out to join her. He would be finishing his studies, and after he had read law with King for a time . . .

In their frequent exchange of letters, she had not mentioned her plans for a political career for him. It was all well and good for him to be a lawyer, but Agnes was never deceived into thinking he had King's business ability. She certainly didn't want him falling into the rut Andy Hart was in, with his shabby little office down on J Street.

No, politics was where he belonged, and with her growing fortune behind him there was no reason why he might not some day become governor or senator. But there was plenty of time for that . . .

1853

CHAPTER IX

DELANEY WAS DRUNK. He had been drunk for a week, or maybe longer. It was hard to think now and he could not quite remember. When he was drunk, the sharp edge of pain that constantly cut across his consciousness dulled for a time. Memories ran together so that the pleasant mingled with the melancholy and all were one, diffused and shifting. Each time he woke up he felt the stab of pain again and made haste to remedy it with whisky.

He had been north in the mining country since late spring and it was July now. Was it July? Yes, he was quite sure of that. Here in the little mining camp of Crosseye-George, time seemed to have lost its meaning. One day was so like the next. So reminiscent of the day before.

The Peacock saloon was empty now except for the bartender, a large, lanky man who had the appearance of having once been stout. Skin hung slack about his jowls and under his eyes. It was pallid, almost greenish. He stood behind the rough bar examining the bottles, now and then picking one up and holding it to the light to examine its contents. Delaney sat at a table, and a few feet away, at another table, a scrawny little man shuffled a dirty deck of cards.

The bartender looked over at Delaney and shook his head. He walked around the end of the bar and ambled over to the table, his shoulders hunched slightly, his soiled apron flapping about his ankles.

"Gettin' late, Delaney." He sat down and poured a drink from the bottle on the table.

Delaney roused himself slightly. He tipped his head back in order to have a better view of the bartender and opened his eyes with effort.

"What time, Baldy?"

"Close to midnight."

Delaney's head dropped and he frowned as he digested this information.

"Late all right."

Baldy poured a drink for Delaney and downed his own.

"See a light down in Bessie's tent still. Why'ncha take a walk down?"

Delaney shuddered with distaste. Baldy persisted.

"Bessie likes you first-rate, Delaney."

"Not tonight." Delaney drank the whisky the bartender had poured for him.

Baldy turned the glass speculatively in his hand. "Why'd you come back this time?"

"Got a good prospect. Gonna get started tomorrow. Get everything all lined up."

"Oh, hell," Baldy said laconically. "Diggin's here are dryer'n an old maid's tits."

"No, now I got something pretty good lined up, Baldy."

"There's nothin' good left in Crosseye. I'm pullin' out myself."

Delaney raised his head again in some alarm.

"You going, Baldy?"

"Sure am. Gonna finish off the whisky myself, or throw it to the rattlesnakes, and light out."

"Where to?"

Baldy shrugged. "Anythin's better'n here. Think I'll carry the stink of it to my grave. Never seen such a stinkin' place in all my life. Stinks from mornin' t' night. I even dream how it stinks."

Delaney was thoughtful. "Yes, it stinks all right."

Baldy poured himself another drink and refilled Delaney's glass.

"I'd clear out if I was you, Delaney. You got a good home in Sacramento City. You oughta clear out. This place ain't good for a man. No woman in sight but Bessie, and that damned stink from morning to night and even in your sleep."

"Well, I don't know . . ."

"Don't you miss home?"

"Yep, I miss it."

"Should think you'd miss the wife, too. Got a good-lookin' wife, they say. Hell, Bessie's goodhearted, but she's wore out."

"Oh, Bessie's all right."

"Hell, you gotta wife of your own and a nice house. What d'ya wanna hang around this hole for?"

"No, I gotta look this proposition over, Baldy. Seems like I always go home empty-handed. I got so I got the damnedest feeling, always going home empty-handed."

"You ain't the only one. Remember when you first come how it used to be?"

Delaney nodded.

"Used t' clean up a thousand a night," Baldy went on reminiscently. "God damn it!" There was a touch of triumph in the exclamation. "You'd never think it! Right here in Crosseye."

"Seems like a long time ago."

"Three years."

"That's long, out here."

"Remember, Delaney, how they used to be lined up here at the bar? The Peacock was some place then! Yammerin' and shootin' twenty-four hours a day. Remember?"

"Sure, I remember." Delaney had lost the thread of the conversation. He was thinking of Agnes again. It got so you hated going home empty-handed all the time.

"You take my advice, Delaney," Baldy went on sagely. "Get the hell outa this place. It's not as if you need the money. Why, hell, everybody knows you're a rich man and about the property you own in Sacramento City."

Delaney drew himself slightly more erect and again made the effort to open his eyes. He overdid it, opening them so far that he had a startled expression, then narrowing them quickly to slits.

"That's true. I got plenty of property. Money too. Bank in Sacramento's full of it. President of the bank tips his hat when he sees me. All in my name, you know. I have quite an account there." He sat even straighter, leaning back in the chair so that it began to tip.

"Set forward, Delaney," Baldy ordered. Delaney obeyed; his manner was meek and childlike.

"My wife," he went on, growing garrulous, "she's always saying stay home. What's up there in those rotten camps that you gotta go traipsing off all the time. That's how she talks. Always wanting me to stay home with her."

"Well, that's the way women are."

"Oh, sure. Misses me, all right. Keeps writing me letters saying come on home. Wants me to stay there in Sacramento with her. She doesn't like it, being left alone. Writes me the damnedest long letters. Every mail there's one, till I get sick of reading 'em."

"Sure, Delaney."

"You know how women are. Always writing such damned long letters and keeping after you till it makes you dizzy."

"Yeh, sure does make you sick. But that's women for you. Say listen, Delaney. Know what I'd do if I was you? I'd take a walk down to Bessie's. Then tomorrow, or first chance I got, I'd light the hell outa here."

"I don't know. I got this good lead. It looks pretty good this time."

"Take my advice, there's no gold left in Crosseye. Listen, I know. You take a walk down to Bessie's. You'll see it different tomorrow."

Delaney frowned thoughtfully. "You think she's still up?"

"Oh, hell, up or down, she's there. Go on, now. It's late."

"Well . . ." Delaney paused. "I just might walk past her tent." He put his hands on the table, palms down, and pushed himself up, steadying himself for a moment when he got to his feet. He kept one hand on the table and groped for his hat. Baldy shoved it within reach and he put it on crookedly.

"See you, Baldy."

"Yeh. You do like I said, Delaney. Get the hell home." The bartender watched as Delaney maneuvered his way out of the saloon. Then he got up, shaking his head slowly, and took the bottle and two glasses behind the bar. The little man who had been shuffling the cards looked up.

"What's eatin' him?"

Baldy cast him a scornful look.

"What's eatin' anybody in this stinkin' hole?"

Delaney walked slowly down the broken, rutted street that slashed through Crosseye, dividing it into two parts. There were three or four deserted saloons along the way, a few tents where the hopeful still lingered, and several canvas and lumber shacks with the roofs caved in. From every side rose the stench of garbage and offal, mingling and becoming a part of the night air. The heaps of refuse were silhouetted in the pale light. At the end of the street stood a tent in front of which a small red lantern blinked and swung with a beguiling frankness. Delaney walked toward it.

Agnes Delaney looked up and smiled. Her throat and shoulders were unbelievably white and cool in the stifling theater box. King smiled back at her.

"Don't," he said.

"Don't what?"

"Don't start looking like that if you expect me to sit through this thing without going crazy."

She looked away archly. "I don't think the heat agrees with you."

"You know what agrees with me."

"King!"

"Don't put on airs with me." He leaned toward her and slipped one arm around her tightly corseted waist.

"King! People are looking."

He withdrew the arm. "I was just curious. How can you wear that thing in this heat?"

"Don't you want me to look nice?"

"You know what I—"

"King, please! I know someone will hear. Now do be nice."

He leaned back in his chair and sighed.

"Why are you breaking your neck to see Lola Montez tonight? I thought you were going through a cultural phase."

Agnes fanned herself. "Well, of course she's not real *theater*," she replied languidly. "Nothing like the Booths, or the Chapmans. The Chapmans simply ridicule her, you know. But she's set the whole town talking, and, of course, she is colorful."

"Such benign superiority! Agnes darling, how you have

changed. Not only do you drag me off to the theater my first night in Sacramento, but you make me buy the most expensive box."

"Sh—do behave now. I think she's coming on soon."

The theater was unbearably hot. Below, in the pit, fashionable evening clothes mingled with sweaty flannel shirts, for no one with the price of admission was excluded. The theater was noisy and full of the smell of unwashed bodies. Voices were high and excited; occasionally an impatient stamping broke out from some corner, to be taken up by the entire audience until the vibrations shook the very rafters. Agnes continued to fan herself with a slight, regular motion. Eyes returned repeatedly to her as she sat framed in the foremost box in her rose-colored muslin gown with its dipped neckline. Her head tilted back in its habitual position from the weight of her coiled hair. Three years in the West had not aged her; indeed, if anything, she seemed younger and more radiant than in those early days. King looked down at her proudly.

The stamping in the theater rose to a crescendo and several of the more impatient spectators fired guns at the ceiling. Decidedly, they were going to give Lola Montez a royal welcome.

The fabulous Lola had arrived early in the month, honeymooning with her third husband, Patrick Purdy Hull, a San Francisco newspaperman. Lola, the Countess of Landsfeld and erstwhile mistress of King Ludwig of Bavaria, had given the town some of the best food for conversation in years. She and her handsome bridegroom were staying at the Orleans Hotel and all Sacramento had laid out the red carpet for them. The theater had been packed at every performance of her famous "spider dance" and the flimsy building shook nightly with applause.

The drop curtain quivered expectantly and a hush came over the audience. It began to rise slowly, and there was an ear-splitting burst of applause as an empty stage was revealed. The backdrop was a painted forest scene with a stream cutting directly through the center and several gaudy birds were perched indiscriminately on low-hanging branches. The orchestra struck up and after a moment a dark-haired young woman in a full-skirted dancing costume entered. Without acknowledging the shouts and cheers she went directly to the center of the stage and started her dance. There was no particular finesse in her motions, but it was clear that she was simulating the gestures of a terrified woman. The reason became apparent as whalebone-and-rubber spiders began dropping from the folds of her costume and she started to crush them ruthlessly, shaking them out with abhorrent motions.

The applause was tumultuous as she finished. Agnes applauded politely but without too much eagerness. King leaned forward again and whispered into her ear.

"Not real *theater*, of course."

"Don't make fun of me."

"Is there more to come?"

"Of course."

"Do we have to stay?"

"Don't you want to?"

"No!"

"Well—"

"Come on. Just think of the distinction it'll give you, walking out on Lola Montez."

Agnes considered his words. "All right."

"Come on now, confess. You don't want to stay any more than I do."

There was a slight pause. They got up and started toward the rear of the box. Her skirt made a rustling sound as it swished past King's legs.

"Oh, King, I *have* missed you!"

It was noon. The Peacock saloon at Crosseye-George was empty except for Baldy and the man who had been there the night before. The latter was seated at the piano, playing softly, swearing under his breath each time the soundless F sharp above middle C made a gap in the tune. It was like a missing tooth. The red calico that lined the interior of the saloon hung dismally but the nude young women whose pictures adorned the walls still beckoned enticingly with over-the-shoulder looks. Baldy sat at a table and poured himself a whisky. Two miners came in and stood for a moment in the doorway.

"How 'bout some whisky, Baldy?"

"Help yourself," the proprietor replied, not stirring from his seat.

The men stared at him in surprise. Then one of them walked over to the bar and returned with a bottle in each hand. They joined Baldy at his table.

"What're you doin', drinkin' in the middle of the day?" one inquired.

"Gettin' rid of the goddam stuff. I'm lightin' outa here. Did you git a wagon?"

"Slap-Ass is gettin' one. He knows a fellow's got a wagon."

"How much does he want for it?"

"Didn't say. But you gotta have a wagon."

"Give him some whisky. He'll take whisky a sight quicker'n gold."

"You gonna give this whisky away just like that?"

"What I can't drink. I'm clearin' outa here. When's he gonna bring the wagon?"

"He said this afternoon."

"We gotta have it today. It's damned hot."

"He'll bring it today."

"You gonna drive?"

"Me and Shorty."

The two men who had come in lifted the bottles and drank slowly, tilting their heads back so that it went down without effort. Both were unshaven and wore miner's clothes. After a moment the shorter one put his bottle down and stirred uneasily.

"Where is he?" he asked hesitantly.

Baldy jerked his head in the direction of the bar.

"Over behind there."

The man went to the bar and stood on tiptoe, peering over it. Slowly he shook his head. The room was silent except for the tinkle of the piano. The taller man rose and went to look. For several minutes they both stared; then, without speaking, they returned to the table and had another drink.

Baldy cleared his throat loudly.

"Seems like quite a trip, clear to Sacramento City. But I wouldn't hardly know what else to do. It's a mighty funny layout. He was a rich man."

"So they said."

"Wouldn't seem quite fittin' to have him buried up here."

"No."

They shuffled their feet under the table.

"Although I must say he always seemed to belong here. Fit right in, and there wasn't nothin' high and mighty about him."

"No, he was like everybody else."

"Funny, a man with money like that and all."

"Well, you know they say that was his wife's money."

"That so?"

"But I don't know. I always had a feelin' there was somethin' there."

"What d'ya mean?"

"Oh, his bein' away so much, and like that, and her never writin' to him."

"Well, you can't tell with a thing like that."

"No."

"Sure must've been somethin' all right. Funny how you don't get to know what's goin' on inside a person."

"Guess nobody knowed what was goin' on inside him."

There was a little movement of the swinging doors and Bessie came in. She was dressed in black, but as a concession to the heat she had apparently worn nothing under the dress, and the loose, undisciplined lines of her body sagged under the worn silk. Her eyes were red from weeping. Her hair, knotted untidily at the back, had already begun to come loose and was straggling about her face.

She looked about the room quickly. Her eyes, when they moved, showed little red veins and red rims.

"Where is he?"

Baldy jerked his head toward the bar. She went over and stood for a moment, looking. Then her drooping shoulders squared a trifle and she turned to them.

"I got a wagon and a coffin. They can bring it in here and fix him up and then take him out to the wagon."

"What're you fixin' to do, Bessie?"

"Bury him. What did you think?"

"But Shorty and Will here was goin' to start to Sacramento City with him."

"In this heat? You crazy?"

The three men at the bar fumbled uneasily.

"Well, we thought it might be more fittin'."

"Fittin', hell. We'll bury him right here, outside the camp. Get the lead out of your pants. Bring in that coffin."

The two men looked at Baldy and hesitated. Then they got up and started for the door.

Bessie was still standing rigid, her back to the bar.

Baldy took a drink. He shook his head as though to clear his senses.

"I don't know as we're doin' the right thing, Bessie. I don't think you oughta rush it so."

"What's there to think about?" she demanded angrily. "This is where he belonged, and it's where he died. Where else would you bury a man?"

"Now, I don't know, Bessie. You're hurryin' it so. He was well known down there."

"He wasn't well known anyplace but here. Anyway, you're drunk."

Baldy leaned back and sighed heavily, shutting his eyes tight and pressing his palms against them.

"Sure, sure, sure. Wish to hell I'd stayed in Pittsburgh. Wish to hell I'd never seen this here goddam place."

"That don't do no good now."

"Soon's I finish this whisky, I'm lightin' out. I'm through with this place."

"You'll kill yourself on that rotten whisky before you ever have a chance to leave."

Baldy opened his eyes, then screwed them nearly shut again.

"What about them clothes he's wearin'? I don't know if they're fittin'."

"Will you quit frettin' around about what's fittin'?" she snapped. "He never belonged in no boiled shirt. Let him be, will you."

"Have it your way, Bessie," Baldy sighed.

Will and Shorty pushed in through the swinging doors carrying a coffin made of a hollowed-out tree trunk. They set it down on the floor in front of the bar.

"Now, listen," Baldy said with loud defensiveness, "you run this show any way you damn please, but somebody's gotta write his family. I know that much."

Bessie's face took on a troubled expression and she bit her lower lip thoughtfully.

"Yes, that I guess we gotta do," she said slowly. She looked around the room. "Well, anybody here can write?"

The three men exchanged embarrassed glances. Then the tinkling of the piano stopped and the little man who had been playing got up and came over to them.

"I can write toler'ble."

Bessie scrutinized him. "Got paper and pencil?"

He grubbed into the pocket of his shirt and brought out a stubby pencil and a scrap of paper.

"Don't look too clean, but I guess it'll do. Baldy, how 'bout some whisky?"

Baldy made a sweeping motion with his hand and Bessie and the three men went and joined him at the table. For a time they all drank without speaking. At last Bessie wiped her mouth and sat erect.

"All right now. Let's get started. Put at the top: Mrs. Delaney, Sacramento City, California."

The little man wrote laboriously.

"Seems as though there should be a first name. What was his first name?" Baldy inquired.

"Nobody here called him anythin' but Delaney."

"What next?" the little man inquired.

Bessie poured herself another drink.

"Dear Madam. It is my painful duty to inform you—"

"Don't go so fast." The little man struggled with the words, hesitating for a long moment over "painful," finally writing "panefull." At last he looked up. "All right, now what?"

"It is my painful duty to inform you—" Bessie closed her eyes tight and thought. "That your husband, Mr. Delaney, died by accident on July 11, 1853, in Crosseye-George." She frowned. "That Crosseye-George sounds like hell in a letter like this. Make it north of Grass Valley."

"All right." The pencil traced the words. "Is that all?"

"No. Write this: 'He was in good spirits and the best of health at the time of his death. He was given a Christian burial.' "

Baldy spoke admiringly. "That's mighty well put, Bessie, to spare her feelin's and all."

Bessie turned on him angrily. "It ain't for her we're lyin'. It's for him." She glanced at the bar, then looked away quickly.

"Whose name shall I sign?" the little man asked.

Bessie considered for a moment. "I guess maybe Baldy's. He's kinda more in charge here than anybody. What's your real name, Baldy?"

"Herbert Wilkins." Baldy straightened a little with pride.

Bessie repeated it to herself. "Fair-soundin' name. All right, put that."

"I can write it myself," Baldy put in self-consciously.

The little man handed him the pencil and pointed to where the signature belonged. Baldy wrote it with careful deliberation.

"There now!" Bessie said. "That's taken care of. Let's have another drink."

"Shouldn't we be about buryin' him?" Will asked.

"We got plenty of time," Baldy said. "Let's get rid of some of this goddam whisky first. I wanna clear outa here Sunday."

They all drank; eagerly, quickly, because it was something to turn their attention to, something to keep them from thinking of what was behind the bar.

At last Bessie spoke. "Figger on clearin' out Sunday?"

Baldy nodded.

"Maybe I might ride along with you."

PART TWO

Keith

1854

CHAPTER I

IN THE PARLOR of King Delaney's home in San Francisco, Andy Hart, King, Margaret and Elizabeth were having tea. It was early May and a little of the first freshness of spring drifted in through the open window, caught at the curtains and begged to be noticed. Early roses were already in bloom. Their fragrance hung about in a confusion of heady sweetness and some of the languor of the day seemed to have transferred itself to the four occupants of the room. Their actions were slow and without exertion. Cups were lifted with leisurely boredom. On such a day there was time for everything. Their voices, when they spoke, were alert and interested but their attitudes remained casual, as though their bodily reactions could not keep up with the conversation.

"Well, *I'm* not going to be glad to see him," Elizabeth declared. Of the four, she showed the most noticeable trace of vitality, for even as she sat inert in an armchair there was an air of suppressed energy about her, of latent nervous interest.

King smiled lazily at her.

"You'll change your tune fast enough, young lady. I hear he was the handsomest man at Harvard this year."

"Oh—handsome! Pooh!" Elizabeth's face assumed an expression of enormous disgust and she sank even deeper into the chair. In the four years since she had arrived in California she had changed little. Already mature at fifteen, at nineteen she was but an improvement, an embellishment of that maturity. Her fair, smooth-faced beauty had grown out of its girlish appealing quality until it was now aristocratic, fine-featured like Margaret's. But where Margaret possessed an unchanging dignity, a coolness that was not of her inherent nature but of her breeding, Elizabeth was warm and volatile. The product of an uninhibited upbringing, she was, as Margaret had intended her to be, intensely vital and attractive.

Margaret smiled tolerantly at her. "I don't think we need worry, King. One look at that outfit and the handsome Harvard cousin will run for Kingdom Come."

Elizabeth's lips drew together in a scowl.

"Frivolous clothes may be well enough for girls who don't mind

97

spending their entire lives subjugated to the whim of a man. To one who plans a serious career in life"—she enunciated each word clearly and primly—"they are an impediment, a drag and a bore. I thought you were quite aware of my feelings on the subject, Mother."

She got up and walked impatiently to the window.

"And just how," Andy drawled, "would you characterize that outfit?"

He was leaning back in his chair, one leg flung up over the arm of it. His eyes narrowed speculatively as he looked her up and down.

Elizabeth wheeled around and glared at him. She was wearing a pair of full bottle-green trousers gathered at the ankle with elastic. Over them ·was a brown bodice and half-skirt. Her feet were encased in heavy, square-toed shoes. Her yellow hair showed no ringlets, but was pulled back relentlessly into a hard stubby knob. And yet every studied attack upon her femininity only increased her piquant loveliness. She moved with daintiness in spite of the heavy shoes and her young breasts under their drab bodice were full and soft.

"This outfit," she pronounced clearly and acidly, "is not luxurious. Nor is it designed to entice men and send them into ridiculous promises which they would break the minute a woman was safely promised to them. It's sensible, comfortable and practical. It's recommended by Mrs. Bloomer and that's enough for me." She turned her back again and examined something outside the window with studied interest. Her feet were slightly apart, her slender shoulders squared. The knot of yellow hair high on the back of her head stood like a rigid sentinel. Behind her, King and Andy exchanged amused winks for which Margaret shot them a look of silent reproach.

"It's quite nice, dear, as you say," Margaret put in cajolingly. "Now come and finish your tea. And do put it out of your mind that you're going to be rude to Keith when he comes. You are his cousin, you know, and you must make him welcome."

Elizabeth allowed herself to be persuaded and somewhat reluctantly returned to flounce down in the chair. But when Keith was mentioned her mouth became stubborn once more.

"He's a fop and a prig and a dandy and I hope he doesn't plan to stay here long because no one wants him."

"Elizabeth!" Margaret's voice was shocked.

"Well, you know it as well as I do, Mother. He's just like all the rest of the men these days. Oh, not you, Father, or you, Andy.

But you must admit men are interested in nothing but satisfying their own selfish pleasures. And for this we women are relegated to a position of inferiority—treated like chattels. As Amelia Bloomer herself says, women can equal if not exceed men in intelligence if the educational facilities are offered them. But of course men make quite certain that every obstacle will be put in woman's way to attaining such advantages."

"No one's putting anything in your way," King commented. "Nobody said a word when you yelled your head off that you wanted to go to St. Louis to the seminary this fall. And at nineteen, when most girls are married and have a baby or two!" His tone was chiding, but he smiled as he spoke and his eyes rested on his step-daughter with unconcealed adoration. Clearly, a higher education at the seminary in St. Louis was nothing. She could have the moon if she asked for it.

"Oh, I know it, Father." Her voice softened and her eyes became deeply blue with the love she returned him. She got up and went around with a little habitual motion to the back of his chair. "You're sweet and so's Mother. But sometimes I get so disgusted—"

"—that it hardly seems worth going on!" Andy finished dramatically.

Elizabeth stiffened angrily. "Now you listen to me, Andy Hart! If you think this is any silly phase I'm going through you're very much mistaken. I'm deadly serious. It wouldn't do you a bit of harm to do less hanging around Portsmouth Square and more reading—an uplifting kind of literature!"

"The *Lily*?" Andy nodded his head in the direction of a pile of Mrs. Bloomer's magazines on the table. "Spare me!"

Margaret raised her hands pleadingly. "Stop it, you two! This instant. Now, no more Mrs. Bloomer talk, Elizabeth!"

Andy threw his leg down from the arm of the chair and sat forward in a contrite bow.

"My apologies, Miss Margaret. I instigated the violence. Elizabeth, my dear, your outfit is charming, your ideas commendable. May I say that San Francisco's loss will be St. Louis's gain?"

Elizabeth tossed her head, ignoring him. "When's his Highness arriving? Not too soon, I hope?"

"Maybe this week sometime. There's a ship due any day," King answered. "And you might just as well get used to the idea. You knew a long time ago he was coming into the law office with me. And besides, you'll be off to St. Louis before he's even had a chance to lay his hat down."

"Thank Heaven for that!" Elizabeth went to her mother and dropped down by her chair, crossing her legs in front of her Indian-fashion. "He'd probably want to stay here forever and make the house all over. Maybe he'd want us to give it to him outright, like Aunt Agnes did!"

"That's enough, Elizabeth." There was a note of quiet warning in King's voice but Elizabeth did not notice. She was intent on the floor in front of her and she traced the flowered design of the rug with her forefinger.

"Probably wouldn't like the beds because they don't have fourteen-foot posters with carved angels on top."

"Elizabeth!" King's tone was so violent this time that Elizabeth looked up, startled.

"Well, I didn't say anything that wasn't true, Father. You were right here that night she said—"

"Please, dear. Not now," Margaret pleaded. A look of pain had crossed her face. Elizabeth noticed it and her eyes dropped to the floor again.

Andy moved uneasily in his chair, his glance going quickly from Margaret, who looked suddenly smaller and less strong in her chair, her hands white on their fancywork, to King, handsome and robust as ever opposite her. King had lost none of his youthful leanness and his reddish hair still grew back strongly from his forehead. His face was smooth and unlined, although he was nearly fifty. In contrast with him Margaret seemed much older. Her gray hair had more of white in it, and the flesh was less firm on her big frame. Her hands, still strong and sensitive, looked bonier, and the knuckles stood out more prominently. Andy felt a little pang of pity for Margaret. She had never liked the West. She had said she would never get used to it. And yet she had never betrayed to King that feeling of not belonging. It had been hard for her too. Keeping up appearances and never letting Elizabeth find out. Those two certainly were the ones! So out-and-out brazen about their affair that people scarcely were aware of its existence.

That was always the way. The poor little one-time sinners were the ones that got whispered about because their consciences gave them away. A conscience was one thing you certainly could never accuse Agnes Delaney of having. Andy knew a moment of mixed feelings toward King. Dammit, it was hard not to like the man. He was everything his brother had been, only with more suavity and polish. He was vigorous and robust, a good man among men; a smart lawyer, and he had a big heart underneath. Only he didn't understand. He never quite knew Margaret. He thought her contented with the fine new home he'd built her. He didn't know; only in brief flashes like this outburst of Elizabeth's did a streak of truth come through to him. It was the way with him. And he would soon forget.

Andy roused himself from his speculation, aware that a change of subject was needed to clear the air.

"I suppose you've heard from Treese, Elizabeth?"

"Only one letter in ever so long. But I suppose she's terribly busy with plans for the wedding and all."

"Yes, I suppose."

"Tell us truly now, Andy, is she really in love with him?"

Andy gave a contemptuous little laugh.

"Do you think that likely? He's forty, you know."

"Then why?" Elizabeth demanded, outraged. "Oh, it's this everlasting subjugation of women, this grinding them under men's heels!"

"But not exactly in this case," Andy interrupted mildly. He looked over Elizabeth's head toward King. "It's not a man who's forcing her into it. It's her mother."

Margaret leaned forward, her face grave with concern.

"Is it that bad, Andy? Is she really being forced into it?"

King gave a little laugh and shifted in his chair.

"Nonsense. Andy, you're too dramatic. The girl's seventeen, old enough to be married. And Wickham's a decent enough fellow, they say."

"Forty!" Elizabeth stormed. "Oh, poor Treese. I'd just like to be able to talk to her for one day. I'd just like to let her read Mrs. Bloomer!"

"I'm afraid even Mrs. Bloomer wouldn't furnish quite the necessary jolt," Andy retorted acidly. "She's pretty well accustomed to falling in with Mrs. Delaney's ways. Her mother's a very determined woman." There now, he thought, I've said too much. I've hurt Margaret again and I never meant to. Only that damned Agnes Delaney. And to hear King taking her part!

But Margaret did not seem to be thinking of herself. Her fine brow furrowed a little with worry and her fingers stopped at their work.

"I'd hate to see that," she said thoughtfully. "I certainly would hate to see Treese married off to some man she didn't care about. And who perhaps—well, I don't know—might not care enough for her. Agnes is a well-to-do woman now. The dowry would interest even a prosperous man and I understand Wickham's quite without funds."

"Without funds is putting it charitably, Miss Margaret. He's up to his ears in debt."

"Then why is Aunt Agnes so determined to have him for Treese?" Elizabeth demanded.

"Social prestige is a mighty force in the motivation of women," Andy observed sagely. "That's all Wickham's bringing Mrs. Delaney by marrying Treese, but apparently it's enough to suit her. There's not a mother in Sacramento hasn't thrown her daughter at his head. Only, Mrs. Delaney had something better to throw along with hers."

"Andy, how barbaric!"

"Sorry, Miss Margaret, but it's true."

"I can't believe Agnes would do it."

King interrupted a trifle tartly. "Well, it's none of our business and we're like a bunch of old maids talking it over this way. It's not as if Treese is being fed to any den of lions, you know. Wickham may be a shade old for her, but he seems quite creditable. And he's probably in love with her. Now, let's drop the whole thing." There was exasperation in his tone.

Elizabeth sat up straight on the floor and looked at him reproachfully. "Well, you may think it's all right, Father. Personally, I think it's revolting. I couldn't love Treese more if she were my very own sister and if I could be with her for one hour I bet I'd talk her into going east with me to the seminary. I bet I'd talk her into it so fast she'd never know what happened." Elizabeth's voice was rising with emotion. "And if I ever have the chance, even if it's the night before the wedding, don't think I won't try!" Tears glistened in her eyes and King looked uncomfortable.

"Oh, there now, dear. It isn't that bad," Margaret soothed her.

"It is! It's horrible. And you all know it even if you don't say so." The tears brimmed over and streamed down her cheeks. She got to her feet, trembling with indignation, and with a last agitated look at them rushed from the room and out through the little side door that led into the garden. There was an embarrassed silence around the room. Then King rose slowly and with a studied indifference.

"Believe I'll run down to the office to wind things up, Margaret. What time is dinner?"

"Any time you say. Will seven be all right?"

"Fine. You'll stay, won't you, Andy?"

"Couldn't drive me off."

"Fine. I'll be back directly." He went to the hall, took down his hat and stick and left by the front door.

Andy looked at Margaret with amusement. "King's getting conscientious."

Margaret laughed. "He's not going to the office. You know it as well as I do. The minute he's out there he'll sneak around to the garden after Elizabeth. He can't bear to see her unhappy. I suppose he's spoiling the life out of her, but there doesn't seem to be much I can do about it."

"And anyway you like it."

"Yes, I like it." Her eyes took on a misty look and she bent quickly to the work in her lap. When she spoke again it was without looking up. "You're looking remarkably fine, Andy."

"Am I, Miss Margaret? Well, the reason's an old one. A filly won't look twice at an old rattailed stud. And I'm planning on amusing myself royally this trip." As always when they were alone he had dropped the formality of speech he preserved in front of the rest of the family. And Margaret, assiduously mindful of decorum, was not offended, for she knew he meant no disrespect. She liked his easy way of speech, like being included in the warmth of his greathearted friendship. And she enjoyed the opportunity to relax herself, to slip, if only for the moment, from the dignity which habit and years of practice had instilled in her. Now she looked up at him again and smiled almost coquettishly.

"The ladies on Portsmouth Square must have changed if they take that much persuasion."

Andy grinned and settled himself back comfortably, watching her quick capable hands resume their fancywork. It was true that he was looking uncommonly well. He was neatly dressed in a newly tailored suit, black, like all the others he had ever owned but nevertheless with more style and elegance than was customary in his clothes. He had left off his spectacles and trimmed his hair so that it hung neatly to the top of his collar. His mustache was trimmed, his sideburns long and luxuriant, and he had shaved off his beard. He looked younger than he had the Delaneys' first year in California. Margaret commented on it.

"It's strange about you, Andy. Every year while the rest of us grow grayer and look older you seem to become younger. And yet it's not exactly that either. It's more that there's a changelessness about you." She paused thoughtfully. "You take the years as casually as if they didn't exist at all. And because you stay the same when all the rest of us move on, it gives you youth. You're to be envied."

"Madame, you'll turn my head. I only hope the ladies on the Square are as easily swept off their feet."

"I don't doubt they will be. But what is the secret of this eternal youth?"

"It's scarcely that, Miss Margaret. I'm no young blade any more."

"You're only beginning to live."

"Only beginning?" His sharp face took on a speculative expression. "No, I wouldn't say that. I'd say I've never even started to live at all."

Something in his tone made Margaret glance up at him quickly and he hastened on. "And there you have the solution to my eternal devilish handsomeness, madame. No wife to nag me, no home to be obligated with, no children to drag me down, no great wealth to worry me."

Margaret's hands were idle again. She lifted her head to him and searched his face. It was still strangely scholarly, a little pinched. The eyes had a vague look as though they were accustomed to spectacles and had not yet become used to seeing without them. But over all was a lost look, a look of dissemblance carefully maintained but beginning to crumble.

"Still the same, Andy?" she asked softly.

The mask of bantering dropped. "Still the same."

"And that's why you're here this time?"

"That's why. Sure. This time and all the other times, though I wouldn't have you think I don't crave your own sweet company, Miss Margaret."

"Why don't you ask her?"

He shook his head. "I don't know. Every time I'm alone with her, every time I get just on the verge of it something keeps me back and I say some fool thing to tease her so she won't guess. I'm scared she'd laugh, I suppose. I couldn't stand it if she laughed. And then I get to thinking what if she says no right out. Then I'd never feel free to come here again or be with her. There'd be something between us then. At least now I can be with her. I can see her and listen to her voice. Can't you see how it is?" He was pleading for understanding.

"Of course I can see. But you can't go on forever this way. If you love her you should ask her to marry you."

"What about Amelia Bloomer and women's rights? The time isn't very propitious, I'm afraid."

Margaret dismissed it with a little wave of her hand. "You know how long these things last with Elizabeth. She's been going on this way for a month. It's time it spent itself. She told me to throw away every one of her pretty dresses when she had those ghastly Bloomer affairs made up. Of course I didn't. I told her I did and then put them away in my closet. She'll want them soon enough."

"But how could she want me?" Andy demanded. "She knows me too well. She'd never take me seriously."

Margaret thought it over coolly for a moment. Then she spoke slowly, weighing each word. "That's true, Andy. But she's not foolish. In spite of her ridiculous notions she's sensible and good and she has a real sense of values. I'm not saying I know what she'd say. But she wouldn't laugh, if that's what you're afraid of. I can promise you she wouldn't laugh or even feel like laughing. She'd respect you and be flattered and you'd never lose your welcome here. So please ask her."

"You'd really approve of me, ma'am?" Andy spoke shyly.

Margaret nodded emphatically. "She's way beyond her years. She needs someone to look up to and follow. She'd be ten paces ahead of any young blade that's after her now. I'd be most mightily happy if she'd say yes."

"And King?"

Margaret laughed tolerantly and motioned with her head toward the window. Voices were drifting in faintly. "Can you believe he'd deny her anything she wanted?"

Andy sat up straight and squared his shoulders. "All right then, Miss Margaret." He walked to the window and back, his hands in his pockets as though trying to drum up courage. "All right, sir. There it is. And by the great horn spoon, I'll do it. From here on it's me or St. Louis—a fight to the finish."

Andy stayed the week out at the Delaneys. He spent Tuesday, Wednesday and Thursday getting his courage up and Friday laying careful plans. On Friday evening Margaret herded King off on a round of obligatory social calls and Elizabeth and Andy took the occasion to dine together alone in the big dining room of the house and then to walk about the garden.

It had grown warmer and everything seemed to have sprung into bloom at once. The imported camellia trees were fragile and white in the dusk, the rosebushes heavy with fragrance and bloom.

The grass under their feet had a clinging feeling and they seemed to sink in at every step. The evening was still. No sound seemed to penetrate from the noisier quarters of the city and the birds had already stilled their song for the night. They walked along the path that skirted the great new brick house and through a gateway leading into the rear grounds. Andy offered his arm, but she resolutely refused it.

"Women must learn to stand on their own two feet," she informed him proudly. "I'm quite capable of walking by myself."

The dusk hid the tender amusement in his smile. He let her precede him through the gate and they walked on without speaking, finally sitting down on a wooden bench that had been built around an old oak in one corner of the garden.

"Will you be staying until we go up for the wedding?" she asked.

"I think not. I'd better be starting back soon. I do have a business in Sacramento, you know."

"Business! You always belittle yourself so, Andy. It's a profession."

"Well, profession or business, it still takes a little work to bring in the dust. And a man has to live."

"Yes, I know." She was thoughtful, and he knew her mind was elsewhere. As a reluctant concession to his pleas she had permitted her hair to fall unpinned about her shoulders and it curled abruptly into waves and ringlets. The fading light caught it and the breeze which had sprung up made little strands of it blow across her face. Even over the roses and other mingled scents, Andy could smell the freshness of it. For a moment they sat without speaking. Her head was thrown back and she breathed deeply, her breast rising and falling regularly. She was wearing black trousers and a bright blue bodice and skirt, but even in the shapeless costume there was about her a lilting youth, a loveliness that knew no confines of dress. Her lips parted slightly and her eyes sparkled and moved about eagerly. The scent of her seemed to creep over Andy, steeping him in its pervasiveness, edging its way into his consciousness even when he struggled to keep it out. He could look nowhere without being conscious of her. Even when he took his eyes from her, the knowledge of her nearness went with him. She was everywhere he looked, everything he smelled and touched and saw. He felt a tightening in his belly. His palms were cold and moist. She moved slightly to change her position on the bench and a wisp of her hair brushed his cheek. He could feel the silkiness of it, smell the sweetness of it.

He paused for an instant in his breathing and the young night closed in around him, shutting out all that had gone before and all that might be between them now, leaving only the one small orbit in which they sat. He leaned forward and kissed her. His arms went around her. He could feel the smallness of her waist, the exquisite smoothness of her lips. She did not resist, but neither did she respond to his kiss. He was conscious only of an ineffable sweetness, a delicacy that yet held promise of spirit and fulfillment. He took his lips away and sat back, slightly away from her. Neither of them spoke. Finally, when he was about to speak she stopped him.

"Don't say you're sorry. If you do I'll scream."

"I wasn't going to say that. I'm not at all sorry."

"Well, thank Heaven for that. It's what they all say. And you know they're not a bit sorry."

"You're not angry?"

"Certainly not. I knew that's what you were bringing me out here for."

"But that's not exactly true. I never intended to when I came out here. I only wanted to talk. But then to see you like that—so small and sweet—"

"There is a remarkable sameness," she observed cynically, "in the approach every man uses to every woman."

"Please," he moaned softly. "Not Mrs. Bloomer—not now!"

She seemed to take pity on him, for when she spoke again her tone had softened.

"All right, Andy. We're old friends. And I always said you weren't like other men. Of all the men in the world I like you best —you and Father. Now does that make you feel better?"

"A little. Elizabeth, let me say what I intended to when I came out here before I lose my nerve."

"All right, say it." Her tone was kind now and she was waiting patiently for him to speak again.

He drew a deep breath. He was this far. He couldn't back out. It was now or never.

"Elizabeth, would you consider marrying me?"

For a moment he thought she had not heard, she remained so silent.

"Elizabeth—"

"I heard."

There was another long silence. The first fireflies began to blink close about them, little pinpoints of light against the growing blackness. He could just see the outline of her head near his shoulder. It was bent down slightly and he could imagine but not see the smooth top of it. She seemed perfectly still.

"I knew you were going to ask me," she said at last, speaking slowly and with careful deliberation. "I knew it all along—for years, I suppose."

"You knew all that time?"

"Yes. I guess always. Andy, I don't know how to answer. I'm going east, you know. I'm entering the seminary in the fall. It'll be a year at least. More, if I want to finish the course."

"I'd wait."

"But I couldn't promise. Not till I get back and feel really grown and know what I want. I want to do something with my life, Andy. I don't want to throw it away like women do and get old before my time so that no man wants me."

She did not say it flirtatiously nor, apparently, did she see the humorous contradiction in it.

"But you'll think it over?"

"Yes, I'll think it over." Then added quickly, "But I don't want to stir up any false expectations. And I would never keep you from marrying anyone else who might come along. Someone you might fall in love with."

He turned to her sharply, so suddenly that she seemed to withdraw a little in surprise at the very force of his physical presence beside her. The darkness was almost complete. The fireflies darted and shone, spangling the night. Above them a thousand stars had come out. There was, for once, no trace of fog. It was clear and diaphanous. The breeze carried the slightest suggestion of a chill, and Elizabeth shivered suddenly beside him. He seized her by the shoulders and pulled her to him, not tenderly this time but with abrupt and uncompromising passion. He could feel her bewilderment in the soft vulnerability of her lips as he parted them, and when he released her she let her breath out in a little rush that was like a sigh, and that was, he satisfied himself, not without a suggestion of wistfulness.

"I'll wait," he said quietly, releasing her.

He awoke late the next morning. Sunlight was already streaming full into the spare bedroom where he slept, shooting the polished floor with glinting gold and setting streaks of light glancing off the slender burnished posters.

There was little difference between the new house King had built her and Margaret's first home in San Francisco. It was larger, to be sure, and more imposing. Gabled and dormered, it rose three stories and boasted a conservatory, a two-story ballroom, an enormous dining room, drawing room, numerous bedrooms and private sitting rooms. King had spared no effort or expense to have the finest in material shipped from New England for its construction. But still, in style and furnishing, in the air of quiet good taste that was everywhere, it was very like the old house. There were more rugs but Margaret had not followed the fashion of covering every floor with wall-to-wall carpeting and there were long strips and edges where dark-gleaming floor showed. The very uncluttered peace of it made Andy roll luxuriously over and bury his head in the feather bolster. Then as though driven by sudden remembrance he sat up in bed. For a moment he stared straight ahead of him, thinking, remembering. Unable to contain himself any longer, he threw back the covers and leaped out of bed. He ripped off his nightshirt and ran across the room naked to the washstand, pouring water from the pitcher into the bowl and splashing in it vigorously. He dried himself with a heavy white towel that hung on the stand and surveyed himself in the mirror. He was all right. Nothing wrong with that build. Not a damned thing. Not too husky, maybe, but solid as a rock. Plenty of women had told him. Well, never mind that. That was over now. He leaned forward and examined himself closer in the glass, screwing his face over to one side and rubbing his hand over his stubble of beard. He got out the brush and lathered his face until the foam made him look like a bearded old sea captain. He stropped the razor vigorously and began to shave, pulling his face this way and that, contorting his mouth and skirting around the neat new mustache and carefully cultivated sideburns. He wiped the soap off, stepped back and admired the effect. Damned presentable. Nothing wrong with that face. He'd just neglected it too long. He went back to the bed and began pulling on his clothes, selecting a fresh white shirt and winding his cravat three times before it satisfied him. Ready at last, he went out into the hall with a light bounding step and hurried downstairs.

He saw only Elizabeth when he entered the dining room. Her bright hair was pulled back smooth and the top of it made a shining cap over her head. She looked up when he entered.

"Here's the lazy stay-abed! Do you know it's way past nine?"

"My apologies. I hope you didn't wait for me."

"We went ahead with breakfast, Andy," Margaret put in. "And we have a visitor. Just arrived this morning. Mr. Hart, my husband's nephew, Mr. Keith Delaney."

For the first time the focus of Andy's eyes traveled outside the small circle which encompassed Elizabeth and he saw that there was a stranger at the table. He was easily the handsomest young man Andy had ever seen.

He must have been twenty, certainly no more. He was not tall, but he was slim with the slimness that precedes full maturity and Andy guessed that his waist was like a girl's. He rose lazily from the dining-room chair and extended his hand.

"Delighted, sir."

"Welcome to San Francisco, Mr. Delaney," Andy said. He seated himself at an empty place next to the new arrival and continued to stare at him.

In everything except the soft, resilient plumpness that characterized Agnes, Keith Delaney resembled his mother. He had the same pale, translucent coloring, the dark, wide-set eyes, the black hair that grew far back from a white forehead. His mouth was full, his nose short and straight. There was no trace of the robust Delaney coloring about him, nor of the Delaney bulk. His hands were slim and white, the nails tapered to ovals like Agnes's. His feet, which Andy could just glimpse from under the edge of the table, showed a well-defined arch, his legs a straight contour. Andy sucked in his breath. God, but he was like her. At least in everything that showed on the outside . . .

"Keith was just telling us something of his ocean trip," Margaret said pleasantly.

The young man had a full collegiate mustache. His sideburns, carefully shaped, almost met the ends of the mustache at the sides of his mouth.

"Pretty bad going?" Andy inquired as the maid filled his plate with bacon and kidney stew. Already his eyes were straying to Elizabeth. What did she think of him? How did she look?

"Miserable. Half the crew down with scurvy or dysentery and the passengers running the decks like mad for fear they'd be left to shift for themselves in the next squall. Weather was abominable and everyone simply green with it. Next time I'll come by stage!"

Andy drew his eyes quickly back before he had a chance to see Elizabeth.

"I'm afraid you'd find stage equally distasteful, Mr. Delaney," he said, forcing a sociable tone into his voice. "Dust and Indians and heat till you're near crazy. Neither way's a bed of roses, eh, King?"

"Right you are, Andy. And it was even worse in the old days when we came out."

"Of course Harvard graduates are no doubt used to all the comforts of life!" All eyes turned to Elizabeth and Andy was glad for the excuse to look at her without seeming to be obvious. She was glaring with a kind of vindictive triumph at Keith, her eyes shooting a challenge, it seemed. He looked at her for the first time since Andy entered the room, a look so full of supercilious condescension that Andy longed to stuff a fist down his throat. Well, at least she wasn't swept off her feet by his high-and-mightiness. Thank God for that.

"You might say so," Keith replied slowly. "But I'm not exactly a graduate. Skipped off my last term without finishing. Boston was getting me down." He spoke flippantly in the manner of college boys relating pranks which they consider indescribably bold.

"How terribly brave!" Elizabeth exclaimed with sarcasm.

Keith looked away, ignoring her last remark. He had apparently come west with the idea of taking San Francisco by storm and the intention was in evidence this morning. He wore a black broadcloth frock coat. His shirt was of silk, with an amount of frilling that just missed being gaudy. His satin cravat was wound twice about his collar and tied in a graceful bow. He wore a green damask waistcoat with gold-threaded fleur-de-lis worked in a delicately repeated design. His buff-colored trousers nipped in smoothly about his waist and fitted snugly over his thighs so that nowhere was there a wrinkle or crease, no smallest indication of improper fitting. They tucked into his hand-tooled boots whose two-inch heels narrowed fashionably at the bottom and whose glossy finish was without a scratch.

Margaret smoothed the conversation over.

"It's so nice you've come in time for Treese's wedding, Keith. They'll all be quite wild with joy."

"I'm not sure Mother'll be too wild. I don't fancy she liked my running out before graduation, but I couldn't wait to leave the East. It's a man's world out here."

There was a clatter as Elizabeth's spoon dropped to her saucer.

"Indeed it is, Cousin Keith!" Her tone was scathing. "It seems every world's a man's world, here or in Boston or in China. But it won't be for long, mark my words! Women aren't going to sit around taking a position of servility forever. There are women stirring already. Women who realize what place we deserve in society and can win if we stick together and stand up for our rights!"

"Elizabeth reads Mrs. Bloomer," King cut in gently.

"Oh!" The expression was of tolerant amusement, as though the explanation cleared up everything.

Elizabeth tossed King an angry look. "Yes, oh! I suppose the boys at Harvard don't approve of her. They scarcely would, when she threatens their own insipid male superiority!"

"I can't say that I've ever heard your Mrs. Bloomer discussed. No doubt her importance hasn't yet permeated the halls of higher learning."

Elizabeth flushed scarlet. Andy saw that her hands were wringing furiously at her napkin.

"Well, now you arrive at an opportune time for many reasons," King said smoothly, glossing over the exchange of words by acting as though it had never taken place. "After the wedding, there's to be a big Democratic convention in Sacramento. I'll be up for it and unless I'm mistaken your mother will be expecting you to go. I rather fancy she has politics in mind as a field for you."

"And I rather fancied I'd take a bit of a holiday before settling down to anything serious."

King smiled wryly. "A pleasant notion, I'm sure, but I question whether your mother will approve. I think she has in mind to put you in my office directly reading law, and to apprentice you out to me as a neophyte politician as well. Now the convention in July should give you a good start."

Andy listened with half an ear as King's voice went on, discussing the Broderick and Gwin squabble, explaining the various factions who would be represented at the convention. His eyes strayed back to Elizabeth and rested there.

Her blue eyes were wide, her mouth soft and tremulous. She watched Keith as he ate and replied to King, as he dabbed at his mouth with a napkin. Once he turned and caught her eye. Andy thought the look he returned her was almost insolent. She dropped her eyes again and one small hand made a fist that she pressed close to her between her breasts.

That night Andy caught the steamer back to Sacramento.

Elizabeth dressed for dinner. She wore a pale-yellow tarlatan lined with deeper yellow shimmering silk. Its myriad flounces— twenty in all—caught the candlelight and a tiny green leaf pattern embroidered around the bottom of each scallop quivered and trembled.

All through dinner she talked little. She sat listening demurely as King and Keith continued their talk of politics, once in a while raising her eyes to Keith's and then dropping them with a slight fluttering of her lashes. King looked at her with only partially concealed amusement but there was a little crease of worry in Margaret's forehead as she watched her daughter. When the men took out their cigars she suggested that they retire to another room.

"Oh, I don't mind, Mother!" Elizabeth pleaded. She sat back, picking up her small yellow fan from the table and looking over it as the talk went on. Margaret sat resolutely in her place at the foot of the table.

"Do go on without me, Mother darling, if the smoke annoys you," Elizabeth pleaded.

"It's quite all right, dear." Margaret's tone was pleasant and unruffled but there was a firmness in it that indicated a hundred cigars would not have driven her from the room.

"Broderick's out to tie up this state, all right," King said, leaning back and taking deep drafts on his cigar. A servant poured brandy for him and Keith. Elizabeth held out her glass pleadingly but Margaret cast the servant a warning look and it was left unfilled. "Knows what he wants and he's out to get it. But what it's come down to is an out-and-out tussle between him and Gwin."

"But of course Gwin's southern, isn't he?" Keith inquired. "And Broderick being a Tammany man, that would put them on opposite sides of the slavery issue."

"Oh, slavery, hell." King looked up as if to apologize to the ladies, but thought better of it. If they could stand cigars, he reasoned, they'd have to stand the talk that went with them. "It's nothing more than a personal feud between two ambitious men. Slavery talk may cloak the issue, but that's all it is underneath, mark my words."

"But who is this Broderick anyway? Where's he from?"

"Came out here just before Gwin was elected to the Senate and organized a rival political machine. His father came over from Ireland and Davey was apprenticed to the old man as a stone mason. Didn't take him long to realize, though, that molding men was more to his liking than molding foundations. He got his training with the boys from Tammany back in New York. Where Gwin got his pointers from old Andy Jackson and sticks pretty close to traditions, Broderick claims he wears no man's collar—strikes out pretty much on his own. He was a saloonkeeper here in the early days, you know."

"That so?" Keith was obviously beginning to acquire an admiration for his uncle's vast knowledge of political intrigue.

"Sure. Now, you take Gwin. Couldn't find a bigger difference between two men. He's from Tennessee. Studied to be a doctor and somewhere along the line switched to politics. Knows the boys in Washington inside out and he's a shrewd one, all right. Came out here during the rush and helped the legislature frame the constitution. They rewarded him by a full term as senator. The boys supporting him are mostly all southern and western Democrats."

"Chivs?"

"That's what they call them. Hold for a more aristocratic kind of government. Proslavery and all that. Broderick's faction makes a great show of democracy and claims to hold no truck with slavery. Most of them are Northerners, of course. But down underneath, as I've said, it comes down to Broderick and Gwin; slavery be hanged. It's just a whipping boy for them."

"So that's the Democratic party." Keith shook his head in bewilderment. "But which side are we—I mean, how can you tell—"

King threw back his head and laughed. "You mean which band wagon are we going to jump on? Well, you're not quite ready for that yet. Look around a little, get to know the people. You'll be able to see fast enough which way the wind's blowing. Play your cards right but don't worry too much about it. You've got a couple of years ahead of you before you need make a choice."

Keith sighed wearily. "Uncle King, do me a favor."

"What, son?"

"Try and talk my mother out of politics as a career for me."

King roared with laughter.

It was after midnight when they retired to their rooms. Keith was given the room Andy had occupied down the hall from Elizabeth's and directly across from Margaret and King's. Margaret and King retired immediately and Elizabeth undressed and sat in her nightgown and wrapper near the window. Her hair had been brushed until some of the curls had begun to lose their tightness, making it stretch down her back and hang loosely over her shoulders. She leaned far out, her elbows on the window sill, breathing deeply of the fragrant night air. So that was Keith! And she had been so sure she would dislike him! She had been so deliberately rude and insulting to him this morning at breakfast. But how could she know? Everyone had said he was like his mother. Like Aunt Agnes. Elizabeth made a little face in the dark. And it was true. He did resemble her. But how much there was about him that was different! She tried hard to think but she could not picture precisely what there was about him that was different. Surely, there was something. She was simply too addled to concentrate now. For never in all the world had Aunt Agnes looked and talked and moved as Keith had. Or maybe she had but there was still a difference. There was something, *something*. And oh, but he was infernally handsome!

A light low knock at the door drew her up so suddenly that she bumped her head against the window.

"Damn!" She said it under her breath. Margaret did not think swearing befitted a lady. She tiptoed in her bare feet to the door and flung it open, thinking Margaret had come with some last-minute words of advice about her conduct. Mother was a darling, but there were times when a girl—

"Keith!"

"Hello." He was standing in the doorway, lounging with a kind of nonchalant insolence. He had not undressed, but he had removed his coat and cravat. His shirt hung open part way down and his hair was slightly rumpled.

"What are you doing here?" she whispered angrily, fearful lest they would be overheard.

"I came to watch the moonlight with you." He smiled down at her and she felt a strange turning-over in her stomach.

"But here! In my room. Keith, do go, please."

For answer, he stepped inside and closed the door brashly behind him. Elizabeth gasped.

"Keith, for heaven's sake! What will Mother and Father think?"

"They won't know if you stop yelling."

"I'm not yelling," she whispered indignantly. "But you've no right to come here like this. It's the worst possible taste and if you don't leave this minute I certainly will yell. I'll bring everybody in this house running . . ."

Her voice trailed off as she looked up at him. He was standing directly over her, a lamp in his hand. While she watched he took his eyes from her quite casually, set the lamp on a small table and blew it out. She felt herself beginning to tremble violently and she knew she must scream and cry out, but her voice seemed to have left her. Her throat was dry and constricted. The darkness was close about her. She was not sure where he was. She could not see him in the blackness. Gradually her eyes became accustomed to it and she could see his silhouette against the white-painted door.

"What did Mrs. Bloomer ever have to say about this?" he asked softly.

Before she could protest he drew her to him, pressing her so hard she could not breathe and his lips came down hot and searching, parting hers urgently and kissing her until she thought all the life had drained out of her. She collapsed weakly against his chest and as he took his lips away her cheek pressed against the smooth silk of his shirt. Her breath began to come back unevenly, in short gasps, but she clung to him as though for support. Holding her with one arm, he pushed her back slightly with the other, tipping her chin up with it. Her face was dim white, but he could distinguish the loose yielding of her lips, the wide lost quality of her eyes.

She struggled and tried to pull away from him.

"Don't get so outraged, my little crusader," he whispered as she started to pull her wrapper tight about her. He took the darkened lamp with him and disappeared into the hall. The door closed noiselessly behind him.

CHAPTER II

ELIZABETH wore her demurest lavender-sprigged muslin at breakfast the next morning and kept her eyes cast down with virginal modesty. When he entered the dining room she blushed furiously and gave him a prim nod, sitting a trifle straighter in her chair and concentrating on her bowl of mush as thought it were a rarity, the first of its kind and texture she had encountered. But her reproachful innocence, if it had been intended to make him feel contrite and humble for last night's boldness, might as well have been left undisplayed. He paid her no attention beyond a polite good morning, but went immediately into conversation with King and Margaret, discussing legal matters and the business of his apprenticeship, complimenting Margaret on her hospitality and swearing he had never spent a more restful night. His debonair boredom, which he had obviously affected for the purpose of making a first impression, had been discarded, but there was still a certain supercilious aloofness about him, a coolness that seemed to lift him a little from his surroundings and to give warning that while he was a good enough fellow on the outside, there was really no approaching him. His attitude toward Elizabeth seemed to indicate that he had kissed a hundred girls in as peremptory a fashion as he had her and that if she insisted on attaching some ridiculous importance to it, she was kindly to keep such thoughts to herself.

Margaret, as was her custom, began to outline the day's duties with brisk efficiency.

"First we'll go over the list of things you'll be taking to the seminary. There are some of them that can be packed now so there won't be all that to take care of after the wedding. You'll be quite worn out with the dancing and balls. Some things will have to be made up and the sooner they're started the better. I suggest that we go to your room first thing and get it settled."

She got up from the table and started for the stairs. Elizabeth rose slowly and followed her. St. Louis and the seminary, which yesterday had glowed with the vivid nearness of a cherished dream close to realization, were today quite without importance in her life. She would not go. She knew without a moment's hesitation that she could not, and yet she had not yet hit upon a way to break the news to her mother. A whole new future with limitless and breath-taking possibilities had opened up as if by magic. She had not been conscious of actually making a decision on the subject. It was simply that when she awoke this morning, she *knew*. She could never leave now.

"Elizabeth! Are you coming?" It was Margaret calling from the top of the stairs.

Elizabeth started guiltily, thinking her thoughts must surely reveal themselves on her face. She picked up her skirts and almost ran to the top of the stairs, arriving out of breath, flushed and panting. Margaret preceded her down the hall.

Margaret turned in the bedroom door and went across the room, seating herself on a small tufted chair by the window and taking out a piece of paper from the pocket of her black apron which she habitually wore in the morning.

Elizabeth's eyes went to where she and Keith had stood the night before. It was there—in that very place. Just inside the doorway and a bit over toward the corner. She had stood there and he had looked so tall looming over her . . .

"Three pairs of long underdrawers," Margaret stated, running a pencil over her list.

Elizabeth looked up, startled. "What, Mother?"

"Winters in St. Louis get quite chilly. You'll need three pairs of long drawers at least. You can have them lace trimmed if you like. Now, let's see. Twelve white muslin petticoats. We'll pack those unstarched and you can have them starched when you get there. Two chemises and a corset. Four flannel underpetticoats—"

"Mother!"

"Four flannel petticoats," Margaret repeated firmly. "Then I think four principal petticoats will do you. You have four, haven't you, with quilting and whalebone?"

Elizabeth nodded.

"Then take those. No use getting new things where the old will do. Then if you like, two petticoats with crinoline flounces. Several pairs of heavy cotton stockings for everyday and one of white lisle for dress."

"Two," Elizabeth pleaded with all the sincerity she could muster.

"One is plenty. Now, are you still crazy to have that patent tilter?"

Elizabeth was surprised her mother brought the subject up. They had had an argument over whether or not her wardrobe should include one of the new tilters. Margaret had been firm against it, maintaining that for winter cold it would be impractical. It was formed by graduated rounds of resilient steel wire held together by tapes and its function was to flare the skirt out. It was weighted by half a pound and required only one stout petticoat over it beneath the skirt of the dress. Margaret's contention had been that Elizabeth would go without the proper amount of underwear in cold weather if she possessed one. Elizabeth's surprise showed in her face and Margaret seemed to feel an explanation was necessary.

"Your father would never forgive me if I didn't let you have everything the latest. Maybe some of the other girls will have them and he'll be furious if you don't measure up to them. So if you still want one—"

Elizabeth ran across the room and threw her arms around Margaret.

"Mother darling, if you aren't the sweetest—" She felt her eyes filling with hot tears which she brushed away quickly behind Margaret's back, and she knew she was crying, not because she was touched by her mother's concession but because of her own deception. She felt wicked and sly and she longed to blurt out the whole truth but something kept it locked within her. It wasn't the time yet. If she could only wait. If she could only stand it to be patient until the right time came!

Margaret smiled in the soft way she had and detached Elizabeth's arms. "There now. It's no cause for commotion. Only be sure you wear your warm drawers every time you put on the contraption. We're not spending all this money on you simply to have you come down with lung fever. Now, let's see." Her pencil ran down the list again.

Elizabeth's original intention, when she decided on school, had been to wear her Bloomer outfits exclusively. But Margaret, who knew how quickly attitudes changed when a girl saw another girl looking lovelier than herself and receiving more attention, had wisely ordered some other clothes for her. They were at the dressmaker's waiting to be fitted.

Elizabeth listened wide-eyed to her mother's description of the dresses, in whose creation she had taken but scant interest up to now. Why, with all those dresses! and if she didn't have to go away she could wear them right here in San Francisco. If he wasn't mad about her now he soon would be, or she'd know the reason why! She exclaimed with rapture as Margaret described each detail and hugged her impulsively at frequent intervals.

There would be four pairs of slippers: one a dusty rose to match the ball gown (and oh, how she could swirl around the floor of the ballroom with him and show those slippers and the white stockings over her ankles!), two pairs of gaiters for the street, and one pair of stout boots for traveling. There would be one pair of ankle boots which laced up the inside of the ankle and had a tassel on the top.

When they came to the bonnets Margaret hesitated warily and asked, "How many?" It had been another point of contention with them, for even in her most ardent Bloomer moments, Elizabeth had never quite abandoned her penchant for pretty bonnets.

"Fifteen," she replied without hesitation. "You simply can't *exist* with less, Mother!"

"It seems to me *I* existed quite well with two when I was your age," Margaret said sternly. "But if you're set on fifteen, I guess you may as well have them."

Elizabeth gasped at the ease with which her mother gave in. She had expected a fight to the finish on the bonnets. Margaret was certainly being agreeable now that it got right down to facts.

"I imagine four pairs of gloves will do. And of course you'll want ribbons for your hair and for sashes. You can take some and then you'll be buying others out there. Now—you'll want two warm shawls. Take your dark woolen one with the heavy fringe and your plain one with the colored border. For good we'll order a cashmere in Paisley and then you'll probably be wanting one of those vest-front affairs with the fitted back and turnover collar. I suppose the girls will be wearing them. How about your Bloomer costumes?"

"Oh, well, of course, _ wouldn't want them to think I was behind the times. Of course I'll take one."

"Only one?" Margaret's eyebrows raised slightly. "Well, of course. Just as you say. I believe that finishes up the list. Then I'll tell Mrs. Humford you'll come for a fitting tomorrow? Those dresses will have to be finished up in a hurry. If you like you might take the rose ball gown with you to Sacramento when we go for the wedding. I imagine there'll be a great deal of dancing."

"Oh, Mother, you're so sweet and I know I'm going to adore all of them!" Elizabeth had risen and was bouncing first on one foot, then on the other in her eagerness. He would be there at the wedding and for all the balls and affairs. He would see her in the rose dress!

"And may I wear the new cashmere shawl for the trip up? And the green dress?"

"We'll see. Perhaps if we go by steamer. But if we decide to take the stage it'll be quite ruined by the dust. We'll wait and see." Margaret started for the door and Elizabeth skipped after her.

"Mother!" Margaret paused at the door and turned back. Elizabeth came up and embraced her, holding her cheek close to her mother's for an instant. "Mother, aren't you going to miss me terribly when I go to St. Louis? If I really was hasty and if you'd rather I stayed—"

"Elizabeth." Margaret's voice was cool, almost stern, and she looked at her daughter with a firmness to which Elizabeth was unaccustomed. It seemed that little lines had appeared at the corners of her mouth; her eyes were fixed and lacked their usual warmth. "Elizabeth, for a whole month your father and I heard nothing from morning to night but that women were being ground ruthlessly under society's heel and that education was the only factor that could free them. We examined brochures from twenty different seminaries. We listened to excerpts read aloud from the *Lily*. We were plagued, run after, teased and tormented until finally we said you might go. And now, by heaven, you're going!" She turned and left the room.

Elizabeth remained rooted to the spot, staring after her and listening to her mother's footsteps growing fainter down the hall. When they became indistinct and disappeared she closed the door, a puzzled expression on her face.

She spent the entire afternoon preparing for dinner. First she had a bath drawn in the little rose-painted tub on the first floor. She luxuriated in the deep suds for three-quarters of an hour, then dried herself on a thick towel and threw her dressing gown on, scuffing upstairs with her damp hair pinned to the top of her head. For another hour she sat in front of her dressing table applying creams and lotions, rose water and talcum. She washed her face separately at her own washstand with lettuce soap and cold water, a method "guaranteed to leave milady's complexion at its silken best" and dried it on a fine linen serviette.

At five o'clock she summoned a maid to help her with her corset and shouted impatiently when the girl did not pull it tight enough. Then she dispatched the maid to select three camellias from the garden. Margaret's camellias were her particular pride and Elizabeth had had to give the girl two of her best ribbons and a verbena sachet to coax her to perform the mission. She took the flowers and put them floating in the washbowl in clean water. They would be put on at the last minute.

She paced up and down the room, stopping at every turn to look at the little porcelain clock on her dressing table. She drew on her white stockings and the little square-toed gold shoes she wore with her gold gown. She leaned close to the dressing-room mirror and touched a faint smear of rouge (her most secret secret) to her lips, leaning far back then to examine the effect and see whether it was noticeable. After a moment's consideration she seized a towel and rubbed it off. Margaret was forgiving, but there were some things—!

At last she began to put on her petticoats, six stiffly starched muslin ones, one heavily quilted and boned to make her dress stand out, and a top one frilled and ruffled and dainty. Then the dress itself, shimmering and elegant in the late sunlight. She struggled to fasten the back hooks; it would be perilous to ask anyone to help her at this last minute when the whole thing might be given away by a chance word to Margaret.

When at last the hooks and eyes were manipulated, she relaxed, breathing heavily. She pulled the gown down at the shoulders so that a wide expanse of white skin was visible. She piled her hair high on her head so that the curls cascaded in ringlets down the back of her head and tied it on top with a black velvet ribbon. She tied a piece of the ribbon around her wrist with some difficulty, using her teeth to complete the knot and then placed the camellias in a kind of coronet across the top of her head.

For a long time she stood looking at her image in the mirror, stepping back and then forward, turning slightly to one side and the other.

She heard the maid announcing dinner downstairs but she waited until there was an urgent knock at her door.

"Miss Elizabeth! We're waiting dinner for you!"

Her heart leaped to her throat in anticipation.

"All right, Genevieve. I'm coming." She drew a deep breath that sent a little shudder all along her arms and neck and started to walk across the room slowly. At the door she paused, her hand on the knob. Give him a little more time. Just a minute. Finally she opened the door and went out. She descended the stairs slowly, watching her footing and appearing quite indifferent to what might be waiting below. When she was close to the foot she heard a low whistle that sent a chill bounding up her spine. But when she looked she saw that it was King.

"Well! If my girl doesn't look like the finest lady in San Francisco tonight!" He was looking her over with pride and admiration. Elizabeth cast him a swift smile but looked past him searchingly. Beyond, through the big double doors that led into the dining room she could see Margaret's back. But where was Keith? She turned back to King, the smile gone from her face, her eyes dark with apprehension.

"Keith—" she stammered. "Didn't he come home with you?"

King's face grew compassionate.

"Oh, honey, isn't that a shame. Now, I'll tell you. He was anxious to see a bit of San Francisco and said he just thought he'd go along tonight without coming home for dinner. If I'd known you were counting on it, I would have brought him back."

CHAPTER III

CHARLES WICKHAM was putting on weight. Not much, to be sure. If you weren't looking for it you might not even notice. An inch or two around the waist was all but it served to diminish his shoulders just enough so that he had to caution his tailor to give his new coat a good square cut. But of course he had the height to carry it, he told himself each morning as he surveyed himself in the glass.

It was true about the height. He stood six feet four without his boots but there was none of the firm lankiness about him that characterized many of the taciturn pioneers. Although his flesh was reasonably solid with the solidity of care and a prudent amount of exercise, he was not muscular. It was as though he had developed his body as an ornamental rather than a utilitarian thing. He bathed it religiously, clothed it assiduously. It was, together with a slightly clipped speech and a claim to a lineage of dubious nobility, his salient social asset. Beyond that, he had an oval face with a mouth whose full lower lip gave it a look of sensuality, a jowl which already betrayed a certain slackness, a hairline whose position he carefully noted from week to week. His eyes were blue, faded and lacking in brilliance, and they were accustomed to looking about him with a certain listlessness as though nothing outside his immediate orbit could possibly be of concern to him. He kept his hands smooth, the nails neatly trimmed and the cuticles pushed back. They were short and square, however, and he was constantly trying to make them appear longer. It was one of the torments of his life that his hands were not in keeping with the rest of his physique. They were broad, flat; the hands of a peasant. Tended and blanched, they had a singularly useless appearance.

He had set Sacramento society back on its heels from the first week he arrived. It did not take long for anxious mothers to discover that he was quite without funds but this lack seemed only to enhance his desirability. Making money and getting ahead was one thing, and all very well too. But impoverished nobility! Before he had been in Sacramento a week he had been feted at three balls, two afternoon socials and a steamer excursion. By the end of the second week the whole story of his background had been well circulated. With convincing reserve Charles allowed it to be drawn out of him that his estates in England were of a size that a city like Sacramento would easily be lost in them. No, they were still intact, but for the moment he was quite at a loss as to how to recover them. Well, no, it was not exactly financial. There had been a little matter of a certain Lady Pamela Frisbe-Smythe. Lord Frisbe-Smythe, the lowest kind of boor, had made the most distasteful row over finding himself cuckold. Ended up in a duel—pistols, naturally —and he'd had to leave in the middle of the night for Liverpool and get away on a miserable freighter. Simply with the clothes on his back. No, he certainly was not going to let it go at that. Just as soon as he'd assembled his resources—here the dissertation grew vague—he was going back there and recover his confiscated property at the point of a gun, if necessary!

Gold, it appeared, had been his first thought when he arrived in California but in short order it became apparent to him that bodily exertion and the prolonged use of a pick and Long Tom were required to net results. He had immediately fallen back on his personal desirability and here he had struck fertile ground. If gold was hidden and elusive, anxious mothers were to be had tenpenny a dozen. During his first month in Sacramento he was rumored engaged to at least five girls and by the end of the second month it was a fairly well-established fact that he would marry Hazel Carlton, daughter of banker Louden Carlton. Charles made no effort to deny the story until one day he heard of a certain widow, Mrs. Agnes Delaney, who was reputedly worth more than all the rest put together. She was still in mourning, he learned, but it might be worth waiting for. He signed his hotel bill and stayed on.

The story of the engaging Englishman who was taking the city by storm had filtered through the drawn portieres of Agnes Delaney's new frame house and after six impatient months of mourning, she promptly ordered her daughter to resume her regular apparel and even ordered a dozen new dresses made up for her. She then held her first "at home" with a carefully phrased invitation to the newcomer she had never met. He would not consider her presumptuous, she hoped, but naturally all Sacramento had heard of him. She would be most honored, she and her daughter.

Charles was pleased and excited over the inclusion of a reference to her daughter. This was better than he had anticipated. Widows were fine, but they were apt to be strong-minded, especially where money was concerned, and from what he had heard of this Agnes Delaney, she was more strong-minded than most. No one had mentioned her daughter. It was doubtful whether she was very desirable but quite likely she would prove at least manageable and the dowry, from what he had heard of the Delaney resources, should be most compensating. Charles spent two slow careful hours dressing and arranging himself to appear in his best light and then set out for the Delaney house. Three months later, early in April, his engagement to Miss Treese Delaney of Sacramento, late of Boston, was announced.

Charles was quite satisfied. He might have wished, if the truth were known, that it was Agnes and not Treese he was marrying. Hardly looked more than a girl herself and that way she had of swinging her hips when she walked! Even in the black mourning dress there was something subtly tempting about her. Hardly looked griefstricken to *him*. But there was no doubt about it. Under that inviting plumpness something firm and purposeful showed itself in brief revealing flashes. Like the persistent queries she had made regarding the exact state of his affairs in England. There was no putting her off with generalities as he had the other mothers. He had the disquieting feeling when she finished with him that she was not under the slightest deception, as to either his resources or Lady Pamela and his nocturnal flight. He caught himself wondering why she was so anxious to have him for a son-in-law until his pride returned to him with something of a jolt and he recalled the immense attractiveness of his person and the note of Old World culture he injected into the crass bourgeois atmosphere that was everywhere evident.

Actually Charles had not hit far from the truth. Agnes wanted him for a son-in-law because every other mother in Sacramento wanted him for a son-in-law. She also wanted him because she felt Treese's future to be dubious in the extreme unless she developed either a more likable personality or a better bustline, and neither possibility seemed imminent. And there was another reason, less tangible but perhaps even stronger than the others. Following King's advice in business matters had won Agnes a respect not accorded other women in Sacramento but she was not yet satisfied. The dread she had brought with her from Boston of living out her life as a dry goods merchant's daughter was still present. She was held in awe, covertly admired by most husbands and respected, if somewhat grudgingly, by most of their wives. But not in the four years she had spent there had she ever quite reached the social plane she had set as a goal for herself. Charles would be the final step in the attainment of that status and regardless of the fact that he was a penniless fortune hunter (Agnes had not been deceived from the first) she wanted him for Treese.

After the initial thrusting and parrying, they had spoken quite frankly, and she made it clear to him that she would undertake his obligations only after he was soundly married to her daughter. Charles, who had half expected at least a minor advance on the dowry, was slightly disgruntled but he accepted the terms with reasonably good grace and comforted himself with the pleasant diversion of anticipation. All in all, he was well satisfied. He did not dislike Treese although he might have wished for something a little less bony and uninviting physically and now that his future had been assured, he felt free to relax for the first time since his arrival in America.

Treese's reaction was less relief than apprehension, less eagerness than stoic acceptance. Even the final fitting of her wedding gown held no excitement or anticipation for her.

She looked at herself in the mirror. The gown was fashioned after that worn by the Empress Eugénie earlier in the year. It was of white satin trimmed with lace, its long train covered with lace in a design of violets. She was to wear a girdle of silver cloth about her waist and a coronet of brilliants in her hair. The long lace veil was thrown carefully across the bed. The orange blossoms which were to be intertwined with the coronet were being shipped in especially for the occasion and had not yet arrived.

In four years she had changed little. She was taller but scarcely less thin. Small mounds of breasts showed but her hips were still flat and without form. Her heavy red hair was pinned high on her head to be out of the way during the fitting. It felt clumsy and as though it was about to tumble down at every move. Her freckles had not disappeared. They still stood out militantly across the bridge of her nose and sprinkled her forehead. There was no fullness in her face; her cheeks showed hollow under their high jutting bones. Her mouth was too wide, her eyes frank and gray as Delaney's had been. She was not a pretty girl. But Charles Wickham was not marrying her for her looks and she knew it.

All around her the bedroom was a litter of preparation. Swatches of materials hung over chair backs and were tacked to curtains. Tiny bits of thread clung to the carpet and a pair of scissors had been left on the floor close to her feet. The curtains of her canopied bed had been flung aside and half-completed garments, all turned inside out, lay across it together with the veil. Some were pinned, some basted with long running stitches; some lacked sleeves.

"All right, again," the dressmaker commanded. "Turn. Turn. Now stop."

Treese obeyed and stopped, this time with her back to the mirror. It was early June and the heat was not yet severe but in the heavy satin gown she could feel perspiration start under her arms and trickle down her sides. The long sleeves were tight over the crook of her elbow. The heavy girdle of silver cloth started a little ring of perspiration around her waist.

"Are we almost done, Mrs. Fitch?"

Mrs. Fitch, a dry colorless woman, bobbed her head in smiling approval, sending the pincushion that was suspended by a tape about her neck into a bobbing little dance.

"I think we are, Miss Treese. One more day should finish this off. The train and veil will have to be adjusted, of course. My!" She rocked back on her heels in admiration. "I'm sure the Empress's couldn't have been a whit finer! Not because it's my own handiwork, mind, but I must say it's got style to it."

There was a brisk knock at the door and Agnes entered.

"Well! How's it going, Mrs. Fitch?" She walked to within six feet of Treese and then circled around her, examining the dress critically. Younger looking and more vigorous than on the first distraught night when she landed in Sacramento City with three young children and a firmly clutched satchel of gold dust and slugs, Agnes Delaney was at thirty-eight the handsomest woman in Sacramento as well as the richest.

"Very nice, Mrs. Fitch." She continued the circling walk. Each time she passed Mrs. Fitch the little dressmaker drew herself back deferentially, sucking her breath in. "Do you think it compares well with Eugénie's?"

"Oh, Mrs. Delaney! Only a minute before I was telling Miss Treese here: If the Empress's was a whit nicer, I'd have to see it myself!"

"Of course one doesn't get the materials here as in Paris—"

"But the style!"

"Yes, the style seems quite suitable." Agnes halted and examined her daughter head-on. As always under direct scrutiny, Treese blushed and cast her eyes downward.

Mrs. Fitch raised herself, her joints making little snapping noises, and hobbled stiffly to the table. She had been on her knees for the better part of the last hour. She examined the well-thumbed picture of Eugénie that was lying on the table. The Empress was posed in the gown from which Treese's was copied, except that the silver cloth girdle had been substituted for a belt of brilliants.

"Pearls," Mrs. Fitch stated. "A double row."

"Pearls." Agnes digested the information. "You think they go well with the silver?" She spoke impersonally and as though she and Mrs. Fitch were alone in the room.

The little dressmaker shrugged ever so slightly. "Well, Eugénie . . ." She let her voice trail off meaningfully.

"Yes, I think pearls will be fine," Agnes decided abruptly. As though as an afterthought she added, "That suits you, Treese?"

"Oh, yes. Fine."

"Well, then." Mrs. Fitch bustled back to her charge and began to undo hooks and remove pins. "That finishes it."

Agnes dropped down on the edge of the bed and watched as the heavy gown was undone and allowed to drop heavily off Treese's flat hips. Holding the gown over one arm, Mrs. Fitch held out a wrapper and Treese slipped into it. Her hair had fallen down in the final tugging and pulling and it streamed now in a red profusion down her back and over the pale-blue wrapper.

"Have you heard further from Keith, Mother?" She went and sat on the window seat, pulling her legs up under her.

"Nothing today. But they should be coming soon. Heavens, how the time drags waiting!"

"Oh, Mrs. Delaney!" Mrs. Fitch was bustling about the room collecting scraps and pins. The pins she stabbed into the little cushion that bobbed on her scrawny chest. The scraps she wadded into a little ball. "I just can't tell you the talk that's going around town about your son, Mr. Keith. Not a house I sew in but what they've heard about him and want to know when's he coming and what do I hear about him. And then order up a new dress for their daughter! Oh, they're sly ones all right!"

"Do they really ask that?" Agnes was pleased. Her mouth softened and curved upward slightly as she thought of her son. Ever since she learned he was in California she had ached with longing to see him but she wrote him a letter telling him not to come to Sacramento until King and Margaret and Elizabeth came up for the wedding. It was as good an opportunity as he would ever have to ingratiate himself with King and the two of them seemed to be getting along well. And Elizabeth, too, from what she'd heard.

"What else do they say, Mrs. Fitch?" she asked, her painstaking dignity giving way to womanly curiosity.

Mrs. Fitch hung the wedding gown carefully against the wall where it billowed and rustled for a moment and then hung, rich and limp and shining.

"Oh, heavens, if I was to tell you all they said, why, I'd be here till morning. Well, that they heard how handsome he was and all and taking San Francisco quite by storm. And many of 'em says Mrs. Delaney sure is the lucky one, having a son growed and mighty near a lawyer and still looking like a girl herself!"

Agnes's eyes shone with pleasure.

"Such drivel!" She bit her lower lip and curiosity fought a losing battle with decorum. "What did Annie Carlton say?"

"Near talked my ear off, Mrs. Delaney, and that's a fact. Wanted to know what all the talk was from this house about when he was coming and all and then went and ordered up two new watered silks for her daughter Hazel—with padding."

Agnes gave a delighted little laugh. The periodic visits of Mrs.

Fitch, from which she gleaned the latest boudoir and fitting-room gossip of Sacramento's top social level, were one of her chief delights. Invariably they began as prim discussions of sleeves and fabrics and ended up over a cup of tea with Mrs. Fitch rambling on effusively and Agnes leaning forward, her lips slightly parted, her eyes sparkling with avaricious interest. Treese, familiar with the process, watched indifferently from the window seat. Hazel's padding and Mrs. Carlton's eagerness were of no importance to her, but the coming of her brother Keith was. Ever since she had learned he was in San Francisco, she had been seized with a shy intoxicating expectancy. All during the long year that followed Delaney's death she had been conscious of a heavy loneliness hanging over her that was like no loneliness she had ever known before. Her betrothal to Charles had done nothing to dispel the feeling. She was hoping that the arrival of Keith would.

"So, naturally there wasn't much I could tell them," Mrs. Fitch continued animatedly, proud of being the center of attention. Her manner suggested that she was relating only surface incidents. If she wanted to tell it, there was much more. "Just said I supposed he'd be up with his aunt and uncle in time for the wedding and all. Of course many of 'em inquired as to why he hadn't come right on to Sacramento in the first place and that I couldn't tell 'em, not knowing myself."

She gave the end of the sentence a slight upward emphasis that was polite inquiry. Agnes knew what she wanted but did not speak. It was nobody's damned business and she certainly wasn't going to talk it over with this old busybody.

Mrs. Fitch sensed the rebuff and for several minutes went about the room briskly making it orderly and getting her materials ready for tomorrow's session. Her dry, colorless mouth was slightly pursed, but she was holding herself in check through obvious effort. Her watery eyes darted with a suppression of excitement and her soft withered cheeks heightened with color. At last the pièce de résistance broke through.

"You know about Mrs. Bement taking a party to the new Metropolitan Bath House tomorrow night?"

In spite of herself, Agnes felt her mouth dropping open. For the hundredth time since Delaney's death she felt the frustration of widowhood binding tightly about her. Before, she had been the one to make social innovations. Now every simpering upstart in Sacramento was trying to steal her thunder.

"A ladies' bath party?"

Mrs. Fitch nodded. "Reserved a private room, so I hear it. The party's to be modeled on old Roman lines. I did up the costumes for it myself soon as the grand opening of the bath house was announced. Wasn't much sewing to it. Kind of a sheet affair but all in different colors. Cost a pretty penny, too. Couldn't buy cheap goods for fear the color'd run in one of those steamy rooms. They say that's quite the place. Four apartments for the general trade and a private parlor for ladies. Mrs. Bement rented out the whole parlor for the opening night."

"You don't say."

"Oh, yes, quite elegant for fair. Hobbses is catering, but they had to hire all lady waiters, because naturally there won't be any gentlemen admitted."

"Naturally." What a silly kind of entertainment! A lot of women sitting around together draped in sheets and not a man to notice! Still, she wished she could have done it.

She changed the subject abruptly. "You haven't told any of them about the wedding gown, have you?"

Mrs. Fitch sucked in her breath with horror. "Oh, heaven above, Mrs. Delaney, you know I never give away a confidence of one of my clientele! And I wouldn't for the gold in all California spoil the effect. Nor of your own gown, either."

Agnes had hit upon the happy plan of coming out of mourning for the first time at her daughter's wedding. She was impatient to be out of black and had worn it this long only because the stylish black gowns Mrs. Fitch fashioned for her were particularly becoming and the little bonnets with their wide-edged veiling poignant about her face.

Mention of the wedding seemed to remind Mrs. Fitch that Treese was still in the room and she turned to her banteringly.

"Aren't you going to be the fine one, Mrs. So-and-so, with your big enormous wedding and your trip to Europe! I guess we just won't even be in it with you when you get back."

Treese made a self-effacing little gesture. She was still on the window seat staring out into the treetops and turned only in answer to Mrs. Fitch's voice. Her eyes were large in her thin face; her hands under the ruffled sleeves of the wrapper were like a boy's hands, slender and muscular, the bones clearly defined.

"Oh my, look at the dreamer!" Mrs. Fitch made a gesture of mock impatience toward Agnes.

Treese reddened and turned back to the trees that rustled and whispered softly outside the open window. There was a lazy clack of hoofs and grinding wheels and a voice rang out proclaiming that ice was for sale.

"Well, it's a shame and a pity that poor Mr. Delaney couldn't have lived to see this happy day," Mrs. Fitch mourned. "A Christian shame and a pity. He was such a fine man."

"Indeed he was," Agnes agreed, forcing sobriety into her tone. She made every effort to let her grief appear genuine, for she knew that her coming out of mourning so soon was going to set every tongue in town going. But she'd be damned if she'd show up at her own daughter's wedding in some shoddy black. Everybody would be looking at her and the one thing she did not want to appear was motherly. And King would be there. At the thought of him something inside her took a quick gulping dive. They had had to be discreet during the past year. A widow had to watch her step and she had her business to think of. But there was nothing wrong with a brother-in-law paying a visit to the house now and again. Oh, those visits! And now he would be here in a few days. Of course Margaret would be with him.

But the week after the wedding was the convention and surely she and Elizabeth would go home by that time while he stayed on. And with Treese on her honeymoon and Keith—she caught herself up guiltily at the thought of Keith. It was his coming she should be thinking of, not King's. Of course she wanted to see Keith! The very thought of him made her almost burst with pride and affection. But with King it was something different. Something that simply refused to be denied. It came from deep inside, boiling and bubbling over in a ferment of pain and wanting and longing. She wrenched her thoughts away from him and tried to look composed, aware that she was under Mrs. Fitch's close scrutiny.

"Would you care for a cup of tea, Mrs. Fitch?"

"Why, that's real kind of you, Mrs. Delaney. I don't know but what a cup of tea would touch the spot right now."

CHAPTER IV

IT WAS QUITE dark when Treese awoke. For a moment she could not think what day it was or what had made her waken. The darkness around her was the heavy gray-black silence of night. In it she could discern familiar shapes and objects that told her she was in her own room. The wedding dress hanging against the wall, the washstand with its stark white bowl and pitcher, the dressing-table mirror that caught and shot back an eerie shaft of moonlight. She lay quite still on her back for a moment. Then she threw the covers back and got out of bed. She tiptoed to the mantel where a little antique clock indicated the time. She had to lean close to make out the position of the hands. Her cheek grazed the cool smooth surface of the glass. Quarter after four. As though sensing that it was not yet time for the evil demons of night to give up lurking behind closet doors and under beds she flew back, her bare feet feeling the tickle of the carpet, and jumped under the covers. She pulled them up high over her head and felt the pounding of her heart in the small stifling enclosure. The reassuring warmth of her own body was a protective covering about her. Tentatively she poked her head out and gulped in fresh air. She allowed her tensed-up muscles to relax and pulled both arms out. She folded them under her head and stared up to where the blackness hid the ceiling.

Today he was coming! In a few more hours he would be here!

"Treese! You mean this is Treese? Why, when she left Boston she was an ugly little freckled thing. Can this really be Treese?"

Treese wriggled happily and squinted her eyes tight shut.

"Is this Treese? But of course. I'd have known her anywhere. By her lovely big eyes and her smile. Hasn't she the Delaney smile, Mother?

"I can't believe that I'm really out here in California. It's been such a long time. Treese, has it been lonely for you? I've wished so many times for someone to talk to. And now that we're both here together we'll have each other. Everything's going to be different now."

An inner voice shouted out within Treese until she thought it would burst her eardrums. "But I'm going to be married!"

"Married? What difference does it make? He's an outsider and we're both Delaneys. Isn't that right? We'll be good friends, won't we, Treese? You have to have somebody close to you to understand what's going on inside of you. Somebody you can talk to about everything. Somebody who'll understand."

Treese's arms were beginning to tingle. She brought them down at her sides and the circulation started again. What would he look like? Everyone said how handsome he was. And he would give her away at the wedding. People would be sure to look at Keith instead of at her and that would be good, too. She hated to think about being stared at.

"Yes, sir, this is my little sister. Oh, no, we're not giving her away. We think too much of her for that. No, sir. Just because she's married she isn't going to leave us. Are you, Treese? Well, I guess not. I wouldn't know what to do without her. I'd miss those long talks we have, giving advice and taking it, listening to each other's troubles. Couldn't let that happen, could we, Treese?"

Two tears of happiness filled Treese's eyes and dropped to the pillow. To have someone! To really have someone who was your own and to be able at last to talk and exchange confidences. She dug her head back into the pillow and screwed her eyes tight shut, trying to picture Delaney's face, just how he had looked the last time she saw him. At least once a day, usually just before she dropped off to sleep at night, she drew a mental image of him, fixing it in her memory. She wanted to keep on doing that as long as she lived. If she made it a habit, like combing her hair or brushing her teeth then surely she could remember him forever. She thought of him now, with his heavy handsome face and thick red hair. His eyes had looked tired, though, that last time. The skin around them had begun to show little circular wrinkles and it was bluish instead of firm and ruddy. She tried to forget about the eyes. The mouth was easy. It had never changed. Wide and quick-smiling, sometimes turned down a little with tenderness at the corners. She had never known anyone so wonderfully handsome.

At the thought of Delaney she became aware of a vague discomfort stealing over her. It was a familiar feeling, one that always accompanied thoughts of him. Before, it hadn't been so bad. Now it came oftener and each time it was more frightening. The time it really scared her had been last week in Andy Hart's office. She'd stopped in to pass the time of day with him and say a nostalgic good-bye to the dusty old office where she'd spent so many pleasant afternoons. Then he'd passed the chance remark that she was like Delaney. She looked up at him quickly, the funny uneasy feeling coming over her.

"I am?"

"Sure. Don't you want to be?" Andy leaned back and filled his pipe. He struck a light on the top of his battered desk and puffed. "He was a good man." Andy threw the match on the floor where there were already a number of others.

Treese turned away from him and looked through the dusty window of the second-story office into the busy street below.

"I've had the funniest feeling lately, Andy."

"About him?"

"Yes." She turned back to him questioningly. "How do you think he died?"

Andy's even white teeth loosened their grip on the pipe and he removed it slowly. "Why, now, I don't know. Never gave it much thought."

"He killed himself, didn't he?" It seemed to Treese she was hearing someone else say the words.

Andy was quiet for a long time. Then he spoke slowly and thoughtfully. "Well, now, I wouldn't want to say. You take a man going off to the mining country like he did, anything can happen. You can't just say he killed himself when there's no way to prove it. There might have been something to it we don't know about. Far as I know nothing was wrong."

"You don't have to say that, Andy. I guess I know all right. I knew all along. Those are things you don't have to be told. Then at first I decided it was because he didn't find gold. Lots of men have shot themselves over that. They count on it so much and then when they get alone up in those camps where there's no one to talk to it grows and grows on them until they can't stand it any more."

"Well, sure. That's natural. What could be more natural than that? A man counts on making himself a pile and he never hits it right. Keeps going back and going back, never has any luck and then one day they find him like they did Delaney."

There was a pause. She looked straight at him. Her gray eyes widened and held their stare until he looked down at the floor.

"Only that wasn't it," she said quietly. Say I'm wrong, something inside her shouted. Please say I'm wrong! Andy remained silent. "The real thing was, the world got to be too much for him."

Andy scowled defensively. "Now what does that mean?"

"It's hard to explain. Only I've had the feeling myself. You feel things crowding in around you that you don't understand. Things happen fast and you can't keep up with them. By and by you begin to feel suffocated, like you can't breathe. You try and try but you can't keep up. You know how it was with him, Andy."

"Yep, I know." Andy spoke quietly now, putting away the pretense of not understanding.

"It was all he lived for, the hope that she'd admire him, that he'd do something big for her. Maybe she wasn't to blame, I don't know. He could never keep up with her. And he got to thinking he'd failed her. As if anybody ever could! And all the time it was getting worse and worse, pressing in on him until he couldn't breathe. And she never knew it." There was a short embarrassed silence. "That's what I've been wanting to ask you, Andy. Do you think she knew it?"

Andy cleared his throat loudly. "That's a hell of a question, Treese. How does anybody know what goes on in another person's mind?"

She pressed her hands together and looked down at them. "I wish I knew, Andy. I just wish I knew. I've had the funniest feeling lately. As if I were going to be cut in two. Made into two parts. As if everything I've been up to now, all the things I've known are going to be left behind. As if when I change my name it'll be real. There really won't be a Treese Delaney any more. I used to be afraid at first of changing and being somebody different. Now I'm used to it. Only I wish I could clear up all these things first. Sometimes I think of them so much my head aches. I guess I knew nobody could tell me but I wanted to ask anyway. You were the only one who *knew* him. You knew him better than I did, even, because you're a man and he talked to you. He never talked much to me except silly little things. And I never understood him. I tried to but I never could get through to him entirely."

Andy drew a deep breath, crossed and uncrossed his legs on the desk in front of him.

"Well, if I was to analyze Delaney, I'd say the one thing he lacked was a sense of value. He never could tell black from white. He never could sift out the good from the bad and tell how much of each was in a person. So he got fooled. Pretty bad sometimes. And maybe, like you say, the world got to be too much for him. Puts me in mind of those touchstones the old-timers used to use when they tried to make gold. The alchemist would touch the metal to the stone to see if it was really gold. If Delaney could have had something like that to judge people; if he could have seen past the surface and not been so trusting, maybe he wouldn't have been hurt so bad. But he was like a child, always looking for the good instead of the evil. You have to recognize both, you know, to get along in the world. To keep up with it. Otherwise you lose your will to fight. And once you back down and refuse to meet the fight, then it gets hard."

For a long time she did not answer and the uneasy, scared feeling heightened in her.

"I'm afraid I'm like him," she said at last. "Oh, I know that sounds terrible. I always wanted to be like him. There was never anybody kinder or better. But now when I think of it, it frightens

me. I'm like you said. I haven't any way to judge people and whatever someone else thinks seems right to me."

"Like getting married?"

She flushed. "Yes, I guess so. I like Charles all right. Mother
says I'll never have another chance like this one. I'm not—well,
you know. But now that it gets closer and closer I keep wondering if the same thing is going to happen to me that happened
to him. I wonder whether I'll just keep giving in and giving in,
going along on what someone else says is right until—oh, Andy,
sometimes it does scare me so!"

The little clock chimed the half hour loudly and Treese started
nervously in bed.

Half past four. Half past five, half past six, half past seven.
She could get up by that time. And then at half past eight breakfast. Half past nine—but when would the boat come? How would
she ever wait?

"And is this my little sister Treese? But how she's grown!
Well, no. Maybe not exactly pretty. But character's more important
than looks any day. And you can see hers in her eyes. Oh, we'll
get along all right. Don't you worry. We're going to be friends,
Treese. What do you think of that?"

Treese flopped over ecstatically on her stomach and slept.

Agnes sent a maid to inquire about the time of arrival of the
steamer that was bringing Keith and the Delaneys to Sacramento.
It was due at eleven that morning. The two hours following breakfast were spent in a frenzy of arranging, tidying, putting to rights
a room that had been in spotless order for a week, checking provisions, planning for dinner. King and Margaret and Elizabeth
would be coming for dinner. They would be going directly to the
hotel now. Agnes's house was not large enough to accommodate
them all.

Agnes wore an unaccustomed flush of excitement as she flew
about the house. Her eyes shone happily and her lips were perpetually parted in a half smile. She had forgotten about King now
that Keith's arrival was imminent. Her Keith! At last he was
coming! She even called out gaily to Treese and included her in the
overflow of her effulgent good spirits. Treese replied politely but
with reserve. Camaraderie with anyone, and in particular Agnes,
was too alien to her to be picked up readily. Inside, she was seething
with expectation. Her palms were wet and she kept wiping them
on a wadded-up handkerchief. Her nose became shiny and she kept

wiping it off. She went to the mirror twenty times in an hour and tried to arrange her hair so that it did not straggle down about her face. She almost cried wishing she might look pretty just for this one day. The angular planes of her face stood out glaringly. She had never felt more awkward. Twice she tripped over the edge of the carpet entering the parlor. Her arms seemed too long for the sleeves of her dress. Her wrists hung out, red and bony.

At fifteen after eleven a hackney coach drove up in front of the house and Agnes went flying out the front door and down the steps. She looked small and girlish in the black dress whose skirts billowed about her as she ran. She picked them up to keep from tripping. Treese hung back, watching from the doorway. A tall young man whose face was a white blur stepped out of the hack. He looked up for a moment, then held out his arms and caught Agnes up in them ,holding her close and then swinging her lightly around so that her feet were off the ground. Treese could see that Agnes was crying. The tall young man held her with one arm and with the other paid the driver and took a valise that was handed to him. They walked together toward the house. His arm was still tight around Agnes's waist. Treese shrank back in the doorway. They mounted the steps.

"Well, hello! Can this be Treese? Yes, it's Treese all right. And damned skinny, too, but she'll fill out soon enough, eh, Mamma? Come on, honey, give us a kiss."

CHAPTER V

ON THE SEVENTH of July Treese Delaney became Mrs. Charles Edward Brooks-Wickham. It was the biggest wedding Sacramento had ever seen and it was notable not only for the fabulous attire of the bride but for the appearance of Agnes Delaney out of mourning for the first time since her husband's death. For the ceremony, which took place in the parlor of their I Street home, Agnes wore a dark-green silk with drop shoulders and sleeves which ended in a bell-shaped flare with a tight undersleeve. Black onyx earrings, heavy and elaborately designed, hung in her ears and a black onyx brooch glistened on her bosom. Her costume was the cause of only slightly less comment than the bride's.

Treese walked down the stairway slowly on her brother's arm. Guests remarked how unlike herself she looked. Instead of wearing her usual self-conscious blush she looked strangely pale and somehow smaller. She spoke her vows clearly and without faltering but when the ring had been slipped on her finger and she turned to face the crowd, everyone was disappointed. They had expected a transformation into sudden radiance. She looked no different. She responded with quiet smiles and soft-spoken remarks when they crowded around her demanding kisses and dabbing at their eyes with perfumed handkerchiefs but there was no light in her unmoving gray eyes. Annie Carlton commented that marriage had made a grown-up lady of her already.

Every person of prominence in Sacramento had been invited, including Mayor Johnson and not a few of state prominence. Agnes's guest list had been carefully prepared with an eye to prestige and political opportunity and she was at her charming best greeting them, making conversation, calling them by name, flattering and cajoling them, brushing aside compliments and fluttering over Treese. She and King avoided each other's eyes but there was no mistaking the quiet intensity with which Margaret watched her. Intensity, but no bitterness. Andy Hart, who received his invitation from Treese's own hand, donned his good suit and attended, but he showed a noticeable lack of enthusiasm over the more formal aspects of the occasion. He slipped out shortly after the ceremony was performed and no one noticed. He was letting his beard grow again.

The food was like the rest of the wedding particulars; it was overdone. Agnes had meant to dazzle the populace and she succeeded. While the sun rose higher and beads of perspiration started out on foreheads, under arms and across backs, throats were cooled with sparkling burgundy and champagne chilled on ice that had been brought down from the Sierras. This was in addition to the cognac, brandy, whisky, Madeira, claret and sherry. There were punches for the ladies, fragrant fresh-ground coffees and imported teas; every well-known brand of cigar for the gentlemen. Everyone said it was the most successful social affair the town had ever seen. Two newspapers sent representatives, both of whom toiled industriously with pencil and note paper, going from room to room, from group to group.

Elizabeth, who had acted as attendant to her cousin, was singularly quiet during the whole day. Once or twice she stole a look at Keith, who, as King remarked, was looking handsomer than any young blade had a right to look. But for the most part she kept her eyes down.

When he came down the steps with Treese on his arm, Keith

had the feeling Elizabeth's eyes were accusing him. When Treese turned around after the ceremony he was conscious of another twinge of uneasiness. He along with others in the room had expected more of a show of exuberance from her. He had a moment of sinking self-reproach and for the life of him he could only think dramatically that he had thrown a virgin sacrifice before an alien, lecherous idol. Then it passed and he was himself again, joking and teasing the girls whose mothers saw to it that they were shoved into close proximity with him, making numerous gallant trips to the punch bowl, politely squiring chesty old women to points of vantage on the side lines. But when Agnes fluttered up to him and ran her palm caressingly along the side of his face, he shrank back with an uneasiness that was a sudden crystallization of resentment against her. He saw the entire panoply of the wedding as an event willed and directed by Agnes and forming a suitably lavish backdrop for her own determination, with Treese pitifully lost, a properly placed item in a well-rehearsed tableau.

After the daylong refreshments there was dancing with hired musicians furnishing the music. Treese and Charles danced the first dance. Charles looked enormously pleased with himself and cut a fine figure twirling about the floor, coattails flying. Treese did her best to keep up with him, but she was every second conscious of her perspiring palm pressed hard against his back and of the way her body now and again was brought against his as they maneuvered a turn. This was now, she thought wildly; and with a houseful of people. What would it be tonight? Terror swept over her, shutting out the music and making the faces of the onlookers a blur. She swirled and turned without seeing the room or knowing where her feet were. She was conscious only of Charles, the closeness of his body and the enormity of his face over hers.

The new intimacy and companionship with Keith to which Treese had been looking forward had never materialized. Sometimes during the hectic days preceding the ceremony she wondered whether she had ever actually believed it would. Certainly she was almost as much relieved as disappointed. From the first his brash flaunting handsomeness completely awed her, and though she admired him breathlessly she was in mortal terror of appearing stupid or awkward in his presence. She had withdrawn more than ever into herself. Only now—today. If there were only someone! Once she caught his eye across the room and he looked away quickly. The music sang out. Treese stole a look at Charles. He was smiling benignly, the picture of a loving and happily anticipatory bridegroom. But there was that fullness of his lower lip. Sensuous, suggestive. She imagined it could become sullen at a moment's notice. How quickly it had all happened and how irrevocable it was! When his face came down close to hers she saw a little line of sweat on his upper lip and caught the faint odor of whisky. She felt weak and sick.

Early in the evening they left for the steamer. Treese had changed into a going-away costume of dark-blue velvet, modeled for traveling with a fluff of white ruching at the neck and two tiny plumes on the matching bonnet. Around her neck she wore a pendant which had been Charles's gift to his bride. It was a gold lion head suspended on a heavy chain; a head-on view showing face, mane and front paws. The mouth was distended, its long teeth forming prongs which imprisoned a diamond set in the mouth. Each paw upheld a ruby and the total effect was one of glistening ferocity. Agnes had frowned slightly when she first saw it. It *might* be an heirloom, as Charles insisted. Then, again, it might be a highly inept piece of local craftsmanship. She was more inclined to suspect the latter. But in any event she had paid for it, one way or the other, and Treese was to wear it. She explained its family history to inquiring guests.

"Perfectly charming, isn't it?" she whispered to Annie Carlton. "Dear Charles has the most devastating taste."

Divested of the subduing virginal white of her wedding dress, Treese seemed also to return to her own natural corporeal form. Although the traveling dress had been painstakingly fitted to her, she had an air of not quite belonging in it and she seemed unsure of her footing in the voluminous skirt. She stumbled getting into the carriage. Ten carriages followed, accompanying the newlyweds to the steamer landing and she was seen aboard by a flurry of well-wishers bearing flowers, fruit and bonbons. The men cornered Charles at the head of the gangplank and began offering him advice, whispering ribaldries and clapping him smartly on the back. Charles, not at his best when mingling with other men, accepted the attention with reasonably good grace and took the various obscene little tokens they handed him with cordial if not effusive thanks. He managed to wink broadly as they took leave of him and went away thinking himself a capital fellow, really a very good sort.

Treese said good-bye on deck to the crowd that had accompanied her. Agnes pressed her close in an effusive but well-timed bit of maternal anxiety and whispered quite audibly, "My little girl." Elizabeth flung both arms around her and kissed her but she did not speak. Treese could feel her sobbing. When she turned to Keith he kissed her cheek lightly and then looked at her for a moment. It was growing dark and she could not see what was in his face. Andy was not there. As she turned away, Treese caught sight of a solitary figure near the rail, hands in his pockets, just turning away. It might have been Andy but in the dusk it would be hard to say.

She took a long last look at Sacramento when they left her to thread their way back down the gangplank. The street flares had already been lighted and in spite of its advancing civilization it began to take on the curiously barbaric aspect it had worn the first night she saw it. Figures moved with excited animation, sounds came bodilessly as though plucked out of the air instead of manufactured in human lungs. She felt lonely and afraid. It had never been home to her but it was the only home she knew. Now she would not see it again for a year. And Europe was a world away. She felt Charles at her side and half turned to him. He was motioning for her to wave and she did so. The darkness seemed to grow denser; she could not distinguish one figure on shore from the next one.

Neither did she see the man who lounged against the ship's railing a few feet from her. He had stood there during the whole ritual of farewell, had watched as first one, then another took leave of her. Now his eyes were on her. They traveled slowly from her to Charles and back again. They took in the slender angular line of her body as it pressed slightly away from the man at her side. They watched the forlorn little wave of her hand, the quick swallow that convulsed her throat. The man reached into his pocket for a cheroot, took it out and broke it in half, replaced one half and lighted the other. The crack and flare of the match made Treese start and look in his direction but the gesture was an instinctive one. She did not see him. The great wheels began to churn with gigantic splashes. She turned and followed as Charles led the way below.

Steve Mallott had not changed much outwardly since the day four years before when Treese had seen him leaning against the rail of the *New World*. His mustache was clipped to less flowing proportions, his sideburns trimmed neatly. He was still lean of face and the lines in his cheeks might have deepened a trifle. His hair was still short, his body slender. His clothes were radically altered, but whether this change had come about as a result of outward or inward compulsion was not immediately evident. He now wore a fashionable but conservative black suit, no jewelry, and a shirt only slightly ruffled.

All in all, except for the new inconspicuousness of his attire, he was easily recognizable as the young man who had hurled two struggling girls into the water. And from the expression on his face, it would seem that there had been little if any inner alteration. The curve of the mouth suggested amusement most of the time. Not a happy amusement but scarcely bitter enough to be termed sardonic. A detached interest which at times touched a humorous chord inside him might have explained it. He had lost a little of the studied boredom he carried with him in 1850; additional years had carried him safely through that phase. But there was still a certain aloofness about him, an aloofness that was clearly not acquired but inherent. It spoke from every action and from the erect manner in which he carried himself. It was as though he wished to keep himself forever a little apart from his fellow human beings, not so much from a sense of his own superiority as from a desire to retain his own sphere of independent movement. He did not wish to thrust thoughts and confidences before the attention of others and he trusted they would return the favor in kind.

His profession was admirably suited to his temperament. Gambling allowed a maximum of freedom. The river gambler was of necessity a rover. He mingled with others but remained always apart. He was never one with the solid transplanted burgher who had brought his solidity to California with him. And the money was good. Not as steady as some positions, perhaps, but ample. If there were times when he lost, there were twice as many when he won. The up-and-down nature of the game only added to its interest. And there was no use deceiving himself. He only lost to make it interesting occasionally. He knew more ways to trim and sand a card than any other sharper on the Sacramento.

A Californian for more than four years now, he was an established Westerner, an old-timer. Yet the memory of another life he had known was still strong inside him.

His mother had come to New Orleans from Charleston at fifteen to work as a domestic in the home of a wealthy merchant and his wife. Within an astonishingly short time Julie Mallott discovered herself to be pregnant and it was not long after that the mistress also became cognizant of her condition. She was summarily turned out of the house, and left to wonder where the next meal for herself and her unborn child was coming from. Not being in a position to pick and choose, she was only too ready to accept an offer of marriage from Ilo Beaumont, a Frenchman of dubious origin to whom the prospect of a well-kept home and tastily prepared meals was attractive enough so that he was willing to overlook her pregnancy.

She named the baby Stephen after the master of the house where she had worked, not as a sentimental gesture, but as a chastening reminder of her past. Her husband, whose indifference toward his newly acquired son was magnificent, boasted loudly in the streets of his virility, claiming the healthy boy as his own and stating that he had only to walk into the bedroom and his wife became big in the belly.

After the first baby more followed in rapid succession. Steve, as he grew older, began to sense that Ilo was responsible for his mother's almost constant pregnancy. He resented the man who caused her to be always heavy and slow and tired. The resentment began to manifest itself in open acts of disobedience and rebellion and Ilo, for the sake of his fatherly pride, was forced to beat him frequently. On one such occasion Julie stepped in to protect the boy and received such a blow that she had a miscarriage that night. Her peasant sturdiness began to wane after that and even for her children she could not muster up the same good humor, the stolid acceptance of the inevitable. Steve became "handy" about the house in numerous ways. He helped with the washing, rocked the cradle of the latest addition to the family, changed diapers and lent a hand in cooking. He was a quiet serious boy, prematurely old and possessed of an adult disillusionment which showed in his quiet brown eyes. He was a man already grown in mind, waiting only for his thin body to catch up.

One day when he was ten, Julie, already large with her eighth child, felt the familiar thrust of pain and took to her bed. Steve sent the older children outdoors to play and prepared supper for the younger ones. Then he went next door for help. When he could find no one, he returned alone to the house and went to Julie's bed. He stood by comforting her and helping her as best he could to deliver the baby. His thin pinched face was pale with fear but he managed to bring forth the baby, a little girl. Afterward he went outside and promptly collapsed, lying by the side of the house unmoving until long after the moon had risen and a damp breeze started up.

The new baby was named Annette. It was Julie's last child and Ilo's particular favorite. Only for her did he come home at night and maintain any semblance of a home. It seemed that Annette had some quality the others lacked, a bright alertness, a charming manner even as a child.

When Steve was eighteen Julie died, tired and thin, old before her time. He helped to bury her and then turned to Ilo with a new independence and announced perfunctorily that he was leaving. If he did not go now, he might never get away. He could still remember their faces. Ilo's red and distorted with anger over being deprived of Steve's wages as a dock hand; the children in various stages of screaming and wailing, and little Annette, the only quiet one, looking after him with black eyes that were wide with concern. Several times in the years since he had left he wondered about it, had felt, in looking back, that she alone of that noisy brood was like him.

He could not quite decide whether or not the prospect of seeing her again in a few hours pleased or displeased him. He had followed her success in the East, in Chicago and St. Louis. California would love her. Only, he was glad she was independent and established. People on the stage were apt to be individualists and that suited him.

The steamer *President* was a floating palace, replete from stem to stern with the finest in gilt, plush and crystal. When Treese and Charles boarded her the dinner hour was in progress and they were escorted directly to the dining saloon where a dinner ordered in advance by Agnes was served them. Other late diners glanced over their shoulders, nudged each other and then stared quite openly. The Delaney wedding had been all the talk for more than a month up and down the river. Treese felt embarrassed by their attention and could scarcely eat a mouthful. But Charles downed the food with gusto, remarking on the excellence of the cuisine but adding the qualifying conjecture that if one has the money to pay for it, there is very little one cannot command. When they had finished, they watched the waiters clear away the tables, pushing them off to one side so that a large open space was left in the center for dancing. A fiddler took his place on a small dais at one end of the room and several couples took the floor as he struck up a tune. Treese noted with a feeling of temporary relief that Charles seemed well satisfied with the meal and the music. He was lounging back in his chair, his body slack and inert with well-being. So far, it seemed to say, everything was running on schedule. An excellent meal, a spot of music, a good cigar—the ashes from the latter dribbled down and caught in the folds of his ruffled shirt front—and then of course what was to come later. Treese shivered a little as a breath of cold night air off the river whisked in and surrounded her with its dank clamminess.

Charles's eyes were half closed with sleepy self-satisfaction. He slipped even lower in the chair and his glance took in the low-cut dress of a young girl who went about the saloon selling confections and coffee. Treese followed the look and was suddenly glad for the sensible white ruching that covered her own neck. From the adjoining room, the social hall, came the loud laughter of carousers around the bar and occasionally chiming in with the sound of revelry came the rattling of money and the sound of voices at the card tables. The social hall, or Main Saloon, with the bar at one end and the floor dotted with brass spittoons, was the chief lounging place for gentlemen passengers, and convivial travelers from every walk of life gathered there in the evening. Treese had caught a glimpse through the doorway as they entered. Men in evening clothes and tall hats, men in expensive sporty traveling clothes and soft rolled-brim hats, white-aproned bartenders, quiet black-clad dealers and gaudily appareled professional gamblers with their fabulous jewels and shirts. She leaned forward slightly at the table and looked toward the doorway but she could not see into the next room from where she sat. The voices and laughter intrigued her.

"Charming, isn't it, dear?"

She jumped. Charles was sitting straighter, smiling across the table at her.

"Yes. Lovely."

"You're enjoying yourself?"

"Oh, yes, Charles. Everything is fine."

"Wait till you see the ship that's going to take us to England. And wait till you see England! Grass so green it's unbelievable. And the cities, the social functions! Perfectly magnificent! There's nothing in America to compare with it. I have a number of cousins who'll see we're invited to all the best houses, meet absolutely the right people. It'll be quite an education for you."

Treese, whose chief instruction outside of a few lessons at home had been six months at the Young Ladies' Institute on L Street, looked down at the tablecloth. Charles reached across the table and took her hand.

"Come now. I didn't mean it that way. Only there are things a lady of breeding should know. Not from books, of course. Heavens, anything but an educated woman! They're absolutely insufferable. But the social niceties, the correct procedure. You'll learn all that.

Oh, you'll be quite the fine lady next year when we return. Maybe you might even have a baby by that time."

Treese stared at him in frightened astonishment. He had said it casually as though it was a matter of small incidental importance. Something inevitable. The correct thing. A baby!

"There now. I mustn't rush you. All in good time." Charles leaned forward to knock the tip of ash off his fine Havana.

Treese's eyes followed the motion. The delicate poise of the cigar between thumb and middle finger. The gentle tap of the third finger to dislodge the ash. How white his hands were. Blunt and flat and pale. Her hand went instinctively to the neck of her blue velvet traveling dress, pulling it closer together.

She was not sure what to expect tonight. She had not been told anything outside of the fact that she was to undress modestly, behind a screen if there was one, and get in bed. Past that point she was in complete ignorance. She had never associated with girls her own age who might have given her inaccurate but at least illuminating information. On several occasions she had walked past houses in downtown Sacramento where heavily painted women leaned out of windows and beckoned to men passing by. It had given her a sense of uneasiness, the fear of the unknown, but she had never understood its actual implications. Once when she was fifteen she had come running into the kitchen at night for water and had stopped short with terror at finding Bessie the maid on the floor with a man, straining in ecstatic embrace. Treese had stopped only long enough to catch a flash of white buttocks in the dim-lit room, then had fled. She did not tell Agnes what she had seen, but three months later Bessie was dismissed and Treese wondered whether her dismissal was in some way connected with the scene she had witnessed. She never found out.

She was fairly enlightened on the subject of babies. They were common enough table talk and Agnes and Mrs. Fitch were forever reviewing which of their acquaintances were "caught" or "that way." She knew that the process of having a baby required several months and that during that period a woman became bulky and misshapen. Logical reasoning had completed the picture for her, although geometrically it seemed an impossibility. What was still lacking in her cycle of information was the man-and-woman relationship involved. She had started to question Agnes timidly on the subject just before the wedding but Agnes had given her a look of withering disapproval.

"You'll find out soon enough and from the proper source—your husband" was her caustic reply. Treese had blushed red to the roots of her bright hair and kept silent.

Now, sitting here at the table, she could not look directly at Charles but she sensed him leaning over the table toward her and felt his eyes on her. She was conscious of a weak watery feeling in her legs as though they might refuse to support her when she rose. Her stomach was a hard knot of fear. Her mouth was dry and there was a constriction in her throat.

"Well, my dear?" His hand closed tightly over hers. "Perhaps you're ready to retire?"

She opened her mouth to speak but no words came. She tried to swallow, and as she did so a shadow fell across the table.

"Mr. Wickham?" They both looked up, startled.

"You'll forgive the intrusion, I'm sure. It's most impertinent of me, I know, but you're quite the talk of the ship and I felt I must introduce myself before we dock."

The man standing beside the table was lean and dark. His eyes moved quickly from Charles to Treese and back again but his manner was polite in the extreme. He was bowing slightly and there was the suggestion of a smile on his face. His upper lip seemed to tighten a little as though he were controlling the smile with effort.

Charles rose. "I'm sorry, sir. I don't believe—" He looked annoyed.

"No, naturally you wouldn't know me. But may I say, sir, that there is no one from here to San Francisco who is not familiar with your name and that of your charming bride."

"Oh." Charles was beginning to be somewhat mollified. He turned to Treese. "May I present my wife, sir. Madam, this is—I don't believe I caught—"

"Mallott. Steve Mallott."

"Mr. Mallott, dear."

Steve Mallott bowed low. "Your servant, madam."

Treese dipped her head slightly. Her heart was beating fast with excitement. She had not many memories in her mind which she could look back on with pleasure. Her mind was a neat catalogue of day-to-day events, carefully arranged without variation. There were a few instances which stood out stark and terrifying and black, and these she kept well to the back, seldom taking them out for examination. Besides these there were only a few, a very few, which she treasured and preserved and kept in good condition. And one of these was an afternoon years before, of sun shining on water, of shouts and cries and noises and smells, a great boat that seemed new and wonderful, and a man leaning against a ship's rail, a wrist with short black hairs that lay back and caught the sunlight. Her eyes, which were on the middle button of the man's waistcoat, dropped to his wrist. It was nearly hidden by his coat sleeve but she could see the short dark hairs, the slim brown strength of the hand and fingers.

"Mr. Wickham, don't tell me you were going to journey all the way to San Francisco without once crossing cards with me? Why, I should be insulted. And with everyone telling me there's no finer player in California! 'Get in a game with Wickham,' they all tell me. 'He'll show you up fast enough.' "

Charles, whose losses in gambling were the major item of expense left on Agnes's shoulders, was puzzled but flattered.

"Why, I'd consider it an honor, Mr. Mallott, but as it happens, I'm on my honeymoon."

Steve Mallott refused to read an implication into the remark.

"Fine! And what better way to start off married life? No gentleman of consequence can afford to neglect his gambling these days! As I'm sure your lovely bride would be the first to concede. Come now, Mrs. Wickham, how about it? Will you permit me to steal your husband for an hour? The men in the card room would never forgive me if I didn't bring him."

She lifted her eyes. He was looking straight at her and behind the polite sobriety of his expression shone a light of such ill-concealed amusement that for a second she caught her breath and suppressed a desire to shout with laughter and relief. Because she had never in her life shouted with laughter for any cause whatever, she did not. But when she returned his look her eyes were level and steady. For once she was not blushing before a stranger.

"Why, it's most kind of you, Mr. Mallott," she said slowly. "I'm sure I couldn't help but forgive you. Charles, do go along. I'll find my way to the cabin."

Charles, torn between desires of the flesh and the intriguing seduction of flattery, hesitated. Steve Mallott stepped into the breach without hesitation.

"Fine!" He reached out and took Charles's arm. "I'll see that the captain himself comes in to escort you to your cabin. Come along, Mr. Wickham. Would you favor twenty-one? Or perhaps poker? Personally, the old games suit me better. Poker may be the up-and-coming thing but give me a good old game every time. A good box of faro or a turn of roulette. But of course one has to watch the wheel. There are so many sharpers these days. Now twenty-one . . ." His voice faded out as they walked away toward the social hall. Charles, who at first had hung back, was walking briskly along, taking an avid interest in what Steve was saying to him. After all, he appeared to be thinking, she will still be waiting in an hour or two hours. And a little delay will only increase the pleasure. They disappeared into the adjoining room.

True to his word, Steve sent the captain into the dining saloon for Treese and she was escorted with flourishing style to the large cabin they had engaged. When she was once more alone she slipped out of the heavy velvet dress and hung it up carefully. She began untying the eight petticoats she was wearing underneath and stepping out of them, picking each one up neatly as she went along and folding it once lengthwise to lay over the back of a chair. When she had finished the chair was a heaping mound of muslin and lace. No part of its own structure was visible. Next came the corset. She unlaced it with some difficulty and stepped out of it with a sigh of relief. It topped off the pile of petticoats. She stood for a moment in her lace-trimmed drawers and chemise. At last she went and sat on the edge of the bed.

The cabin Agnes had engaged for them was the finest on the *President*. It was twice as large as any of the others and was ordinarily rented by either the very wealthy or the very influential. Besides a large double bed securely anchored to the floor so there would be a minimum of pitching, and rolling, there were a secretary, two bureaus, a large corner wardrobe and a dressing table. The floor was richly carpeted in green. The oil lamps were fastened to the walls and each had a chimney adorned with scrolls and cutwork.

Treese felt strange in the cabin. She could feel the slight motion of the steamer under her, hear the roar of the engine and the thrashing of the wheels. She had never felt more alien to herself and her surroundings. It was as she had told Andy; she was no longer Treese Delaney. This was Mrs. Charles Wickham bound for San Francisco and Europe. And if she was Mrs. Wickham in name only now, in another hour or two or three the picture would be complete.

She tried to steer her thoughts into a clear channel that would better prepare her for what was to come; she skirted perilously near the looming figure of Steve Mallott, then shied away. Well, what harm to think of him? she asked herself boldly. He's nothing to me. I passed only a second's conversation with him. *But why had he done it?* What had been the meaning of the look he had given her?

And why did she even now feel such a curious lack of embarrassment? Ordinarily, a strange man sent her into a panic of blushing and stammering. With him she had felt only a comfortable, knowing familiarity. She knew without being told what he was thinking. She knew what he meant to do for her. The reason was, after all, not important. Perhaps he was doing it for his own amusement. To torment Charles and deprive him for a time of the nuptial felicity he was obviously so eager for. Men had ways of playing the game with each other, she supposed. And there was no doubt about it; he had been laughing inside when he looked at her. Even now Treese could feel the shadow of a smile on her own lips. Well, if that was the reason, it was good enough. Or if there was another reason—but of course there wasn't. Only it had seemed, just for the fraction of a second, that there was something more behind the polite smile he turned on her. Something more than amusement, more than a sardonic whim. Something kind, and infinitely knowing. An hour or two of reprieve would not mean much, after all, but it was something. It would give her a little time. Just that much longer to get used to an idea that was still new and terrifying. She sank wearily back on her bed and flung one arm up across her eyes.

CHAPTER VI

THE SOCIAL HALL of the *President* was ablaze with lights from the two rows of wall-bracketed lamps that lined either side of the long room. At one end the bar was crowded three deep. Men laughed good-humoredly or drunkenly as their condition of sobriety warranted, one foot on the railing, their hand around a glass. On the floor a table of faro was the hub of another little circle of activity and the clack of the casekeeper's buttons and rods mingled with the snap of cards. A roulette wheel spun a few feet away, the little ivory ball rattling and bounding before it came to rest at every turn. Besides these, there were several tables at which two or more men sat, engaged in private games. Some had small crowds of onlookers shouting to applaud a good play or offering over-the-shoulder advice. At one such table, in a far corner, sat Charles and Steve Mallott. A little group had gathered around them, nattily dressed young men who made it a habit to spend the whole of any river trip in the social hall. They were easily distinguished by the expensive, somewhat extreme cut of their frock coats which they refused to remove in spite of the warm summer night, the heavily ruffled shirts and gaudy silk cravats. They all wore two-inch-heeled varnished boots and their trousers were slick against their thighs, held taut by a strap below the instep.

Both Charles and Steve had removed their outer coats and were sitting in their waistcoats and shirt sleeves. There was a bottle of whisky and two glasses on the table between them and each time Charles drained his glass, Steve unobtrusively filled it again without refilling his. Charles was already quite drunk but he was making a valiant effort to conceal it. He had spilled some whisky down his shirt front, staining his ruffles. His shirt had pulled partway out so that it gaped from between his waistcoat and the top of his trousers. He was slouched in his chair, his posture displaying to the worst advantage the inches he was putting on about the waistline. His lower lip protruded slightly. It was moist and petulant, and his eyelids were half closed in a squint as he examined his cards.

"Card," he said thickly. His voice was muffled from the whisky and he breathed heavily.

Steve dealt him a card.

" 'Nother."

He took it and examined it.

"I'll stay."

Across the table, Steve looked at him narrowly but with amusement. In his shirt sleeves Steve looked less slender than in his black nipped-in frock coat. The chest and shoulder muscles under his fine white linen shirt were heavy and firm. Only his hands showed a trace of delicacy. They were strong and brown and wiry but their movements as they flicked the cards were effortless. The nails, neatly but not obviously manicured, were white-tipped ovals. As he dealt the cards to himself he watched Charles. From the corner of his mouth hung the stub of a cheroot and he squinted slightly against its smoke as he observed the other man. Charles never took his eyes from the play of Steve's hands on the cards.

"Hah!" he exclaimed delightedly. "There's eighteen already!"

Steve looked at the cards. "One more, I think."

"Go ahead!" Charles roared. "Go ahead! See what happens!"

Charles had already lost a hundred dollars.

Steve flicked the card off.

"Deuce."

"See? What did I tell you?" Charles gloated.

"One minute till we see what's in the hole." Steve turned over the remaining card that was face down. "Ace. Twenty-one."

Charles scowled blackly. "I'm done for," he muttered, starting to rise. Six eager hands pushed him back. The young dandies were anxious to see the game continue.

"Your luck'll change, Wickham. Stick it out!"

"Come on. Get back at 'im!"

"Give it to him! You can do it."

Charles sank back into the chair. "Got a little bride waiting," he mumbled.

"She'll be there when you get back," Steve said soothingly. He was shuffling the cards easily, still squinting slightly against the smoke. "You want to go back a victor, don't you?"

"God damn it, I want to go back with my shirt!"

"You'll take this one. Want to raise the bet?"

"No! Keep it twenty!"

Steve shrugged.

"Poor little bride." Charles's eyes filled with sentimental tears and Steve poured him a whisky.

"Can't she wait?" one of the onlookers shouted. There was a general hoot of amusement.

"That's what I'm afraid of, dammit. Should have picked that mother of hers instead. I don't know about this one. Looks colder than yesterday's porridge to me."

"It's more fun that way. Where's the sport if there's no resistance?" another asked.

"Sure, ask Jack! He's tried 'em all, up and down the Sacramento. Leaves a trail of despoiled virgins behind him."

"Oh, the hell! Leave off it! You've had your share."

"Ready?" Steve, who had been watching Charles closely all the time, sat erect with the deck in his hand.

"Ready."

Steve dealt a card face down, then a ten up. Charles swore and examined the hole card.

An expression of crafty satisfaction stole over his face.

"Stay," he announced triumphantly.

Steve dealt himself a card face down, then a three face up. A five followed and an eight.

"Out," he said briskly, flicking over the first card, a nine.

"Twenty!" Charles roared gleefully.

Steve leaned toward one of the dandies and whispered something in his ear. The young man threw back his head and laughed with delight. He hurried off.

Charles rubbed the palms of his hands together and then reached for the whisky Steve had poured for him. He downed it in one gulp, choked and sputtered for a second and then wiped his mouth with his sleeve.

"Same bet?" Steve inquired.

"Make it fifty!"

Steve went out again. Just as he was preparing to deal a second time there was a slight rustling noise behind Steve and the girl who had been selling confections in the dining saloon sidled up behind him. She was pretty and lively with dark curls and an unusually white skin. Her pink satin gown was cut to expose her bosom and underneath its tightness the firm line of her figure showed. She leaned over Steve and the dandies whistled as a little more of her breasts became visible.

He whispered something into her ear. Her face fell.

"Oh, Stevie, I thought it was *you*!"

"As a personal favor, Louise? How about it? A personal favor and fifty dollars. There. How's that?" He counted out the money and tucked it deep between her breasts.

"Oh, all right. Only when—"

"Next trip up, honey. I promise."

"All right, Stevie. Only you'll have to fix it up if the captain hears anything. He gets mad as all get-out, you know."

"I'll see to it he doesn't hear anything."

Charles had reared back slightly in his chair and was watching the girl from under drooping lids, his head tipped back. It took a moment for him to bring his vision into focus. Then he started out of his seat.

"I say!" He fell back, unable to maintain his balance. Louise was standing just back of Steve, her hands on her lips, smiling at him. Steve looked from one to the other and smiled faintly. He shoved his chair back and rose, pulling on his coat. The young dandies had made a circle around Charles and Louise.

"All right, boys," he said briskly.

"Ah, hell, Steve. Why break up the party?"

"Come on."

"This is gonna be good!"

"I said let's go."

They pulled out of the little circle reluctantly. When they had begun to drift away Louise advanced a step toward Charles. She reached for the shoulder of her dress as though to adjust it but instead let it drop quickly to expose one breast. In an instant she had pulled it up again. Charles staggered to his feet, his eyes popping from his head. She smiled and looked at him from under lowered lashes. Then she turned and hurried out through a side door. He lunged after her.

CHAPTER VII

SACRAMENTO was the state capital now; had been since February. J Street as far as Patterson's Hotel ten miles east of the Embarcadero was planked with Oregon fir three and a half inches thick which protected it from the bottomless mud. It was fitted with plank walks from the levee to Twelfth Street. Plank walks also lay along K Street as far as Eighth; and Second, Third and Eighth streets were planked between J and K. The first telegraphic message had passed between San Francisco and Sacramento the previous October. The municipal waterworks had been completed and Agnes Delaney was one of the holders of the more than a quarter of a million dollar bond issue which made up the water loan. She held stock in the new California Stage Company, which had begun operations early in the year and she had bought up "levee scrip" bearing interest at two per cent a month when the raising and strengthening of the levee was decided upon.

R. P. Johnson, a Whig, was mayor, and big business in the form of the California Steam Navigation Company had appeared on the scene. The year 1853 had been a peak one for shipping; in all, 630 craft of all descriptions had entered Sacramento—barks, brigantines, schooners, sloops, steamers. Early in 1854 the Steam Navigation Company set out to control every type of river traffic. Independent boats were already finding it rough going. While light-draft steamers carried trade to the Yuba and Feather and upper Sacramento and merchants' committees built and fitted out opposition boats to handle their own supplies and produce, Agnes went ahead and with King's intercession bought and fitted out two steamers for her own use.

It was this and other business matters, King explained to Margaret, which made it necessary for him to remain for a time in Sacramento after Treese's wedding.

"Business," Agnes announced firmly, "is simply wonderful everywhere."

King sighed patiently and slid far down in the veranda chair. It was early evening, but still oppressively warm. On the low table between them stood lemonade and two glasses and a warm rich spice cake dripping with white icing.

"It looks wonderful on the outside, as I've been trying to tell you all week," he said dryly. "Actually the depression's already here. The majority of the people don't know it, which is just as well. If they knew it every bank between here and San Francisco would be closed tomorrow. In San Francisco property's already down to a quarter of its value."

"Well, I simply can't see this business about taking all my money and investing it back east." Agnes's mouth grew firm with displeasure.

King reached toward the pitcher and poured himself a drink.

"Eastern mills and railroads are the safest investment in the world right now."

"Send my money east to God knows where," Agnes muttered. "I wouldn't even be able to keep my eye on it."

"Let me worry about that. Haven't I managed all right so far?"

Agnes's black eyebrows drew together worriedly. "What has all this to do with me? I don't own any property in San Francisco."

"It's not going to stop in San Francisco. It'll be here too. Everybody with an ounce in his pocket is speculating. The whole state's riding along on speculation. It can't last. It's worse in real estate but it's everywhere. Can't get away from it. And the trouble is that it doesn't just stop there. There are interweaving threads, complications, entanglements in politics. Take Harry Meiggs, in San Francisco. Up to his ears in real estate and on the Board of Aldermen to boot. Now, you can't tell me he's not pulling every string at his disposal to promote that North Beach property of his. And he's so far in debt it'll take a miracle to pull him out."

"But what does that mean?" Agnes demanded. Business matters beyond those of her immediate scope seemed involved and puzzling to her. She was alert enough in figuring actual debit and credit where it concerned her, but more indirect ramifications escaped her.

"It might not mean anything. Then, again, the lid may blow off there without any warning. I'm just as glad I don't hold any city warrants. If he should take a notion to lay hold of them and start using them to pay back his own debts they won't be worth the paper they're written on."

"But my money's safe enough. I've got my steamers and so far the Steam Navigation Company's not bothered me. And I'd just like to see them try it!"

King laughed with amusement at her defiance. "If they take a notion to, honey, just don't get the idea you can buck them.

They're a pretty big outfit. Maybe they'll be content to ride along this way. If they are, so much the better for you. But if they decide to do something about it, you'd better have an ace in the hole."

"But I have my property! I've got plenty to fall back on."

"And I just told you property's going to take a drop one of these days that'll set your head spinning. It's already started in San Francisco."

"But I don't see why I can't keep it in California! For God's sake, that's what I came west for—to get away from the East."

"Stop being so dramatic, honey. I told you why. California's going under."

"Going under!"

"Oh, not for good. Don't get so alarmed. California's got a future like no other state in the Union. But people are trying to milk too much out of her at once. When everyone else is going begging you'll have money to start over."

"But I don't want to start over! I've worked hard to get this far!"

"That's what I'm trying to explain to you," he reiterated patiently. "The only way you can keep it is to send it east. Surely you've noticed the falling off in your shipments to the mines this spring."

"Well." Agnes hesitated. It was true her shipping business had not been as profitable as usual during recent months.

"It's been a dry season. Mining's fallen way off because of lack of rain and as a result the miners suffer. They can't afford to buy your goods and they ask for credit, which you naturally refuse."

"Naturally," she snapped. "What would you expect? I can't carry every miner in the Sacramento Valley on my shoulders."

"Exactly. But doesn't that demonstrate to you the futility of having all your investments in one place?"

"But sending it east! That's what I don't like."

"It could be only a temporary arrangement, if that's what you want. Then in a year or two there's another little idea we might be working on."

"What?" she demanded, immediately interested.

"Ever hear of hydraulics?"

"No. What on earth is that?"

"A new method of mining."

"Oh." Agnes's voice dropped with disappointment. "Heavens, I'm no miner. I don't know the first thing about it."

"That's where hydraulics will be different from ordinary mining. It'll not be individual operations. It'll be corporation mining. The day of the individual miner is soon going to be over, Agnes. A couple of years at the most."

Her eyebrows lifted slightly.

"It was tried two years or so ago up towards Marysville. Two fellows rigged it up with wooden boxing and sailcloth. It's the coming thing, all right. And with good equipment like I could get hold of there'd be no stopping us. It's been slow catching on, that's all, because it's so revolutionary. People are timid about trying it, and then too it takes an investment. As long as a miner can scrape out a few ounces a day with a pan he won't go into anything that involves a little risk."

"How does it work?"

"It employs the principle of pressure. First you construct a ditch that holds running water. Then you build troughs to carry the water. We'd get piping, of course. More efficient. Then you take the hose and to the end of it attach some sort of nozzle. The water's forced through it. You direct it anywhere you like and it eats into the soil as though it was so much sugar. Blasts the whole thing away, or will with good equipment. The soil is washed down into sluice boxes that sift it; hold back the gold and let the soil wash through. What could be simpler?"

"Well, I don't know." Agnes's mind was working rapidly, examining the idea from all angles. "Is it going to be practical, do you think?"

"Doesn't it sound practical to you?"

"But you don't own any mines and neither do I."

"Plenty of the placer diggings are being exhausted. Men would sell out a claim in a minute if the price was offered them."

"But if the diggings have petered out—"

"That's just the point! We could get at what's under the surface. What they can't reach!"

Agnes's eyes were beginning to glow with eagerness.

"King! Could we really? I mean, would it work?"

"Of course it would work. We'd be taking more gold out of the state than anyone even dreams of today."

Agnes was staring thoughtfully over the veranda railing. "It might work out all right," she said. She was speaking rapidly but keeping her voice controlled, as though some part of her resented showing too much enthusiasm for this new project of his. "I could send Charles to the mines to represent my interests."

"You mean you'd trust him with anything more valuable than your daughter?"

"King! What a contemptible thing to say!" There were times when she found herself able to hate him fiercely, when she sensed that his knowing of her was deeper and more penetrating than her knowing of him. She hated it when he said short unexpected things that reminded her of little places in her conscience that were uneasy.

"Charles will make Treese an excellent husband," she said icily. "Heavens, she should be pleased to have a mother who'll take an interest in her affairs, not simply throw her to the mercy of every fortune hunter in California."

"So that's the new line of reasoning! Last time we discussed it you claimed she'd never get any sort of husband at all. All right, darling. Turn the logic of it any way it suits you. Only take my word for it and don't expect to get too much work out of that crested nobleman. I have an idea he's going to come back here sooner than you think and expect to be supported in style."

"Supported! Well, he can get that out of his head in short order. The debts I paid off for him still make me see circles every time I think of them. His tailor, his hotel, his food, his gambling debts. And the dowry!"

"Quite a price for that new crest on your dinnerware. And, confidentially, you think it's fake the same as I do."

"King!"

"All right. Let's talk about your son instead."

A pervading warmth crept over Agnes, bringing out color in her cheeks.

"Keith?" she said softly.

"He's got a lot to learn," King went on thoughtfully. "I don't think he gives a damn for the law right now, or politics either. But he'll come around. He's still young and all taken up with himself."

"But what do you think of him, King?"

"He surprises me a little."

"Why?"

"He's so little like you."

Agnes's face reddened with anger and hurt.

"Not like me! Why, he's the image of me! Everyone says so!"

"Oh, he looks like you enough. And he has traits that are like yours. An enormous confidence in what his looks will get him, for one thing. But underneath it I sense something different."

"What, for heaven's sake?"

"Maybe you might call it lack of sureness in himself. I have the strangest notion sometimes that he's a bit lost."

"He's nothing of the sort!" Agnes exclaimed scornfully.

King went on as though he had not heard her. "I don't know—with you everything is confidence and sureness. You have such a way of brazening things out. Your flaunting way is your stock in trade. With him, the same manner, the same mannerisms seem like a cover-up. They're not the means by which he gets his own way, although often the result is that. They're rather the thing he hides behind."

"Oh, posh! You're talking ridiculous notions. He's like me every inch of the way. I know he is. Why, I know him better than I know myself, he's so much like me. We're cut from the same cloth, just the way Treese took after her father in everything."

He looked at her, tilting his head a little curiously. "Have it your way, honey. Only someday you may find out different."

"Nonsense!" She was angry with him for what he had said but she had missed him too long, wanted him too hungrily, to let it last. She wanted to get back to the delicious warm confidences, the soft talk, the secrets that were between them. "Tell me. Are he and Elizabeth really . . ." She let her voice trail off suggestively.

"I think he's asked her to marry him."

"Not really!" Agnes was astounded but pleased. It was part of her confidence in herself that she had never for a moment thought that marriage would separate her from Keith. He was too basically hers, too like her. King was ridiculous when he said those other things. It was there; anyone could see it. And from the time she first heard that Elizabeth had taken a liking to him she had hoped Keith might decide to marry her. She was quite frank in admitting the reason to herself. Since he would undoubtedly marry someone someday, he might as well make a match that would react to her own benefit. And surely nothing would draw her more permanently to King than to have Elizabeth married to Keith. So far she had relied, and happily, on herself. But she would not always be thirty-eight and looking twenty-eight. Later she might wish for some insurance, some more binding guaranty. With Keith married to Elizabeth . . .

"Did she say yes? Is it settled, do you think?"

"That I don't know. I should imagine, from the look in Elizabeth's eyes, that it is. But she's to go away to school, you know. She begged and teased to be allowed to go and now I imagine she's begging and teasing to stay home. I rather imagine Margaret will insist on her going though."

"Why?" Agnes demanded indignantly.

King shrugged slightly. "I guess her mother wants to make sure he's really in love with her, that he'll wait."

Something inside Agnes flared with angry resentment. It made her hot and prickly all over to hear King refer to Margaret that way—"her mother." A world of deference and respect seemed to go with it. And then to have the nerve to say that Margaret wanted to be sure! Well, nobody would ever be sure of Keith! That puling Elizabeth might marry him and give him nineteen brats but she'd never be sure of him. The thought gave Agnes a curious satisfaction and she hoped again, but this time for a different reason, that Keith would really marry her. It would seem like some sort of retribution. She'd never quite got over hating Elizabeth. With decorous control she managed to keep her temper hidden.

"Well, the idea might have some merit. They're both young, of course."

"Yes, there's no hurry about it." King spoke now as a father, a fond family man. It made Agnes uneasy and depressed. She wanted to get back to the plane of intimate laughter and easy kisses, of touching and feeling and merely being together. She looked at him with a sidelong smile.

"King, do you know what I want?"

His face lost the look she hated and she felt self-confidence and ease returning.

"What, my darling?" He leaned forward in his chair and kissed her just under the ear. It tickled and she shuddered with the pleasant feeling.

"I want a new house. What do you think? Shall I build one?"

CHAPTER VIII

STEVE MALLOTT stepped out of the hackney in front of the Hotel Arabique and turned to pay the driver. The afternoon was warm but the cooling winds off the bay gave San Francisco its customary feeling of freshness, the heritage of some cities by the sea. The dusty street billowed turbulently under the turning of wheels and the flat twang of hoofs. Noises were muffled in its thickness, colors mitigated by its constant sifting and settling. Only the sky shot back clear and brilliant, its blue ruffled close to the horizon by a little breastwork of squatting clouds.

Steve had discarded his customary frock coat for the lighter and more comfortable sack coat. It was short and shapeless, of rough-woven material. With it he wore gray trousers that showed a thin plaid pattern and a folded silk cravat that all but concealed his shirt front. It was a conservative outfit, but expensive. He had spent half an hour deciding on it before he left his own rooms.

He hurried up the broad flat steps of the hotel and into the lobby. It was cool and dim and cavernous inside. Everything in its decorative scheme reflected the pseudo-Near East atmosphere from which the name derived. Great dim tapestries which might have been authentically imported, or which could have been shipped at almost the same expense from an eastern mill, hung from every wall, some flat and expansive, some draped and swagged. Luxuriant carpets covered every inch of flooring. From the ceiling hung huge globular chandeliers composed of hundreds of smaller bulbous chimneys which protected the candle flames. Each tiny glass was shaped like a minaret or ornately domed in the Byzantine style. The chairs and settees, obviously built to specifications, were low, elaborately carved about the arms and legs and backs, and upholstered in woven tapestried material.

The men who were the hotel attendants circulated about the lobby carrying messages and luggage, bringing drinks to transients reclining on the low furniture, or answering the summons of a chime struck at the central desk facing the main entrance. Even the chime had a lyrical, minor sound, a slightly Oriental twang. The attendants were garbed in ankle-length trousers which tightened in at the bottom and billowed silkenly about the legs. Their shirts had full-flowing sleeves and they wore short embroidered vests that were uniformly elegant.

Steve stood in the doorway for a moment, letting his eyes accustom themselves to the dimness of the interior. Then he crossed the floor and presented himself at the desk.

"Miss Beaumont's rooms, please."

The man behind the desk looked up sharply over his pince-nez and drew himself a trifle more erect. His trim black suit, his conservative unruffled shirt fairly shouted loyalty and pride in his employer.

"*Mademoiselle* Beaumont?" he queried with reproving emphasis.

Steve nodded shortly. His expression had lost much of its casual confidence since last night's trip to San Francisco on the *President*. Now it was somehow younger, less intrepid. The lines of faint cynicism about the mouth were less visible. He looked apprehensive and a little uncertain.

"Mademoiselle is expecting you?" The man's glance took in his attire from head to foot and then fixed itself closely on his face.

"I'm her brother." The words sounded strange as he said them. Ten years was a long time.

"Oh." The man's disappointment was manifest. "Well. Her brother." He summoned one of the silken-trousered attendants. "Suite Nine." He motioned with his heard toward Steve. The attendant gave a nodding little bow and started toward the staircase. Steve followed.

He was left at the end of a long carpeted hallway on the second floor. He knocked tentatively on the door. For a moment there was no answer, no footsteps. Then, surprisingly, it opened. The woman who faced him was neat and immaculate in a maid's dress of gray muslin, over which she wore a full-gathered white apron. She was probably past middle age but there was a youthful erectness in her bearing that made it hard to say for sure. Her skin had golden-tan tones and it was as smooth as a girl's. Steve guessed that she might be an octoroon or a quadroon. He had seen many of the same appearance in New Orleans. Everything about her dress and manner was sober and subjective, from the quiet folded position of her hands across the front of her apron to her neatly laced black shoes. Only in her hair was there a strange bizarre note. Interwoven among the heavy black braids that wound thickly about her head was a flash of scarlet ribbon.

"Monsieur Mallott?" she inquired. Then, without waiting for confirmation, "Please come in." She spoke with no trace of an accent but her voice had a precise quality. Her words were formed carefully, making them sound almost pedantic.

He followed her inside and allowed her to take his hat.

"Mademoiselle has gone for a drive. She is expecting you and will be back directly. At three." Her eyes, large and gold-flecked, went to the clock on the mantel. Steve looked too. It was eight minutes before three. He was glad Annette was not there. It would give him a few minutes more to accustom himself to the idea. His stomach was tense with a strange anticipatory excitement and he could feel a cold sweat in the palms of his hands. He was a little disgusted at his own lack of control.

"Please make yourself comfortable, monsieur. You may smoke

if you like." She seemed to sense his discomfort, and though the polite deference of her expression did not alter, he thought he could sense a smile in her light eyes. He liked her instinctively.

"Thank you."

She turned and disappeared through a doorway into an adjoining room and he sat down.

The room had apparently been completely redecorated for its present tenant, for it bore not the slightest resemblance to the rest of the hotel. Here were no traces of ornate manufactured artistry, no ponderous Oriental effects. The high-ceilinged paneled room was painted a mellow ivory tint, the ceiling pale blue. The floor was carpeted with an indefinite design in which soft grays and blues predominated. The furniture seemed diminutive. There were no heavy pieces in the currently popular walnut. Instead, everything had the appearance of individuality, as though it might have been styled for a particular person. Many of the small upholstered chairs had white enameled frames. There was a little white enamel writing desk near the windows, a white piano in the corner just beyond the fireplace. Over the fireplace itself, the focal point of the room, hung a life-size portrait. It was this which Steve now studied closely.

The girl in the portrait looked young; perhaps sixteen. She was dressed as Juliet, in a deep crimson gown of velvet with a low gathered bodice and flowing sleeves. She wore a crimson jeweled cap on her head and her hands were clasped in front of her in an attitude of supplication. Her hair, parted simply in the center of her forehead, fell in heavy black waves and ringlets about her shoulders. Its radiant darkness caught lights from the artist's brush and glistened against the white of her skin.

Steve let his head rest against the back of the chair and squinted as he examined the picture. It was not professionally perfect. The proportions could quite possibly have been improved. But it was recognizable; even after ten years he could see that. And there was something else. Something that shone through inept artistry and gave it quiet domination over the whole room. It was an impression of energy, of activity, as though the subject had been too volatile for mere painting and the artist had had to content himself with catching the faintest suggestion of it on the canvas. Was it in the hands? Steve wondered. Something in their clasping of each other seemed to suggest life ready to burst into being. Or was it the great dark eyes? It was impossible to define it. It was everything about the girl in the portrait. It seemed that she must surely be only pausing in this room. This was but a temporary arrestment. In another moment she would be gone. Steve shut his eyes and looked back at the portrait. She was still there. He felt a little foolish.

He took deep breaths to relax himself and let his thoughts turn to the night before. He wondered where Mr. and Mrs. Charles Wickham were today. Probably here in San Francisco waiting for a ship that would take them on the long voyage around the Horn and thence to England. A long lonely voyage for a frightened young girl. Long and lonely, full of fears and the unknown. Although by today it was probably no longer unknown. Steve wondered why the thought should make him uncomfortable. He was not one to concern himself with the troubles of others. And she was not a beautiful woman, one to incite him to bravado and gallantry. Scarcely more than a girl; thin, awkward, unsure. But lonely. It was that loneliness he seemed to keep coming back to. Did he see in her some reflection of a mood that had been more and more with him lately? He put the thought aside. It made him uneasy.

The clock on the mantel chimed and he gave a start. Somewhere he heard a woman laugh, a low-pitched, uninhibited laugh. He leaned forward a little and listened. The thick carpeting in the hotel muffled footsteps but it seemed to him someone was coming down the hall. He heard the laugh again, then a man's voice. He could hear both of them talking now quite plainly but the words seemed to run together so that only the voices carried. He got up from the chair and stood with his back to the fireplace, facing the door. It opened slightly and stayed that way as though someone outside were hesitating, keeping one hand on it. He could hear the words now.

"When will you come back?" It was the woman's voice and it was incredible. Low, husky, a theatrical voice with a thousand shades of warmth and life, deep-flowing, strong. It sent a little chill up Steve's spine. My God, what would it do to an audience?

"When you want me, my little one. Like always."

"Come for a little supper before the theater."

"No. You got company."

"But I want you to meet him if he's here. Come about seven, Dio."

"Whatever you say. You should rest a little too."

"I will."

"You always say that. Come now, I mean it."

"I promise."

"That is better. I will be back at seven."

"Good-bye, Dio."

"Good-bye, little one."

The door opened the rest of the way, then closed as she came in. She saw him immediately. For a moment she stood there, her back against the closed door, surprise and pleasure and a touch of self-consciousness mingling on her face. Steve felt the same sensations mirrored in himself.

"Steve!" she said at last. She almost whispered it but her strange husky voice made it carry so that it seemed she was standing next to him instead of a room away. Steve shifted nervously.

"Hello, Annette."

She crossed the room and took both his hands in hers, holding them and staring up into his face. He wondered whether he should kiss her. He disliked family scenes.

She settled it for him by straining up on tiptoe and touching his cheek lightly with her own. He felt relieved. For a moment he stared down at her, making a rapid mental comparison between the girl in the portrait and the girl in front of him. Annette was eighteen; she looked no older than the sixteen years of the portrait. She was not over five feet but she held herself erectly so that it was hard not to think of her as taller. She was not as pretty as the girl in the picture. Obviously the artist had wanted to make a concession to beauty. Her huge dark eyes were almost too large for her small heart-shaped face. Her skin was pale to the point of sallowness. Her mouth in repose seemed thin-lipped and without character. But when she spoke or moved something else became evident. The quality that had puzzled Steve in the portrait. The illusion of arrested motion, of controlled energy. It was all about her, injecting itself upon him slowly, unfolding like a spring fern in the mellow dank of the forest, pressing itself upon his consciousness, forcing him to recognize it. When she spoke, the mouth that had seemed drab and unappealing became mobile and soft, the canvas for a hundred subtle and fleeting expressions. Her large eyes became alight with points of eagerness or enthusiasm or tenderness. Even her translucent skin seemed to show an underglow of color and light.

Her one point of perfection was her body; though small, it was perfectly formed; full round breasts rising from a slender waist. Her shoulders were not sloped according to the current female craze but squared slightly with what Steve thought was a touch of independence. She moved gracefully and her whole body seemed to move with her, not like the stiff-legged, ungracious movements of most women. Even her hands were part of it. They were a part of the over-all control, the pleasant studied unity of her bearing and manner. Their movements were not fluttering, but quick and sure. Restful, Steve thought. It was a good word for her. Restful and reassuring. And yet there was something else. He knew now why the newspaper accounts had called her beautiful, even though she was not so in the accepted sense of the word.

He was aware that she was watching him, waiting for him to speak.

"It's a little hard to get used to," he smiled. "Having a family again."

She laughed and pulled him by one hand to the little sofa that fronted the fireplace. With the other hand she untied her bonnet strings and threw it to the table. She was wearing a dark-blue afternoon dress of taffeta shot with narrow stripes of silver-gray. It was cut to a deep V in front but filled in with a fluffy white insert of lace. The same lace was repeated in the tight puffs that covered her wrists under the flowing bell-shaped sleeves of the dress. When she moved, the room seemed to fill with the whisper of the material and an indefinable fragrance moved with her.

"I kept you waiting," she said apologetically. "How wicked of me."

"I was glad. It gave me a chance to prepare myself." He was beginning to feel more at ease.

"Prepare yourself! Heavens, how ominous. I'm not that bad, really. You'd like a drink, wouldn't you?"

She turned and called over her shoulder. "Pelu!"

He was glad she'd brought the subject up. He could do with some whisky. The golden-tan woman appeared quietly from an adjoining room, bearing a tray. Steve had the curious impression that she was like a bit player in a stage play waiting off stage for her one small piece of business. She set the tray in front of them on a low table and went out again. Annette seemed to see nothing strange in this bit of prescience. She poured a tumbler a quarter full of whisky and handed it to him. He was grateful for the size of the glass. It made him feel as though he was drinking with another man. There was nothing traditionally feminine about Annette. Nothing cramped and strictured, made to fit into a mold of convention. And yet he could not have imagined a more thoroughly womanly person. He gulped the whisky gratefully and drew a deep breath. He could feel the drink seeping down, burning his throat, then settling in his stomach and throwing off little rays of warmth

that traveled out and upward. He could anticipate her next words.
Now tell me all about yourself.

She settled back on the sofa. From under the edge of her skirt
he could see one small blue slipper with a high polished heel.

"Now tell me," she said, watching him lazily, "where you got
that haircut!"

For a moment he stared at her. Their eyes met and it was a
moment of understanding. He could see the suppressed laughter in
her eyes, feel it mingling with the whisky in the pit of his stomach.
He threw back his head and roared. The laughter, too big and
hearty for the dainty feminine room, bounced and echoed around
it. She laughed with him. Her laugh was like her voice, low and
husky, theatrical without being artificial. They let the moment
linger, wear itself out. Then he stopped laughing and looked at her.
He was smiling with admiration.

"I was afraid this was going to be conventional."

"Shall I tell you something in strictest confidence? I was every
bit as scared as you were."

"I wonder why. Women usually—I don't know. They like tears
and reunions."

"And I was deathly afraid you were going to want to protect me."

"Why do you suppose—I mean, it's funny, isn't it?"

She nodded. "Maybe because we're a couple of independent
cusses. But I am glad you're here. When did you get in?"

"This morning. I spent all forenoon reading your notices in the
papers. I'm sorry I didn't get here for the opening. They were con-
quered by you."

"Yes, I was very pleased." She spoke of it matter-of-factly. "But
I've been here two months. You must have been gone a long time."

"I've been sojourning inland. But it's not too profitable. It's an
off season for mining. Think I'll stick around here for a while."

"You have a place here in San Francisco?"

"Well, not much of a one. Enough for me." He began to feel
uncomfortable again, as though they had started off by trying too
hard not to pry into each other's personal lives and now there was
nothing left to say.

"I kept track of you these past years," he said finally. "In the
newspapers and like that. It gave me a good feeling sometimes. At
first it seemed hard. It seemed to me you were so young to be out
on your own like that." He wondered if he was sounding foolishly
sentimental.

"Fourteen. That's how old I was the first time I went on the stage. Maybe it was a little young. Not for the stage, so much, but for the other things you learn."

He was not sure what she meant and he did not want to inquire. But she did not seem reticent and continued talking. There was a note of reminiscence in her tone.

"Before you get to be important there isn't too much you can do about it. You're pretty much at the mercy of those in a position to help you." She saw his expression change and went on quickly. "Oh, heavens, it's not so bad. Not if you're quick on your feet. Which I was." She laughed softly. "I can even look back on it now and enjoy it, knowing that it's over."

"I guess it was conscience that bothered me," he said. "There were times when I felt I'd run out on everybody."

"Oh, no! Don't ever think that," she assured him hastily. "I'd have done the same thing. And we managed all right. Ilo was killed two years later, you know."

"Killed!" Steve sat up straight.

"We never knew exactly—" She gave a little wave of her hand. "You know what those brawls are. But we made out all right," she hastened to reassure him. "Betsy got married to John Carreau. Did you know that? We didn't want her to at first. We thought she was only doing it for us but she said she really loved him, and I guess she did. She has three children now, all boys. We moved in on her. I felt sorry for poor John but you'd be surprised how he took it. He was wonderful to us. And then as soon as we could we got out. That's why I went north when I did."

Steve was watching her with absorption. It struck him as odd that he felt no kinship whatever with the others in the family. They were like strangers he had never known. It had always been so. Only he and Annette had seemed related.

"Wasn't it—I mean at first—"

Her mouth curved in a smile that was thoughtful, half sad.

"I guess it was. It's funny how you forget those things."

Remorse welled up in him. "You should have come out here!" he cried. "We could have—well, we'd have managed some way."

She shook her head. "I think it was better this way. We each found out for ourselves. And maybe we're the better for it. Self-sufficiency comes in mighty handy sometimes."

Her answer quieted the remorse, made him feel relieved. He did not want responsibility. He disliked being entrusted with anyone's well-being. But he liked to be reassured that he was not shirking.

His eyes roamed about the blue and ivory room. "You've done well for yourself." He could have kicked himself then for saying it. It sounded inquisitive and he had not meant to pry.

She studied him momentarily as though trying to make her mind up about him. He felt that she was wondering how much to tell him of herself, how much to keep back. She was wondering what sort of person he was underneath. Or perhaps—he twisted a little uneasily and took out a cheroot—perhaps she knew already. He struck a light against the sole of his boot and lit half the cheroot, replacing the other half in his pocket.

"I've done all right," she said quietly. She hesitated.

Then she asked, "Do you know Dionys Pelekis?"

"Know of him." Pelekis was a great handsome Greek, about forty, Steve judged. He owned ten water-front saloons in San Francisco and was worth a small fortune.

"He's a friend of mine. He's been very kind."

This time Steve carefully avoided saying anything that might sound like a query. What she did was her own business. He did not want to hear it, not because he was not interested, but because a confidence usually expected a confidence. And there was nothing he wished to confide in anyone. He merely nodded. She went on.

"I was hoping you might have dinner here tonight, before I go to the theater. Dio is coming and I'd like you to meet him."

She seemed to be seeking his approval as any sister might ask a brother's judgment on an admirer. While the front of Steve's mind told him he was displeased and that he did not wish to be entangled, some remote back part admitted sheepishly that he was really pleased and flattered. For Annette had a way, not of imposing herself upon a person, but of weaving her way in subtly so that before you realized it she was firmly entrenched somewhere inside you and you could never quite get rid of her. He imagined it would be very hard for a man to refuse her anything.

Seeing her together with Pelekis at dinner in her rooms that night only affirmed this impression. The utter devotion the big man showed her, his infinite pains to please, his gentleness were only the outward signs of his love for her. When he sat watching her talk, his face was like a face turned toward the light. When she moved, his eyes followed her every step. And yet, while she surely must have been aware of it, she showed no hauteur toward him, no touch of aloofness that would have displayed cognizance of her power. Strange, Steve thought, how impossible it is to command homage. It has to spring spontaneously like this in order to be genuine. All other forms must have some weak spots which sooner or later are their downfall.

He guessed that Pelekis was supporting Annette, that they were intimate. And he was a little surprised to find that the conclusion did not disturb him in the least. He wondered whether his indifference sprang from lack of family cohesiveness, the attenuated brother and sister ties so long neglected that they were practically nonexistent. He did not think so. He thought, rather, that in the few hours he had become reacquainted with Annette he had already developed an attitude toward her and that the essence of that attitude was confidence. There was a sureness about her that made it seem whatever she did was right. He did not think she was in love with Pelekis but she showed a genuine fondness for him that she made no effort to conceal. Steve guessed that she gave more of devotion to him than many women ever gave their husbands.

Pelekis, a giant of a man with huge muscular shoulders and arms, black curling hair and a broad, handsome, earthy face, seemed to like Steve from the start. Steve sensed that it was not so much for himself, however, as for Annette. The smallest person or thing that touched her life would be important to this man.

"Gambling, eh?" Pelekis commented speculatively. "A good business. Everything is a business to me. Doctors, lawyers, they like to call themselves professional. Professional, bah! It is all the same. They want the same thing like me. And it is all business to me. But if you want to get something nice and steady be a saloonkeeper. I never regretted it. If you got a head for it, it is steady as the sun."

"I'm not sure I'm cut out for anything steady." They had finished dinner and were seated opposite each other in front of the open windows that overlooked the bay, waiting for Annette to dress for the theater. They had lighted cigars and the fragrant mist of smoke that circled and curled around their heads added to the bluish haze of the twilight.

Pelekis gave a little laugh. "And look at me. I got my saloons. I got all the money I want. I got one of the best houses in San Francisco all built ready to move in. Am I satisfied?" He shook his head. "Nothing I like better than the steady life. Home and a family. But—" He shrugged and motioned with his eyes to the closed bedroom door— "She will not marry me."

Steve was momentarily surprised. It seemed to him this man had everything to offer that a woman would want, especially a woman who had known the pangs of insecurity and struggle in the past. "Why not, I wonder."

"You wonder!" Pelekis laughed good-naturedly. "I am crazy in the head trying to figure it out. She says it is something hard to explain. Something about the stage and life and excitement. She says it is hard to settle down after that. To know you are settling down for good and all. I told her she will not have to, but she said no. It has to be one or the other with her. So I settle for the next best." He said it quite frankly and without any undertone of meaning. "Just to be with her when I can, to see her, be in the room with her. You know how it is." Steve did not know but he could guess. And he decided suddenly that he liked this big man.

"Maybe she'll change her mind," he put in.

Pelekis laughed a little wistfully and shook his head. "Well, maybe. I always have hope. But if not, I take this much. She is a different kind of woman. Gets in your blood so you cannot get rid of her and even if you could you would not want it." He said it quite simply as he would make a statement of accepted fact.

"I guess not," Steve agreed.

Pelekis straightened a little self-consciously in his chair as though thinking he had said too much that was intimate and of no interest to anyone else.

"But you remember what I said about the saloon business. Gambling is fine and a good living. But you get tired of riding those boats all the time, seeing nothing but the river and always men with no sense. You pick yourself out a nice little piece of property and then let me know. I will show you how."

"I used to think about it sometimes," Steve said thoughtfully. "I guess it's easier to keep drifting and that's why I never did anything about it."

"Sure that is why. Takes a little pulling in to get a thing started. Pull in your belly and say you are going to do it. That is all. You try it sometime and see. You will not be sorry."

Steve laughed. "One of these days."

The bedroom door opened and Annette came out. She was clad in a long hooded cloak of black velvet which hid the costume she would wear for her opening scene as Pórtia in the *Merchant of Venice*. She had appeared the night before as Juliet and would play in *Twelfth Night* the following day. Then would follow a week's rest and a repetition of the schedule.

Both men got up as she entered. Pelu came in from the vestibule with several sprays of camellias which Annette gathered up in both arms and pressed close to her.

"Dio, you darling. You always do things in such a nice way."

She threw him a look that was an affectionate caress and the big man blushed with pleasure.

She gave the flowers back to Pelu to be put in a vase. "Beside my bed," she instructed the maid. Steve saw Pelekis seek her eyes for a fleeting moment and something seemed to pass between the two. Annette turned briskly to a table that was piled high with opened envelopes.

"Have I read all these, Pelu?"

"I think so, mademoiselle. The late ones I read to you while you were bathing."

"All from heartbroken admirers?" Steve inquired banteringly.

"She is the cruelest woman alive," Pelekis commented, never taking his eyes from her.

"And how would you like it if I weren't?" she teased.

"You do not need to ask."

Steve was beginning to feel like an extra person in the room.

"They saw her as Juliet last night," Pelekis explained. "Now they want to die for her. But if it is all the same to her, they would rather take her to supper."

Steve grinned. He liked the easy companionship, so free from malice, that seemed to lie between the two. He had the impression that Annette was quite free to come and go at will, and that if she did not, it was of her own choosing.

She picked up an envelope lying beside the others, unopened. "This looks like a recent arrival." She opened it and read it. Her face took on a musing expression, a suggestion of a smile. "The same thing. Only a little more desperate and a little better written." She looked up toward Steve, throwing the note aside. "You don't know anyone named Keith Delaney, do you?"

CHAPTER IX

DOWNSTAIRS in King Delaney's home a maid was lifting a taper to the vestibule chandelier. She balanced the slender stick carefully. The wick was slow taking the flame. She removed the taper, put it back to the candle for an extra moment to make sure, then brought it down and blew it out. The other candles, which had ignited with much struggling and sputtering, were now burning strongly. Still the maid hesitated. She turned toward the stairway and paused, holding her breath. Sounds of voices came distantly. She strained slightly but they were upstairs and behind a closed door half a house away.

She tiptoed into the parlor and lit the oil lamp on the large table. The strong smell of the oil seeped into her nostrils and made her grimace a little. She replaced the globe and took the long taper with her into the kitchen where the cook was having her supper. The dishes that had been cleared off the dining-room table were stacked unwashed at one end of the table.

The cook, a stout, red-faced woman with fleshy forearms and strong, stubby hands, lifted a cup, took a generous mouthful of coffee and swished it around in her mouth, swallowing it with a gulping sound. She looked up as the maid entered.

"Still at it?" she inquired.

The girl nodded. The cook shook her head.

"Never hardly touched the roast. If Edgar comes later you can give him a mite of it."

"Thanks," the girl said.

The curtains in Elizabeth's bedroom were closed, the dark blue velvet portieres drawn. The lamp on the table near the bed cast a circle of illumination close about it, but beyond all was in shadows and half-light. Scarcely visible in this outer dimness sat Margaret, quiet and gray and immovable as one of the shadows herself. Her hands were folded in the lap of her black silk gown. Her face looked pale and unhappy but there was resolution in the tight lines of her mouth. Her eyes were on the bed.

Elizabeth lay across the rumpled counterpane, her face buried in the pillow. Her dress was wrinkled, her hair disheveled. She was crying the dry, coughing sobs of weariness and exhaustion. For several minutes Margaret watched her, saying nothing. Elizabeth turned furiously in impotent anger and flung herself down on her back. Her eyes were puffy and swollen. Her lips had lost their contour in the distortion of long weeping. Both hands tore at a small damp handkerchief. Her cheeks were streaked with tearstains but there were no tears in her eyes now. They looked instead hot and burning and feverish, and small red veins were visible in the whites.

She raised herself on one elbow and emitted a sound that was a groan and a cry, a sound of furious impatience.

"If I could only make you *see*, Mother!" She flung herself back down on the pillow and covered her eyes hard with both palms.

Margaret did not change her position in the armchair.

"I do see, Elizabeth."

"You don't! You don't!" Elizabeth screamed. "You keep saying that, but you don't. You wouldn't make me do it if you understood."

She collapsed into a fresh tumult of weeping and Margaret waited again.

"I don't know how you can treat me this way," Elizabeth moaned chokingly. "You always let me make my mind up about things. You never said I must do this or that. And now when it comes to something really important you won't even listen to me!"

"I have listened to you, dear."

"You haven't! You let me talk but it doesn't mean anything to you. You've made up your mind beforehand and nothing I say makes any difference. I'm nineteen! That's too old for school."

Margaret did not answer.

"And don't bring it up to me about Mrs. Bloomer again. I couldn't stand it!"

A mixture of sadness and amusement flickered briefly over Margaret's face and disappeared.

"You'll make yourself ill, Elizabeth."

"I'm ill already. I couldn't feel any worse! Mother, please!" She drew the word out agonizingly, sitting up in bed and facing Margaret once more.

Margaret sighed deeply. "I wish you'd stop, Elizabeth. You're wearing yourself out."

"I don't care! What difference does it make anyway? I might as well be dead as in school in St. Louis!"

"There'll be plenty to do. You'll be busy with your studies and I don't doubt there'll be parties and dances. I don't imagine any of the girls will have prettier dresses than yours."

"Oh, who cares about that? What's the good of dresses anyway? I want to get married!"

Margaret's lips tightened.

"Mother, you don't understand! Why can't I make you see it? He's asked me—he's asked Father. He wants me now, not next year!"

"A year isn't long." Margaret knew when she was saying it that it sounded trite and ineffectual.

"Not long!" Elizabeth ripped the handkerchief straight across. "But I love him. I'm old enough to be married! Any other mother would be glad to get a daughter off her hands. Aunt Agnes certainly was and I'm two years older than Treese!"

"Your aunt Agnes and I see things differently." Margaret's tone had grown acid.

"I wouldn't want you to be like her. I didn't mean that." Contrition forced itself into Elizabeth's voice in spite of herself. "But I love him so!"

Margaret refused to grow impatient. Her look said she would sit in the armchair all night, if need be, until the thing was settled.

"I know you do, dear."

"But I can't expect him to wait forever."

"Why not talk it over with him? Explain it to him. I'm sure he'll understand. If he doesn't—"

"If he doesn't, why, let him go and good riddance, is that it?" Elizabeth's mouth twisted with bitterness. "Well, I'm not going to let him go. I know what you think. Maybe it's true. Maybe if I go away for a year I'll come back and find he doesn't want me any more. You wouldn't want me to marry somebody who didn't think any more of me than that, would you? Well, I can't help it! I love him and I want him. I want him now!"

"There are other things besides physical love," Margaret said calmly.

The shock of it, coming from her mother, silenced Elizabeth.

"You may not think so now. It seems hard to believe when you're young. I'll tell you the truth, Elizabeth. I think Keith does love you in his own way. You're pretty and lively and attractive to him. And you're in the family almost. That makes it easier, too." She knew she was hurting the girl but she could not think how to soften what she had to say. "Everything about such a match would be to his advantage. It would be socially acceptable to all concerned. It would be very right, essentially. You'd make a good couple, everyone would be pleased. But if he wouldn't wait even a year for you, what can you think your marriage would be like?"

"It would be different then! We'd be married. We'd be together always. There'd be something between us. Not like this!"

Margaret shook her head. "If I thought he loved you enough—"

"It isn't that at all!" Elizabeth exploded angrily. "You want me to marry Andy."

Margaret drew her breath in painfully. Something tight and hurting seemed to bind about her chest.

"Elizabeth, it isn't that, believe me. I don't care whom you marry. I only want to be sure you'll be happy. I feel that if Keith is willing to wait—if he still wants to marry you next year—"

"Oh, next year! Mother, please try to see!"

Margaret sat unmoving in the chair.

Keith made a manly show of disappointment when Elizabeth broke the news to him the following afternoon. They were alone in the little back parlor off the dining room. The drops from a recent brief shower glistened on the windowpanes. The sun had not yet pushed through the overhanging grayness and the room seemed dreary. It was too warm to light a fire.

"Of course I can understand," he said thoughtfully. "She might easily feel that way. You mustn't be too upset."

Elizabeth bit her lip trying to hide her disappointment.

"You're sure you don't mind waiting?"

"Well, I guess I mind, all right." He smiled at her and tried to act as if he really did mind. "Sure, I do. But if you can, so can I."

"You really will wait?" She was angry that she was humiliating herself but she could not hold the words back.

"Of course I will." He said it earnestly and he did actually mean it. He would be glad to wait; more than glad. It would give him an extra year. One more year to himself. Why the hell had he ever asked her anyway? Just because he had felt lonesome and a little bit lost when he first got here. He was getting his bearings now. There were things he wanted to do. Other women—

"Oh, Keith!" She breathed his name in an outpouring of her love for him. She crossed over to where he sat and slid into his lap. He let his arms go around her waist, pulling her close to him, kissing her mouth and then letting his lips slide over her cheek and back to her ear. "Keith, if you want me, I'll marry you now. I don't care what they say. Once it's done they'll forgive us." She was whispering rapidly, not taking a breath.

The soft warmth of her body was making him feel a little light-headed. He could see why he had proposed to her. And he did want her. He really did. When she came back. In another year, then he'd be ready to settle down.

"Honey," he whispered. "I want to marry you. Plenty. But I can wait. I don't want your mother and father down on me. You go ahead and do what she says. Maybe she knows best, after all. A year isn't long. And we'll have that to look forward to and plan on."

"Darling, are you sure?" She was still whispering, her lips close to his temple. "Because if you aren't—I mean if you don't want to wait, I wouldn't care. I mean even if we weren't married—" She broke off in a confusion of embarrassment.

He drew back and held her away from him, staring at her.

"You don't mean that." He was trying to be impressively rational. "I couldn't do that, Elizabeth. Honestly, I don't mind waiting."

She bit her lip inside so hard she could feel a tiny bitter drop of blood squeeze out.

"No," she said finally. Her voice had lost its eagerness, became expressionless. "I don't either."

CHAPTER X

KEITH LEANED against the bar and ordered whisky. While it was being poured he turned toward the double doors that opened into the hotel lobby and wondered what was keeping King. He turned back to the bar, put one shiny boot on the brass rail and adjusted his smooth-fitting gray trousers. Hot as hell. That must be one of the prerequisites of political conventions. They had to be held on the hottest day of the summer. He had come without a coat, over Agnes's protests, and already he could feel dampness soaking into his thin lawn shirt between the shoulder blades. The ruffle down the front was wilting with steamy perspiration. Whisky was a fool idea on a day like this, but it couldn't make matters much worse. He drank it down and grimaced.

He had not wanted to return so soon from San Francisco. If it hadn't been for that damned political convention he wouldn't have, either. But Agnes had her mind set on his going to it. Thought it would be a good initiating experience for him. Christ, politics! The word meant nothing to him in relation to himself. He thought of it only as applied to others. Men with side whiskers and mustaches who whispered to each other in anterooms and smoked cigars. Men with big comfortable bellies who talked of tickets and campaigns and platforms and then after hours pinched fandango girls on the behind. Hell, he wanted some fun out of life. That's what he had come west for—not to be nabbed the minute he set foot off the boat and shackled to some career cut out for him ahead of time.

He was finding that his attitude toward his mother had taken a peculiar direction. He had always thought of her affectionately. When he was younger she had never denied him anything. She

had interceded on his behalf with Delaney and always won. Often he
carried little stories to her to make her laugh and they seemed to
delight her. There was an intimacy between them, not founded on
anything fundamental or inherent in either of them, but on surface
incidents and on the fact that they were so alike outwardly. He had
thought her different from other mothers and had loved her for it.
The two of them had comprised a unit in the family. The others
had never been particularly important to him. The two little girls
had been mere babies. They had meant nothing to him. And Delaney and Treese had seemed to form another unit but one which did
not interest him and which he made no effort to understand. During
the four years they had been away he had preserved this pattern of
remembrance. He had thought to find everything the same.

Now he was confronted by facts and situations that puzzled him.
Agnes seemed the same as ever outwardly. But underneath he
seemed to sense a strong undercurrent of purpose, a hard-driving
intensity concealed by the charming exterior he had always known.
And Treese—grown and married. That was irreconcilable, too, with
the picture he had preserved. Agnes made it all seem natural and
right. But Keith knew. Some sharp inward insistence kept telling
him that it was not right. There had been a look in Treese's eyes
after the wedding. What was it? Reproach? A plea for help? There
had been a clutching desperation about it. And yet he had done
nothing. What should he have done?

He would have liked to stay in San Francisco another week or
two. If he could have had that long—even a few extra days might
have been enough—he was sure he could have persuaded Annette
Beaumont to go out with him. He'd never known a girl yet who
held out so long. But she was vulnerable too. They all were. And
one way or another he'd have persuaded her.

Maybe he was crazy not to have taken Elizabeth when she
offered herself to him. Maybe it would have reassured him, made
him feel better about himself. He was not quite sure why he had
said no. He'd hurt her saying it, too. But if only he weren't so sure
of her! Maybe that was it. Because the more she let him know she
was crazy about him, the more he kept thinking of Annette Beaumont. He felt guilty about it but he couldn't help it.

He was glad Elizabeth was going away to school for a year. A
lot could happen in a year. And he needed that year for himself.
Everything was rushing at him too fast. He needed time to think,
time to sort out these things that were confusing him. Maybe this
year would give him a chance. At least he wouldn't have this feeling

of being rushed and cheated out of something. Out of what, he wondered? He didn't quite know.

"Didn't take you long to acquire the ways of the West, did it, Mr. Delaney? I daresay you wouldn't have thought of that back in Cambridge."

Keith looked in the mirror directly back of the bar and saw that Andy Hart had slid in beside him. He was unshaven and slouching, and the glint off his spectacles had its counterpart in beads of perspiration that stood out along his temples and trickled down his uneven sideburns. Without meaning to, Keith made a slight involuntary motion of moving away. Andy did not appear to notice.

"I'll have the same, bartender. But a bottle." He looked at Keith and nodded toward a table near an open window. "It'll be more comfortable over there." He paid for the bottle, seized it by the neck and started for the table. Keith hesitated for a moment in confusion, then followed. Andy did not seem to regard anything as out of the ordinary. He pushed out a chair with his foot, slid into it, and planked down the bottle on the table in front of him. Keith sat down opposite him.

"I daresay," Andy began, "there are things to be said against drinking in the middle of the day—" His voice trailed off as he took the top out of the bottle and poured them each a shot. He lifted his airily. "May the best Democrat win." Keith nodded, still staring curiously at him, and drank. He would have to go easy, he thought with something like panic. And even as he though it he knew he was not worrying about showing up sober at the convention. He was afraid of letting Andy see how unaccustomed he was to whisky. He wondered why he cared.

"I'm waiting for my uncle to come downstairs," he said. He was aware that Andy was regarding him critically from behind his spectacles. And yet it was more than criticism, too. There was something a little sardonic there. Was Andy laughing at him?

"King Delaney," Andy announced with studied irrelevance, "is a great hand at conventions." He paused to pour them each another whisky. "And what do you think about politics?"

This time Keith nursed his carefully while Andy drank. "I don't know. I don't think anything one way or the other. They tell me I'm to make a career of it out here."

"And how does that sit with you?"

"I don't much care. I suppose one must do something. And politics has a certain dignity—"

"Wishful thinking. Of all callings, it has least dignity."

"You think so?"

"Such has been my experience. The politician sets himself up as a demigod; the poor man's messiah—and don't forget to go to the polls six times tomorrow, friend—but underneath he has no claims to homage."

Keith scrutinized Andy narrowly and wondered whether he was drunk. There was nothing in his manner to indicate it. He seemed composed and he spoke thoughtfully.

"I never gave it much thought," he said.

"However, I can see from here that you're the type."

"That's encouraging. When you're being pushed into something blindfolded it's at least nice to know that you're the right type for it."

"And not without wit. What I had specific reference to was your rescuing the picture from the courthouse the day of the fire. The pieces about you in the paper rang most masterfully when read aloud. I trust you clipped and saved them as a reminder of your first step toward public acclaim?"

Keith felt a little twinge of irritation.

Andy's reference to the city's destructive fire of five days before cut with faint pique into Keith's vanity. It had occurred on the day of his return from San Francisco and he had flung himself zealously into the fight beside the firemen, climaxing the day by rescuing from the burning courthouse an oil painting of George Washington.

"I really didn't do it for political reasons," Keith said.

"Oh, I know, you were thinking about the portrait itself—"

"Nor of it either. I did it quite on an impulse, and because a great many pretty girls were watching."

Andy opened his eyes wide and let his eyebrows shoot up. Then they leveled themselves once more. "I don't," he announced, "particularly like you. But I perceive a certain honesty that has heretofore escaped me. Shall we drink on it?"

They lifted their glasses and Keith took a small swallow.

"May I ask what you have against me?"

"About fifteen years—no more, no less. California is a young man's country. And there are other things that are a young man's province as well. However, that's no talk for a July midday. There's Louden Carlton over there."

Keith followed his glance and saw a stout, affable, side-whiskered man enter, trailed by a younger man with a nearsighted squint and a head that showed signs of early balding. He looked questioningly at Andy.

"President of Carlton-Jamison banking house," Andy explained. "That's George Stanley with him. In charge of real estate at Carlton-Jamison. At the moment rumor has it that he is unofficially betrothed to Hazel Carlton. And may I take this opportunity to say that I would sooner get into bed with a hayrake than with Hazel. Mr. Carlton, won't you join us?" His voice rose on the last sentence, and there was a scraping back of chairs as he and Keith rose to greet the newcomers.

"Mr. Carlton, may I present Mr. Keith Delaney—late of Harvard and with modest aspirations in a political way. Mr. Stanley, Mr. Delaney."

They shook hands and Andy dragged two chairs from an adjoining table. Louden Carlton sat down mopping his forehead with his handkerchief.

"Devil of a day. Going to be hell to pay over there at the convention. Don't know why in thunder they don't put it off till fall."

"This is Broderick's idea," Andy put in.

"You drinking whisky? Devil of a day for it. Mr. Delaney, you're a new arrival here." He pronounced each sentence with an air of finality as though it was something he had just made up his mind to.

"Yes. I'm still getting the feel of things."

"Fine. Always need new men. Read about you in the paper, rescuing the picture and all. Devil of a business, that fire. Damned destructive."

"But good for real estate," Andy put in, filling Keith's half-empty glass and then his own. "Won't you join us in a drink?"

Louden Carlton began fanning himself with his handkerchief and unbuttoning his waistcoat. "Not for me. Too damned hot. You've got the right idea, Delaney, leaving off the coat. Wife wouldn't let me out of the house—that is, Mrs. Carlton is quite a one for form—you know how the ladies are."

"To be sure. But where would we be without them?" Andy inquired politely. He allowed his glance to slip to George Stanley and winked broadly. George Stanley blushed and seemed to be trying to draw his skinny neck into his collar.

"I was saying to George here only today that what we need in California is more family men. More settled life. This damned vagrant miner business has got to stop. Got to get more families out here, more law and order."

"You have the right idea entirely, Louden," Andy agreed firmly. "Although I myself am a fine living example of human flotsam."

"Are you interested in politics, Mr. Carlton?" Keith inquired politely.

"Only unofficially, my boy. Quite unofficial. One has to keep an eye on these things. Finger to the pulse, and so on. What happens in politics has a good deal to do with what happens in business. I never miss a convention. Breaking George in, too."

"And George is beginning to look well broken, too. Or is that just the heat?" They all turned as King approached the table and stood there, immaculate in a clean white shirt and looking cooler than any of them. "Keith, I can see you're in bad company. Louden, I wish you'd quit tempting the lad. He needs a fatherly hand."

Louden Carlton chuckled. "We just got here. Waiting for you so we can start over there. Though God knows I don't relish it any. Pull up a chair. I haven't got my breath yet."

King drew a chair in so that the five of them were around the table.

"Would that be whisky?"

Andy handed him the bottle and King called for a glass. When it was handed to him he filled it and tossed the drink down.

"I've got seats reserved for us over there, if that means anything. There'll be about five hundred jammed in that place. I daresay the Fourth Street Baptist Church will see scenes that will make its carpets curl up."

"What do you figure will happen?" Louden Carlton's small eyes squinted warily as he watched King.

King took a cigar from his pocket and bit the end off. "Hard to say." He leaned forward while Andy struck a light for him. "Broderick's pretty sure of himself, but there are a great many factors he's overlooking in his enthusiasm." He leaned back and inhaled the fragrant smoke. "I shouldn't wonder if it works itself into some sort of stalemate."

"Devil of a business. That might mean a deadlock in the legislature too."

"Well, it's a little early to tell about that. Might even swing votes to Gwin."

"So it might, of course. But dammit, King, you know what interests me. Where's the money on this thing?"

"Anybody that bets on this one is crazy."

"That's what I thought." Louden Carlton allowed his pale bulging eyes to wander vacantly out the window. He was disappointed in not knowing what stand to take. He brought his glance back to King warily.

"You committing yourself?"

King laughed. "All in good time, Louden. Don't rush me. Keith's mother has entrusted him to me for schooling in politics. You wouldn't want me to set a bad example by flying off half cocked, would you?"

"Oh, devil take it. No, I guess not. You're too cagy for me, King. But dammit, this is a hell of a confusion. Now, I've nothing against Broderick. The man might be one hundred per cent as far as I know. But that gang of hoodlums he's got supporting him! Now, you take Gwin. He's got the stamp of a gentleman—"

Louden Carlton went on talking. A fly which had buzzed in through the open window circled once around the uncorked whisky bottle and perched on its rim. It sat up and rubbed its front legs industriously together, then flew in a wide circling sweep to the half-full glass in front of Keith. Keith watched as it prepared to alight on the rim. He lifted his hand and brushed it away with the motion, sending it into a wild angry buzzing and directing it toward the window. Halfway there it wheeled around and came back, this time lurking just about their heads, malevolent and sulky.

"Keith's mother has entrusted him—" Keith began to feel the spinning effect of the whisky coupled with an increase in the heat. He struggled to keep his eyes focused close at hand, but they were showing an alarming tendency to wander off vaguely, almost, it seemed to him, in opposite directions, so that to persons watching him he must certainly appear walleyed. The fly took a diving turn in the direction of the small faint bald spot on George Stanley's head. Keith watched George duck and swat at it. He chuckled silently and thought to himself that he must soon arrange to see what Hazel Carlton looked like. Then he thought again and decided that it really wasn't necessary. That hayrake description of Andy's could probably not be topped by anything in the flesh.

"Well, personally," Andy was saying, pouring himself another drink, "I can't see that it makes a hell of a lot of difference who's elected senator right at this point. In another year California'll be in the middle of a depression."

Louden Carlton bristled indignantly and his side whiskers seemed to stand out at right angles from his face, giving him the look of a disgruntled porcupine.

"In the middle of a depression, eh? Listen to me, Andy Hart. Do you know what sort of men go around saying things like that? Fatalists and no-accounts. That's who. I'd like to hear you repeat 'em next year when this state's enjoying her greatest prosperity within memory. Do you know that there's no other spot on the face of the earth with the inexhaustible resources and limitless possibilities for the future that we have right here in California?"

Andy yawned wearily. "Have it your way, Louden."

George Stanley began to fidget uneasily and King's eyes took on an amused twinkle. Louden Carlton grew voluble.

"I can only speak for myself, of course, but let me tell you— Carlton-Jamison is built on rock. Solid rock! Why, there's gold enough here to float currency for the whole world. There are new homes being built, new families settling. There are supplies being sent from the East, and it won't be long before we have enough of our own mills and factories to support our people. And good hard cash to pay for everything. Does that sound like failure to you?"

Andy leaned back in his chair. Little damp marks of perspiration were beginning to show on the front of his shirt. "There are also," he said slowly, "a hell of a lot of people trying to get rich in a hurry."

"You sound as though industry and hard work were things detrimental to a community rather than its lifeblood."

"Whose industry and hard work?" Andy snapped back. "Chinese labor? Poor damned would-be miners who couldn't find gold and came back to the cities to break their backs in some tannery or lumberyard?"

"Poor would-be miners who're getting damned good pay for what they do," Carlton retorted. "If they don't get pampered and fed with a spoon they organize into these damned labor groups and unions—"

"Industry and hard work," Andy went on as though Louden Carlton had not interrupted, "are not exactly the same thing as speculation and gambling. What else do you think the boom here and in San Francisco came from?"

"Where matters of business are concerned," Louden Carlton said icily, "I would suggest that you let well enough alone, and allow those who have made it their life's work to absorb the shocks and hold the reins. The legal mind, the professional approach, are sometimes hardly adequate."

"Touché." Andy grinned good-naturedly. "Take off your coat, Louden. You're working up a sweat."

"Devil take it. I believe I will." Louden Carlton began to struggle out of his frock coat, with George Stanley's help.

King smiled across the table at Keith. "How does it strike you, being on the inner circle?"

Keith drew his attention together with an effort, clutching the tatters of his former debonair pose.

"It strikes me," he declared, "as highly confusing."

Louden Carlton leaned across the table toward him with an air of confidence. "Listen, young man. I hope you haven't been listening too close to Andy here. You've got a great future in California. Any young man has if he's got any gumption and aggressiveness. There's plenty for everybody. I take an interest in seeing young men get a good start. Took George here under my wing and got him a good start in the real estate line"—Keith tried to keep from smiling —"and stood him on his feet. You're a lucky fellow yourself. Got an uncle like King to take an interest in your career. Just don't go chumming around with boobs like Andy who'd sooner get themselves a bottle and a pretty girl than a good steady job." Here he leaned across the table in the other direction and gave Andy a good-natured poke. Andy shook his head and laughed.

"My day's complete," he announced. "I've been insulted by the president of Carlton-Jamison. Adds to my stature. Don't worry about him, Louden." He nodded across toward Keith. "When his head clears he'll be smarter than the lot of us." The smile that he directed at Keith was partly a taunt, partly admiration. Keith reddened with humiliation and wondered which was genuine. He'd not done as well as he supposed, then, holding the whisky. Dammit, what was Andy grinning at him like that for? He knew a moment of blind helpless anger. Then suddenly something else surged through it, came to the surface and bobbed before him like a cork on a crest of wave. Something hung suspended in Andy's look, sharp and aware and knowing, and Keith felt it knifing through the confusion that had clouded his mind earlier. Then in a moment it was gone, leaving only the sense of its having existed, only the awareness that it had once been there, leaving an abrupt, complete soberness. The effect of the whisky was gone. He rose to his feet quickly.

"Hadn't we better be getting to the fracas?" he asked.

They did not speak again until they reached the church.

At the crowded entrance they paused. Louden Carlton was puffing heavily.

"Well, what do you say, King? Do we get seats?"

"We can try. I've got scouts in there holding them down, if that means anything. Looks to me as if every seat that doesn't belong to a delegate is being fought over. Ever see so many pistols and bowie knives on display?"

They struggled through the mob outside the church. King put himself in the lead and plunged through, clearing a path. Louden Carlton came second, panting and red, holding both arms out in front of him for protection. George Stanley was close behind, warding off blows and jostles from the rear and clutching Louden Carlton's coat. His thin neck had begun to perspire and stain his collar. Andy and Keith brought up the rear.

"The sacking of Troy," Andy Hart announced philosophically, "was nothing compared to what a bunch of Democrats can accomplish when they get together."

Seats had been saved for them, but there was a momentary scuffle to claim them. Several enthusiastic Democrats charged forward and demanded to know whether they were qualified delegates. Keith was a little surprised at how quickly King managed to smooth the situation over simply by talking with them in a low voice.

When they were seated Keith looked around the packed church curiously and leaned toward King.

"Will Broderick be here?"

"He'll be here, all right. Wait—there he is now. See—up front there." Keith followed his eyes. A stocky man who had been talking in a little knot of delegates near the front of the church turned halfway toward him so that part of his face was visible.

"Is that Broderick?"

King nodded and a half-smile made his face thoughtful and a little enigmatic. "That's Broderick."

David Broderick had been at King's hotel that afternoon. It was a visit which King had not expected, but which nevertheless did not particularly surprise him. He answered the knock at the door himself.

"Hello, Dave."

"I'm glad I found you in. Have you a few minutes, King?"

That was Broderick, King thought. Never any equivocation or evasiveness about him, whatever his other faults might be.

"As much as you. I think we're headed for the same place today. Have a chair. You don't smoke, do you?"

Broderick shook his head and took a chair near where King had been sitting. King reached for a whisky bottle on the table and poured himself a drink. "Or drink either, I believe," he smiled.

"No."

"You're a good man, Dave. But there are certain pleasures in life you seem intent on passing by."

"That depends on what you call pleasure. There are other things in life I make a point of not missing."

"Quite right. My observation was too narrow to be universal." King sat down with the glass in his hand and scrutinized his guest.

David Broderick was a tall, well-built Irishman. Before he had become engrossed in politics, he had wrestled and boxed, and it showed in his superb physique and heavyhanded grip. He had a ruddy brown beard and slightly darker hair. Strong white teeth showed under a heavy upper lip. His eyes were steely blue, not glittering and calculating but with a steadfast, stubborn depth. His nature was well known to King. In his mid-thirties, Broderick was a lonely, embittered man; positive, unrelenting, dogmatic. His face was not a cheerful one. It bore an expression of perpetual thought, introspection and decision; the face of a man who resolves and then acts without counsel from anyone. It was difficult to disagree with him. Even his taciturnity had a positive, domineering quality. He spoke distinctly and with deliberation, seldom smiling.

"I've come to ask a favor of you, King."

"What kind of favor?"

"I want your support. But before you consent, I want you to understand the nature of that support."

King smiled inwardly. Sure as hell of himself. Before you consent—he has me all sewed up already. Aloud he said, "Do you want me to leap to the platform this afternoon and champion the Broderick cause?"

Broderick did not smile. "I want nothing now," he said slowly and deliberately. "I believe I have this convention where I want it. I believe they will nominate me. If they do, then the legislature is sure. They'll elect me senator."

"Sort of a rush job, isn't it?"

"There is such a thing as picking the propitious time. Gwin's term doesn't expire till next year, and of course that would be the normal time for the election. I managed to have it set forward because I believe I hold more cards now. The legislature is favorable to me. In another six months, who knows—the tide might have turned again. One has to ride in with the tides."

"You've wanted this for a long time, haven't you, Dave?"

"I have wanted it," Broderick replied, "since I first arrived in California in 'forty-nine and saw the future that lay here. I still want it. I believe this is my year. If it proves to be otherwise, that is of small importance. There will be another year. But I am making an attempt now because I believe I have more to throw into the scales to offset Gwin's influence and patronage than I may ever have again."

"It'll be Sacramento and San Francisco who elect you if you do get in."

"I know that. I know where my strength lies, and my weakness. I know I have no strength outside the cities. The federal patronage belongs all to Gwin, of course. He has the state as a whole where he wants it. But there are other factors—"

"The governor?"

"I elected Bigler singlehanded and he knows it. He'll be there this afternoon to speak for me."

"If they let him."

Broderick looked up quickly. "You think they might not?"

King shrugged and drank his whisky. "The place will be packed with Gwin men. You'd expected that, hadn't you?"

"In a way, yes. But there is a tendency in these things to look on the bright side. Dangerous, I suppose—"

"Not particularly dangerous. But a little foolish, I think."

"What do you mean?"

King got up and filled his glass again, then returned to his chair. "I mean that you're too early, Dave. I don't think you'll make it today. I don't think you can get a majority."

Broderick showed no reaction. "It may be. However, I believe it is worth the try. And I am quite confident."

"Then more power to you." King lifted his glass in a salute but did not drink. "You said you wanted my help."

"Yes." Broderick leaned back a little in the chair but his body did not seem to relax. "And that is quite a story. Mostly about Gwin."

"I know about Gwin."

"Then you know what I mean," Broderick said quickly.

"No, I don't."

"Put it this way, then. You know what Gwin's beginnings were —in the South with Andy Jackson. You know what he stands for here in California. Southern aristocracy, the age of chivalry. They even call his men Chivs. They're southern and western Democrats and they want to keep the government aristocratic—a kind of closed society open only to those who measure up to their standards. Well, the Democratic party isn't big enough for both of us." For a moment something fiercely bright seemed to stand behind Broderick's shrewd eyes. Then he was as calm and deliberate as before. "It's been a battle between us ever since the early days out here. Most of the time Gwin's been on top. But it won't end that way. It won't end until one of us steps out of the picture. And I won't step out, unless—"

"Unless what?"

"Unless they kill me." He had said it quite without emotion, but for a moment it seemed to King that something dark and chilling passed through the plain hotel room, touching both of them and then moving on.

"That's strong talk, Dave."

Broderick seemed not to have heard. He sat forward again, resting his elbows on his knees and examining his broad hands as though they contained a mystery.

"My men," he said thoughtfully, "are mostly Northerners. You know about that. I'm a northern man myself, Tammany trained. They're not like Gwin's bunch. They're outspoken—sometimes they're rough. You don't control two cities like these without being rough at times. You know what I was—a stone mason's apprentice. But there are things we believe in. We believe that a government belongs to the people. And we believe that slavery has no place in America."

"I've never been quite sure of that," King said, twirling his glass so that the whisky banked up against the sides and then fell with little red-brown ripples.

"Why not?"

"I always discount talk about ideals. I think you want to be senator, Dave, and to hell with what you believe in."

"Naturally I can't argue with you. I'm not senator and I'm in no position to prove anything that I've said. But these are things I believe in. They're things I would work for—no, fight for—if I got to Washington."

"You don't have to give me the campaign build-up."

"It's not that. But I want you to know. You could be very important to me, King."

"How?"

"I want to use your name for what weight it would carry. I would like it to be publicly known that you support me. Nothing more."

"Nothing?" King could not hide his surprise.

"Nothing."

"Not even money?"

"That's up to you. But I'm not after money."

King finished his whisky and put the glass down on the floor near his chair. "Why?"

"Because your name carries prestige in California. You're respected as a man of law, and your social standing is secure."

"You mean my wife's social standing."

"It might have been that at one time, if we're speaking frankly. But I think that's past. I believe you yourself have claims to distinction in polite society. You have qualities that others of us lack. Poise, adaptability. You could stand up to any of Gwin's men and be taken for more of a blueblood."

"This is all very flattering to me, and I think you know it."

"I am only saying what is true. Now can you see how you could help me?"

"In a way, yes."

"There are things that I have to live down. Not because they carry any personal shame, but because Gwin's men can turn them to good advantage. I owned brothels in San Francisco."

"That's a ridiculous quibble."

"Nevertheless, it has been used against me and will be again. It is of such small things that the case against me is woven, but the whole fabric is enough to make me appear an upstart, a presuming pimp. Do you see now why I need your name?"

King grinned quite openly. "You have appealed to the one thing in a man which can defeat him—his vanity. And how well you know it! But since you know it, and since we're old friends, I can at least save us the farce of equivocation. You have my support, Dave."

Broderick gave a little sigh. Not of relief or triumph, it seemed, but of accomplishment. A good job well done. A deal satisfactorily concluded. "Are there conditions?" he inquired.

King shook his head. "No conditions. But there is a certain risk on your part."

"I know what that risk is."

"Then you know me better than I thought."

"There is the risk," Broderick said slowly, "that I may not emerge victorious in this thing. That all my talking was for nothing and that Gwin will still defeat me. In which case I will no longer have your support. Is that what you mean?"

"Exactly. You spoke of tides before, Dave. Well, there we are in agreement. I, too, ride with the tides. And yours is coming in. Not today, perhaps, or not this year. But you'll have your day. However, that's only my opinion. I'll be with you as long as it profits me and as long as it's safe. After that, I cannot promise."

"That may be long enough. You're a fortunate man, King."

"Why fortunate?"

"Because there are no ideals to keep you awake at night, no scruples to trouble you, no loyalties to make your life hell. And yet you're a good man."

"How can you tell that?"

"Not by anything explainable. Just by something I feel."

"Then your feelings are more acute than my own."

Broderick rose briskly. "Well, I must get over there. It's been good to talk to you again, King." He held out his hand. King took it and together they walked to the door. Just before going out Broderick paused and asked, "How does it feel, being launched into politics?"

King smiled and leaned against the open door, his hands in his pockets. His shirt was open against the July heat, and a little perspiration had started out on his neck from the whisky he had drunk.

"You know, Dave, you and I are very much alike."

"Are we?"

"Both Irishmen, sprung from the sod, so to speak, both trying to get ahead and jealous as hell of Gwin and his damned aristocratic heritage."

Their eyes met, and a rare smile crossed Broderick's face.

"How do I like being launched into politics?" King paused. "I find it very entertaining."

Next day the citizens of Sacramento read in their newspapers how the Democratic convention had broken up late at night in a stalemate, with David Broderick unable to command a majority of votes. Going back to San Francisco King Delaney read it too, and his expression was thoughtful.

CHAPTER XI

EARLY IN AUGUST Elizabeth left by overland stage for St. Louis and the seminary and Keith moved out of his uncle's home and took a small suite of bachelor rooms nearer the center of town. He had imposed long enough, he explained when Margaret protested. He could not think of accepting further hospitality. He celebrated his new independence by inviting two other young gentlemen about town and three young women to a late supper which he had sent in. The party lasted until daybreak and Keith awoke to find himself in a decidedly pleasant frame of mind. An excellent future stretched itself ahead of him. He was engaged to a girl who was not only of the best family in San Francisco but who was passionately in love with him. He had money enough to live comfortably; Agnes had been more than generous on that score, and he had his freedom. At least figuratively speaking; independence within a certain sphere of movement.

He turned his thoughts resolutely away from Annette Beaumont, who had refused two more invitations from him.

King made periodic trips to Sacramento to help oversee the building of Agnes's new home, for which the first ground had been turned late in July. No expense was spared to make it the finest house in Sacramento.

Pure white marble for the mantels was brought in from the middle fork of the Cosumnes. Bricks of first quality were obtained locally for ten dollars a thousand. Ornamental stonework was done by Mr. Aitkens, and Mr. Rogers provided the tin, copper, zinc and sheet iron required. Agnes made it well known that she was distributing her purchases locally. She imported only that which Sacramento could not provide.

In December she moved in. It was a big brick house at Eighth and O streets, an enormous high-ceilinged, ornate affair. The parlor was long and narrow and one end of it was entirely taken up by two floor-to-ceiling windows covered with lace curtains and mounted on top with heavy gold-leaf scrolls. Between the two windows was a full length pier glass, also mounted with gold leaf. It made the forty-foot room appear twice as long. The floor was carpeted from wall to wall in crimson and a heavy crystal and gold chandelier hung from the ceiling.

It had been an eventful autumn. By December the word depression was being whispered about but no one was willing to admit openly the possibility of such a thing. Public confidence was still exhibiting a bold front; speculation was rampant. Behind the surface, however, small fissures were beginning to appear. The first had come in San Francisco in October. True to King's suspicions, Harry Meiggs of the Board of Aldermen had awakened one morning to find himself completely insolvent due to the decline in realty prices and in order to save himself financially had resorted to the forgery of city warrants to be used as collateral security for his loans. Before long he realized it was a losing battle. Detection was certain. On the 6th of October he fled the city and the news was not long in leaking out. Holders of the forged warrants marched on the City Hall to see what they could realize on them. The town was in a furor of apprehension and excitement. Hundreds of investors, small and large, were affected. When a complete check was made it was found that the debts and forged warrants had cost the creditors nearly a million dollars. The moneyed interests were frightened, the small investors desolate. No one dared lend funds even on the most rock-ribbed security. By December banks were refusing to discount for any but their depositors and others were obliged to pay exorbitant rates of interest for temporary loans.

Still the anxiety was beneath the surface. Ostensibly, California was still riding the crest. Agnes, whose money was safely withdrawn and invested in eastern mills and railroads, was scarcely aware of what was taking place around her, except for the brief moments when she stopped to consider her own good fortune and to think herself an extremely astute businesswoman.

On New Year's Eve she held a gala housewarming in her new home, her first formal entertainment there. She had wanted King to come but Margaret politely declined for both of them and Agnes tore the letter angrily in two, comforting herself in the knowledge that she did, after all, hold the upper hand where King was concerned. The thought was solace for a time and Agnes repeated it defiantly to herself. Only once did she experience the little familiar qualm that started deep inside her and made the back of her neck uneasy. The frustrated anger she knew in the moments when King referred to Margaret as "Elizabeth's mother." She tried to drive it away but it kept returning.

Everyone had evidently come determined to start the new year off gaily and to forget the uneasy talk that was in the streets and behind the counters. The women eyed the lavish furnishings and made mental estimates on the cost. The men followed Agnes with their eyes as she passed from room to room to chat with her guests. Everything went off with clockwork precision. The group of singers Agnes had engaged for entertainment was loudly applauded and called back for encores. The musicians played for dancing and wide-ruffled skirts whirled and dipped around the long parlor, where the crimson carpet had been rolled up. There was a clamor of shouting and good wishes at midnight and the party went on. Only later did the thing happen that they spoke of afterward, that they mentioned to substantiate what they regarded—each of them—as proof of their own inherent foresight. A gale from the southeast blew up and a rain started. It was scarcely noticed until it began to increase in volume so that it could be heard whistling and shrieking eerily about the corners of the house. Then one of the great windows at the far end of the parlor blew open, sending the lace curtain into a mad flapping and shooting a cold shaft of rain and wind into the room. Some of the candles were blown out, leaving the room in semidarkness, and the dancers paused uncertainly to look first at the window, then at each other, chilled by the clammy air. It was remedied in an instant. Servants scurried to push the window shut and adjust the curtain. Others lit the candles and Agnes herself motioned for the startled musicians to resume their playing. The dancers took up where they had left off and everything seemed to be as it had been. Except for the strange feeling that seemed to touch all of them, even though they would have felt ridiculous admitting it. The feeling that whatever had entered the room in that furious nocturnal gust was still with them. It had not been shut out with the closing of the window. It had been shut *in* and it was dancing beside them now, turning when they turned in careful time with the music.

1855

ON FEBRUARY 22 it happened.

The San Francisco house of the Page, Bacon & Company banking firm closed its doors following the collapse of its St. Louis house and a heavy run on its own resources. Frightened citizens began to fill the streets, to mill and surge aimlessly, angrily. The whole city was sleepless during the long night. February 23 dawned dismal and chilly, but the indomitable populace took heart with the coming of light. It was a new day; it would all come out right. Then came the final blow. Adams & Company had failed to open.

The streets were thrown into an uproar; panic surged through the city as depositors stormed the banks demanding their money. As though at a signal the scene was enacted simultaneously in Sacramento. Banks whose doors were closed were beaten upon with angry fists. Voices were raised to shouts. The streets were crowded. Carlton-Jamison & Company failed to open its doors and at noon angry depositors battered them down with a heavy oak log to find only the slumped-over body of Louden Carlton at his desk, his head blown half away.

They remembered the day afterward as "Black Friday." It was a financial collapse that brought a spectacular close to the era of "flush times" in California, when fortunes pyramided from one bag of gold dust and speculation of every description was rife. It ushered in a more staid and conventional type of business dealing, equally unscrupulous but available now only to the few instead of the many. Those who had come out of the panic comparatively unscathed such as King and Agnes, whose losses were minor compared to the majority, formed the top stratum of this new business order.

It was an arrangement which suited Agnes well.

Even more predominant in Agnes's thoughts, however, during these first chilly days of early spring, was the news that had come in a letter from Treese that she was expecting a child. It would be born in England, the letter said, but they would sail for America as soon afterward as possible. It was a quiet letter, short and without visible exuberance except for one sentence, a burst of confidence which seemed strange coming from Treese; even stranger because it was Agnes in whom she was confiding. "I am sick at heart; and it is no sickness of this child or my body—I am sick for the sight of California."

Agnes read the letter over her morning coffee in the dining room, then took it upstairs to her own room and sat by the fire, took it out of its packet again and reread it. Her first instinctive annoyance at having spent several thousand dollars on a trip to England which Treese neither enjoyed nor appreciated was short-lived. It was replaced by something that was partly pride and partly a vicarious loneliness for her daughter's plight and which, had she been more analytical, she might have recognized as remorse. Superseding all these nuances of feeling, however, was the pride that rose in her at the thought of a grandchild. Strangely, the thought of being a grandmother held no terror for her. She dismissed it as a dread which others might hold, but which she would surmount in her own sweeping stride. If she must be a grandmother, well and good. She would be like no other, that was certain. But long after she had put the letter away, the thought of a grandchild persisted. It was a warm, glowing thought that sometimes faded away, only to recur sharply, but that never entirely left her during all the days that followed.

Treese's longing to see California again resulted in such a complete change in her that on the voyage home Charles vacillated between alternating spasms of relief and alarm.

"You'd think," he said pettishly, "that I'd been keeping you among savages for the past year."

Treese stood up straight by the small anchored crib where she had been adjusting the baby's bedclothes and faced him across the stateroom.

"Don't be ridiculous, Charles." She smiled.

"You're certainly delighted enough to be seeing America again." Charles went to the big steamer trunk that stood against one wall, lifted its cover and began poking inside. "Moping about and drowning yourself in tears half the time we were there. And now look at you. Personally, I think we might very well have taken another month or two. Starting right off with a young baby isn't the wisest thing in the world, you know."

"I think it was wise." Treese looked down at the small form in the crib, then tipped her head slightly to one side and looked back at Charles, bent over the trunk with his broad posterior toward her.

"Well, you needn't have been so insistent about it. I don't think everyone took it too kindly, after they hadn't heard two words out of you all the time you were there."

"Perhaps they didn't take it too kindly because they didn't relish seeing the last of your pocketbook."

Charles stood up, red-faced, and turned to her. "Now, that is gratitude! That's a fine interpretation to put on family kindness and hospitality."

"Oh, Charles, I didn't mean to sound unkind," Treese said lightly. She walked across to the big double bunk where Charles had just thrown a discarded shirt and cravat. She picked them up and stood for a moment holding them. Then she turned to him. There was a new fullness in her figure, a new erectness of bearing that belied some of her former timidity and self-consciousness. "But can't you feel it too, Charles? Honestly, can't you? Isn't it like going from one world into another? I never was so aware of it before, that feeling of newness and growth that's everywhere in California. And when you realize that, it leads to other realizations that are all so new to me. About the men who made it—how very courageous they were. Men like Delaney—"

"Well, as to that—" Charles began, then broke off, looking sharply at her and trying to decide whether it would be wise to make a comment. He decided against it and turned to the trunk again.

Treese did not seem to notice. "That's what's so incredible to me," she went on. "Everything was so unlike what I expected. I expected fine airs and manners and a great way of living—oh, I'm not saying they weren't polite and all. They certainly do make a show of who sits at the head of the table and that sort of thing. But for real consideration—real understanding of people—why, Delaney would have made them all look like novices. And if it's the grand manner they're looking for, Uncle King could give them more real polish than all the dukes and counts put together. Oh, Charles, I don't mean it because they're your relatives. But look at it yourself. It's the way they live, and what they've been brought up on. They've so much behind them that they have to consider— in California that doesn't count at all. It's what you are now and what you can make of yourself. California is all the future. Surely you must see the difference."

"Hobnobbing with bootblacks doesn't quite hold the attraction for me that it does for you, I'm afraid." Charles's voice was muffled in the trunk.

"Charles, you're being obstinate about it. How could anyone not see it? Everything about the West—about California—that's fine and great is that way because of all the men who made it. Not just a few of them, but every one; the ones who were successes, and the ones people called failures. They were all part of it. There's nothing like that anywhere else in the world today. Nothing that's so young and growing, so alive somehow."

"And nothing so corrupt and greedy, I daresay."

"I'm not denying that. But what amazes me is that I can see it now. All these months I've had to think and be away from it have shown me so many things about it that were right in front of me before and yet I never noticed. Why, the West doesn't belong to people like Mother. She's taken what she could from it—I guess no one could blame her exactly—but there wouldn't have been anything without all the others—all the people who built it up for her." Her voice dropped a little. "Even people like Delaney. They were all a part of it." She looked across toward the baby, who had started to whimper softly. "My son will be part of it. And I will be. I am now."

"He's my son too, you know," Charles said with a touch of

irritation. "Treese, where the deuce is my muffler? I'd like to take a turn on deck."

Treese went over to the crib, lifted the baby and wrapped a blanket around him, balancing him competently against her shoulder. Then she went to a chair and took the muffler from where it had been thrown across the back of it.

"Here, Charles. Why didn't you tell me what you were looking for?"

Charles cast her a look that was less gratitude than suspicion.

CHAPTER XII

TREESE'S RETURN from Europe in the summer of 1855 was accomplished much in the manner she would have wished. It was completely overshadowed by something else. The week before, Elizabeth had come home from St. Louis and her engagement to Keith had been announced. Treese was delighted at the news.

There were other factors which tended to reduce her importance in the general scheme of things. There was Agnes's fabulous new house, in which she and Charles were also to make their home. Its magnificence startled her, then awed her. She felt uncomfortable in it but she was grateful for its imposing magnitude. Persons and their problems assumed a smaller stature beside it and this was the way she liked it best.

Charles was almost immediately sent north to the Marysville region as Agnes's business representative in the matter of obtaining suitable land for hydraulics operations. There were no decisions involved. His work was cut out for him. He had only to negotiate the purchases as anonymously as possible. Even so, going to work had come in the form of a major jolt to him.

"Why, I don't know," he had answered Agnes shortly after the return from Europe. "I hadn't exactly thought about it one way or the other."

Agnes kept her tone pleasantly determined.

"Surely you must have had something in mind, Charles. Some way to earn a living?"

"Why, I—well, I hardly know what to say. In England these things are put on a different basis."

"Yes. All the same, this is not England. And I shall expect you to go to work."

"Work!" The word carried shock, horror, fear of the unknown.

"Yes. Immediately."

Treese was covertly delighted with the arrangement, for it meant that Charles was away now for weeks at a time, and with Agnes much preoccupied with business it gave her an unaccustomed new freedom. Actually, she did very little with it except to enjoy it. But after the long dreary months in England during which she had been forced to visit one threadbare relative after the other, all clinging to a semblance of vanished and now bankrupt nobility; after watching one family heirloom after another packed and crated for shipment to America (all somehow like Charles—authentic on the outside but dingy and spurious underneath), she was ready to enjoy any arrangement in which she was simply left alone.

Agnes's eagerness over the baby surprised Treese a little. It seemed as though this was the only issue out of all their relationship together wherein their thoughts seemed to touch and merge, to achieve some semblance of understanding. The baby was immediately installed in an upstairs bedroom which had been converted into a nursery and Agnes herself supervised every detail of his readjustment to normal living after the long ocean voyage.

"It's a mercy to me he ever lived through it, Treese," she said scoldingly one day. "That was a terrible chance to take with such a tiny baby."

"I knew it would be best for him," Treese said simply.

"Well, it's done now, and I must say he doesn't look any the worse for it. But it's a scandal that you haven't named him yet. People are asking, and it's dreadfully embarrassing."

"I wanted him christened here in Sacramento. He'll be called Delaney."

Agnes considered for a moment. "Well, a family name is always good. Though I should think Charles would have forbears he'd want considered in the matter. They set such store by those things in England." She bent over the crib and missed the slight smile that curved about Treese's lips.

"He's not being named for the family, Mother. He's being named for Delaney."

Agnes looked up, not quite comprehending for the moment. "For Delaney? Oh, yes. Well, but isn't that rather odd?" She did not wait for an answer, but leaned over and grasped one tiny hand in her own. "Well, no matter. He's my baby now too. Isn't he, dolly?" She shook the little fist. "Isn't he?"

The smile faded from Treese's lips and a small shadow flickered across her eyes.

Late in the summer when Charles was away, Agnes insisted that Treese take advantage of the extra time at her disposal to go to San Francisco and visit Elizabeth. Treese hesitated, allowed herself to be tempted, then agreed. She did long to see them all again.

Margaret, King and Elizabeth were delighted to see her. It was more than a year since they had said good-bye to her at the Embarcadero after the wedding. Elizabeth insisted she had changed.

"It's something—I don't know. You look grown up!" She and Treese had gone up to talk in her bedroom. She left Treese standing in the middle of the floor and walked in a circle around her.

Treese blushed. "It's my hair, I guess." She wore it low on her neck after the fashion of the young matrons.

"No. Not just that. Something else too." Elizabeth cocked her head curiously to one side, then gave up. "I don't know. Come on sit down." She went and plumped herself down on the bed, propping herself up against the bolster. She patted the space beside her in invitation and Treese came over and climbed up. The bed was high and the motion of scrambling up gave her a look of peculiar but attractive childishness for the moment. It was true what Elizabeth had said about her being changed. Where she had been blundering and youthfully awkward, she seemed now to have become nervously alert. The motions of her hands were often quick and surprising. Her eyes were darkly intense and moved quickly, wanting to take in everything at once. She seemed never to relax completely.

"I guess you won't ever change, Elizabeth. Nobody'd want you to, anyway. You're just right the way you are." She looked at her cousin affectionately, admiring as she always did the smooth tilt of her neck, the way her blonde curls fell in profusion from the top of her head, the way the little hairs close to the nape of her neck sometimes clung damply to it.

Elizabeth returned the look and the two girls smiled at each other, suddenly conscious of their privacy and the long afternoon for talk and confidences that stretched ahead of them. Elizabeth dug her back deeper into the bolster and looked up at the ceiling.

"I guess I ought to be ashamed to say it, but I can't wait till Keith and I are married. All the time I was in St. Louis it was just killing me, thinking of him out here and no way to see him for a year. Sometimes I'd have the most awful feeling that when I came back he wouldn't be here or something. Or that he wouldn't want me."

Treese laughed. "You are silly. As if anybody wouldn't want

you." Her admiration for Elizabeth was so genuine that her incredulity showed in her voice.

"It's not so silly." The unexpected bitterness startled Treese. "He's seeing some woman."

"Keith? Who?" Treese sat up straight. She was incredulous. Well-ordered lives bordering on hers somehow never experienced deviations of this sort from the norm.

"An actress. Annette Beaumont, her name is. He takes her out. To supper and like that, after he leaves me." Elizabeth was struggling to keep her voice under control. "And she already has another man she isn't married to."

"Oh, Elizabeth!" The exclamation carried shock and pity.

"That's why I wanted to get married right away. Mother kept insisting next summer and I said no, so we compromised on Christmas. I wish it was Christmas now." There was a childlike wistfulness about her face as she said it.

"But he loves you, Elizabeth. You're the one he wants to marry," Treese insisted, trying to convince both of them.

"Well, maybe." The childishness had vanished and Elizabeth was coldly ironic. "I'll die if anything happens to upset things."

"Silly. Nothing's going to happen. You know how men are. It's awful but there's no getting around it. I guess just about all men are alike."

Elizabeth grasped at the straw. "I know. That's what I tell myself. And it's true too. Why, sometimes I've even thought that Father—"

She cut off the sentence and Treese felt self-conscious at having known something for years that Elizabeth was only now stabbing at in the dark.

"Of course. It's ridiculous to worry over it. And it'll be different after you're married. Keith's still young. He wants to have his fling and get it all out of his system before he marries you." Treese was struggling as she went along to sound plausible.

"I guess that's right." Elizabeth bounced over and lay on her stomach, raising herself on her elbows to face Treese. "Treese, tell me about your baby. I do wish you'd brought him."

"He's traveled half around the world already. He needs a little home life."

"I know. But what's he like? Is he like you?" Elizabeth sounded inordinately hopeful. She had never liked Charles.

Treese thought for a second. "I think so, a little. He's beginning to show reddish hair. He'll be like the Delaneys, I think."

"Do you really? Oh, that's exciting. Treese, you've no idea how much it's improved you, having that baby. You even *look* different."

"I don't suppose it was all the baby." Treese wondered whether Elizabeth would understand if she told her about her new feeling toward the West, the feeling that was both belonging and proprietorship. The pride in homecoming, the excitement, the new awareness. She rather imagined Elizabeth was too absorbed in her personal problems now.

Elizabeth began pulling absently at the threads of the coverlet. At last she raveled one out in a long strand, wadded it up between her thumb and forefinger into a tight ball, unwound it and then began rolling it again.

"It's nice to have you here to talk to, Treese. Will you stay a long time?"

"I can't stay very long. I should be back by the time Charles comes back from the mines."

Elizabeth was struck with an idea. "Why not wait until Keith goes? Go back with him."

"I didn't know Keith was going to Sacramento."

"Oh, yes! In another month. Why, I thought you knew. Father's sending him to Sacramento for a while to do some work for him there."

"Is he going to stay there?"

"We don't know yet. Father didn't say."

"Oh, I wish he would! Then you might even live there after you're married and we could visit back and forth! Only I guess maybe you wouldn't like to move away from San Francisco."

"I wouldn't care," Elizabeth said frankly. "Just so I was with Keith I wouldn't care. And it would be nice to live near you, Treese. And I'd only be a little way from Mother and Father." She warmed up to the idea suddenly. "It *would* be fun, wouldn't it?"

Treese nodded. "Maybe I could stay until Keith goes up then and go with him. I'd like to stay."

"Father says he's sending Keith up there so he'll be out from underfoot while the wedding preparations are going on. He jokes about it like that. Only I think it's for another reason. I guess he's heard, too."

Elizabeth broke off the sentence and Treese self-consciously avoided her cousin's eyes. Then she sat up again in her original position, alert and full of news once more.

"I knew there was something I was forgetting to tell you!

Treese, do you remember that gambler I was in love with when you first came west—Steve Mallott?"

Something dry caught in Treese's throat.

"Why, yes."

"Well, he's still around, you know. Debonair and wicked as ever but of course Keith is the handsomest man in San Francisco now. Anyway, Steve Mallott is going to be a neighbor of yours. He's building a big saloon and gambling house in Sacramento. The Red Tent. It's going to open this winter and it'll be the most fabulous thing outside of Portsmouth Square, they say. Andy told us all about it. Now, can you imagine? A thing like that happening in Sacramento?"

Treese stayed until Keith went to Sacramento. They made the trip back together and Treese remembered it long afterward as a pleasant interlude, set apart in her scanty collection of memories. They sat on deck or in the dining saloon. Once they danced together. Keith was sociable and polite with her and he laughed often. If they seldom touched upon subjects close to either of them, Treese did not mind. It seemed nicer this way. No rough edges, no worrisome places to avoid. She was more glad than she had realized that Keith was marrying Elizabeth, and she was convinced that the woman in San Francisco was exactly what she had told Elizabeth —a last fling before he settled down for good and all. When they docked at Sacramento on the last day of August, life seemed indescribably good to her, full of prospects and possibilities that all but obliterated what she had come to regard as the debit side of the ledger—Charles and Agnes. She was secretly excited and stimulated beyond words at the thought of seeing Steve Mallott again but even this was not pressing and immediate. It was a nebulous thing surrounded by the haze of the future, pleasant to speculate over and weave dreams around. Her more immediate concern was for Keith and Elizabeth and the prospect of their happiness was a thing she lived vicariously, savoring every moment. She was particularly pleased over Keith's good humor, for it seemed to her he could not possibly be brokenhearted over leaving his new amour, the way he laughed and joked and talked. The truth was not brought home to her until just as she stepped off the gangplank onto the Embarcadero and looked up to see if Keith was behind her. Before she could turn, her eye caught a huge billboard that had been plastered across one of the Embarcadero's open-air vending shacks. In large glaring letters she read:

Coming September 15
to the
Acadia Theater
Mademoiselle Annette Beaumont
The Belle of New Orleans
An Extended Inland Engagement

Her eyes traveled again slowly over the last line. "An extended inland engagement." She turned and waited for Keith, who was struggling down the gangplank with their luggage. The gossamer tracery of her dreams folded limply around her.

Steve Mallott spread the drawings out on Annette's bed and slapped them with his pencil.

"This," he said emphatically, "is going to be the fanciest saloon Sacramento, or any other place for that matter, ever laid eyes on."

"How modest of you, dear." Annette went on laying out dresses on the half of the bed not occupied by the drawings. A large trunk stood opened in the center of the floor and the whole bedroom was topsy-turvy. Shoes were scattered about the floor, unmatched stockings littered the dresser. Pelu came and went through the doorway with methodical regularity and purpose, each time on a specific errand, each time bringing a small touch of order into the chaos. She had just taken a dress from Annette's arm and was folding it neatly and placing it in the trunk.

"Those which may crush," she explained, "will go on top."

"All right, Pelu. Any way you want to do it."

"Pelekis has the right idea," Steve went on exuberantly. "Give 'em what they want but soak hell out of 'em for it."

"That seems sensible."

"Now look here." He pointed with his pencil and Annette looked over his shoulder. "Three stories. Carpets on every floor. Crystal chandeliers. Pillars down the center of the main floor here. Bar on one side, tables for gambling on the other. Private dining and sitting rooms on the second floor. The third floor's for me."

"The whole thing?"

"Naturally. I have to live better than the others."

"Did Pelekis tell you that too?"

"I thought it up. But he said I was absolutely right. The impression's everything, he said."

"I suppose it is. What about the money, though?"

"He said it should pay for itself in a month."

"Is he lending you any?"

"No. He offered to but I didn't take it. Why?"

"I just wondered."

"Why did you ask?"

She turned and picked up a stray stocking from the dresser, examining it for flaws absently.

Steve watched her for a moment. "You're crazy," he said at last. "You ought to know Pelekis better than that. If he did anything he'd do it for me, not because of you. You wouldn't be under any obligation to him."

"I know. He's awfully good. But you know how I'd feel. He does so much for me anyway."

"Because he enjoys to."

"Yes, but all the same . . . I do like him a lot, Steve."

"You sound as though you're having an attack of conscience."

"Nothing of the sort!" She was indignant.

"Do you still want to go to Sacramento?"

"Oh, yes!" Her answer was a shade too eager. "I mean it's a wonderful engagement. A very good offer. And it's months now since I've been on the stage. I'm dying to get back to it."

Steve shied away from the discussion as he always did when he felt he had ventured too far into something that involved personal problems. He rolled up the drawings, took out his watch and examined it.

"I'd better be moving."

"You just got here."

"You don't show the proper respect for my new station in life. I'm a businessman now. And at the moment I'm supposed to be pricing bricks and lumber."

She laughed and came over to him again. "This has been good for you, Steve. I'll be glad to see you settled down."

"That's an odious phrase. You might as well want to see me married."

"Well, now, it's not that bad!"

He looked at her with elaborate glumness.

"Only I wish you'd tell me one thing," she went on. "You've got all of San Francisco to pick and choose from for this new venture of yours. Why on earth are you going to Sacramento?"

He hesitated, looking hard at her, and in spite of herself she colored a little.

"Why are you?" he asked softly.

Pelu examined the whole matter in the light of philosophical reasoning after Steve had gone.

"Once you have your affair with this Keith Delaney," she stated succinctly, "you will be satisfied. That is all it needs."

"Pelu, you put things abominably."

Pelu began matching up small ribboned and flowered shoes in pairs and stowing them neatly in the racks provided for them in the big trunk.

"Pelekis is a good man," she said simply.

"He's wonderful, Pelu. That's the only part of the whole business that makes me feel terrible." Annette sat down disconsolately on the edge of the bed. She was in a red-and-white striped taffeta wrapper with little red pompon slippers, her long black hair was loose over her back. "I want so much to be good to him and not hurt him. I'd like to repay all the nice things he's done for me."

"He expects no more than what you have already given him. And if you had not wanted to give him that much, it would have been all the same. It is the manner of the man."

"He *is* good, isn't he?" Annette seemed to want to torment herself with the reminder.

"He would still marry you." Pelu let her voice rise suggestively.

"But it wouldn't be fair, the way I feel. And it's not just Keith, either. I don't feel that I'm ready to give up the stage and just settle down for good. I'm young yet."

"Did he ever ask you to give it up?"

"Well, no."

"Or to settle down?"

"Not exactly, but—"

"The affair would do it. It's the lack that you feel. The incompleteness of it. Where there is further to intrigue, then there is continued interest."

"If I were only sure! I want so to be fair to Dio."

"That is only your conscience speaking."

"At least I have one!"

Pelu paused thoughtfully. "It may not be so unwise, this trip. It may be the best thing." Her quiet hands were folded for the moment over the front of her white apron. "Once you see for yourself that one is very much like the next, you may want to come back and marry Pelekis."

Annette stretched both her feet out close together and stared at the little red fluff on the toe of each slipper.

"I don't know," she said thoughtfully. "I just don't know. Sometimes when Dio is here I think it's all I'll ever want in the world, to be with him quietly like that, have him take care of me. But when I see Keith—"

"There is the matter of ages. You are both young."

"If it were only that! I just don't know! How is it I can't tell, Pelu? When I've known so many men and always known myself so well? How is it I can't tell this time?"

There was a knock at the outer door.

"That's Dio," Annette said. She got up quickly from the bed and hurried to brush her hair in front of the dressing table. Pelu scooped the dresses off the bed and hastily tidied the room, then went to open the door.

When he came in Annette had turned and jumped up to meet him. Her hair streamed in long dark waves and curls over her shoulders and fell across her breast. Her cheeks were glowing pinkly and her mouth had shaped itself loosely and naturally into a greeting that was affectionate, even a trifle penitent. The red-and-white striped taffeta rustled as she ran across the room to meet him. His big body filled the whole doorway and his black curly hair shone where it caught the light from the parlor. He had to bend far over to kiss her.

"My little one," he said softly. "You look beautiful." He slid his cheek over hers caressingly. "I am going to miss you."

There was a little throaty catch in her voice when she answered. "I'm going to miss you too, Dio."

CHAPTER XIII

IT WAS the after-theater supper hour at Bellamy's in Sacramento. The fashionable eating place was crowded with richly turned-out ladies and gentlemen who had come as much to be seen by others as to enjoy one of Bellamy's superb late suppers: clear golden consommé in a heavy tureen, boiled salmon, plump canvasback duck nestled in brown potatoes and vegetables, green salad, piles of crusty French bread which the waiters kept replenishing, fruit, Cheshire cheese, bitter black coffee in tiny cups, and finally brandy. Talk circled and hummed, rose from little groups and then swooped down as voices were lowered in strictest confidence to repeat a rumor that everyone on J Street would know the following day.

A tiny young woman moved through the crowd in front of her

escort, pausing when she was stopped by a greeting or compliment, smiling graciously or dropping a word. She wore a dress of sea-green taffeta, full skirted and cut wide and low at the neck so that the white curve of her shoulders was visible. Around her neck was a gold medallion on a slender black ribbon. The young man behind her was handsomely attired in a cutaway tail coat of the finest black broadcloth, with squared shoulders and a nipped-in waist with broad silk lapels that emphasized an already sturdy chest. He looked handsome and proud, and his eyes followed her every minute. They were seated at a table in full view of the whole dining room, and while she adjusted her wide skirts and made room on the table for her fan and flowers, waiters bustled around them bringing the heavy white tureen of soup with which to start the meal.

Annette leaned toward him slightly. "Are they still staring?" she whispered breathlessly.

"They'll never stop staring until you leave Sacramento."

"Heavens, how shall I ever eat my soup. I feel like a museum piece."

"Not a very apt comparison."

"Well, anyway, I'm hungry and I'm going to eat."

"That's the spirit."

The tureen was uncovered and the fragrant soup ladled into shallow gold-rimmed dishes. They had scarcely dipped their spoons into it before a waiter came up with a note for her. She read it and scribbled a hasty answer on the reverse side with a pencil the waiter handed her. The whole dining room watched interestedly.

Keith raised his dark eyebrows inquiringly. "Love letter?"

She laughed a little. Her laugh was always surprising, always pitched lower than you expected it to be. "Love letter. Desperate. But not as original as yours, I'll admit. If yours hadn't been so terribly interesting I'd never have accepted your invitation finally."

"Is that why you refused so long? To keep me writing those notes?"

"Maybe."

"What did you tell him?"

"Who?"

"This one just now."

"What did I used to tell you?"

"And I thought you showed me some originality." He pretended offense but he could afford to be generous tonight. Every eye in the place was on her. Every man was hating him for his monopoly of her.

There were two more notes during the duck and three while they lingered over their coffee and brandy. Keith lighted a cigar and watched with abstract, tolerant interest as she scribbled the refusals which he knew from experience were polite, interested, and heartbreaking. He observed her as she sat across from him, her skin illuminated by a flush of excitement, but translucent and fragilely white except just under the wide cheekbones. It was those bones, together with her small pointed chin, which gave her face its arresting heart-shaped appearance. Her eyes, now on him, now on the table or the notes, were so dark it was hard for him to tell always whether they were brown or black. There was a wide innocence about them that was tempered with knowing humor when she laughed, giving her a strangely mingled appearance of naïveté and worldliness.

A group of musicians played at one end of the room. The song was slow, appropriate, digestive. Most of the diners would have begun to filter out by now ordinarily, for it was midnight. But something made them linger. A sense of expectation, perhaps merely a peculiar sense of interest and aliveness which Annette's presence seemed to create in the room. They still watched her and even the mere watching was diversion. The room had settled down to a subdued pattern of muted sound. The unnoticeably suitable music, the lowered voices, pleasantly tired, pleasantly fed.

The pattern was abruptly shattered at precisely eight minutes after twelve when ten men from Confidence Engine Company Number One (Pride of the City of the Plains) burst in the front door grandly. They were in full fire-fighting regalia—red shirts with blue trimmings, black pantaloons, leather belts. As one man, they whipped off their Philadelphia fire helmets bearing the company's motto: *Douse the glim!*

While the room sent up a gasp of surprise and speculation they marched without hesitation in a body to the table occupied by Annette and Keith and formed a semicircle around it, standing in two rows. One member stepped out slightly, raised his hand and hummed a pitch. The hand made a vigorous circular motion and then descended and the ten men burst forth grandly, singing to the tune of *Oh, Susannah!*

> Oh, we've come to take the lady home,
> To squire the lady home;
>   The toast of Sacrame-en-to
> On Engine Number One!

> Heave along, comrades!
> Roll that engine free,
> 　　Oh, in all of Sacrame-en-to
> The fairest flower is she!

There was a burst of applause of the entire dining room and at a signal from their leader the firemen bowed as one and obliged with several more stanzas. Annette was watching them delightedly yet modestly. It was a look that told them she had wanted nothing on earth more at that precise moment than to be serenaded by a group of such splendid firemen and yet which denied in the same instant that she was worth any such honor. Keith looked from her to the firemen with amusement. He felt flattered but also a little unnecessary. No one was paying any attention to him.

When the song had run its course and the last applause had died, the leader made another motion and a short stocky fireman in the first row stepped forward and bowed from the waist. He was apparently the lyricist and Annette returned his bow with a smile and an inclination of her head. The dining room, roused from its lethargy and taking part in the scene, began to clamor for her.

"Give us a song, mam'selle!"

"Give us the *Petty Wazzeau!*" (*Le Petit Oiseau* was the ballad she sometimes sang as an encore or as an afterpiece at the Acadia.)

"Come on, mam'selle!"

Clapping was augmented by stamping. Annette glanced at Keith. He was sitting stonily now, not looking at either her or the crowd. His sense of proprietorship was dispelled. He was not only unimportant, he had become somehow ridiculous. He was only another follower in her wake. Another admirer, where before he had been the chosen one. Now they all claimed her.

"Do you mind?" she asked timidly, knowing he did.

He kept his lips tight so that they did not form outlines for his words. "Suit yourself. But I don't like being made a show of. I'm not used to it."

Anger at his unreasonableness flared in her. He had reminded her of what he considered her to be and of how he considered she should deport herself. He had reminded her too, in some way, of that girl in San Francisco, who was waiting for him and who fulfilled the proper qualifications. The "right sort" of girl. The musicians had struck up *Le Petit Oiseau*. They were calling her name. They wanted her to sing.

Without another moment's hesitation she rose and permitted

herself to be escorted by the firemen to the small raised platform where the musicians sat, still sawing over the introduction to the song. She smiled to acknowledge the applause, then began to sway lightly from side to side with the slow suggestiveness they wanted.

"*Le petit ouiseau voit tout*—" she began. The room grew silent. "—*s'assait dehors, voit dans la chambre*—" She began to go through the pantomime which accompanied the song. The suggestive movements of a woman preparing for bed, pretending to remove petticoats and stockings. Her small white hands fluttered gracefully and the green taffeta skirt swayed and sang with her. She lifted it slightly, just over her calves, when she came to the stocking part, and an appreciative hoot rang out as her white silk hose with the embroidered green clocks came into view. She looked affectionately at the firemen, at the clustered admiring waiters, at the musicians. She distributed her love over the entire audience, made them feel it and warm to her. Her mouth had become full of color, her dark eyes flashed with innuendo. She had not yet looked toward Keith. The small hands struggled with imaginary corset strings, the round little bosom sighed with relief when it was accomplished. The voice grew lower, huskier. It was an unbelievable voice. No respectable woman had a voice like that, the women whispered to each other, and yet each of them would have killed her for it had they not been spellbound themselves.

The song was concluding and on the last bars she swept down in a deep curtsy, bending her neck and leaning far forward so they could see just enough down the front of her dress. Applause thundered around her. Flowers were snatched from table arrangements and flung at her feet. Pieces of gold added their clatter and even the glitter of jewels showed now and then. Some of the gold pieces made heavy clanking sounds. They were five- and ten-dollar coins. She acknowledged it all again and again, modestly, pleadingly. She wished they would please not do so much, her look implored. She was not worth it really. Not worth it at all. Their shouts and bravos roared in denial. As they shouted, she accepted a proffered hand from each side and raised herself and this time she looked at the table where they had sat. Keith was gone.

She was escorted home in triumph by Confidence One, sitting in a place of honor atop the engine, which was drawn with white ropes by the men themselves. Her lap had been filled with flowers and the firemen formed a retinue carrying the gold and favors which her small hands could not accommodate. Another crowd assembled at the entrance to her hotel and she was detained a quarter of an hour trying to thank them all and make a graceful farewell. She left the flowers on top of the engine, making it resemble a parade float, and begged that the firemen keep the gold they were carrying. They refused loyally and carried it inside the hotel for her, where it was put in charge of a flustered but pleased manager. She carried two of the jewels with her, a square-cut emerald pendant and a little diamond brooch. She had no idea of the identity of the donors. The hotel clock read half past one when she finally got away and upstairs to her own suite.

Keith had lighted a fire and was standing in front of it facing the door when she entered. She could sense his anger. It filled the whole room. She did not speak immediately. Instead, she placed the jewels carefully on the table and threw off her wrap as though that action were an important, urgent thing requiring all her concentration.

"Well?" His voice cut through the room.

She could feel her anger rising to meet his and tried to hold it back. "Well?" There were sharp edges in her own tone. She had never accounted to anyone for her actions and she did not intend to do so now. And yet the set of his shoulders against the firelight, the glint of his hair—

"You certainly made a fine spectacle of yourself."

She did not answer.

"Making an indecent show in front of all those people."

Her low voice answered sharply. "Did you think it indecent when I did it at the theater?"

"The theater is a different matter. There's a time and place for those things."

"It would be the same anywhere."

"You were with me tonight. And you made me look ridiculous."

She laughed a little. "I feel sorry for you. Your feelings are fragile."

He grew irritated. "That's hardly the point. I'm not in a position to be snickered at."

"I'm chilly," she said. "Do you mind if I enjoy the fire?" He was blocking it belligerently with his body, arms behind him, legs apart.

He stood stiffly to one side. She came over and spread her hands to absorb the warmth. "You really shouldn't take on so." She smiled, trying to pass it off lightly. "I'm sure everyone noticed that you left."

"Did you expect me to ride on the fire engine?"

"It was fun." Now she was tormenting him and she knew it.

"Fun for someone not too discriminating." He knew the minute the words were out that he should not have said them, but now that it was done he straightened himself even more, looking angrily defensive.

He had expected her to flare up. He was not quite prepared for the sound blow that made his face, from his left temple to his jaw, quiver and smart. He seized both her wrists furiously. She did not resist him and he knew he must be hurting her. She was looking directly at him, her eyes blazing with fury.

"Damn you!" he said angrily. "What are you trying to do?"

Something in her tense immovability made him release her, but she did not move away. She remained in front of him, so close her wide skirts brushed about his knees, staring at him. When she spoke her voice was pitched lower than ever.

"Everyone has a dignity of his own," she said slowly. "I value mine as highly as you do yours. I didn't intentionally slight you tonight. It was a question of offending you or offending everyone else there. I was sure you'd understand. And about that other, it may very well be. You are not the first man I've cared for, but you are the first who ever insulted me. The first I ever parted with unpleasantly." She started to turn away from him but he caught her back roughly, holding her arm.

"What do you mean—parted with?"

"Exactly what I said."

"You mean you want me to go?"

"It's all the same whether you go or stay. You know what I mean. Tonight should have at least proved to you that I'm quite capable of getting along without you."

"I see." It sounded lame but it was all he could think of. He found himself wanting to stay and yet to do so would be to accept humiliation. She had turned away from him, facing the fire again. He became conscious of the fragrance that had entered the room with her, the nearness of her, his own desire. She seemed to have taken it for granted that he was leaving. She had dismissed him. Anger and pride flared up in him again. He seized her by the wrist and pulled her to him, bending down to kiss her. She neatly avoided his lips so that they just grazed along her temple. He thrust her from him.

"Christ!" he exploded. He seized his hat from the chair and strode to the door. She did not look at him. When he had his hand on the knob he turned back to face her.

"Annette, what is all this anyway?"

"All what?"

"Oh, hell. Don't give me answers like that! What's making you act like this?"

She spoke to the fire. "I'm not acting any way. I've scarcely said a word."

"You slapped me. That was ridiculous."

"You were rude."

"Well, I'm sorry if I said anything."

"It's all right."

He took two tentative steps back into the room; not enough to admit reconciliation but enough to indicate there was more to say.

"Well?" he demanded stubbornly.

She turned to him. She was standing quite erect, a small compact figure in the little circle of firelight. Her face was serene. "There's no one keeping you."

He slapped his hat vengefully against his thigh. "You can't talk to a woman."

"If there was anything to say— But you don't want me as I am, apparently, and I have no intention of changing. It would hardly be worth while. I've had no complaints up to now."

"I wish you wouldn't make it sound so commercial."

"I hadn't thought of it until you reminded me a minute ago."

"I already apologized for that. And you don't need to throw your other friends up to me."

"You're in a very bad mood tonight. Why don't you run along?"

"Will I see you tomorrow?" He spoke stiffly, hating himself for giving in that much.

"Not unless your temper's improved. I don't like scenes. Good night." She turned her back on him, went into the bedroom and closed the door.

He stood uncertainly, still two steps inside the room. At last he jammed his beaver hat on his head violently, went out and slammed the door behind him. In the hall he hesitated again. It was the first time he had ever quarreled with her, and he was beginning to feel a strange empty sickness. He hadn't realized how upset it would make him to be angry with her. And, after all, he had acted like a fool, trying to run her that way. She had a lot of spirit. You couldn't just bully a girl like that around the way you could— Sharp conflicting loyalties made him leave the comparison in mid-air. He put his hand out for the doorknob and turned it noiselessly. He wondered if she was crying now. That was the usual procedure,

he supposed. Flinging oneself across the bed and weeping. He'd
like to know, that was all. If he heard sobs he'd turn and go right
back out again. He pushed the door open a crack. No sound. He
shoved it all the way open and looked inside.

She had come back into the living room and was standing again
before the fire, the light behind her silhouetting her. She turned as
he entered. Keith saw she was not crying.

He threw off his hat, not stopping to see where it landed, and
crossed the room in long strides. He caught her up in his arms and
swayed back and forth slightly, pressing her tight against him, feeling the pressure of her rounded thighs against his through the
petticoats and silk.

"I didn't mean to act that way," he said at last, mumbling it
into her hair. "I don't know why I was jealous. I didn't mean to be."

She did not answer and he leaned over to kiss her. This time
she did not avoid him. Her lips had a desperate sweetness about
them that he seemed to notice for the first time. He kissed her
again, harder and more slowly. Then he drew her inside the bedroom and closed the door.

"I don't know why," he repeated. "It just seems that whenever
there are outside things pulling us this way and that we get upset.
With ourselves and so with each other. When we're alone there's
never anything."

She smiled and walked away from him, unfastening the ribbon
around her neck. "I know. It does seem that way. When we're alone
it's perfect."

He followed her to the dressing table where she stood, and put
both hands on her shoulders, leaning over to kiss the back of her
neck. "I love you."

She looked at him reprovingly.

"It's true," he insisted, on the defensive.

"Well, it may be true with reservations. But it's those reservations. I begin thinking of them the minute you say it."

He threw his coat off and walked to the bed, lying down on it
with only his legs hanging off the side. He folded his arms under
his head so that it was tilted up slightly and watched her undress.
Every motion she made was graceful, expressive, co-ordinated.
There was no wasted energy. He began to feel how cheap his performance had been. How childish he had been to resent the harm-
less song she had sung. He watched her take off her corset and sit
down in her chemise and ruffled drawers to take down her hair and
brush it. He liked her best like that, partly because it showed the

neat calves of her legs, which were usually covered, but mostly because it gave her an odd ingenuousness that delighted him. He let himself relax completely as he watched her, feeling more at peace with himself than he had felt in a long time. And he did love her. He wished he could make her believe it. But it was not too surprising that she was skeptical. He was only beginning to get used to the idea himself.

CHAPTER XIV

TREESE LIFTED the foot-high blue china cats, one in each hand, and stood for a moment trying to determine where she might place these newest arrivals. The packing box in which they had been delivered was on the floor at her feet. She stepped over it gingerly and approached the already full sideboard. Again she paused. Directly in the center was a huge crystal punch bowl with a ladle resting in it and twenty-four glasses clustered around it. The arrangement was flanked by a set of ivory satin pillow covers embroidered with violets and lilies-of-the-valley. There was a large leather-bound Bible from which trailed markers for family events—births, deaths, marriages; there were a small gilt foot warmer, a crocheted bedspread, an ornate silver coffee urn.

Treese set one of the cats down, shoved the Bible over a few inches and made room on either side of it for a cat. She left them and bent over the packing box, scooping up paper and straw, pressing it down firmly and carrying the whole thing into the kitchen where it would eventually be used for kindling.

When she returned to the dining room Agnes was entering with another package. Treese sighed wearily. Another litter of paper on the floor, another gift for which room would have to be made.

"Mrs. Carlton and Hazel," Agnes said by way of explanation.

"Oh." Treese knew Agnes had been waiting for the Carltons' gift. Hazel and George Stanley would be announcing their engagement soon. It was nearly a year since Louden Carlton's death and George was doing fairly well in the independent real estate line. Agnes wanted to appraise the value of what they were sending Keith and Elizabeth, so that she could send something just a trifle better.

She untied the package and opened it on one of the dining-room chairs.

"Hmm." She pulled away the tissue wrappings and held up a heavy gold-encrusted meat platter. "Well—"

Treese wondered whether she was expected to make comment. As usual when in doubt, she remained silent. Agnes tipped her head to one side, turned the platter over and examined the back.

"Hiller & Andrews. Well, I suppose it's rather good."

"It's quite lovely, isn't it?" Treese said, furnished with her cue. "Elizabeth should be pleased. So many nice things."

Agnes did not appear to hear her and Treese began to collect the wrappings and press them back into the box, making another weary trip to the kitchen and back. Agnes was still holding the tray when Treese returned, but now she was eying the blue china cats critically.

"Who on earth—?" she began.

"Mr. and Mrs. Spencer."

"Atrocious, aren't they? And quite cheap, too. Push them back, Treese. And the Bible, too. We'll put the platter more to the front."

"I don't think there's room."

"Then put them over there on that server, out of the way."

Treese obeyed.

"Goodness, if these things don't stop coming I don't know what we'll do." Agnes's pride was thinly glossed over by the feigned irritation.

Treese's loyalty was quick and instinctive. "I suppose ever so many were sent to Elizabeth in San Francisco, too."

"Oh, well, naturally." Agnes left no doubt that her son was the important half of the whole affair. "There now." She placed the platter on the sideboard. "Write them a note, Treese. And one to the Spencers too, I suppose, for those abominable cats. What on earth would you do with them?"

"On the mantel—" Treese suggested tentatively.

"Abominable," Agnes repeated. "You won't forget the notes?"

"I'll do it right now." As Agnes left the room Treese sat down at the dining-room table. It was littered with note paper and ink, with cards received and cards to be posted, with lists, half of whose items had been neatly crossed off. Treese bit the tip of the pen thoughtfully, then started to write: "My dear Mrs. Carlton and Hazel—"

It was the week before the wedding and the Delaney household was preparing to pack up and leave, bag and baggage, for San Francisco. It had been a week of such frenzied preparation that each individual seemed momentarily to lose his identity in the welter of hurrying and bustling. For a time it seemed to Treese that no order could possibly emerge from the orgy of fitting, ordering and packing that went on from daylight to dark, and she wondered with an ever-increasing sense of amazement what it must be like at Elizabeth's, where the ceremony would actually take place.

Clothes were the prime consideration. There must be new outfits for both Agnes and Treese: dresses for the teas that would precede the ceremony, dresses for the balls, dresses for the ceremony itself, new traveling outfits, new underthings, new bonnets. Mrs. Fitch spent every afternoon now in one of the upstairs rooms sewing and fitting with frenetic haste, the small cushion of pins bobbing on its tape about her neck. For once both she and Agnes were too busy for confidences.

It had been so all during the fall and early winter. Time seemed to have flown by until it seemed to Treese it must surely be only last week that she had come up from San Francisco on the boat and seen the poster. When this recollection cropped up in her mind she hurriedly pushed it down again. She knew that everyone in town was gossiping about Keith and the actress. She knew there were many nights Keith had not come home at all. And yet she told herself resolutely that once Keith was married to Elizabeth it would all be right again. These things happened. They were nothing to be too concerned about. Once he and Elizabeth were married it would all be right. Men had strange attitudes in such cases but it meant nothing. She had repeated the formula to herself nightly and several times each day until its meaning had become dull even to her.

She knew that Agnes must be aware of the situation and yet her mother had never reproached Keith in any way or reprimanded him. Only occasionally had Treese noticed a tenseness in Agnes's manner, an anxiety that she seemed to be keeping under rigid control. And during the past week, with preparations going into their final stage, even this seemed largely to have disappeared.

It had been a fairly ordinary autumn, punctuated here and there by a few events of noteworthy significance. The new courthouse had been completed and was to be rented by the state as a capitol building. The former courthouse, the one partially destroyed by fire the previous summer, had taken on the adjective "old" as a designating description. A gaspipe line had been laid and the city was momentarily awaiting the first turning on of the new street lights. The Sacramento Valley Railroad had been completed and was operating regularly as far as Patterson's, ten miles away. On the same day Treese was writing the note to the Carltons, it was to open for regular business to Alder Creek, a distance of eighteen miles. There were other milestones; all of them cause for civic pride, none of them quite as important to Treese as the fact that Steve Mallott's Red Tent was having its gala opening on Christmas night.

Agnes bustled back into the dining room.

"Did you thank the Hobbses for the relish server?" she inquired anxiously. "I certainly never saw anything cheaper, goodness knows, but Emily Hobbs can talk more than any woman in Sacramento."

"I wrote them a note."

"Oh. Well, all right. Have you seen Keith?"

"He came in a while ago. But I think he's going out again. He said something about not being here for dinner tonight."

"Where's Charles?" Now that Agnes had on her mind the additional duties of preparing for her son's wedding, she seemed to delight in showing that all the details of household management, even unimportant ones, fell on her shoulders, and she consequently magnified all of them, gave them all a sense of urgency they did not actually possess. Treese twisted the pen nervously in her fingers.

"I don't know. I haven't seen him since breakfast."

"You haven't! Well, I can't imagine . . ." Agnes's tone indicated this to be a personal shortcoming on Treese's part. "Maybe he's gone to make arrangements for the stagecoach. I told him to, but he might not have remembered." She snatched up one of the lists from the table. "I've been looking for this." She pinned it with brisk efficiency to the bosom of her green silk dress. "Now let me see!" She closed her eyes and pressed her thumb and middle finger over them, concentrating. There was a loud knock at the front door and she gave a little start. "Heavens, if that's another package—!" She started for the hall. "I'll go, Nellie. I'll answer it!"

Treese bit the end of the pen again.

"—perfectly charming and in the best possible taste—"

Once she had walked by while Steve Mallott was still building. She remembered it because it was one of those perfect fall days before the wet weather set in. Clear and bright with color, warm in the sun but prescient with chill where the shadows fell. She had been walking on the opposite side of the street and she had stopped to watch for a moment. There was not much form to it yet, mostly scaffolding and raw lumber. It was a big building. She could make out three stories. At first she had been so preoccupied with watching a workman perched hazardously near the top, busying himself with a hammer, that she had not seen Steve. He was standing on the ground near what would be the front entrance, one foot raised on a wooden sawhorse to balance the papers and drawings he was examining. He was wearing laced knee boots and trousers of a rough dark material and a plain brown sack coat that came almost to his knees.

She had fastened her gaze on the back of his neck, feeling as she did so a peculiar sensuous excitement, out of place against the blatancy of the afternoon sunlight; unfamiliar to Treese in any surroundings. Fifteen months slipped away from her and she was conscious again of the strange fluid quality of her brief association with him, the thing that made each touching of their lives seem like a continuation of the last time.

She remembered the morning after her wedding. How Charles had stolen softly into the cabin at dawn and how she had pretended sleep; the strange feeling of a body beside her in bed as he crawled in and fell asleep. It was nearly noon when he awoke. There was remorse, apology. But now it was no longer formidable. Even the caresses which she suspected he felt obligated to bestow did not frighten her now, for it was daylight and by day there was nothing frightening about Charles in his nightshirt. She had never stopped being grateful to the stranger who had given her that extra time.

Steve was half turned away from her that autumn day. She watched the ends of dark hair curl up slightly from under his wide-brimmed felt hat, noticed the slight stoop of concentration in his shoulders as he studied the sketch in front of him. His left hand was visible to her and she watched with fascination as it moved, tracing a diagram on the paper, resting with something that was never quite relaxation. Even without looking she would have remembered the leanness of the wrist, the visible sinews, the dark little hairs that lay back and caught the sunlight.

She did not notice that he had turned his head and was looking at her. When she did become conscious of it, it was an instinctive knowledge, a gradual realization that seemed to start from an inside rather than an outside source. She raised her eyes hesitantly and as they met his he took off his hat and gave a slight bow. When he straightened she was still looking at him. She didn't want to, but it seemed almost to be the action of an ungovernable second party lodged within her. Gathering her skirts quickly around her she hurried off down J Street. She was surprised to notice how weak her knees had become.

"It was the boy from the milliner's." Agnes came back carrying two large boxes. "I was beginning to worry about those bonnets."

She put them on the table and Treese shoved over to make room for them. Agnes began to untie the strings.

"Did you finish that note to the Carltons?"

"Almost. Just a second till I sign it."

"Because I think I'll send it over by messenger. Looks a little better than just posting it. What do you think of this?" She held out a rust-colored velvet bonnet with satin ties and satin rosettes perched under the brim.

"Quite nice for traveling, don't you think? Just enough. Yours is in the other box."

"I'll look at it as soon as I finish this."

Treese scribbled hastily at the note, suddenly not caring whether or not she duplicated worn phrases. She signed it, folded it, careless of wet ink, and thrust it into an envelope. Agnes had replaced her bonnet and opened the other box.

"Well, I don't know. I suppose this will suit you, Treese." She turned the little green bonnet around in her hands. "It does have style." She lifted her head with quick instinct. "Keith!"

He had just slipped past the dining-room door on his way out. He returned looking sheepish.

"You're going out again?" She was trying to keep the sharpness out of her tone.

"Yes—to see the first run to Alder Creek. It'll be quite a show." He was wearing a long black greatcoat and a brushed beaver with a high bell-shaped crown in the latest style. He was affecting a walking stick, and this together with his buff leather gloves were in one hand.

"You're not coming back for dinner, Treese says."

Treese felt vaguely traitorous.

"No. I expect to make a day of it."

"And a night, too?" It was more than Agnes ordinarily reproached him, and Treese had the impression she was keeping herself under control only by the most vigorous self-restraint.

"Please don't worry about me, Mother. I'll make an exemplary husband, I promise you."

"Why, of course, dear."

"Only I'd like to enjoy my freedom—what there is left of it."

"Naturally, darling. But I don't know why you speak of it that way. Dear Elizabeth is quite—well, after all, it isn't as if—"

"I may be late." He had turned away from the doorway and they listened to his footsteps recede, punctuated by the bang of the front door. Agnes turned back to the bonnets and fumbled obviously with them, making unnecessary motions and looking overly brisk. Treese sealed the Carltons' envelope and addressed it, glad for the excuse not to look at Agnes. Treese had noticed the change in attitude between Keith and Agnes ever since Keith came to Sacramento early in the fall. Their former easy companionship seemed to have developed edges that made for rough spots and awkward lapses between them. Or scenes like this one. She felt uncomfortable because she knew Agnes's concern was not for Elizabeth's feelings. It was for something that had to do with Agnes herself. Agnes felt too deeply about it to have someone else's interest at heart.

She shoved the envelope across the table toward her mother. "There," she said.

Agnes did not see it. She was working absently at the string of the milliner's box with her fingers, but her eyes were not on it.

"I'll be glad," she said rather obscurely, looking past Treese to the crowded sideboard, "when this is over."

Keith had the strange impression when Annette met him at the door that both of them were acting out prearranged parts, going through motions established beforehand. They were projecting themselves into new characters, becoming what they were not, and doing it quite expertly. There were only a few rough edges, and with rehearsal those could be smoothed out. Only there would be no rehearsals. This was the performance, and once it was done . . .

"I guess I'm late," he apologized, coming in and taking off the new high-crowned hat. "I stopped to buy these." He handed her a little nosegay of violets and larkspur.

She took them and thanked him.

"And this," he added, though now he was beginning to feel uneasy, as though he had done too much. The flowers would have been enough. He held the box out to her and she took it and opened it, lifting out the narrow cameo bracelet. He thought for a second how nearly her small pink nails matched the cameos in the bracelet.

"It's beautiful. You shouldn't have done so much." She had noticed it too, then. He felt more ill at ease than ever.

"It's nothing. I hope you like it."

"I do. Will you put it on for me?"

His fingers were cold and clumsy as he fumbled with the catch. He had not kissed her yet, as he usually did when he came in, and it seemed to him the omission must be noticeable. He leaned forward and touched her lips tentatively with his. They were yielding, warm. Nothing was changed, really. Everything was the way it had always been. And yet he felt no buoyancy today, no pleasant sense of expectancy. He caught her by both arms.

"Annette—" What did he want to say? He could find no words.

"Don't you want to take your coat off? It's quite warm in here with the fire."

She smiled pleasantly at him and he let go her arms. He threw his coat over a chair and followed her to the window. She was wearing a deep-red velvet dress that he had not seen before and the little gold medallion she was fond of hung about her neck on a velvet ribbon.

"I've been at the window all day watching the men working. You see down there? It's the gaslights. They're going to turn them on Christmas Eve."

"It ought to be quite a show."

"I don't know. I rather liked the old ones. But these are quite the latest, they say."

He was stricken with quick remorse. "Where will you be Christmas Eve? I mean—will you be alone here?"

She continued to watch the street below. "I don't know. I expect I may put in an appearance at Steve's place on Christmas. I'm so anxious for everything to go off well for him."

It seemed strange to be speaking so casually of a time when they would not be together.

"He's a queer one," Keith said almost angrily. "Spending all his time on that building and letting you stay alone here. Someone should be with you." It was a relief to transfer to another some of the guilt he felt.

"I've always taken care of myself." There was a trace of sharpness in her tone and he sensed that he had said the wrong thing. He was always underestimating her.

"Will you stay in Sacramento for a while?"

"I think I may. The Acadia will sign me for six months if I like and probably longer after that. I rather like it here. I've had more of a feeling of belonging."

Guilt rushed over him again, making a little spot at the base of his skull tingle nervously. It would almost have been easier if she had said she was going away, that she could not bear to remain here now. Her attitude gave their whole past relationship a strangely unsentimental cast, made it appear less important than he had imagined it to be. What he planned to say to her had become somehow unsuitable and shabby. He dreaded saying it and so pushed it back, procrastinated.

"I'm leaving tomorrow."

"Yes."

He noticed how new hairs showed soft and curling at the back of her neck and remembered how many times he had kissed her there, making her laugh and squirm away from him. A desire that was quite out of place in the atmosphere of the afternoon came over him and gave him the impetus to say what he had held back.

"I'll be living in Sacramento, you know." Something still kept him from saying "we."

"Yes, I know." He had not dreamed she was capable of such cold, withdrawing dignity. He wondered whether he dared continue. "I thought perhaps—there's no reason why we couldn't—" He broke off because she had wheeled around to face him. He thought he had never seen her so angry, even that night when they had quarreled. Her eyes darkened and they moved quickly, the pupils distended. Her face was pale. She kept her hands tight together in front of her as though to quiet their nervousness. Her usually soft, moving mouth was rigid and controlled, so that she seemed to be speaking through her teeth.

"You Delaneys seem to have a way of overestimating your importance," she snapped. "We both knew what the situation was. We planned on it. Now that it's done, it's done."

He felt taken aback, obliged to defend himself.

"You certainly never were one to moralize!"

"I'm not moralizing now. I'm being perfectly sensible. Don't try to give the whole thing an importance it never had."

"Never had! I certainly thought—"

"You thought wrong, then."

Her look was a plain invitation for him to leave, but he hesitated because he did not want to go, to break this last tie irremediably. To be with her, even to feel her anger, was something. She turned her back on him again. With studied carefulness he picked up his coat and put it on. He buttoned each button with precision because it would take a little longer and turned his hat in his hands for a moment.

"Good-bye," he said at last. He made his voice rise a little so that it sounded like a question.

"Good-bye."

He walked to the door, opened it and let himself out, closing it carefully behind him.

A little patch of early-morning sunlight shone on the spot where he stood watching them load the great egg-shaped Concord stage. From his seat high on top the driver shouted orders, brandishing his whip and glaring with supercilious authority at his underlings who rushed to make fast to the front and rear "boots" the baggage, mail and express chests. In all California there was no person of quite so much individual importance as the stage driver. He assumed quite as a matter of course that he never carried a passenger quite worthy of his society, and as a result his manner was condescending in the extreme. If his language at times became offensive in the heat of an arduous trip, there was none who would venture to reproach him, for in difficult situations he was known to be capable of unbounded chivalry.

This one was typical, Keith thought as he watched. Brawny, red-faced, big-muscled, but with a jaunty aloofness that set him somehow apart and gave him dignity. He shouted down to one of the loaders.

"Casey, you son of a bitch! Give 'er an extra twist! She'll slip out sure on the bumps. Harry, you check the 'braces? Take another look! Hand that up here! Valuables? Hand 'em up here! I'll put 'em under the box. Anybody wants to get 'em'll have t' move my tail!"

Keith leaned against the post where he stood and listened with a sort of relief. The man's raucous voice had a peculiarly soothing quality as background for his thoughts, even for the pounding headache he had awakened with.

He had been drunk the night before. He did not remember in what saloon or with whom. Waking up this morning before dawn in order to make the early stage had been less idyllic. There had been the quick shot of pain piercing through his skull when he sat up, the cottony dryness of his mouth, the dizzy nausea when he got to his feet. And then remembrance. That was the worst. It had swept through mercilessly and then settled down to a steady throbbing reminder that fell in with the beat of his aching head. He found himself washing and dressing, selecting a cravat. He even studied with surprising objectiveness for a moment the two greatcoats in his wardrobe, balancing their merits and deciding which was more suitable for traveling. When he had put one on, it struck him as slightly ridiculous that he should have cared. And then he realized that actually he had not. He was merely going through gestures and thought processes that were by now second nature. Marrying Elizabeth would be like that.

Something out of the past recurred to him with a jolt. He had seen Treese once in a bridal gown that had made her look small and pale and indefinite. He had thought of her then as one of the movable pieces in the arrangement Agnes had made of all their lives, and he had not defined the why of it, except to suppose subconsciously that Treese's will was nonexistent or buried under the long years of habitual yielding. But he was different. He was himself, and he had a will. But where was it now, and why was he getting on a stagecoach and making a trip that he did not want to make? Why was he leaving the best part of him he had ever known somewhere behind him in a hotel room that was more truly home to him than any other place he had ever known?

Agnes, stylish and nervously alert in her brown merino, wearing her rust-colored bonnet, bustled over to him. She carried a small leather box in both hands.

"What do you think, Keith?" she asked under her breath. "Would you trust this with him?"

"What is it?" He could not rid himself of the feeling of detachment from his surroundings, of going through motions unconnected with reality. He was looking at Agnes as though she was an irritating stranger accosting him there at the depot.

"Why, my jewels!" Agnes was too preoccupied to concern herself with attitudes. "Would you dare let him take it? He said all valuables up there in front, but—"

Reference to the stage driver held out a thread of the present that Keith could recognize. He felt a sudden unaccountable loyalty to the man, as though he had been a friend of long standing.

"He's all right," Keith replied with peculiar fervor. "You can trust him with your things."

Agnes glanced at him, surprised at his quick definiteness. She had not actually wanted advice, but chatting excitedly about her many responsibilities heightened her sense of importance.

"Well, I don't know." She hesitated. The hesitation made Keith irrationally annoyed.

"Go ahead." he said sharply. "Let him have it."

"All right. I suppose . . ." She let her voice trail off as she hurried over to the stage and held up the little chest for the driver to take. He leaned down with hearty gallantry.

"You'll take good care of it?" Agnes asked anxiously, fixing a beguiling smile on the man.

"The best, ma'am." He swept off his hat, holding the box in one hand as if it was weightless.

She looked up at him and leaned toward the step where his big boot rested, letting him have a long last look at her before she turned away.

Then Keith watched her disappear into the hotel that served as headquarters for the stage company. A moment later she reappeared with Treese and Charles. She was telling them something with an important, confidential air. Charles, neat and resplendent in his long traveling coat, was stroking his mustache, giving her half his attention. Treese did not appear to be listening at all. Her eyes traveled quickly, absently over the other passengers loitering outside near the stage, over the stage itself, the driver, the men loading. They rested for a moment on Keith, then flickered off.

Charles was talking now and Treese inclined her head slightly out of habit more than interest. His voice reached Keith.

"Not exactly the most comfortable way to travel, but with all the steamer explosions lately—"

"Goodness, yes!" Agnes cut in importantly. "I wouldn't set foot on one of those wretched boats!"

"Two a week or more you hear of." Charles seemed determined to outdo her in decrying the situation. "But of course they've improved these things a good bit." He nodded toward the stage. "Better thorough-braces and all. And good ash wood, every inch of it."

Treese nodded politely. "It does seem light, though, doesn't it, for such a long trip?"

"Light!" Charles roared, happy for a chance at refutation. "Twenty-five hundred pounds or more, if you call that light!"

"My!" Treese shook her head incredulously, humoring him. What constant dissimulation between a man and woman, Keith thought, to keep things running smoothly. He had never thought of Treese as either capable or subtle. Now all at once he realized that she was both, and so practiced at it that it was second nature to her. He had never been conscious of pretense where Annette was concerned. He wondered how it would be with Elizabeth.

Agnes came over to him again, taking quick little steps and holding her skirt above the muddy ground with one hand. It was going to be a bleak day, chilly and damp; the early promise of the sun had disappeared. Thick puffy clouds hung grayly, now and then moving enough to cast into damp shadow the spot where Keith stood. Agnes drew her cloak around her.

"Well, I guess we're all ready." She was still looking around busily. "Just as soon as they finish loading."

Keith nodded and looked toward the stage, which had in some way become a looming, important factor in his life. With the peculiar sense of self-removal he had felt ever since last night, he examined the wide, egg-shaped body, the elegant gold scrolls which adorned its sides, the damask curtains at the window. He thought with a bounding little thrill how simple it would be not to step on the stage with the rest of them. How simple to remain behind. In their eagerness they would scarcely notice. The thought was pleasant and he clung to it, turned it over in his mind for a moment.

The horses were beginning to stamp and snort, and the driver called out to them affectionately, using a tone more deferential than that usually employed toward passengers. The last bags were strapped on, the door held open, and the little waiting groups began to look busy and concerned and nervous, to gravitate with backward glances and last-minute admonitions toward the stage. Treese and Charles walked toward them. Charles was still discussing the construction and merits of the Concord. Agnes moved excitedly.

"We'd better hurry before all the inside seats are taken. Are we all ready? Treese, pull your skirt up. It's muddy there from so much walking. Ready, Charles? Come on, Keith."

Keith's hesitation was so slight as to be unnoticeable. As he followed the others toward the open stage door the master of their destinations roared down from his exalted position, "Get a move on! We ain't got all day!"

CHAPTER XV

ANNETTE MOVED WAKEFULLY and opened her eyes. She recognized the room, the bed, the little night table, the washstand. A circle of light, bright in the center, spreading and diffusing at its outer edges, moved along one wall. That would be Pelu carrying a lamp. It was her room and Pelu was with her. It was night. But what night? She had no idea what time it was, even what day. She did not know how long she had been sleeping. It seemed there was something she was supposed to remember but she could not for the life of her think what it was.

"Are you feeling better, mademoiselle?"

She could see Pelu bending over her, could read the anxiety in her strong, fine features, golden now in the lamplight instead of tan.

"I feel quite well." She said it experimentally, testing her voice. "What day is it?"

"It's Christmas Eve."

"Christmas Eve!" Something important was to happen then. Some event that had been on her mind. All she could think of was the gaslights. "Have they turned on the new lights yet?"

"Not yet. A little later."

It seemed to Annette there was something more she wanted to ask but what it was escaped her. Already she was beginning to feel tired.

"I think I may sleep," she murmured.

"Yes, sleep. Your brother has been here to ask for you. He's here now."

"Steve? I'd like to see him, but—" The present seemed to be slipping away. She tried to keep her eyes open. The darkness was soft and restful. She let herself drop back into it. Then something important occurred to her and she struggled to keep awake long enough to say it. "I'd like to see the lights." She thought she had spoken it but her lips had only formed the words.

Pelu adjusted the covers around her, smoothed the black hair that was flung in disorder about the pillow and turned away, taking the light. She went out of the bedroom but left the door slightly ajar so that a shaft of light would streak in and keep it from total darkness.

"Did she wake up?" Steve looked up as she entered the room.

"Only for a second."

"Did she ask about him?"

"No. I think she did not remember."

"I'd like to kill that bastard."

"There were no others like him. The others all wished to marry her. It was the little one who did not want it."

"Damn him. If I could get him back! If there was only something we could do!"

"I think it is too late for that anyway. He was married this afternoon."

"I wish there was something I could do. If you need anything, or if there's anything she wants, send a messenger over."

"Good night, monsieur." She saw him to the door and then watched him from the window.

Annette's eyes opened and instinctively sought out the narrow shaft of light that came in from the parlor. They fixed upon it, narrowed, remained unmoving. Something was different this time. She knew she had not moved, that she was in the same room, the same bed. Pelu, if she called, would be just beyond the doorway. What was it that was different? From far in the back of her mind something seemed to be pushing forward. The thing she had tried to remember before was stirring. She could feel it and its imminence gave her an uneasy fear. She had tried to remember before. Now she did not want to. She closed her eyes tight and tried to lose the thing in the ensuing blackness. But still it came on, moving steadily forward, growing larger and larger until she was forced to recognize it.

"Pelu!" It was an agonized scream that shot through the bedroom and came back to her from the four walls.

The shaft of light widened as the door opened and the circle of lamplight came in. Annette was sitting up, her hands behind her, balancing her. Her hair was wild about her shoulders and her eyes were wide and black.

"Pelu!"

The older woman moved close, put both arms around her and held her close for a minute.

"It was today!"

"Yes."

"Oh, Pelu!" It was a cry of desperation, a half-groan. She wrenched herself away from Pelu and flung herself sideways across the bed, her face down. Her small body shook with sobs that were like no weeping Pelu had ever heard, deep and throaty and anguished. Each one seemed to tear from deep inside her. Pelu watched, helpless.

It was the day after Christmas. The front parlor of King Delaney's home was curtained and almost dark, although it was early afternoon. There was no fire lighted and dampness hung in the air, sending off musty odors from the upholstered furnishings. This in turn mingled with the scent of flowers which were banked against the walls and around the fireplace, looking for the most part fresh but showing here and there a curled brown petal. The total effect was one of depressing solitude, of intended gaiety halted or averted without warning. Agnes shivered as she entered and looked around. She pulled her bright wool shawl close about her shoulders and sat down, not relaxing, keeping her body tense.

"Hello, Agnes." She gave a start and turned. King was just coming into the room.

"I thought I might find you down here."

"Really?" There was no particular cordiality in her tone.

"Yes. I think I know quite well when you fancy being by yourself."

"Do you, now?" She could not keep out a trace of sarcasm.

"And one of the times is when you think you're going to be held to account for something."

"Well, of all the ridiculous notions! Now, what could you possibly hold me to account for?"

"Nothing. That's just it. I can't understand your attack of conscience."

"Heavens, you do twist a person around. I thought you left your lawyer manner in the courtroom." She was feeling uncomfortable, as though they were strangers. All their shared intimacies seemed to have slipped away or become in some manner blurred and hard to remember. She knew a moment of bitter resentment against Keith for doing this to her.

"I thought we might have a little talk." He had strolled to one window and was looking out, holding aside the heavy draperies.

"About what?"

He dropped the drapery, crossed the room and knelt down to light the fire. Then he straightened and looked down at her. He seemed enormously tall, looming over her. For an instant she thought of Delaney.

"About how soon you plan to get your son back here to marry Elizabeth."

Little darts of flame jumped up, licked around the kindling with a bright blaze, then settled down to the more subdued glow of the logs.

"Well!" She could not think how to answer his directness.

"He will come back, of course," King went on easily, turning away and leaning against the mantel, his back to the fire, both elbows crooked up to support him.

"Of course."

"He wouldn't have proposed to Elizabeth if he hadn't wanted to marry her."

"Naturally not."

His voice snapped out sharply, "Then what the devil did he run away for?"

Agnes felt a little tightening of fear at her throat. She remembered feeling the same thing years ago when she had first gone to Sacramento and Florabelle and Violet had died. Fear of Delaney. Only it had always been easy, somehow, to defeat Delaney. She tried to pull herself together with some dignity.

"How should I know?" She made her tone intentionally heartless to match his. Why wasn't he thinking of her feelings? Didn't he know she was suffering too?

"I guess you wouldn't." His expression had become sardonic. "You never did know your children very well."

"You don't have to be insulting!"

He did not seem to notice her indignation. His mind seemed to be rushing ahead, thinking of other things.

"It was that actress, I suppose."

"Yes, I suppose it was."

"There was a good bit of talk about it. I sent him to Sacramento so he'd be away from her, but apparently they thought of a way to continue this little affair."

"He's young, King."

Again he did not appear to listen. "There are two ways to do it. I'll leave it up to you. You can let it run its course or you can drag him back here by the scruff of the neck now. I think it might be wiser to wait. These things have a way of playing themselves out. When he's had his belly full he'll be ready to come back and it may be the kinder way. Talk will have died down then and we can arrange a quiet ceremony. I'll send them to Europe for a while."

"Whatever you say."

"I'm only concerned about Elizabeth and Margaret."

Agnes felt a sharp twinge that was both hurt and anger.

"I don't like to have them humiliated this way." He seemed to be directing the accusation at her more than at Keith. "Elizabeth's hurt more than anyone knows. It's unfortunate she was so fond of him. Margaret's taken it like a soldier, of course."

It was the "of course" that raked hurtingly over Agnes's bruised feelings. There was so much of tribute in the way he said it. Something hot and uncontrollable rose higher and higher in her until she could no longer sit still. Like a nervous animal she leaped up from the chair and walked a few steps, then turned and walked back to face him.

"Margaret!" she said scornfully. "Margaret's taken it like a soldier!" The words were acid-tipped. "How would you expect her to take it? She never wanted them to marry in the first place. She never thought he was good enough for her precious daughter because he wasn't one of the first Philadelphia families. Taken it like a soldier, has she? She's upstairs right now telling Elizabeth it's good riddance. Laughing up her sleeve at the lot of us!"

King's voice was surprisingly calm. "I doubt that, Agnes."

Agnes was too angry to pay attention to him. "And, what's more, you'll have a nice time trying to convince her when Keith does come back. She'll want to forget the whole thing."

"Don't concern yourself about that. Elizabeth wants him and she's going to have him. I'll see to it."

Agnes's exasperation was complete. "Not even your own daughter and you treat her as though she was breakable. Anything she wants—even my son! Lord, you'd think a man would have more sense than to make a complete fool of himself over another man's child."

For an instant a bleak, tired look came over his face.

"It's been unfortunate," he said in a queer flat voice. "It's been bad all the way around. All those people who knew—and the gifts. You'll see to those matters?"

She watched him and love for him flowed through her, strengthening and chastising her, making her feel a shame and repentance that were almost welcome.

"Yes, I'll see to it." She was happy in feeling subservient to him, grateful that he leaned on her, if only for this.

There was a light step in the doorway.

"Mother, have you seen Charles? I wanted to ask him if he'd made arrangements about the luggage—" Treese stopped and looked from one to the other, seeing Agnes's irritation and King's apparent indifference. She took a tentative step forward. "Your afternoon paper was in the vestibule, Uncle King."

He smiled his thanks at her and she crossed the room and handed it to him. She looked tired, worried, anxious. He put the paper down on the low table in front of him without looking at it.

"Thank you, dear. Have you seen Elizabeth?"

"Aunt Margaret's with her."

He nodded and looked down. There seemed nothing more to say. Agnes did not look at her, as though seeking to drive her away by indifference.

Suddenly both women were aware of a change in King. He seemed to stiffen slightly and grow taut. They followed his eyes to the newspaper, watched it with a slow sense of growing horror as he picked the paper up and unfolded it. For a moment he read silently. Then he threw it down and looked at Agnes, seemingly unaware that Treese was still there. He had grown almost pallid with something that might have been rage or grief, or a little of both, but which to Agnes seemed like a denial of everything they had been to each other in the past. It was stolid, completely impersonal. When he spoke it was the voice of a stranger.

"Your son, madam," he said slowly, "was married last night."

PART THREE

Treese

1856

CHAPTER I

"THE CONVENTION of Nigger worshippers came together in this city yesterday." Charles smiled and looked over the newspaper he was reading, around the dining-room table from Treese to Agnes. The May night was warm and they had finished a meal which none except Charles had eaten with any relish—saddle of mutton, boiled potatoes smothered in heavy gravy, mashed, watery turnips. Agnes was taking occasional sips from her demitasse but Treese only stirred hers listlessly.

Charles continued with the newspaper article he was reading.

"Resolutions and policies bordering on dangerous fanaticism were drawn up, chief among them being opposition to the extension of slave territory and slave power, the welcoming of 'honest and industrious' immigrants, speedy settlement of land titles in this state, and construction of a transcontinental railroad with aid from Congress.

"This newspaper's only surprise is that the Congregational Church would permit its sacred precincts to be so far violated as to house these hoodlums who with much braggadocio are calling themselves the first state Republican convention. Prominent in the organization of the new party are the merchant Leland Stanford and E. B. Crocker, who is chairman of the gathering."

Charles paused again.

"Is that all?" Agnes asked. Since Charles had developed the habit of reading choice bits of news aloud from the paper after dinner each night, she had cultivated a sort of disinterested patience which seemed to her the easiest way out of the situation. Treese accepted the after-dinner ritual placidly, but she seemed almost never to really listen, and only roused herself enough to answer when a question was put to her or when some comment seemed expected of her. Yet her indifference was not a quiet state. It was seldom that her hands were quiet or that her eyes did not move restlessly about the room. Agnes often became irritated to the point of speaking sharply to her, as she seemed nearly ready to do now.

"Well, no, there's more. But all in the same vein. They say they wouldn't be surprised to see it broken up the way the other meetings and debates were this spring."

"My."

"Even if the Republicans never amount to much, they'll still keep the vote split. And Broderick's not out of the running yet, don't forget."

Agnes sighed. "Heavens, I wish they'd elect that man senator and be done with it. All that ridiculous wrangling last year in the legislature and then leaving us with only John Weller in the Senate and all because they couldn't agree."

"Oh, he's not through yet, don't you worry. He's as strong as he ever was here, and in San Francisco too. Only that fellow King's giving him plenty of trouble right now."

"King?" The name shot through Agnes, brought her spine up rigid.

"James King of William. Edits the *Bulletin* there in San Francisco. And he's got it in for the Broderick crowd. I understand they're betting in the streets on how much longer King'll stay alive. Broderick doesn't like that kind of fooling around. But King won't let up. Keeps blasting away every issue of the paper."

Agnes relaxed. This sort of thing was of little interest to her. It was stuffy in the dining room. The oil chandelier hung low over their heads and seemed to concentrate the heat. The smoke from Charles's cigar was sucked up into the shaft of light every time he exhaled. She looked at Treese, whose small silver coffee spoon tinkled against the cup as she stirred. The sound made Agnes edgy. She was getting too jumpy lately. Nothing had been the same since December. It hadn't been easy, either. Never seeing Keith except on rare occasions like the time in the street when he was with that woman, his arm around her and laughing down at her. Agnes could have cheerfully clawed her eyes out, but instead she swept by, barely nodding. Afterward, though, she had had a peculiar feeling of loneliness and frustration, as if the slight had hardly touched them. And then having to face every woman in town, go to teas and the theater and parties and keep her head up and never let on how she'd been hurt. Even that she could live through, though. It was this thing with King that was killing her by inches.

"—certainly going to see some fireworks in San Francisco one of these days or I miss my guess."

"You really think so, Charles?"

His reply slipped past her, unheard. You'd think King would have sense enough to see she wasn't responsible for what had happened. Oh, it wasn't so much outwardly. They were still in the hydraulics venture up north together, but in that Charles acted more or less as a plodding go-between. And he had been to visit her once. Only once. She remembered how she'd gone out of her way to have everything as usual for him. And yet all the time she'd had the feeling things were different between them. After he had gone she had looked at herself in the mirror and noticed for the first time the ever so slight extra bulk around her waist, the barely noticeable layer of loose skin and tissue under her chin. For the first time she faced the fact that she was forty years old.

"And by the Lord, you mark my words, if much more happens, Broderick's going to find his back to the wall and all his machine won't help him. They may say the old Committee of 'Fifty-one is dead. But William Coleman isn't dead, and neither are the Vigilantes, or I'm off my guess. Wait and see."

Charles was reddening with the heat of his own one-sided argument and his cigar was growing frayed where his teeth clenched it.

Strange, to think that Charles was forty-two. A son-in-law two years older than herself. That was a good thought. It made her feel younger. But he was certainly putting on weight. It gave him a sunken, underslung look, especially when he sat at the table like this and let his belly slump forward. His hair was thinning too, growing back to two deep points of bare scalp on either side of his forehead. Well, in all honesty she couldn't envy Treese a man like that. It was remarkable the way King had kept his youthful vigor and trim build.

Charles relit the dead butt of his cigar and drew in. He always asked the ladies if they minded his smoking and then proceeded to light his cigar without waiting for the automatic assent.

"Oh, by the way, had you heard anything about Margaret taking Elizabeth east, Agnes?" Charles brought this up casually, but the crafty sideward glance he shot her showed that he had been saving it.

Agnes's lower jaw dropped slightly and even Treese sat up straighter and began to pay attention.

"Taking her east!"

"So I heard. Just a bit of gossip on the street. And you know how unreliable those stories are apt to be. The way I heard it, she's been moping around so ever since what happened that Margaret is worried about her health. So they're both going back to Philadelphia for a few months. And I suppose to get Elizabeth a husband."

"Elizabeth doesn't need to have anybody 'get' her a husband." Treese spoke for the first time, a trace of indignation in her voice.

"Well, my dear, you know what talk is. I'm merely repeating what I heard. And, according to this party, Elizabeth is absolutely wild over it. Refuses to stir one foot out of San Francisco till it looks as though they'll have to tie her up to get her on the stage."

"What wretched gossip!" Treese exclaimed. Her gray eyes looked large and dark tonight in her face.

Charles was instantly agreeable. "Isn't it, though? The sort of things people repeat. Absolutely revolting. But I suppose there must be some truth in it. What do you think, Agnes?"

Agnes was no longer listening. She was staring straight ahead, her eyes blazing with excitement, her mouth trembling slightly. Margaret going to Philadelphia! And taking Elizabeth with her! That would solve everything. That would be just the opportunity she had been needing. With both of them out of the way and with King all to herself, she was sure to win him back.

"Are you sure?" she breathed.

"As sure as you can be on the strength of a bit of gossip." Charles was obviously enjoying the reactions he had drawn from both of them. He felt the evening was a success.

"Well!" Agnes said. She breathed out heavily, and there was triumph in every line of her face. "Well!"

At the same moment, in the dusty room that was both legal office and living quarters for Andrew J. Hart, attorney at law, Andy was sitting back in a rickety chair, his feet propped up on the scarred oak desk, reading and interspersing his reading with long rambling periods of introspection. He was not really interested in the written matter before him. It contained a list of grievances drawn up by an irate client against his neighbor, who, it seemed, "had caused to be erected without the knowledge and consent of said client a stout wooden fence, partition or barricade separating the properties of the two said individuals. And whereas the neighbor had in said manner annexed without the will, knowledge or consent of the said client a fine apple tree bearing excellent fruit which grew at least three feet within the property of said client as surveyed by Thomas P. Link-letter, licensed surveyor as of October third, 1854—"

Andy rubbed his eyes, pushing his spectacles back to accomplish the business. Then he straightened the spectacles, blinked, and

looked back at the paper. But he was no longer reading. His eyes
had lost their focus, become distant. The night was too warm for
legality. For the letter of the law. A good case, now, with ramifications that were not on paper. That he would welcome. But these
goddam fences and horses and wives. Well, people were made up
of such everyday things. It was the fabric of their existence. And
their eternal small possessiveness, their bickerings, their jealousies,
these were the bread and butter in Andy's gaunt belly. Well enough
to be superior and bored about them. They were what he lived by.
He supposed his attitude was a form of intellectual snobbery, and
wondered a little at finding himself guilty of it. But many things
were different now.

He swung his legs to the floor and stood up. He walked across
the room, took a bottle off the shelf over his narrow bed and
uncorked it, taking a healthy pull. He replaced the cork, returned
to the desk and methodically resumed his previous position. Funny,
a man never seemed too old to go through phases. When he had
first come west he had been a lascivious bastard, going after every
woman who caught his fancy, living every day—how did they say
it?—up to the hilt. Then he had been by turns an ingenuous suitor,
a disappointed lover. Now he was what? The lean ascetic. That
sounded good. He repeated it to himself. Only he could have said a
frustrated lonely man and it would have been equally true. Except
that he didn't like the words as well. They were too blunt, too lacking the sheen of vagueness.

Well, she was going away. When she came back, if she ever did,
there'd be another young man, handsome and vacuous and appropriate. And it would be as final as it would have been with Keith.
Only he couldn't help being glad it wasn't Keith. He didn't know
why, exactly. Except that he'd been glad when it happened. Sorry
for her, but that was only an obligatory feeling. Beyond it, behind
and far inside of him had been a rejoicing so loud it threatened to
split his eardrum. She hadn't married him. She didn't belong to him
and she never would. Theoretically, she was still free, still available.
Knowing that she would never belong to him had not troubled him
greatly. That was a factual point, like something established by
precedent in the law. It was there, inflexible, but over and above it
was the human element, the atavistic human relationship that made
her fair game for any man who might win her. Knowing that it
would never be he had somehow not seemed important to Andy.
The lean ascetic. He repeated it to himself with a certain morbid
satisfaction.

"—and that the produce from said tree has been sworn, avowed and attested to as a not inconsiderable factor in the annual income of the said client—"

Andy tossed the paper down and folded his hands across his chest, staring up at the ceiling. The whisky he had drunk was taking effect in small relaxing ways.

He and Steve Mallott were a lot alike in some ways, he reflected. Both wanting women so bad it was twisting their guts inside them, yet always just beyond the pale because the women they wanted were not for them. And he had thought to find a new equality in the West! Well, it had been here for a while. It had been here in those first raw days when gold was the measure of a man's success, and when a man who had been a chimney sweep back east might own the best horses and the best women in town here. Now gold was still the measure, but in a different way. Something more went with it. Steve Mallott had plenty of money but he wasn't in it with the Delaneys for class. That was the whole thing right there. The social distinctions and barriers that had been built up. Artificially, of course, and by women like Agnes Delaney, because they raised her own stock in the town. You had to hand it to that young Keith, though, he'd stood up on his hind legs and done something about it. God, how that must have made Agnes Delaney squirm!

But of course it wasn't fair really to compare his own case with Steve's. Treese was married. And people like the Delaneys didn't get divorces. Besides, Treese was timid and shy and reticent and she'd never even spoken to Steve alone. With Steve it was more a visionary business. But with him—with Andy—he'd kissed Elizabeth once. No, twice. Felt the warmth of her next to him. Smelled her hair, watched it glisten palely in the dark. That put him in a class by himself, he thought, almost triumphantly. Then he laughed a little. Even in frustration there were classes.

The knock at the door was so soft that at first he thought he had imagined it. When it came louder he frowned and got up, tucking his flannel shirt into his trousers. If it was legal business, he was in no mood for it. He wouldn't answer at all except that whoever it was must have seen the crack of light under the door.

He crossed the room and flung the door open. His heart leaped up and started a pounding that he felt sure must fill the whole room.

"Hello, Elizabeth."

"Andy. May I come in?" She was standing there, tired and pale and disheveled in her black traveling cloak. Her yellow hair was down about her shoulders. He thought she had never looked so beautiful, so desirable.

He held the door aside for her and motioned her to the narrow bed, the only comfortable seat in the room. He took a chair near. But not too near. He was wary, on guard, now that the first thrill had spent itself.

"Aren't you out late?"

"I took the stage out of San Francisco." There seemed no more to explain. Her voice was tired but there was a thin-drawn note of desperation in it.

"You're going to visit here for a while?" He knew she was not here on any ordinary visit, but asking conventional questions seemed the only line of procedure.

"No. I want to stay here."

"Stay here?"

"Andy, Mother wants to take me east." Her eyes had a pleading quality. Pleading for what?

"So I'd heard."

"I can't go. I couldn't bear it. I'd die."

"You die easy." He smiled as he said it but he knew it was cruel. Why did he want to hurt her?

"Andy, please understand. I can't go. I want to stay here. Once you—a long time ago—" She stopped. It seemed more difficult than she had thought it would be. She plunged into it. "Andy, do you still want to marry me?"

Andy thought it strange that he was so unsurprised. Something about the way she had stood in the doorway had given him a wordless warning. He had known then that it would be something like this.

"You want to stay near him," he said thoughtfully. He was amazed at his own rational calm.

"No!" Her voice rose high. "There's nothing to talk about. I only want to know whether you still want to marry me."

Something warm started inside him. Something that was no longer rational or calm. Something that was the wanting of months and of years. And now it was being offered to him. He could take it or not as he chose. But he knew he was only putting it that way to be dramatic. He knew there was no doubt about his answer.

"Yes, I still want to."

She looked at him, relief and tiredness and a sudden limpness in her face and body.

"When?"

"Right away?"

"Tomorrow."

"All right, tomorrow." She started to draw her cloak around her. She had settled her business and in a matter of seconds. The deal was concluded.

"But you can stay here tonight," Andy said. His voice was as taut as hers had been, as full of frayed undertones. She looked at him and her face said that she understood. It was not an invitation, it was a condition. That much she would have to give him.

CHAPTER II

THE TALL YOUNG MAN opened the door of Andy Hart's law office and walked in hesitantly. Once inside he removed his wide felt hat and turned it in his hands while he surveyed the interior. Books were piled on the floor for want of shelves, and a patina of dust served to neutralize the color and appearance of the entire room. The oak desk, littered with papers, had an empty whisky bottle for a paperweight. The young man cleared his throat and shuffled his feet uneasily. He might have been a little over thirty and he had a kind of saturnine good looks that showed in dark hair, heavy brooding eyebrows, a thin mouth and deep-set eyes that seemed to burn intensely, giving his face a pointed, purposeful look. He was wearing what was evidently his best suit. The black coat had been brushed and pressed, and the trousers, tucked into shiny boots, had a preserved look about them. His sleeves were short for him; the wrists that protruded from them were red and bony. His hands were big-knuckled and calloused.

There was a sound from the small room adjoining and the door opened. Andy emerged in his shirt sleeves, a decrepit coffeepot in one hand. He waved it at the young man in greeting.

"Morning."

"Mornin'."

"Make yourself comfortable. I'll be in directly."

Andy disappeared and the young man seated himself gingerly in one of the straight chairs, trying to keep the dust from coming in contact with his trousers. He continued to turn his hat in his hands. His gaze was fixed on the door through which Andy had disappeared. In a moment Andy returned. He went to the desk, flung himself down behind it and raised his feet to its top.

"You won't mind if I don't put on my coat? I charge extra for it anyway."

"No, sir. It don't matter."

Andy's now clean-shaven face looked worn and there was weariness in the slump of his thin body as he slid down in the chair. He was accustomed to summoning up affability for the least of men or animals, but this morning it was plainly an effort. Nevertheless, his grin, which fitted into well-worn grooves at each corner of his mouth, seemed to put the young man at ease. The latter relaxed slightly in the chair but his face never lost its look of concentration.

"I need some legal advice," he said with deliberation, spacing each word thoughtfully. "Sign outside says you're a lawyer, and by the looks of your place here you wouldn't charge too high." Andy grinned.

"Continue."

"I come to see you on a matter about my land."

Andy's eyes swept him quickly. "You farming?"

The young man nodded. "Name's John Trask. I got a place along the river up Marysville way."

"And what's this matter about your land?"

"I aim to sue somebody."

"Who?"

"The Delaneys."

Andy paused and stared, and let his breath out in a whistle. "No wonder you got up early."

"That's why I come to you. I figgered you could handle the suing for me and maybe not charge too high. I got the money, mind, but I don't aim to get mixed up with any crooked lawyer'll take my eyeteeth."

"Wait a minute!" Andy was still staring at the young man in disbelief. "You want me to sue the Delaneys for you?"

"That's the idea. You want to take the case?"

"But I don't understand. What are you suing them for?"

"Damages. To my land."

"How did they damage it?"

"With their damned mines. That water poundin' and roarin' every minute of the day till it makes your head spin. It washes into the river, all the runoff from the sluice boxes; the water's startin' to rise already. And it comes off the ridges too. Their land's a mite higher than mine. Over my fields and washin' my topsoil away. I aim to sue 'em and put an end to it."

Andy was thoughtful for a minute. He got up and walked to the unwashed window and looked out. He put his hands in his pockets and faced the young man, who had turned in the chair to follow him with his eyes.

"Well, I'll tell you, John—" He hesitated.

John Trask's voice shot back contemptuously. "Scared of 'em?"

Andy strolled back to the desk and perched on the edge of it.

"No, not scared. I just don't want to see you throw your money away."

"I can get a lawyer who's not so fussy!" John started to rise.

Andy reached out and shoved him back into the chair. "Who?" he asked. "Think you'd find a lawyer in Sacramento'd take a case against King and Agnes Delaney? Not a chance, my friend."

"I didn't come for no advice I don't pay for."

"Don't be so damned independent. I'll take your money if that'll satisfy you. All I say is, don't go off half cocked and think you're going to win any case against the Delaneys, because they'll take the skin right off your back. You'll be lucky if you get out of that lawsuit with your shirt, much less your land."

"It's my land. Nobody's takin' it."

"I wouldn't be too sure. King Delaney knows the judge by his first name. Any judge in California."

"If a man's got the price of a lawyer he can get what's his by right. This is a free country."

"Well, it sounds nice to say so. But take my advice and don't tangle with the Delaneys."

"I don't aim to break my back over that farm and then stand by and see it all washed to hell."

"What do you do when the floods come?"

"You expect the floods. You look for 'em and build a levee and then when the waters go down it's over. It's not like this. This comes and stays. Not all at once like a flood, but just a mite at a time. Just an inch maybe, but you can see it comin'. And it don't go down. It stays. And what about the water that washes down the ridges? Am I goin' to build a levee around that? Around every field I own?"

"The river isn't high yet, is it?"

"Not yet. Not even hardly to notice. But I can tell. It's creepin' up slow-like, and one of these days all hell'll break loose and my farm'll be floatin' down the Sacramento."

"Maybe not for years. Maybe never."

"I don't aim to take chances. I got two boys'll get this farm when I'm gone, and I aim to leave it in shape for 'em, not two feet under water."

Andy frowned thoughtfully. "You're a man of forethought, John. In twenty years maybe every farmer in the Sacramento Valley will see what you see now and be mad as all hell about it. But the damage will be done. There's a disadvantage to being foresighted. It puts you into a peculiarly frustrated position. Nobody listens until it's too late, and then there's not much to be done."

"I don't aim to wait," John repeated doggedly.

Andy walked around the desk and sank back into his chair, swinging his feet up. "Take my advice and don't go to court."

"If I'm goin' to fight 'em, I want to do it legal."

"Oh, it'd be legal, all right. Only thing is, it'd be their law. I know King Delaney. Known him for years. And he's all right till you tangle with him. But he couldn't lose a case in California if he tried. Do what I say and stay out of court."

The young man's shoulders sank dejectedly. Andy grew cajoling. "Why don't you dig up your own land and look for gold? It's probably right under your feet."

John Trask scowled. "There's gold there, all right. Only it's not under any ground. It's right there on top and I put it there with my two hands. I'm no miner, I'm a farmer."

"Well, in that case you'd better resign yourself."

"To what? Doin' nothin'?"

"I wish I could help you—"

John Trask's deep eyebrows grew black across his forehead. "I don't give a damn what you say. They're not goin' to get away with it. I'm not the only one whose land's at stake. Other farmers will be in it too. And the rivermen don't like it much either, I can tell you. That river'll be too damned shallow in a few years for anything bigger'n a flat-bottomed scow. I can talk to them."

"I'm afraid I was right the first time. You're too early. By several years."

"Never mind that. I'll do somethin'. Only you might have been right about one thing. Maybe takin' 'em to court ain't the way to get things rollin'." John seemed to be talking to himself now, his mind working rapidly ahead of his slow deliberate speech. "Maybe there's a better way. Maybe if I go round and talk to the men. Make 'em see."

"Well, maybe. But I wouldn't count on it. The fellows in the labor unions tried it and didn't get far. Too damned much labor. For every man that quits or strikes they can bring in a Chink to do his work for a quarter the wage."

"They can't do that with us. They've still got to eat. We've got 'em there. If we can get an organization strong enough so's they start worryin' about their stomachs they'll listen to us, all right."

"That takes money."

"I got money."

"And leaders."

The two men looked at each other hard. Then Andy shook his head slowly. "Not me."

"Then I'll get leaders."

"Your leaders must be men of experience and education. They've got to know the ropes. They've got to know people like the Delaneys. Not from the outside, but from the inside. Where would you find anyone like that?"

"I calc'late if I look hard enough I'll find one."

Andy sighed and shook his head hopelessly. Something in him went out to the grimly determined young man. He felt a tightening in his chest, a sudden surprising longing to feel as intensely as this young man did about anything in life. To know it again. To feel its throbbing once more. Anything but this dull defeatism, this feeling of everything worth struggling for being past. Tired out and nothing gained. And yet certainly he could not take a case against his own father-in-law. Fancy him anyway, battling in court against the smooth flow of King's ready oratory, aligning himself with ridiculously feeble armor against King's formidable array of power and prestige. Even though he knew King would only laugh at him and refuse to bear a grudge. Even so, it was unthinkable. He paused and smiled wryly at the sophistry he was permitting himself. A year ago—six months—he would have taken the case.

"I wish there was something I could do," he repeated ineffectually.

"I wish there was," John said thoughtfully. "But I reckon dif'rent men is made outa dif'rent goods. That's the way the world runs. You probably got your reasons for not wantin' to mix in it."

"I told you my reasons. You're twenty years too soon."

John's grasp was strong, calloused. "Much obliged." He opened the door and went out.

Andy watched him go, followed his progress up the street. There was only one person in Sacramento who'd be damned fool enough to take a case like that. He wondered if John Trask would think to go to Keith Delaney.

He walked back to the desk and dropped heavily into his chair. He took out paper and pen and spread them in front of him, but for several minutes he sat without writing anything.

In loving Elizabeth hopelessly he had had more than now. He had had buoyancy, his freedom, the leeway to hope. In winning her he had been so utterly defeated. How had it happened? She had been different before. There had never been a moment when she was not exhibiting some definite reaction to the world around her. Delight, exuberance, anger, dismay. She had always been demonstrative and it was this utter frankness he had so loved. Now it was gone, completely and as blankly as though it had never been. And there was only the eternal indifference that lay between them. He wondered whether things would have turned out differently if he had not been demanding of her that first night she came here to his office. If he had proceeded more slowly, allowed matters to take their course, waited until they were married. And yet of all the nights that was the only one in which she had ever given herself to him completely, showed him any responsiveness at all.

John's coming had brought it all into sharper focus, had added to the burden of hopelessness the sharp edge of bitter irony. For he knew that six months, a year before, he would have leaped at the chance to stand up for John, to beat his fists against King. It was the sort of thing he loved. Not because of any particular altruism on his part, but simply because of the challenge it offered. Even against his better judgment he would have taken it.

And today he had not accepted the challenge. Was it really for the reason he had given John Trask, that the farmers' cause was premature? There was no mistaking the wisdom of that. Or was it because King was Elizabeth's stepfather and because she had always been fond of him, and because Andy himself could not have borne the anger that he might have risked adding to her coolness? There seemed to be no fight left in him. Everything in him that was responsive to the world and man, causes and challenges had somehow seeped away. It must have been a gradual process, for he had been unaware of either its beginning or its progress. All he knew was that he was faced with the accomplished fact. It was this realization that was hardest of all. This, and the knowledge that John Trask might go to Keith Delaney, and that if he did, Keith would make him welcome and listen to his story and think for a minute and then say, "Tell me more." He knew, although he scarcely knew Keith, what the outcome would be. He felt bitterly alone, an outsider, aligned against both of them, wanting desperately to be one of them.

He picked up the pen wearily, held it poised over the paper. How could he say it? How could he explain the unexplainable truth?

He wrote "Dear Miss Margaret:" then paused again. At last he began the body of the letter, writing with many pauses and hesitations.

"I know you must have been looking for word from one of us, but the truth is that business and legal matters have been keeping me much occupied—" This was the embroidery, the false cheerfulness that propriety demanded. "Until at last I feel thoroughly ashamed for so long neglecting you. I trust Elizabeth has written before this. I feel I must tell you, however"—getting into the meat of it—"that her constant preoccupation gives me some cause for concern. I do not wish to alarm you, but I would consider it more than a kindness if at some near future date you could arrange to pay us a visit. I think having you near might do much to alleviate the melancholy that I see every day in her . . ."

He stopped writing, examined the words. He threw the pen down and let his head rest forward in both his hands. In the grubby little room around him sunlight was fighting its way into corners, nudging through dust, catching in the drifting motes. It made a pattern of light and shadow on the floor, created vagaries and illusions on the scarred desktop. It caught luminously in the inkwell and slipped over the half-written sheet. Only when it reached Andy did it seem in some manner halted, for the whole of his figure was shadowy, clothed in a darkening nimbus. For the first time Andy Hart looked quite out of place in the cheerfully dusty, sunlit old office.

He had not intended to tell Elizabeth about John Trask's visit, but when they were alone in their room that night with the long silent evening lying before them he did bring it up conversationally. Her reaction surprised him.

"Why didn't you take it?" she asked sharply. She was sitting in a chair near the lamp, her workbasket on her lap but her hands idle and uninterested.

He looked at her curiously. "I don't know. For any number of reasons. Because it wouldn't have done any good, for one thing. There's not enough strength behind it yet to get anywhere. It would take years for those farmers to gather enough force to fight such a case. Even with the rivermen backing them up, as they eventually will."

"And for another thing"—she smiled a one-sided smile—"there's the matter of Father."

"It wouldn't have been very tactful on my part. To get into a big family feud."

"If the thing had been reversed, Father wouldn't have hesitated to fight you."

Andy spread his hands and shrugged. "Well, that may be."

"I don't want to ever influence you, even indirectly. Whatever you think is right"—she paused and looked down at her lap—"is all right with me too."

If she had said it tenderly, he would have bounded across the room and kissed her. But she said it matter-of-factly and without emotion. And even at that he found himself holding tight to the arms of the chair to keep from leaping up and going to her. It was so little. But it was something.

CHAPTER III

AGNES WENT to the door of the hotel room and opened it.

"Well!" she said. She stepped back to permit him to enter the room. She said nothing while he threw his beaver hat on a chair and walked to the windows, unbuttoning his coat, but her attitude was plainly belligerent. Her hands, tightened into fists, were on her hips. Her mouth was pursed angrily. He looked out the window for a moment, pulling the lace curtain aside to do so.

"Hot tonight."

"I'm sure you didn't come here to discuss the weather." She strode over to him. "Although why you did come is a mystery to me. After letting me wait here—sweltering in this abominable hotel room for four days—"

"Three. And I didn't invite you here." King let the curtain drop and sagged wearily into a chair. His face, in spite of the heat, had a cold grayish pallor. Deep lines had appeared about the corners of his nose and mouth. His eyes were bloodshot. Looking at him, Agnes fought back a wave of maternal pity that was strangely mingled with desire. Anger rose quickly to the surface again.

"Well, I'm glad I did come. We're going to have this thing out once and for all. The way you've been treating me ever since

Christmas! You act as if the whole thing had been my fault. I don't see why any of it makes any difference about us. And I'm sick and tired of wasting away in that revolting wilderness—"

He smiled faintly. "Come now, my dear. No city boasting a mansion with the proportions of yours can quite adequately be called a wilderness. And don't you think it was a bit indiscreet of you to come here the minute Margaret left to visit Elizabeth?"

"You never were so worried about discretion before!" She was still standing defiantly, looking down at him.

He shook his head, still with a kind of humorous sadness. "Alas, my past recklessness returns to plague me. Agnes dear, sit down. There are so many things I have to tell you."

She made a little switching motion with the skirts of her pale-blue dressing gown as though from irritation at his slow deviousness.

"For heaven's sake, get to the point! What's changed between us? Why aren't things as they used to be?" Sensing that it was not as simple as all that, for all her direct insistence, she dropped into a chair near him, wishing that it was not so warm. She was conscious that her face was shiny, her hair becoming disarranged. She felt she needed the full resources of her beauty tonight, and almost unconsciously she tilted her chin slightly upward to conceal the new plumpness of her throat.

"Agnes—" He stopped, pressing back his hair at the temples, a line appearing between his brows. How gray he was becoming, Agnes thought. But, then, she'd seen him so little lately. She let her chin drop a trifle so that she was more comfortable.

"Agnes, have you heard of the Vigilantes?"

She let her breath out in an impatient rush. "Oh, Lord! Is there anything else to hear of these days? The men can't talk of another thing. It's the Vigilantes this and the Vigilantes that, and William Coleman and Sam Brannan this and that until we're ready to die from it."

Again the wry smile, so strange to King. "That may be more accurate than you know, Agnes."

"For heaven's sake! I didn't come here to—"

"I know." He closed his eyes wearily, then opened them with effort. He raised himself a little in the chair as though it required great exertion. "Well, now, Agnes, there are many things I have to tell you. Some of them you may not understand. I had hoped our relationship might taper off gracefully, that we might avoid some of this. But apparently—well, women have a way of enjoying death struggles."

"King!"

He did not appear to hear her. "So, that being the case, it appears we must have one. And I don't doubt ours will do the long history of parting lovers adequate justice." He hitched forward in the chair, folding his hands and resting his elbows on his knees. "To begin with—well, yes, I was emotionally upset over Elizabeth last winter. She'd counted on the wedding so much. It just about finished her off. I'm still not sure that it hasn't. It went pretty deep with me. You know I always thought of her as my own. And I couldn't reconcile myself to her unhappiness. Still can't, but the world seems to be moving on in spite of it, and we must move too. I suppose that's why I didn't come to see you oftener. Not so much that I felt you to be personally responsible, but that I was in no mood for love-making, to put it bluntly."

Agnes winced, but she remained silent.

"Margaret and I began to grow together more. We found resources in each other that we'd long since forgotten. Or at least I had. We found comfort in each other. It was—well, something you wouldn't understand, I'm afraid. It was more than I deserved, to have her there, to know her comfort and compassion. And she never reproached me. She must have known that would have been the breaking point with me. I couldn't have taken any more—not just then, though God knows she took a lot more all these years."

Agnes was close to explosion.

"That was the reason, actually. And it might have gone on that way. For truthfully I couldn't bring myself to miss you. I don't mean to sound heartless, but how else can I make you see? That was the way it was until May. There was no incentive for me to continue seeing you. And in May the thing that happened made it impossible altogether."

Something in the finality of his tone clutched at her throat.

"What?" she said. Her voice was smaller than life size.

He looked down at his hands, placing the tips of his fingers together and studying them carefully.

"The Vigilantes."

She stared at him in frank astonishment. "The Vigilantes! What in heaven's name have they to do with it? The Vigilantes got themselves a lot of guns from some place and strung up two murderers. That's all. They surely didn't come over to you and threaten you at the point of a gun to stop seeing me!"

"Practically," he said calmly.

"King, are you out of your mind?"

"This is the part I knew would be difficult, because it involves trends and attitudes and people themselves, none of them subjects in which you have a deep and perceiving interest."

"If you're trying to call me stupid in a nice way—"

"No, my dear. We have all made the same mistakes. We've taken too much for granted here in the West. We've assumed people as a whole are louts and blunderheads and that anything can be put over on them—"

"Who's we?" she demanded suspiciously.

"Let's say everyone who finds himself in my shoes today. That's obtuse enough to keep you wondering until I finish my explanation. Well, we've held the reins, the purse strings, most of the cards. And now it's run out. We've worn it thin and it won't work any longer. There are thirty-five hundred armed men up on Sacramento Street at Fort Gunnybags who say it won't."

A little cloud of worry showed in Agnes's dark eyes. When he began to talk like this of issues and men and guns she could take a concerned interest; worry for his safety if need be. These things had no bearing on them or their love. "King, why in the world are you telling me these things? Is it because you're in danger? You've never done anything wrong. Why should you be afraid?"

"Right and wrong," he said gravely, "are questions of the moment. What is eminently right in one set of circumstances might be fatal in another. That's how it was in the West when we first came here. Every man was a law unto himself, and the devil take the hindmost. You couldn't steal a horse without risking your neck, but you could kill a man and still be reasonably sure of getting off in time for supper, if you had a good lawyer."

She spoke breathlessly. "Like King Delaney?"

He smiled faintly. "So far, at least, you follow me. Yes, I did well for myself. Murder was common enough so that I made out quite handsomely. And on the side there were claim-jumping issues and property disputes, and of course there was always real estate. Never mind if the building was built over running sewage or sinking ground; sell it at a thousand per cent profit and move on."

"You sound so virtuous and repentant all of a sudden."

He looked at her with something that was almost amusement showing in the tired lines of his face. "It's a case of the devil being sick and trying to act the saint, I suppose. No use saying I didn't know what I was doing at the time. I did, and I was glad to do it. I was glad to be rich and have the best house in town up on the hill. Glad to give Margaret and Elizabeth the best of everything.

Oh, I hadn't any regrets then. And I haven't any now, I suppose. Not real ones. Only, the reckoning has come."

"What reckoning?" Agnes had forgotten her earlier anger in this new anxiety.

"People like me are on the black list. They're on the way out. Law and order has ushered itself in with a vengeance, Agnes. And this is no political purge. Those men have guns."

Agnes had grown white with fear. "But they're taking the law into their own hands! They can't do that. What's the governor doing to stop it? They've no right—"

"Who can say who has the right?" King asked slowly. "The right belongs to whoever has the power. Broderick and his machine had the power for a long time. They aren't through even yet, and Broderick himself won't be touched—he's too big a man. The Vigilantes will let him alone. But the rest of us, well, we'll have to stand and answer charges. One afternoon in a hotel room, a long time ago, Broderick asked me for my support. I told him I bet only on sure things—that I'd stick with him as long as he was winning. I found out later you don't get out of a thing that easily. And I found that I was stuck with my dubious loyalty, like it or not."

"But what does that mean to you? To us? What difference can it make?"

"It means, my dear, that I'm going to become the most respectable lawyer this side of St. Louis. I'm going to defend widows and orphans, contribute loudly to every charity I can find, be a family man, attend the Episcopal church on Sundays and do my best to turn in this fairly trim physique for one with at least a slight potbelly. And along with my other pleasant vices, I'm giving you up."

"Me!" The fury rose again, white and uncompromising.

"Respectability's at a premium in San Francisco, Agnes."

"I don't care about respectability! You can't just throw me away like that!"

He tried to keep his voice gentle. "I wanted to do it easily, Agnes. I didn't want a scene. Unfortunately, there's no way out. Do you realize the city's virtually under martial law now? The governor's powerless to act. Admiral Farragut's out there at Mare Island now. The governor ordered him to bombard the city and disperse the Vigilantes, and Farragut refused. Major General Wood refused to send arms and ammunition from Benecia to use against them. The whole state's behind the Vigilantes. It's no puny insurrection. It's a popular revolution. Do you think I have a fancy for being caught in the middle of it?"

"So you'll throw me away with no more consideration than that!"

"I can be respectable and save my neck, or I can take my chances with you."

"And you haven't the gumption—"

"Let's say I haven't the inclination. It suits me better to be respectable. I'm over fifty, you know. Not old enough to be senile— I could still enjoy your bed a lot, Agnes. But old enough to have a certain longing for security. I have a lot of good years ahead of me. I want to have some kind of insurance for their tranquillity."

"Well, of all the insulting—" Genuinely hurt now, she was close to tears. He saw and tried to be gentle.

"If I've told you harshly, my dear, it's because I believed no other course except honesty would work with you. I haven't meant to hurt you. You've given me some of the happiest moments I've known. Some of the most painful too, perhaps, but that's all past and we'll keep only the good with us."

She grasped at a straw. "You can't leave me like this. We're business partners! What about that? What about the hydraulics? What about all the money you've invested?" Her tone carried a certain triumph.

He seemed to be bracing himself for another reluctant task.

"We—are not—exactly—partners," he said slowly, spacing the words with effort.

"Not partners!" Her laugh ridiculed him stridently. "Why, we've been together in it from the very first. What do you mean— not partners?"

He paused, then chose his words slowly, speaking without looking directly at her. "There were certain precautions—certain measures, shall we say, which I considered it wise to take from the very first. Not, perhaps, that I anticipated an eventuality of this sort. I looked for nothing so drastic. But I could see disadvantages, encumbrances, to any binding agreements for either of us. I felt that investments, separately handled, would be of greater benefit to us both. It would give us greater leeway. Frankly, I felt that such a partnership would also be too open-faced an insult to Margaret."

The veins in Agnes's plump neck stood out angrily.

"I took it for granted," he continued, "that you would understand and respect my judgment. I trusted that in the long run you'd approve."

Agnes strove for calmness. This was business, and nothing she felt personally must dim her perspective of it.

"Exactly what is the arrangement?" she inquired coldly.

"Simplicity in the essence. Half the holdings are yours, half are mine. Separate deeds. The machinery is mostly yours. What little is in my name I'll gladly turn over to you. The mines themselves you may buy from me—at a sum which I promise will be nominal— or I am prepared to sell them to a London firm with which I have been in correspondence. You may take your time in considering it."

Agnes, whose whole world seemed suddenly to have slipped into a bleak and yawning abyss, gripped the arms of her chair for support. There was a blackness all around her, a kind of void through which she heard King's voice repeating absurdities, but she knew she must not let go. Some fragmentary pride that had not spoken or protested when she made the wretched dusty flight to San Francisco to see him, which had not argued when she stayed miserable nights in the hotel waiting for him to answer her note, stood now in rigid defiance and demanded recognition. It was this pride, speaking through Agnes, which answered.

"I'll buy the mines. Charles will come to San Francisco and negotiate the price with you." There was dismissal in her tone. "Is there anything else?"

King looked a little relieved. He could stand scorn better than hurt from her. "There's only one last detail. Before this—crisis came about, I had been negotiating for a mining engineer to run the show for us up north. Something like that is absolutely essential in hydraulics. It demands too much technical knowledge and skill. The few efforts we've made were amateurish at best. I realized almost from the start that we'd need professional advice. Charles seems to be willing enough, and I believe he's actually beginning to take an interest in the mines, but he's no engineer. So I engaged a fellow, a Richard Miles. Supposed to be a first-rate engineer and knows the latest wrinkles in hydraulics. I assume he'll be acceptable to you. But if you'd like to see him and talk to him first I'll leave you his name and the hotel where he's staying." He took a piece of paper and pencil from his pocket, jotted something down and handed it to Agnes. She took it stoically. He looked at her with a familiar provocative twinkle in his eyes. "I think you'll like him, Agnes."

She turned the piece of paper in her hand without looking at it. She knew she had behaved quite satisfactorily. She had pleaded, but not too much. She had let him know how much she wanted him, but she had shown him she could get along without him. She had done it well; at least she had that satisfaction. That offer to buy the mines was a good touch. Let him see she still had her mind on business.

She looked up as he rose and reached for his hat. Something dark and fathomless and empty rose up before her again and she felt her self-will slipping.

"It's as easy as that—" she began, wanting to keep quiet but unable to let him go so quickly.

He looked down at her, smiling with something that was very much like the old tenderness but that bore the strange stamp of finality.

"I'm afraid it is, Agnes. I wanted you very much, and what we had was exciting—quite wonderful. But I've reached the point where there are other things I want more. I want to be on the right side of the social fence for once—to be one with the McAllisters, the Colemans, the Athertons. Broderick and his gang may still be strong, but the southern element, the aristocracy is on the ascendancy in California. I intend to straddle the fence sedately for a time, until what connections I had with Broderick are forgotten, and then swing tactfully in line behind the Chivs. But respectability is of the essence. And so, my dear—"

He straightened, adjusted his coat, smoothed the lapels, put on his hat and rapped it once smartly to give it a straight, irreproachable set. "This is farewell."

She turned her head away but kept it high, listening to his footsteps, the sound of the door opening and closing, a sound which meant the drawing of a curtain on everything that had been her life. She phrased it so in her own mind and took note of the tragic melancholy implied. It gave her a certain morbid satisfaction.

But if Agnes's grief came from causes other than she supposed, it was nonetheless genuine. She told herself she had lost the one love her life had ever known. What irked her more, though she did not admit it, was being dismissed with all the consideration due a chambermaid who has been caught shoving dust under the carpet. She let herself weep a little over the tragic aging of King, his gaunt weariness. What really annoyed her was the obvious relief he had shown just before he left, when all his business had been satisfactorily concluded. She lamented over the fate that would make them live apart, lonely and wanting each other till life ended. Actually she was displeased over the possibility that he might very well strike up a peaceful and enduring association with Margaret. But though she might be refusing to see actualities, preferring instead the gilt and honeycombed embellishments of her own imagination, she was hard hit emotionally. She had seen her own life stretching ahead of her, inexorably intertwined with his. She had known the full measure of his devotion. She was still comparatively young, a vigorous, sensuous woman not ready to relinquish any of the pleasures of living, much less of loving. She would miss him. For as love interpreted itself to Agnes Delaney, she had loved King; loved him still.

She half turned in her chair and pressed her cheek against its green satin upholstery, weeping voluptuously, openly. Tears spotted the upholstery, ran down her cheeks, glanced off the bosom of her blue dressing gown. Her hair began to straggle down. Her handkerchief became damp and wadded. But she felt better. After ten minutes, try as she might, she could not wrench out another sob. And it was then that she looked for the first time at the crumpled piece of paper in her hand. Richard Miles.

Agnes had never been lacking in decisiveness. She had more than once applied the term euphemistically to her impetuousness. But for good or ill, it was inherent in her. And now, precisely eleven minutes after patting the last cold earth over her dead love, she made up her mind again. If she had lost King, at least she still had the mines. And as long as she had earthly possessions she could keep her head high, hang onto her self-respect. But material possessions were not held by the same easy ruses one used in love-making. Actual brainwork and energy were essential. She had leaned on King from the first moment she had arrived in the West. She had taken his advice in all matters, with the single exception of the long-ago deal with William P. Leamer, now only a dim but pleasantly remembered shadow of experience. But if she had been able to do it once, she would be able to do it again. She would bend all her efforts to making her investments pay. When she had bought King's share of the mines she would own land in two counties, Yuba and Nevada. She would be the biggest holder of the new hydraulic workings in California.

She wondered why King was willing, even anxious to sell out. Surely that was too high a price for his respectability. Shrewdly, she guessed that it was not so much respectability he was seeking in getting rid of the mines as relief from responsibility and uncertainty. So far, the hydraulic experiments had not been howling successes. Too much was dependent upon water power, which froze in the winter and dried up in the summer, which had to be laboriously piped in. There had been trouble with the machinery, and it had eventually appeared that they were proceeding at too fast a rate, trying to extract gold before they had made the necessary preparations. All of which would mean a further layout of money, sizable investments. But if Agnes had needed convincing when King first proposed hydraulics to her, she was now its devotee, its missionary. She was zealous in the belief that it was the coming means of mining gold. As she sat in the stuffy hotel room, only half hearing the noises in the street below her, not noticing as the summer dusk closed in around her, she became conscious of a new resolve forming in her mind. If she had needed incentive, here it was. She had lost King, but she had been offered the opportunity of a lifetime. Richard Miles, eh? She scanned the paper again. Well, he'd better be on his toes if he intended to work for Delaney Enterprises. Now, this summer, while the mines were immobile, would be as good a time as any to prepare things, get everything in order for the fall work. Charles was no good; never would be. But as a glorified errand boy he would come in handy. Agnes began skimming over a kind of itemized mental list. She would have to contact the bank as soon as she got home. Let them get in touch with her eastern bank for her. She'd have to have her fingers on every asset, know just what was at her disposal. And the next thing—she stood up and began slipping out of the dressing gown—was to have a talk with this Richard Miles.

She dressed quickly, slipping into the dusty brown dress she had worn on the stage coming down. She tied her hair up hastily and bunched it under her coal-scuttle bonnet. Then she hurried downstairs and ordered a hackney. The attendant at the door eyed her worriedly.

"You'll be driving out alone, madam?"

"Yes. Please hurry with it." He stepped to the curb and signaled a hackney, then glanced at her again.

"If you don't mind my saying so, ma'am, a lady like yourself takes a bit of a risk venturing out alone of an evening, once dark comes on. There's been a good bit of feeling in the town since spring. Good bit of gunplay."

Agnes, who had not been listening to a word, got into the hackney without assistance and instructed the driver tersely.

The hotel where Richard Miles was staying was a shade less elegant than Agnes's, of a type which catered chiefly to out-of-town drummers and small mineowners. Its façade was only meagerly impressive, and its lobby had a worn quality about it. There was a little path in the carpet from the door to the main desk. Agnes followed it and confronted the night clerk.

"If Mr. Richard Miles is in his room I should appreciate your sending him a message," she said authoritatively.

The clerk, a stout, balding individual, gave a little jump at the sound of her voice. His eyes narrowed suspiciously.

"No women allowed in the rooms," he said severely. "We don't allow no—"

"Please!" Agnes interrupted, more irritated than insulted. "Go find Mr. Miles, if he's in, and tell him Mrs. Delaney is waiting to see him in the lobby."

The name worked its magic. The clerk was at once obsequious, apologetic. So many strangers these days—transients and all—a body never knew who they were talking to. Certainly, he'd find Mr. Miles, and in short order too. If she'd just sit over there on the sofa by the palms— Agnes heard him no more than she had heard the pleasantly worried attendant at her own hotel. She stood rigidly at the desk, her mind whirling with a hundred items she was trying vainly to categorize. When a light-haired young man with a slow drawl confronted her and informed her he was Richard Miles, her only words were, "Thank Heaven! Come over here where we can talk."

She led the way to the sofa, which seemed the most secluded spot in the open lobby, and sat down next to him.

"I understand," she said briskly, "that you've been engaged by Mr. King Delaney as a mining engineer."

"Yes, ma'am, I have."

"He's told you the sort of work—hydraulics?"

"He told me."

"You considered yourself experienced enough to take over such a position?"

He laughed a little. "I don't reckon anybody's what you could call experienced in hydraulics yet, ma'am. It's too new a thing. But I've made a considerable study of it, and I got a lot of new ideas in mind I think would speed it along."

"I see." Agnes was thoughtful for a moment. Then she proceeded impressively. "I came over here to talk with you tonight because I wanted you to know that Mr. Delaney is no longer interested in the hydraulics venture. He has decided to sell out—to me. I'm buying up all his mines." She could not help noticing the little thrill her prospective ownership gave her. "I shall be the largest hydraulics-working owner in California. With what I already own, the property extends into both Yuba and Nevada counties. I want you to take over the management of the mines, install the necessary equipment, take over the running of them. My son-in-law, Charles Wickham, will be your assistant and will act as a liaison between us. Naturally we will have a thorough discussion of every proposed investment, every necessary installation and purchase of machinery. Tell me, do you have faith in hydraulics?" She asked the question abruptly but he was ready with a deliberate, slow answer.

"I do, ma'am. It's the coming thing. It's reaching into the very bowels of the earth to tear out the gold. Nothing can stop it. I've got all the faith in the world in it."

"I, too, have faith in it," she answered, "but we've made a discouraging start. We've realized some gold but there have been countless difficulties, most of them due, I think, to inadequate preparation. It will be your job to remedy these things."

"I got it all in mind, Mrs. Delaney. Just how we should start."

"I should like to be of more help to you, to tell you what's wrong, what's needed. But Mr. Delaney had been keeping his finger on all that. His pulling out at this particular time leaves me"—she sought for the phrase—"singularly unprepared."

"I can see that, ma'am," he said gravely.

She eyed him sharply, then decided there was nothing intended in the remark.

"I understand there has been trouble in obtaining adequate water pressure," she said.

He seemed to relax like a man in familiar territory.

"That's gener'lly the case, ma'am. Hydraulics is a get-rich-quick business, but that's no sign it doesn't take as much preparation as anything else. Maybe even more. It's pretty complex. Water pressure's essential, of course. That's the first trouble you've got to overcome. What most of 'em have done is break their necks trying to pipe it in from a distance. Then the pipes break or give way and the pressure's lost, money and time are lost. The thing to do is create your own source of supply."

"But I don't see how—"

"Dams. Dams and maybe later reservoirs. And we'll try different means of carrying the water. What do you have now?"

"I really don't know."

"Wooden flumes, more than likely. They may do for a time, but when we get into really big operations they won't be strong enough. And we'll experiment with different hoses and nozzles. You can't go into a thing like this hastily, Mrs. Delaney."

Agnes was looking at him with a peculiar directness.

"No. No, I can see that."

"It's a question of comparative values, as I see it, Mrs. Delaney. You can spend a little wastefully, or perhaps a good bit wisely.

You're a businesswoman yourself. You don't need me to tell you which is the wiser course."

Agnes observed his quiet earnestness and wondered how old he was.

"No, indeed. How right you are. But I'm quite sure I shall need you for other purposes, Mr. Miles. I think you may be quite valuable to me."

"I aim to help as much as I can, ma'am. I'll try and take some of the load off your shoulders. Now, here's the first thing we ought to do—"

Agnes listened as he proposed initial investments in machinery, the hiring of Chinese labor, the construction of dams and viaducts. She was listening carefully, but she was also thinking, and her thoughts were not of hydraulics. How soft and slow his voice was, she marveled. How relaxed and boyish he appeared when he was talking of things familiar to him. That artless boyishness concealed by wide shoulders and an intense virility had always appealed to her. How old could he be? Surely not over thirty. And yet she felt a jab of irritation at realizing that he was using the same respectful tone in speaking with her that he probably used toward his mother. Damn! Whatever had made her run over here dressed like a frump —not even a touch of rouge and her hair looking as though she'd just come in out of a strong wind? She hadn't even bothered with a corset on account of the heat. Well, she'd fix that! She looked admiringly at his bland, undistinguished but nevertheless pleasant features, at his fair straight hair, his clean spatulate fingers gesturing. She could feel the shininess of her nose and forehead and inwardly she gave a rousing mining camp curse.

"There's absolutely no limit to what we can do with it, Mrs. Delaney!" he said eagerly. "I don't want to ask you to give me carte blanche in buying this stuff or anything like that—but if I draw up lists and show them to you for your approval . . . Itemized with the approximate cost, of course."

"Of course, Mr. Miles," Agnes murmured. Then, as an afterthought, "You're from the South, aren't you?"

If Agnes had found herself tragically unprepared in her first encounter with Richard Miles, she made up for it in her second one. At her suggestion they arranged to have dinner together at her hotel the following evening. This time Agnes was not caught off guard. She slept late in the morning, and after she had awakened she lay languidly between the thin expensive sheets, looking at the ceiling with its play of sunlight and shadows and at the patterns of morning light upon the deep-carpeted floor. Outside she could hear the sounds of the day's business and play. The call of vendors, the screams of children, the rattle of carriage and wagon wheels, the clump of hoofs, the voices of men together or of women bent on shopping.

It was nearly noon before she felt completely satiated with languor and ordered one of the hotel maids to fetch her breakfast on a tray.

After she had eaten she put her dressing gown on and sat in a chair while she permitted the maid to clear away the tray and make the bed. All the time the girl worked, Agnes was organizing her thoughts. At length she gave the maid her instructions and started the serious business of coping with the day's problem. First she had a tub brought up. She sent out for a woman whose business it was to arrange hair, and while waiting for her to arrive, creamed her face and neck painstakingly and rubbed cologne on her throat and temples. The dress she chose was a pale-ivory taffeta that showed off the whiteness of her skin and rustled with an eerie magic against the silken petticoat. She rouged her cheeks and lips lightly. Then she stood back and observed the result.

At exactly five minutes after six, Agnes swept downstairs and through the lobby. White kid gloves demurely covered her forearms. She held a small pink shell-encrusted fan whose tassel bobbed as she walked. Her head was erect, her plump shoulders gleamed in the early lamplight.

Richard Miles, sitting in a chair near the desk, looked up, then looked again, then rose dazedly. He was later to recall the moment, to look back upon it and try to remember exactly what had taken place within him at that instant of seeing and reacting and rising. But he could never be quite sure.

CHAPTER IV

AGNES BORE her new husband home in triumph, so blatantly the victor that there was an edge of embarrassment to the initial shock Treese felt upon being introduced to her stepfather. Richard took the entire matter calmly; but it was a calm, not of sophistication, but of complete absorption in his bride. When they were in the same room his eyes followed her, never leaving her for an instant, and when she came near him his hand went out to her in an instinctive protective gesture, to touch her gown or to guide her elbow. Treese saw that Agnes was wise enough to guide this adoration along into proper channels. She did not flutter too much over him. She even ignored him for moments at a time to stimulate his desire for her. And this too was a source of subtle humiliation to Treese; this pageant of the pursuer and the pursued being enacted before her eyes, in surroundings that customarily witnessed nothing more sensuous than the ordering of the next evening's dinner.

She liked Richard. His pleasant slow voice, moved to urgency only when he spoke of engineering and the mines, his long, unhurried stride, his straight light hair struck her as singularly boyish and likable. It was impossible not to smile with him, to become enthused over the plans he expounded with such eagerness. But she pitied him too, dreading the day or the night when the pageant would end and the white light of realization would shed mercilessly in on Agnes, when he would no longer want her, but find himself inexorably hers.

Charles's reaction had been, on the whole, less altruistic.

"What does she think she's doing?" he demanded of Treese on the night of Agnes's return. They were behind the closed door of their bedroom, and Charles's voice was lowered to a note of cautious desperation. "Doesn't she know what people will say about her? Can't she realize that now there'll be talk about a lot of things that wouldn't have been mentioned otherwise?"

Treese sat in front of her walnut dressing table with its long oval mirror, brushing her hair and dividing it into two sections for braiding. Reflected behind her she could see Charles standing in his nightshirt, his protruding stomach visible, his lower lip extended angrily.

"It's ridiculous!" Charles exclaimed.

"If you mean about Uncle King," she said, putting down the brush and starting the first braid, "of course they'll talk." Neither she nor Charles had ever mentioned the relationship between Agnes and King. Tacitly, they had of course known, and each was aware that the other knew. It was characteristic of the abstruse quality of their married life that neither had spoken of it, and Treese knew how strong a compulsion must be moving Charles now. She dreaded what she knew he was going to say; not because it would surprise her, but because she knew it so well and hated to be reminded of it.

"Well, doesn't that mean anything to her? Hasn't she any pride?" Charles, scuffing across the carpet in his bedroom slippers, had drawn his forehead into a black scowl that emphasized his growing baldness. The light from the lamp caught the smoothness at the front of his scalp and sent a reflection shimmering off it, lighting up the sparse hairs directly behind it that gave promise of soon following the example of earlier fellows.

"I suppose marrying Mr. Miles was evidence of pride, too, Charles."

Charles stopped and stared toward her, looking not at her, but in her general direction, scowling thoughtfully.

"But what do you suppose happened between her and King? You think he deserted her?"

"Something like that. You know how things have been going in San Francisco. Perhaps he didn't want to take further chances with his reputation." Treese folded one thick rope of hair over the other, grasped it under her other hand, folded the second over and under, over and under. Her fingers moved with the deftness of long habit but they were cold with a nervous dread. Would he say it now? Was it possible that he would have the decency not to say it?

The scowl that creased Charles's forehead turned subtly to a sneer. "I suppose our fine engineering friend has already got his eye on the money."

In spite of being ready, in spite of knowing it without it being said, Treese felt as though cold water had been dashed in her face. She swallowed and said nothing.

Charles was pacing restlessly back and forth, his nightshirt flapping around his calves, his ankles looking white with the sparse hairs standing out about them.

"Filling her up with all sorts of schemes and drivel, turning her head and telling her how much money she can make if she does things his way. She'll find out what it gets her to squander her money on every fly-by-night scheme and then be left by the wayside —money gone and her husband run off with the first filly that catches his eye!"

"I don't think Mr. Miles will leave Mother," Treese said quietly.

"Not leave her! Why, he's nothing but a boy! You don't think any man his age is going to stay with a woman who— Well, how long do you think he can stand it?"

"It's not a question of his standing it, Charles. I'm sure he won't leave her."

"You mean she won't let him go."

"Something like that." She finished one braid and started on the other one. Charles had stopped pacing and was standing in the middle of the room staring at the floor.

"Well, he won't get away with it. He'll never get away with it."
He pronounced the words with a certain vague emphasis, as though
it was something he was sure of, even though he had not yet found
the means to implement the certainty. "I was doing all right with the
mines. I was doing fine. If she had to catch herself another husband,
I don't see why she couldn't have picked one who wouldn't be putting his nose in all the time. All this talk about machinery and
equipment and viaducts. It's too damned expensive and it's risky.
What does he think we've got, anyway, a gold mine?" He stopped
short, realizing the ridiculousness of what he had said, yet not willing to let laughter intrude upon his sternly righteous mood. He
glanced sharply at Treese, making sure that she did not laugh, and
she obligingly did not, although she knew in other circumstances she
would have been expected to, to heighten Charles's opinion of himself as a clever fellow, a wit.

"You may be overestimating the seriousness of the whole thing,
Charles," she said smoothly "You may find that you get along well
with Mr. Miles."

Charles snorted contemptuously. "Him!" he exclaimed bitterly.
"That fortune hunter!"

Keith came to call on his mother, to plead the farmers' case.
Treese never knew what went on behind the closed double doors of
the parlor that afternoon. Agnes refused to see him alone, so
Richard was present during the conversation. The entire visit did
not take more than fifteen minutes and when Keith emerged there
was an expression of set anger on his face. Coupled with it Treese
almost imagined she saw a grim satisfaction, as though he had been
longing for a good fight but was unwilling to take steps toward it
without first trying all possible means of mediation. Agnes did not
see him to the front door, but remained behind with Richard. Treese
slipped past the parlor door and followed Keith out onto the
veranda. She caught his sleeve just as he was about to start down
the steps.

"Keith!"

He looked up, a faint note of surprise breaking into his determined preoccupation. "Hello, Treese."

"Keith, be careful, won't you?" He had never seemed so far
away. How did one go about bridging a gap of so many years?
"I'd like to do something if I could. If there's anything I can do—"

"You?" The surprise deepened, showing in a little line between
his eyebrows. She nodded. For a long time he searched her face,

something that was almost remorse showing in his own. When he spoke again his voice had a strangely tender quality.

"There is something you can do. You can look after Annette for me. I may be away a great deal. She's going to have a baby." He paused thoughtfully. "I'd appreciate it if you'd look in on her often. Will you do that for me?"

His eyes sought hers. She nodded, her hands pressed tight together in front of her.

"Good," he said softly. "That's fine." And he hurried off down the steps.

That night as she lay in bed waiting for Charles to finish undressing and blow out the light her eyes traveled over the shadow-patterned ceiling, something restless behind them. She turned and watched Charles, still in his undershirt and trousers, lean over to pull off his boots. Her eyes narrowed thoughtfully.

"Charles—" There was a grunt of acknowledgment as Charles removed one boot and sat red-faced.

"Charles, last month at Hazel's tea they were all talking about your new lodge—about the Protectors. They said you were important in it." Her voice acquired an unaccustomed smoothness that was almost unctuousness. "I felt so foolish. You never told me a word about it. Why didn't you? Surely you must have known I'd be interested. Charles, tell me about the Protectors—are they like the Vigilantes?"

Treese kept her word to Keith. During that fall and winter there was never a week that she did not stop to call at Annette's little house. She had dreaded the first visit, but Annette had put her at ease immediately.

"It was so good of you to come," she said quietly.

The door had been opened by a woman whom Annette called Pelu, a pleasant-faced tan woman primly dressed except for a flash of red ribbon in her dark hair. It was all strange to Treese, the way Annette addressed the woman in French and Pelu answered.

The woman had made her a slight curtsy and then had taken her India print shawl. Her motions were deft and practiced, not like the heavy-handed country girls Agnes engaged as maids.

Standing in the middle of the pleasant parlor a moment later, Treese looked around her at the walls.

"Have you read all these books?" she asked incredulously.

Annette laughed. Her laugh was as low and throaty as her voice. "Many of them."

The house where Annette and Keith lived was a small one-story building a few blocks from the business section of town. Outside, it was like any other house on the block, indefinite as to architecture, somewhat in need of painting. Inside, it was unlike any other house Treese had ever seen. Agnes's home, the house she was accustomed to, was a haven of well-ordered ugliness, of expensive knicknacks, of decoration done to the limit and then jut a step beyond.

The floors everywhere Treese looked were painted a deep mahogany red and they shone with cleaning and polishing. Scattered over them were woven rugs, bright-hued and haphazardly placed. The furniture was simple and there was little of it. A small sofa, a few rush-bottomed chairs, a piano. And bookshelves against every wall, books everywhere. Treese had never seen so many before. The bedroom, which she could just glimpse through an open door, had a big postered bed and a patchwork spread.

Treese went to one of the shelves and traced along the titles with her forefinger. "What are they all about?" She had known only a few scattered months off and on at the Young Ladies' Institute which left the world of literature largely outside in its effort to instill the social graces into its long-limbed charges. Annette was watching her now a little curiously.

"Many different things. The ideas of different men on man himself. Some of them are plays. They are in French."

"You read them?" Treese reiterated incredulously. No one she knew read more than the *Lady's Book*, or the *California Ladies' Quarterly*. And in French!

"Of course. Sometimes I read them aloud to Keith."

"But he doesn't understand, does he?"

"I tell him what it means. He says he likes to hear me read, even when he doesn't understand. But there are others in English. Sometimes we read a play together and I make him act out a part."

"Keith?"

"Yes. He's really very good. He could have been on the stage. He's handsomer than Booth."

Annette motioned for her to sit down and Pelu brought in a tray.

"I know you're more accustomed to tea here. But in New Orleans we enjoy coffee. I hope you don't mind."

"I don't mind at all."

The coffeepot was silver, ornately wrought and with an old look about it. The coffee cups were small, foreign-looking. There were tiny cakes, each one carefully shaped but with some little asymmetry about it that set it apart from its fellows.

"I've been wondering." Annette sat back in her chair, her cup resting daintily in one palm so that the oval tips of her fingers just curled up over the edge of the saucer.

"What?"

"I've been wondering why you're being so kind to me."

"It's nothing that I'm doing for you," Treese said quickly.

"For yourself then?"

"Yes, for myself in a way."

The explanation seemed to satisfy Annette. She did not inquire further.

"I don't really care what the others think," she said slowly. "About my marrying Keith, that is. I don't feel required to explain it or justify it to anyone. I'd like you to know, though."

"There's no need."

"No, I want you to know. I suppose everyone thought I was after—well, I don't know what. Notoriety perhaps, or the Delaney money. I'd like you to know how it really was. I was so in love with him." She paused. "I'm sorry it had to be this way. I'd be glad to be friends with her." Treese knew she was speaking of Agnes now. "It's easy to talk about living your own life and not caring about anyone else, but down underneath there's an instinct to belong. To be part of a family. Having you here makes it more like that."

"I'm so glad," Treese said warmly. She had suddenly lost all feeling of strangeness in the little house.

During the next few months she enjoyed greater freedom than usual, for the rainy season had started and the mines were busy. Both Charles and Richard were away for long periods of time, and sometimes Agnes made the trip with them, inspecting sites where dams and ditches were to be constructed, listening to long eager recitals from Richard about where new equipment was needed. Then, on her return, she would set about buying it, going to San Francisco to hunt for supplies, writing letters. Once she even took a trip to New York to purchase machinery. This interval of several weeks was one of the pleasantest Treese could remember. She spent almost every day with Annette, sometimes leaving the house even before breakfast, so that she could sit with Annette before the fire and enjoy a cup of the thick New Orleans coffee Pelu brewed. While the rain beat against the windows or swirled wraithlike about the house they would talk, and Pelu would bring more coffee and the hours would seem to vanish until it was time for dinner. Then she would bring in a great silver tray laden with fragrant, foreign-appearing dishes, steaming and savory. Treese began to look forward to the new exciting tang of garlic, the hot Creole concoctions, rich and dripping with tomatoes; fresh sea foods stewed with onion and spices; ham and rice cooked together and embellished with tomato. Sometimes when Keith was in town he would join them at noon, and Treese would watch with a feeling of vicarious warmth as he hovered over Annette or sat across the table from her, his eyes going repeatedly to her, his whole manner a concentration of concern for her. It was this concern, she guessed, coupled with his new sense of responsibility toward John Trask and the farmers, that had produced the change she noticed in him, the slight hard edge that made his handsomeness something less vacuous than it had been before. His dark eyes seemed deeper set, his mouth more sensitive and quick to change.

She knew that Annette worried about him during his long absences and that she never let him know she worried. She maintained a steady, questioning interest in his work. How many men had he talked to? Did they seem receptive? What did the rivermen say? Would they go along with the farmers? Was there a chance of accomplishing anything through legislation? Then the two of them would begin to talk eagerly, sometimes, it seemed, almost forgetting that she was in the room. But she listened avidly to what they had to say, trying to fit the pieces together, conscious of a growing curiosity in herself. If only she had learned before this to listen! How much there was in the world to learn. How much Annette and Keith already knew, and how painfully ignorant she herself appeared beside them. How vital were these matters that concerned the whole future of California! And how would she ever learn?

Often, when Keith had gone, Treese would question Annette. What had they meant about legislation? What did politics have to do with it at all?

Annette smiled patiently. "This is not an isolated issue, Treese. It's all part of something so much bigger. Perhaps Keith and John Trask and the others are ahead of their time. Andy Hart says they are and I shouldn't be at all surprised. It's too big, too growing. There's too much money involved. European capital has already started pouring in to finance hydraulic workings. It isn't only your mother any more. But Keith and the others feel they must put up a resistance—and not only against hydraulics. Rather, against everything, every force that seeks to exploit California, rob her of her future. What do you suppose would happen if California became a slave state? Not only would the inhumanity of the whole system be given a tremendous new lease, but the small farmer and miner would be crushed as completely as if he had never existed. Everything California is today those little men made her. They've plundered and stolen from her too. They've been greedy and selfish beyond reason. But whatever greatness there is about her is due to them. Slavery stands in opposition to all that. That's why Keith can't side with Gwin and his Chivs."

"You're from the South," Treese hesitated. "You talk strangely, it seems to me. At home—" She paused, deciding that it would be pleasanter not to mention home.

"There's a difference in attitudes toward the question," Annette said. "Most people don't care too much one way or the other about slavery, but they know enough to side in with the ones who appear certain to win. My being from the South—I don't know, it never seemed to matter. I was so young when I left, and I saw so many things."

Treese hesitated for a long moment. Then she asked a surprising question. "What does your brother think? What does Mr. Mallott think?" It was the first time she had ever spoken of him aloud, and she experienced a strange detached feeling as though she had heard someone else ask the question.

"I don't know. I've never quite known about Steve. There was such a long time when we lost track of each other, and when we became reacquainted there were gaps that were hard to fill. I only know that he dislikes becoming involved emotionally. He dislikes having other people's problems forced upon him. It's a peculiar independence he has. I shouldn't be surprised if he's the same when it comes to politics. He probably plays a safe middle course on the pretext that it's good business. But what does go on inside him, I don't know. I don't know what he'll do when he has to make a choice."

"Why should he have to make a choice?" Treese inquired, puzzled. "Why should anyone have to if he'd rather not?"

Annette's pleasant smile took on a faint suggestion of irony. "My dear, everyone in California will have to make a choice one of these days."

Keith was away for longer and longer periods at a time. Something ominous seemed to hang in the air, to cloud the very atmosphere they breathed. In desperation, Treese tried to dissipate it by covering as wide a range of trivial subjects per visit as she could rake up. And Annette would sit, sometimes smiling quietly, knowing what was being done for her benefit. One day early in the new year she herself ventured to co-operate and take some of the burden of levity from Treese's shoulders.

"You undoubtedly have," she announced, "the most beautiful head of hair in California. And the things you do with it are abominable. Would you let me fix it this afternoon?"

Treese blushed, but admitted she would be delighted. Not that there was any truth to that business about her hair. Red was a wretched color for a woman. Blonde and glossy black, now, there would be proper material for a coiffure. But red—

"In the theater," Annette interrupted, "that hair would be a sensation. In Europe too. But here in America sloping shoulders and insipid coloring are the order of the day. All the same, I'll show you what can be done. Now, look here—"

So they sat in the living room in front of the fireplace, and Annette loosened Treese's hair from its pins and combs, letting it fall to her waist and catch lights from the leaping fire. Outside a slow drizzle was falling, but inside the flames threw back the light of the polished floors, and the whole interior seemed to take its color note from the bright mass of Treese's hair. Annette brought comb and brush from the bedroom and worked over the hair until it glistened and snapped and shone. She braided sections of it experimentally, then took it out and brushed it again. She twisted a strand around her finger to form a curl and then combed through it. It was a soothing, lazy business that Treese could feel in the relaxation of her whole body. But if her body was easily lulled, her mind was not. All the accumulation of questions that had been in her thoughts for weeks repeated themselves to her with every motion of the brush, growing and intensifying until she felt she must speak.

"Annette," she finally asked, "does Keith think Broderick will ever be elected senator?"

"Why not?"

"Oh, I don't know. No reason really. It's just that he's been trying for so many years. So many people laugh at him."

"Do you laugh at him?"

Treese reddened suddenly, remembering times in the past when she had laughed.

"I guess I have. It was probably very wrong of me. But the others at home always did—"

"It wasn't wrong of you when you didn't know." Annette's voice was not disapproving, and it occurred to Treese that she had never seen in Annette disapproval or superiority over differing opinions. There was rather a constant eager attempt to communicate what she felt, a desire to make something that was of great importance to her understood by another. It was almost as though she felt time was too precious a commodity to be wasted on superficial attitudes.

"Broderick has come a long way since he first arrived in California back in 'forty-nine," Annette said slowly. "He's learned that there are more weapons than truth and conviction necessary to wage a fight in politics. He's learned that it's important for him to be able to wear a cutaway coat with as much poise as Gwin does, so that when he speaks people will listen, not laugh. He's learned to cater to pettiness in order to win his point. He can turn a phrase as well as Gwin, if he chooses, and he's learned which fork to pick up first at a dinner table. Yet, underneath, the great strength of him has never changed. I think it never will, unless they beat him down by sheer physical force."

"But many say he's only against slavery because Gwin is for it. They say he's reduced it to a personal issue. Uncle King has said that many times."

"It might have been in the beginning. I don't know. But I do know that no man could stand up under the personal abuse Broderick has taken all these years unless there was a strong inner conviction fortifying him. When he's elected senator—and I'm convinced he will be—he'll have to take even more. I've never doubted his sincerity. I don't doubt it now."

She put the brush down at last and grasped Treese's hair in both hands.

"I'm going to try it with braids first. Then we'll see what else we can think up."

Treese let her head fall back a little, feeling the rhythmic pull and tug of the strands as Annette began the braiding.

"Annette—" She paused, wondering if she should ask the question that was in her mind, that seldom left it these days. "Annette, what are Keith and John Trask doing all this time that they're away?"

She was not sure whether there was a break in the steady movement of Annette's hands. But the voice that answered was quite as usual.

"Claim jumping. Getting enough men and guns together to take over different mines in Yuba and Nevada counties."

"Can they do that?" Treese was taken aback.

"It's legal. Any unoccupied mine automatically becomes public domain. The first one there can claim possession."

"But are they left unguarded?"

"Guards can be bribed."

Something quick and proper and moralistic sprang up in Treese in spite of her wish to keep it down. How could Annette condone something which, though it bore the stamp of legality, was quite patently dishonest? Annette seemed to read her skepticism.

"Sometimes," she said, "we must make use of their own weapons."

Treese was not sure what she meant. "But it must be dangerous!" she cried. "Don't you worry?"

She could have bitten off her tongue the moment the words were out, but Annette did not seem to lose her composure.

"Yes," she said, as though that was the first time she had given it much thought. "I worry."

There was a moment's pause during which Treese experienced a flood of remorse that brought tears to her eyes. But Annette's next words were quite cheerful and matter-of-fact.

"There, now—such a mess as I made of that braid. Let me try it again." She unwound it and brushed it free again, letting the hair cling to the comb, and pulling it away so that each strand seemed to stand out by itself, alive and charged with color. For several minutes there was no sound except the falling of logs in the fireplace, the crackle of the fire and the little pellets of rain striking against the windows. At last Annette put the brush down again and began separating the hair into sections to be braided.

"Treese," she said quietly, "what do you know about the Protectors?"

A voice boomed at them from the doorway. "Potbellied shopkeepers on horseback!"

Both women wheeled around in their chairs and watched as Steve Mallott walked into the room slapping his wide black hat against his thigh to shake the glistening wet from it. Annette jumped up and ran to him.

"Steve! We never heard you come in! Look how you're soaked. Take that coat off right away and let me hang it near the fire. What a terrible day to come out in."

He let her take his coat and spread it out on a chair near the fire, but his eyes were fixed with fascination on the long sweep of Treese's hair. She squirmed uneasily, reaching back of her and trying to gather it into some sort of order.

"Don't do that," he said sharply. "Leave it."

Annette bustled back from the fire. "Goodness, I don't know where my head is. Treese, I want you to meet my brother—"

For the first time Steve's eyes left her hair and went to her face, meeting her own startled gaze quite directly.

"Mrs. Wickham and I have met," he said.

Annette accepted it in her stride. "Well, that's fine. Now sit here near the fire, Steve, while I finish with Treese's hair. We certainly never expected company on a day like this, did we, Treese?"

"I was thinking about you," he said. "I wondered how you were." He took a chair near them and sat watching the movement of Annette's hands in the red hair. He lifted one leg and crooked it so that it rested on his other knee. Then he took a cheroot from his pocket, lifting his eyebrows for permission.

"Oh, of course," Annette said. "But I told you you didn't have to worry about me. I'm all right."

He broke the cheroot in two and replaced one half in his pocket, lighting the other. The flame cast a bright glare against his features, throwing the deep-set eyes into prominence and revealing the lines at the corners of his mouth. He tossed the match into the fireplace and squinted against the smoke, holding the cheroot in the corner of his mouth.

"Nobody gives me a chance to be lonely," Annette went on animatedly. "Treese is over here nearly every day, and Pelu is always around, of course. I have more company than I know what to do with." She smiled and tugged at the piece of hair she was working on. "And today we're trying something new by way of diversion. Making Treese into a prima donna."

"Sounded like more than that to me. What was all this gossip about the Protectors when I came in?" He shot Treese a look then that was so clearly a warning she felt a little chill up her spine. She gripped both hands together tightly.

"Oh, nothing. I was just asking Treese about them. People do talk a lot, you know, and some of them seem to think there might be more to it than meets the eye. Some even say they're armed." Annette tried to make her tone light and unconcerned.

"That won't do much good. There's not one of 'em could hit the side of a barn with a cannon. And besides, it's just talk."

"Of course it is. But you know we women get hard up for something to gossip about." Annette twisted a braid around to the top of Treese's head and pinned it. "Now the other side." She worked rapidly and finished the second one, then twisted them around each other to form a coronet on top of Treese's head. The effect was to form a kind of frame for her face and to give her added height. It made her hair the most noticeable thing about her, instead of inconspicuous as Treese had always attempted to make it. It called attention to its unconventional beauty in a flaunting, dramatic manner. Treese flushed with embarrassment.

"Look!" Annette handed her the mirror. Treese barely glanced at it, letting her eyes drop instead to her lap.

Annette smiled with amusement. "Never mind, you'll get used to it. And I never want to see you draw it back in that awful bun again. Tomorrow maybe we'll try it another way."

She put the comb and brush aside and sat back heavily in her chair.

"Well, now," she said, "I can tell you one thing. Now that I've got all this company I'm not going to let it get away. You're both going to stay to dinner. We'll make a regular party of it."

"As a matter of fact, dear lady, I came over here for that express purpose," Steve announced. "But there are conditions. No politics, no election talk, no Broderick campaigning."

"Steve likes his women decorative and nothing else," Annette giggled.

"Well, I wouldn't say *nothing* else," he said, smiling slowly and drawing in on the cheroot.

Treese cleared her throat nervously. "Annette, I'd love to stay, really I would, but they'll be expecting me at home. I must be on my way.

Annette's face fell. "Oh, Treese, couldn't you stay? We could have such a gay time of it—"

Steve interrupted. "And it's most unwise not to humor a woman in her delicate condition."

Treese grew redder and Annette took pity on her.

"Steve, shame! What kind of talk is that in front of ladies? But couldn't you, Treese?"

Treese raised her head just enough to catch Steve's glance again. His mouth was smiling but his eyes were urgent and direct. They seemed almost to be trying to tell her something. She hesitated.

"Well, perhaps I might—"

"Good!" Annette got up again. "I'm going to speak to Pelu about it. I'll be right back."

She left the room. They could hear her footsteps going back to the kitchen, and then low voices in consultation behind a closed door somewhere. A little clock on the mantel that Treese had not noticed before ticked loudly.

His voice, low and controlled, came across the room at her. "Just what *do* you know about the Protectors?"

Treese looked at him squarely for the first time, her embarrassment suddenly gone. He was watching her closely, and his body seemed tense and unrelaxed. The recollection of a night long ago aboard the steamer *President* snapped suddenly, bringing her back to reality and the uneasy fears of the present.

"I know enough about them," she said quietly.

He searched her face as though seeking affirmation of something there. "Then don't tell Annette," he said finally.

She nodded. There were footsteps again and Annette reappeared. She moved heavily, but with a certain grace that seemed never totally to desert her.

"All settled," she announced with a smile. "This is really going to be a party!"

By eleven that night the rain had stopped and a chilly wind had sprung up, drying the board walks but making little impression on the streets which had not yet been planked. There the mud still lay, dark and shiny and forbidding, treacherous to both horse and buggy in those sections not lighted by the gas lamps. Steve maneuvered his rig deftly back toward J Street, holding the reins tightly and leaning forward with his eyes fixed on the blackness somewhere just ahead of the horse's swaying rump. Neither he nor Treese spoke while he concentrated on the business of getting the horse to a firm footing. The wind was penetrating, and Treese, sitting huddled in the seat beside him, had pulled her cloak close about her. Once, without looking at her, he said, "There's a blanket there—in back of you, I guess." Treese reached around until she felt it and then wrapped it around her. It felt warm and comforting, and now the damp gusts of wind did not reach her. She stopped shivering and sat a little straighter. The buggy lurched, listed and righted itself, then repeated the process. Treese was thrown first against the opposite side, then against Steve. She struggled to remain erect, but he did not seem to notice. When they reached J Street, Steve said, "There now," and let his breath out in a little sigh of relaxation. He let the horse trot briskly, and Treese did not offer argument when they rode past Eighth Street and on toward the rise of Sutter's Fort.

It had been a nice party, she thought. And Annette had really seemed to relax and enjoy herself. Steve was garrulous all through the meal, filled with entertaining and sometimes slightly off-color stories about happenings at the Red Tent; stories that made Treese's eyes widen with interest and wonder until she could almost see the crystal-lighted scarlet interior, the beautifully gowned women, the gamblers. Steve had looked at her only a few times during the meal, and then there had been nothing in the look that she could interpret. She thought how ridiculously few had been the times their lives had touched, how much importance she had attached to those times, and how little they had actually possessed. A man who spent half his life in association with beautiful women! And yet, coming out of the dining room, she had caught a glimpse of herself in the hall mirror, had noticed the high, startling arrangement of red hair, the tall straightness of her body. She had squared her shoulders and remembered what Annette had said to her. In the theater that would be a sensation. Well, at least it was hers, Treese thought with sudden independence. It was hers and there was nothing in the whole of Sacramento like it.

When they reached the end of the board planking a few blocks beyond the busy section of town, Steve drew the reins in and stopped the buggy, pulling the horse over toward the edge of the street.

"This is good enough," he announced. He fastened the reins at his side and flipped up the collar of his frock coat around his neck. The wind had blown the clouds away from the face of a new moon and a flood of pale-white light burst through the blackness, silvering the flanks of the horse and lighting up Steve's features as he turned to her.

"Now," he said quietly, "what's this about the Protectors?" He was looking straight at her with the same urgency Treese had seen in his eyes at Annette's house.

She wondered why she could feel no hesitancy about answering him, only an immediate overwhelming relief.

"What do you want to know?"

"How many are there?"

"There are about seventy-five men in the lodge. They're the ones who wear the uniforms and give the password—that sort of thing."

"Then there are others?"

"About twenty or thirty. I think closer to thirty. They're hired, and all of them are armed."

"Who are they?"

"Oh—you know how that sort of thing is done. They're mostly riffraff bailed out of jails from here to San Francisco. Hired gunmen, men who make a business of it."

"They have political protection, of course."

"Naturally. There's hardly a political office in the state that isn't held by a Chiv. Many of the lodge members are officeholders themselves. But here's something peculiar—I don't think most of them know what's being done right under their noses. They're footing the bill by their contributions and heavy dues, but I don't think they know what's going on—about the gunmen or any of that. They think it's just another lodge—like the Masons."

"And the ones who do know?"

"The ones who do know only know half of it. They think it's another group like the Vigilantes, protection of law and order, speedy justice and all the rest of it. They think they're doing something heroic instead of just paying up their good money to protect the Delaney mines."

"There's one part of the picture that doesn't fit."

"What?"

"Well—one person who could stop the whole business in a minute."

"You mean Mother?"

"Certainly. She must know Keith's life will be in danger. She isn't that angry with him, is she?"

"No, of course not. But she doesn't realize what's going on."

"Then why don't you tell her?"

Treese drew a long breath and hesitated for a moment, choosing her words, wondering if she could make him understand.

"There are things behind all this that you might not see right away, things that you absorb through living with people and getting to know them pretty well. One of them is about Charles. Mother never took Charles seriously. She saw him for what he was—a fortune hunter, but quite eligible, someone who'd be a social feather in her cap if nothing else. Beyond that, she's never seen anything in him. She doesn't take him seriously, or think he's capable of any kind of planning, any kind of definite action. Underneath, though, that's not the case at all. But Charles knows how she feels, and he's played up to it, letting her go on thinking that he's the way she imagines him to be. He's—he's—how can I describe him? He's a lonely man, a man with a terrible feeling of insufficiency. He wants Mother's money, but he resents everything that puts him in that position. He resents her *having* the money and being able to dole it out to him. He resents Keith, because Keith is everything he could never be. Independent, not afraid of anyone, willing to take what he wants out of life with no help from anyone. That's why this whole Protectors business looks like the biggest thing in his life to Charles. You ask why I don't tell her about it. How can I tell her when Charles does himself? Every night at dinner he talks about it, tells about the password and ritual, the secret grip, the uniforms. Mother sits there with a straight face, pretending to take him seriously, while all the time underneath she's ready to burst out laughing at what a clown he is. If I told her Charles could be dangerous and menacing, she'd laugh in my face. She hasn't ways of knowing things about him, like I have."

For a long time Steve sat quite still, studying her face. Then he let out his breath with a soft whistling sound between his teeth.

"Well, that's that. Now, the next thing is to try and do something about it. In the morning I'll send a rider north—tell him to get there as fast as he can. I know about where he'll find Keith and John Trask—I wish I could be more sure. But it's the best we can do."

"Why? Do you think they're going to try something soon?"

"The Protectors? Not exactly. But Keith and John and the others are. They're going to jump one of the Delaney claims any day now."

Treese gave a little gasp that was both fear and surprise. He nodded, his mouth tightening.

"I tried to talk Keith out of it last time he was in town. Andy and I both did. This whole thing won't do them any good. All they'll get out of it is a bullet right between the shoulders and there won't be a thing to show for it. They can't possibly gather enough strength to fight a machine like that. The farmers and rivermen aren't awake to it yet. It takes years."

"I want him to be all right," Treese said thoughtfully. "I can't bear to think of him being hurt. But whatever happens, I'll always be glad Keith did this. And I think Annette will be glad too. No matter how bad it is. He wasn't anything before. He wasn't even living. Do you know what I mean?"

Steve reached in his pocket and drew out the stub of a cheroot, struck a match against the side of the rig and lighted it.

"Yep," he said laconically. "I guess."

Later, after he had turned the rig around and started to drive slowly home, they talked of other things.

"Once I talked about you to Annette," Treese said musingly.

"She said you disliked having other people's problems forced on you, that you played a middle course. You don't sound like that to me. Why should you be so interested in the Protectors?"

"I'm not," he retorted. "But I am interested in Annette. Now that she's found a little happiness I don't want to see it all thrown overboard."

"Is that all?"

He seemed almost irritated by the question. "I don't know. I thought it was at first. Now I'm not exactly sure." He paused. "I always felt close to Annette. I never quite got over the feeling that she was something special to me. The only family tie I had. That's why it's understandable that I'd take an interest in something that touched her." He drew in on the cheroot and the smoke trailed back over his shoulder in a wisp. The collar of his coat was still turned up so that his face was half hidden from her. She could feel the wind about her head blowing her hair loose and pulling at the pins that held the braids.

"How about you?" he asked sharply. "You had all that information down pat, and I hardly think your husband would approve of your relaying it to strange men. How do I know you were telling me the truth? How do I know I can trust you anyway?"

"I don't know," she said softly. "But I do know that you can trust me. And I'm glad. I think that's what I've been wanting more than anything—just to be able to tell someone. To be able to talk about it."

"How can you go on living in that house if you hate it that much?"

"I don't exactly hate it. I've never known anything else. And I have a child."

"Is that any reason why you couldn't get out if you wanted to?"

"But I don't want to! I never even thought of it." Treese looked at him, startled.

There was a long silence while they reached Eighth Street and turned, the horse picking its way slowly down the dark street toward the big brick house. It was too dark now for her to see Steve's face.

"I saw you a long time ago," he said finally. "The night you got married. You looked as if the world had just taken you by the collar and bent you in two. You didn't have any more fight in you than a rabbit. What happened since?"

"I went to England. I was there a year. Alone. Really alone. There wasn't anybody to talk to—not even someone like Andy or Aunt Margaret, who'd be comforting to have around. And I found

suddenly that I was homesick for California, more tired and unhappy and homesick than I'd ever thought I could be. I didn't think
there were any ties that strong holding me. But over there everything was so different—the dampness and the oldness that clings
about you wherever you go. The sense of everything having been
finished long ago. I began to realize how accustomed I'd become to
a place that was new and growing. And then, because I had nothing
else to do, I began to think more and more about it. And the more
I thought the more I realized that all the strength and greatness
of California is only the result of what men like Delaney put into
it. They came out here greedy and searching—they wanted to find
gold and then head for home. But something kept them here, almost
all of them. And they stayed to build a state and to make something
good out of it—in spite of the Chivs with their class consciousness
and in spite of the political machines that men like Broderick built.
Something good emerged in spite of all that. It isn't done yet. It's
still being fought over, and there'll be more fighting before it's done.
But I wanted to come back here. I wanted to be part of it, and I
want my son to be part of it. This is something I wouldn't have
him miss for the world. They don't realize it in England. Even back
east they don't realize it. They think we're barbarians. They don't
know that we're making something wonderful here. That's why I'm
glad Keith's in it, even if he's hasty and hasn't a chance of winning
this time. Because I know he's caught some of it. He feels as I feel,
and he's fighting to save something that's the most important thing
California will ever have—her land."

"You talk a lot," he drawled. "Why don't you really do something?"

"I do what I can," she flared. "I found out about the Protectors, didn't I?"

"I wasn't thinking of that. I meant that if you really wanted to
you could make your own life. You, and your child too. If there
was something you really wanted badly enough, nobody in the world
could stop you."

They did not speak again until the buggy drew up in front of
the dark-windowed house. Then, quite without warning, something
that was curious and bold sprang up in Treese and she asked, "The
last time you saw me on the *President*, the night I was married,
you had quite a time amusing yourself by keeping Charles away
from me. If you had it all to do over again now, would it be just
for amusement?"

She thought for a moment that he had not heard her. Then

she experienced a second's panic at her own shamelessness. But when he turned to face her there was no suggestion of amusement in his attitude. She could not see his features, but his whole body as he faced her seemed tense. Without saying a word he lifted his arm so that it was on the seat back of her. His fingers touched the back of her neck, then went up through her hair, pulling the braids loose so that they fell down her back. He seized both of them hard so that her head tilted back. Then he leaned forward quickly and kissed her throat where a small quickening pulse beat showed. For a long time he held his lips against it until she began to feel the beat of it growing and filling her whole body.

"Steve!" She wrenched herself away and lifted both hands to his face in the darkness. "Steve—"

His hand still held her hair tight, but this time he pulled her toward him in the darkness.

1857

CHAPTER V

AGNES RETURNED from New York early in March, full of excited reports concerning the machinery she had bought, the equipment that would be shipped west by water. She had been unusually lucky, she said. What she had been unable to buy in the East she had succeeded in locating through the agent of a London firm. Richard was enthusiastic over her success, and Treese could not help noticing that news of the machinery seemed to excite him more than the fact of Agnes's presence near him again. Agnes inquired casually of Richard whether there had been trouble at the mines. No, there had been no trouble. Nothing important. One or two claim-jumping attempts. Treese saw Agnes turn her head quickly away, saw the slight stiffening of her back. It lasted for only a moment. When she looked up again her dark eyes were shuttered and impassive. Gradually, during her first evening home, they began to acquire a luminosity, following Richard about the room, watching him with a mounting intensity. Early in the evening, while he was still eagerly discussing the new plans for the mines, she suggested that they go upstairs; she was tired after the long trip. In the instant's hesitation before he rose and took her arm, Treese read a new reluctance and knew that the inevitable had happened. She felt a strange detached sympathy for him as she followed them out of the room with her eyes.

The equanimity of Agnes's reunion with her husband was to be short-lived. At three o'clock the following morning Treese was awakened by the sound of furious pounding on the front door. She sat up in bed, trying to place the sound. Then she threw back the covers, thrust her feet into her slippers and pulled on the wrapper that lay across the foot of the bed. She hurried out into the hall.

Agnes was standing at the top of the stairs holding a lamp. Her long black hair tumbled over her back and she clutched her wrapper together in front of her. She looked at Treese but seemed not to see her, quickly turning back to watch Richard, who was scuttling down the steps, his feet flapping in their slippers, his robe pulled about him over his nightshirt.

The man almost fell into the hallway with exhaustion when Richard opened the door.

"—rode hard all the way—" They heard fragments of his gasps coming up the stairway. "—Mr. Wickham sent me—said you should hurry and bring men—all the men you can find. He said the Protectors—try to round up the Protectors. They have guns."

Richard shook him impatiently by the shoulder, trying to hold him upright and keep his knees from sagging.

"What happened?" he demanded. His usually slow voice was sharp and urgent. "What's wrong?"

"They jumped the Red Hill diggin's. Bribed the guards and got inside, barricaded themselves in with guns. He said—he said hurry—" The voice faded out as the man slumped over. Richard dragged him across the hall and into the parlor, where there was a thump as of a body being dropped. He returned to the hall and mounted the stairs two steps at a time, losing one of his slippers and not going back for it.

"I'd better get up there," he said curtly. "I'll get all the men I can."

"Richard—" Agnes's eyes were wide in the small circle of lamplight she held, and her face seemed whiter than ever in the black frame of her hair. "Richard, be careful."

Treese heard the sudden lost note in her voice, the lack of certainty. Agnes stood there as Richard hurried into the bedroom and started dressing, seemingly unable to move from the spot, still with her wrapper clutched across her breast. She looked across the breadth of the hall to Treese and for a long moment their eyes met. Treese knew the warning had not been for Richard.

Neither of them went back to bed after Richard had left, but they could not find words to say to each other, so they did not speak. Treese dressed and went down to the kitchen herself and made coffee without arousing the servants. She brought some into the dark chilly dining room to Agnes, and then, noticing the damp predawn gloom of the room, said gently, "Why not come into the kitchen? There's a fire going there, and it's pleasant."

Agnes looked at her dumbly as though not quite understanding, but she followed as Treese went ahead and opened the door. They sat across from each other at the scrubbed wooden kitchen table and drank the hot coffee silently. Agnes was still in her nightgown and wrapper, her hair disheveled, her eyes wide in her pale face. Treese felt all at once capable and in command of the situation and thought, quite irrelevantly, that it was more years than she could remember since she had seen her mother drink a cup of coffee at a kitchen table.

Agnes picked up the cup and held it in both hands as a child might have.

"I'm so afraid of shooting," she said aimlessly. Her voice had suddenly become quite without expression, Treese noticed. Her gaze did not seem directed at anything close at hand, but wandered aimlessly from point to point around the kitchen.

"It'll be all right, Mother."

"You know, there's something very capable about you, Treese. I don't know why I never noticed it before—did you make this coffee yourself?"

"Yes."

"I often thought I should have taught you how to cook and different things, but of course if you can get people to do things like that for you there's not much use . . ." Her voice trailed off. She searched around, picked up a different thread and went on. "I don't know much about these Protectors, do you, Treese?"

"No, not very much."

"Charles talked about them a great deal, but I got the idea it was just some sort of lodge. I really don't know much about it. Why do you suppose that man asked about the Protectors?"

"Some arrangement he must have made with Charles."

"Yes, I suppose so. You know, I really don't like all this violence. I'm accustomed to carrying business on in a civilized way, with papers to sign and lawyers and that sort of thing. I really don't care for violence."

"I suppose sometimes it can't be avoided."

"Oh, that's so grim, Treese. Goodness, there's always a way of settling things." She glanced around again. "I suppose it must be rather early—cook isn't even up yet."

"It's not even light yet."

"Goodness, servants certainly aren't as they used to be. Why, I mind the time when a good cook was up lighting fires and baking bread long before this."

"There's no need, Mother. Cook takes very good care of us."

"Well, yes. But there's a certain dignity to be considered. My, but I can't say that I enjoy being up like this before daylight. Treese, I tell you what I think I'll do, just this once. I think I'll go and get the baby up. It won't do a bit of harm, and it would keep me company. I'll bring him down here in the kitchen and it'll make me a little easier in my mind." She got up and started for the door.

Treese looked at her and experienced a suffocating, overpowering pity. Who had ever called pity a virtue? This lonely, hurting thing, this aching need to reach out and give something to another human being and know that there was nothing that could be given? This aloneness, this complete desolation that she saw in Agnes—could there be anything more terrible? And yet it was nothing that could be traced from actual effect to cause. It was not losing King, though that had been part of it; not losing Delaney, or Keith, although they too figured in the picture. It was not any single loss. It was rather the lack in Agnes herself that had brought these things about. It was the dreadful, consuming need to reach out and control others because there were no resources within herself on which to draw. There could have been so many who would have stood by Agnes and comforted her. Margaret, Elizabeth, Keith and Annette, even Richard, if Agnes would only have let them. But there was no giving in where Agnes was concerned, no exchange of trust, no pliability that would allow give-and-take. There was only the hard, uncompromising core and the terrible need that made her draw her strength from the compliance of others. Now she had only Richard. And how long would she have him? And after Richard, who would there be? Only young Delaney. Only the baby; a new life forming, a new personality growing—

"No!" Treese jumped up from her chair and stood rigid, one

hand clutching the table edge to steady herself. Agnes turned questioningly.

"It's too early. He won't be awake yet." Her voice was tight and full, the words indistinct. "Don't disturb him."

"But why—just this once—"

"Don't go to him!" Her voice rose hysterically. "Leave him alone!"

Agnes looked confused and worried. She pulled at a strand of black hair that had fallen across her shoulder, twisted it around her finger and came back to the table.

"All right, Treese," she said tonelessly. "All right."

When it was scarcely light Treese threw on her cloak and hurried to Annette's house. The dawn curled in a mist around her heels as she ran through the deserted streets. There seemed to be no one up yet except a few early-morning tradesmen who were railing at sleepy, steaming horses. In spite of her anxiety she felt the strange heightening exhilaration of responsibility, of being needed, and she hurried even faster.

There was lamplight from behind the windows of the house as she hurried up the steps and she thought that Annette must have heard, or she would not be up at such an hour. She fell back with a gasp of astonishment when the door was opened, for it was Steve who stood there, his coat off, his shirt sleeves rolled up to his elbow. His cravat was hanging untied about his neck and his collar was open at the throat. The ruffles of his shirt were mussed and limp.

She stared at him for a moment, not understanding. Finally she found her voice.

"Is Annette all right? I came as soon as I could—"

"How did you know?" His voice had a harsh, strained quality and his forehead was drawn together in a frown as though he, too, did not understand.

"A rider came to the house and told us."

"What the—"

"About the mine. About Keith and the other men jumping the Red Hill mine."

"Oh, Lord, that too! Well, my concern is a trifle more immediate. Annette's having her baby."

"What—what can we do?" she stammered.

"Everything is being done," he said wearily, turning away from her and leaving the door open for her to come in. "I'm an old hand at this sort of thing. Pelu is a help too."

"Is there something I can do?" Treese threw off her cloak and followed him into the little parlor with its bright rugs and shiny dark-red floors.

"There's enough work for everyone. I think she'd like to see you, if you'd care to come in."

Annette was on the bed, her white face wet with perspiration, her hair a tangle on the pillow. Pelu bent over her, wiping her forehead with a cloth and speaking soothingly to her. Treese hurried to the bed and bent over Annette, taking both small wet hands in her own.

"Hello, dear. Are you feeling very badly?"

Annette's eyes opened and were suddenly flooded with gratitude. Her voice came weakly.

"Treese! How did you know?"

Treese started to speak, then changed what she was going to say. "I don't know. Maybe I guessed. Would you like me to stay here with you?"

"Oh, Treese!" The name was a plea, a flood of gratitude. For the second time that day Treese felt the peculiar sensation of capability, of being needed. First Agnes, so competent, so untouchable, so uncompromisingly efficient. Now Annette, so small and determined and sure, so ready to help someone else.

Treese felt Annette's hands tighten on hers and saw that her face had contorted suddenly with pain. Pelu kept up the quiet comforting talk and Steve stepped forward, throwing back the covers.

"All right, sweetheart. Let's try it again. Hold Treese's hands." He looked across the bed at Treese. "Hold her tight. Help her to push. Pelu, get her legs."

For a moment Treese could only stand holding Annette's hands, looking across at him in sheer horror. Then suddenly there seemed no time for hesitation. Annette's grasp tightened and there was a low agonizing moan from the bed. Her own humiliation was drowned in something greater. There was no time for fastidiousness. She knew little enough about how babies were born, but she stood resolute, standing firm while Annette clung to her, carefully ignoring what Steve was about. "Push, dear," she said.

The chill of the rest of the house struck her forcibly as she came out of the door, for Pelu had kept a warm fire going in the bedroom. She felt perspiration all over her body begin to cool and make her shiver. Her dress was clinging across her back and she felt the dampness between her breasts. She walked into the parlor, not knowing what time it was. It was still overcast outdoors, so it was impossible to tell from the sun. Probably noon. Maybe later. She felt almost too weak to stand and then remembered that she had had nothing but coffee since the night before. Later she would go into the kitchen and fix something.

She sank down on the small sofa in front of the cold fireplace and dropped her head in her hands, not caring that her face was pale and shiny with fatigue, her hair still hanging down her back in the bedraggled braid she had twisted it into before starting out that morning.

Strange, how little a momentous thing like birth changed the ordinary aspects of the day. There was Annette lying spent in the next room with a new life sleeping beside her, small and red-faced. In that blanket-wrapped bundle was a concentration, a kind of distillation of all the hopes and frustrations that the human spirit was heir to. New material for the mill, she thought grimly. Something unsullied and completely new—hardly an hour out of the womb, and any minute now this new little daughter would know hunger and be fed or cry from the chill and be covered warmly or know internal disturbances and relieve herself quite without conscience or fear of rebuff. Everything would be made easy for her, all her wants attended to. And yet in the same small body there dwelt dormant the pain, the fears, the lack of knowledge that made each one vulnerable in his own special way. And how would they fare within her? Would they be dealt with skillfully so that they might never come to full fruition, to cause tears and torment, or would there be a slip somewhere along the way, even an unintended one, which would open the gate and allow them their full freedom? How was it possible to know the key, to be sure of the solution? How was it possible to be sure you were not making a mistake when you did this or that? How could you know whether a chance word might not have been the wrong one, a chance action fatal, a chance caress the one that was too many?

She heard Steve come into the room, heard his footsteps cross to the window, but she did not look up. She remained in her position of utter exhaustion, her head resting in her hands.

"Treese."

She lifted her head, smoothing her hair back at both temples. He was standing with his back to the window, his hands in his pockets, sleeves still rolled up.

"Yes."

"Are you all right?"

"Yes. Of course. Is Annette asleep?"

"Yes. Pelu's with her. She'll be all right now."

"And the baby?"

"You saw the baby." He seemed a little surprised. "She looked fine to me."

"I know. I was thinking of something else." She leaned against the back of the sofa and fixed her eyes on the line where wall and ceiling joined.

"You were good with Annette," he said. "I never thought you could do it."

"Why?"

"No reason exactly." He looked at her, then walked over to the sofa so that he stood above her. "You should have something to eat. And some rest. Why don't you let me fix you something?"

She smiled faintly. "I suppose I should ask whether you can cook too. But nothing would surprise me today." Her eyes moved distractedly along the line of wall and ceiling until they reached the corner, then they moved back listlessly.

"Would you eat something if I fix it?"

"A little later. Right now—I don't know. I've been thinking."

"About what? Keith?"

"Partly. But mostly about the baby."

This time he showed no surprise. "I know. I've been thinking too."

Her eyes moved to him, catching at the line of his waist and moving up over the slender body that was a shade too taut, a shade too wiry, to the chin with its gray stubble, the deep lines from nose to mouth, the dark mustache, the eyes that were so like Annette's and yet which held no serenity.

"What were you thinking?" she asked.

"Nothing you could put your finger on. Wondering what will become of her and how much happiness will be allotted to her, whether she may someday meet a man, and what kind of man he'll be, and yet none of those things distinctly. Just everything jumbled together."

"She has a good start. She has Annette and Keith."

"Yes, she has them." He walked to the fireplace and kicked at the dead stub of burned wood that had fallen to the hearth. He took a cheroot from his pocket and lighted it. The smoke in the chilly damp room seemed to cut through searingly, filling her nostrils with good dry strength. "I wonder if that's enough though."

"It's important."

"Yes. But there are other things too—"

"Things another person can never quite reach."

"That's what I mean." He faced her again. "There are places in everyone that are his own individual property, his to live with, to examine, to try to understand. I wonder if another person can ever quite get to them, no matter how willing they might be, or how they might try."

"It means a great deal to know that there is someone there who would like to understand. It makes the going easier."

"I suppose it does. I've never had anyone like that."

"Neither have I."

They stared at each other for a moment. Then he smiled wryly. "We're talking in a vacuum then, aren't we?"

"I guess we are." She reached around and drew the disordered braid over her shoulder, loosening it and rebraiding it. His eyes watched the movement of her fingers. "There was someone with me," she said distantly. "A long time ago there was my father. And he came very close to what we were talking about. Someone who was always there. But he in turn drew his strength from someone else, and when that strength failed him, then he failed too. And then there was no longer anyone for me."

"And so the best thing is to not need anyone."

"Yes. But it never quite comes out that way."

"But you can condition yourself. You can make yourself believe it."

"One part of yourself. But the other part, the part we spoke of that is your own property, your personal problem, that part of you knows that you are lying."

"I wonder what that part of a person is. Is it his conscience, do you think?"

She considered for a moment, her hands pausing in their motion of braiding the three red ropes of hair.

"No, not his conscience. I think it is his sense of himself. His sense of being important and a part of something, wanted in some way or by someone. He must have that." Her eyes grew wide and intense. "Everyone must have that, in one way or another. Without that a person is nothing. It was like that with him. With Delaney."

"And how about you? Are you needed?"

She did not answer immediately. Her hands took up the braiding, finished it and tossed the braid back. "I have a child—"

"You say that as if it wasn't enough."

"It's enough in one way. It's a real enough need. I know how much it counts and how important it is. I don't mean it that way."

"Well, then—"

"But it's an accidental need. It's—how can I say it? It happened because I had a child, and that was purely a physical thing—an accident of nature. Or rather no accident, but nature's normal course of affairs. And the minute I had that child he became my responsibility. But it had nothing to do with the thing we spoke of. It's something that comes to every woman who has a child, and yet it's not demanded of her because she has any special skill or anything to give that child. That's why some are good mothers but many are not. It's a responsibility thrust upon her. It is the most important thing in the world, but its importance is centered in the child."

"If you are needed, you are, that's all. I see no difference."

She looked at him. "I think you do see it."

He flicked the cheroot away. "Think so if you like."

"What I mean is—" She breathed in hard and looked at the floor. "I have never been needed for myself alone. I have never had anything to give anyone."

"You've given Annette a great deal."

"Company on a rainy afternoon? No." She lifted her head and smiled ruefully. "No, you don't need to say things like that. I know it isn't true. No one has ever needed me as long as I've lived. And I'm not saying it to make you pity me. I'm saying it because it's quite true and the only thing about my whole life that is real and factual. Now I have a child and I must go on living as always and being as always because I've been handed a responsibility. But nobody willed it. Nobody intended it that way. It just happened. And it will turn out badly."

"What makes you say that?" He was frowning suddenly and his voice cut through sharply in the dim room.

"Because nothing is any different now. Everything is still the same. There's nothing strong or dominant in me that will come to the surface all of a sudden because I need it. I'll be the same as I've always been. And my son will be the one to suffer."

"The other night you spoke differently. You said there were things you wanted to give him. You spoke of California and of the West."

"I know. Those are things I think because they make it easier. There are times when I can almost bring myself to believe them. But they are only dreams and I know it. What have I to give him?"

Her voice had grown bitter and now she was not looking at Steve or at anything in the room, but at something that was far and outside.

"Treese—" His voice was different now, neither casual nor ironic, but suddenly a little uncertain. She looked at him. He was watching her, his eyes troubled. He came over to her and bent down, pulling her up toward him and kissing her, holding her so close that she could feel every line of his body and taste the perspiration on his lips.

"Treese, I want you. I need you."

"No." She moved her face away from him so that the top of her head was against his cheek but still they clung together. "You don't need me. Someone perhaps, but not me."

"I've felt it before—not just this afternoon. I know it. I know it by the way you talk, the things you say that make me realize a great many other things about myself. I know that no one can live by himself, in a world made by himself. There's the same need in you that there is in me—a longing to be a part of something, to be depended on. You could give it to me, Treese. We could give it to each other. Alone we'll never find it."

"We'll never find it together either."

"Why?" He held her away from him by the shoulders and shook her a little, but she would not look at him. "Why can't we?"

"Because things are the way they are." Her voice was so low he could hardly distinguish the words. "Because I'm what I am and you—"

"I'm a saloonkeeper and not good enough for the Delaneys?"

"No. I don't care about that. But you can't change people and you can't change the way they talk. The things they'd say about us—"

"Does it matter that much to you?"

"It doesn't matter at all to me. But it would matter to my son."

"Oh." He let her go at last and turned back to the cold hearth. "And what do you think of a woman who lives out her life giving herself to a man she doesn't love?"

"You know what I think of her. I told you a minute ago. She's not even worth gossiping about. She's not worth anything."

"But she's respectable."

"Yes, she's respectable. That's important to a child."

"Naturally. I'm overlooking the essentials."

She went over to him and looked up into his face earnestly.

"I'm not deceiving myself, Steve. I know that it's not the most important thing, but it's all I have to give him. You can see that, can't you?"

"Just now you said you knew it would all turn out badly. You must have meant something by that."

Treese felt a dry knot forming in her throat, and her breath seemed to burn in her lungs when she breathed. It would turn out badly. Why had she said so?—she had not meant to. She had said it because she was sure of it. She had known it before, but now, since this morning, she was certain. In that dark lonely moment before dawn with a fire burning in the kitchen and coffee black and fragrant on the table in front of her, she had known. She had seen the despair in Agnes's eyes, the lost look, turning, turning, searching for something. Or someone. And it would never end as long as there was Agnes and as long as there were new lives. There would be this baby and then perhaps there would be others—and Agnes would claim them all. But even to give them to Agnes, could it be any worse than having them pointed to on the street, ostracized and hurt, until they would grow to hate her? In this, at least, she would have a refuge. A pat answer for all their questions, a righteous reply for all their resentments. "Your grandmother has been good to you, darling. She's given you a great deal. Ask your grandmother, dear. What does grandmother say?"

"Steve!" The name was a sob, and now all at once she was in his arms again, trembling and shaking, her head thrust against his shoulder. "How can I bear it? How can I know what's right?"

He did not answer, but he held her close, and one hand touched the back of her head and then moved with a gentle soothing motion through her hair at the place where there was a little depression and where all her troubled nerves and sinews seemed to have their root. She began to feel the rhythm of it, to know a softening of perceptions until all thoughts and impressions seemed to run together easily and there were no more obstacles, no more dark places. She put her arms around him and pressed hard against his back as though she would have liked her own being to blend and dissolve in his. She could feel the steady beat of his heart, the smoothness of his shirt against her cheek. All she could see was encompassed by his arms and shoulders and above her his face, tilted downward slightly so that it rested against her forehead.

"Steve, I love you. I never loved a man before."

"I love you too. And I have loved a great many women. Perhaps that means even more."

"When did it happen—and how?"

"I don't know."

"I saw you once. Long before you saw me."

"When?"

"Aboard the *New World,* when we were coming to Sacramento for the first time. You were lounging up on the deck with the most beautiful boredom. Wearing a very wicked-looking chain. Quite the most dashing man I'd ever seen. And then you threw two girls overboard. That impressed me vastly."

"I don't remember it."

"And I've never forgotten it. Do you know what I remember most of all?"

"What?"

"Your hands." She backed away and took them both in her own. "And your wrists. I remember how they looked with the sun on them. I knew you were a gambler by the clothes you wore. But your hands weren't like that. They were brown, somehow, or they gave that impression, and strong. I never forgot them."

"Treese—" He pulled her to him again and ran one hand along the line of her jaw and cheek, holding it there while he kissed her again. Then suddenly he knew that she was crying again and he let her go. She threw both arms around his neck and buried her face in his shoulder until he could feel the tears against his own skin through the thin material of his shirt.

"Steve, will you take me away? Will you take me and the baby away somewhere where we'll never see Sacramento again or anyone that was ever part of our lives?" He did not answer and she clung still closer to him, feeling his hands upon her back where he held her, the smoothness of them through the dress. "If we could do that —if we could go away, Steve, then there wouldn't be any more problems. We'd be by ourselves, making a life of our own. No one would care what we'd been before. We'd have each other, and we could have children of our own if you wanted them, and there'd be no one to bother us or care what we'd been before. Steve, could we go away?"

She lifted her head and looked at him. Her face was streaked with tears but now it had taken on a sudden radiance, a look of hope that was close to desperation.

He let his hands drop so that he was no longer holding her.

"Steve—"

"That would be quite a handy arrangement, wouldn't it?" he said. There was something almost like amusement in his voice, but all the softness had suddenly gone from his mouth and eyes.

"I only said it because I love you so much. I want you so."

He seemed not to have heard her. "I could set you up in style—back east, let's say, or maybe even in Europe. I have plenty of money, you know."

"Steve, don't!"

"You wouldn't have to bother about a divorce, and you wouldn't have to face any of your old friends—"

"I only thought we could be together—"

"My darling Treese." He took both her hands and held them tight, but now there was no warmth in his touch, no caress in his voice when he spoke. "We could be together right now, right here in Sacramento, the place that means more to you than any place on earth, in case you've forgotten. We could make a life of our own right on J Street. A few minutes ago you had me believing something very touching. Something all wrapped up in motherhood and self-sacrifice. You wanted the best for your child. You couldn't bear to have his life jeopardized. That was really beautifully put. Only all of a sudden it comes to me that it wasn't true—any of it. You aren't worried about what's best for him. You're thinking of what would be easiest for you. It wouldn't be easy to renounce the family ties, the Delaney reputation—although what it consists of has always escaped me. It would be hard to throw all that away for somebody whose background is as dubious as mine, even though he might love you like all hell. It would be just a little too hard, wouldn't it? You couldn't quite do it. No answer? I thought not. Well, then, that's that. Oh, I'm not trying to play noble about it. Only for some reason this thing is important to me. And it's one time I'm not running away." He turned and started to walk away from her. She followed him, caught him by the arms and made him face her again.

"Steve, don't go away like this. I didn't say it to hurt you. Please, Steve—"

He took her hands and disengaged them firmly. "In another minute," he said, "you'll be offering to come to me some night for an hour or two in my rooms. Which would be very delightful, I'll admit. But unfortunately it won't be enough any more. I have a certain pride. And more than that, although you probably won't understand it, I have a feeling of pride for you. And I don't want to see you taking everything the world kicks your way. There's a thing in you that I love, that I want. And it isn't that. Cowardice isn't a very becoming quality, Treese."

And then he was gone and there was no sound but the screaming silence of the empty room. She went to the sofa and dropped down on it, dry-eyed for the first time, staring straight ahead of her. In the next room a tiny wail rose.

The office in the rear of the Red Tent was a small bare room, with a desk, several straight chairs, and a cot against one wall. There was one small window high up near the ceiling. Steve struck a light and put it to the lamp on the desk. The room flared into dim light and shadows. Steve flung himself down in a chair behind the desk, tipped back and reached into the drawer for a bottle. The faro dealer stood in the doorway watching for a moment.

"I always wondered about this room," he said.

"Why?" Steve drew the bottle out and poured himself a drink. He motioned with the hand that held the bottle toward another of the chairs. The man closed the door behind him, muffling the noise of the Red Tent, and sat down in the chair across the desk from Steve.

"Doesn't seem to fit in with the rest of the place. Or with your rooms upstairs."

"I planned it that way. For a reason."

"It's only curiosity on my part, of course—"

"I like you because you don't talk too much, Sloane. Most people don't know when to stop. Don't have a way with words, either, like you do."

"This is all highly flattering," Adam Sloane smiled.

"It should be. I don't like many people." Steve lifted his legs so that his heels were propped up on the edge of the desk. "I wish you'd have a drink with me. More sociable."

"I'd like to, but I just never got used to it."

Steve drank the whisky and closed his eyes for a moment. When he opened them they were dark and curious. "What made you give up the gospel, Adam?"

"I never gave it up."

"But you left the ministry."

"That's something else again."

"But to turn to such an opposite extreme. There doesn't seem much connection to me between faro and the church."

"There is no connection. I didn't intend it that way. I was looking for something, that's all. And I found it here."

"What?"

"A certain integrity. Of the soul, I might say. If you wouldn't think that too reminiscent of my former calling."

"Doesn't quite hang together."

"Well, yes, it does in a way. The missionary business was all right as long as I felt that I was accomplishing something. But there's a point of stagnation. Maybe not for everyone, although I rather fancy it does come to all of us at some time or another. With me it came when I was traveling through the mining camps preaching, trying to bring some sort of order into the filth and chaos. But somehow I could never seem to reach the men. For a long time it worried me—gave me a feeling of frustration. Until one day it dawned on me that the trouble all along had been that I was looking down on them. Not in a social way, not as inferiors, but judging them by a moral code that I had adopted second- or third-hand and then embellished with a few of my own hypocrisies. And it didn't fit the time. It was archaic."

"I thought righteousness was supposed to be eternal."

"I thought so too. And that was my downfall. But look at it this way. A man gives up his home, sometimes his family, everything that has meant security to him in the past, and comes west. It might be China, for all he knows about it. That takes courage, you know. Never mind whether it's gold he's looking for. The motive isn't important. Even if it's selfishness, still it took nerve. And a great deal of fight. He'd heard about California. Back east the streets were full of stories, and because he was a man and subject to the desires of man, he wanted to come too and try his luck. You can hardly blame him for that. We wouldn't even know the world was round if it hadn't been for that same spirit in someone else. But when he got here, what did he find? Sometimes gold. Rarely. But he found plenty of other things. Rats and filth and bedbugs and snakes and fever. Polluted water and lonely days, and nights so long they amounted to little separate eternities. And he would have gone home—oh, how he'd have gone! But he didn't have money enough for his fare back. So he'd scrape two or three ounces of gold from the ground and come back to camp with his back aching and his feet sore and his hands broken and split. Sometimes he'd take the money and buy flour with it, enough to keep him going until he could dig out two or three more dollars' worth. And other times he'd buy a bottle and a woman with it. Satisfy his lust and drink himself into oblivion, and then for a few hours he'd be able to drop off to sleep and keep from remembering. And then I came along and was supposed to change all that. Do you wonder I felt frustrated?"

"Doesn't sound like a type easy to convert."

"It wasn't a question of converting. I found myself agreeing with him. What had I to offer him? A substitute opiate. And a poor substitute at that. The wages of sin— What worse hell had I to threaten him with than the one he had already created for himself?"

"So that was what gave you the push?"

"In a broad sense, yes. But to be specific, and honest, well, I'm human myself. There was a woman."

Steve raised his eyebrows in simulated horror.

"Oh, no. You misinterpret me. It was the woman I already had. My wife. Where I sympathized with the poor devils, she excoriated them. She was, in a word, God's little demon. She made virtue a cult. Practiced at it day and night. Especially night. Told me she liked submitting to me because it gave her a chance to ask forgiveness the next day for my multiple sins of the flesh and to feel twice cleansed."

"Was that the immediate cause?"

"The immediate cause was that she said it once too often and at the worst possible moment." Sloane did not smile. "I packed my things that very night and never went back."

"And where is she now?"

The dealer shrugged lightly. "I have no idea. But she is the type who would always manage."

"But why did you become a faro dealer?"

Sloane thought for a moment. "I don't really know. It could have been anything. The principal thing was that I be by myself and have an opportunity to think, to live a fairly normal life and readjust my values gradually. But no—" He hesitated again. "There's something else. The truth of the matter is, I like cards. Always did. I'm fascinated by them. And I like gambling." He smiled now, quite openly. "Is that an honest answer?"

"A long way around, but honest. I wonder if it's that easy for everyone to make a choice."

"Did I say that it was easy? I've misled you then. It was the hardest thing I've ever done in my life."

"You made it sound easy."

"These things are different in retrospect. At the time it's less simple. There are issues to be weighed, small imponderables to be considered. There is, above all, the reluctance to leave the status quo, no matter how distasteful it is." He slid his long frame down in the straight chair to a more comfortable position and looked directly across at Steve. "Did I ever tell you about the first time I met Treese Delaney?"

Steve, pouring himself another whisky, felt his hand jerk and some of the whisky slopped over the edge of the glass. "No," he said.

Sloane's voice went on with pleasant normality. "It was on a boat, the *New World*. That was the steamer we started out on when we landed in California. The cholera steamer, we learned later. We had dinner together at the captain's table. Mrs. Delaney and her children were there. I was quite imbued with the missionary spirit then. Also impressed with Mrs. Delaney's beauty. Looking back on it, I can remember a great many other things."

"Such as?"

"Oh—a little girl very much overshadowed by her mother's charm. A kindly child, concerned over her small sisters."

"Sisters?"

"She had two younger sisters then. And she was most motherly and efficient with them. But she was timid too, rather awkward. A little frightened by the wildness of the new world she suddenly found herself in. But brave. Something about her stayed with me long after the other details of the trip had disappeared."

"There is something about her that a man remembers," Steve said almost to himself. "What is it, do you think?"

"I'm not sure. That was the only time I ever saw her except for once or twice about the streets here. But I should say that it is probably the same thing that has made me remember many different individuals throughout my lifetime. Strength showing through apparent weakness, beauty through external plainness. Those are trite phrases, and yet—"

"Yes, I know," Steve said quickly. "And yet it's not even that simple. There's something else. Something lost, or searching. Some unsureness there."

"Call it that personal integrity I spoke of before. There's the desire for it in every man. And yet everyone does not find it. Some are content to end the search at the halfway mark. They achieve a certain success, financial or social, and they believe that they have found it. I suppose she wants it too. The feeling of her life being worth something, having some purpose. Christianity says we were put on earth for a purpose. To do God's will. I'm inclined to think of it rather differently. To examine life as a justification rather than as something ordained in advance. We might have landed here by some monstrous hoax or freak of nature, but once here we owe it to ourselves to fight back, so that we know at least to our own satisfaction that it was worth it."

"You don't sound much like any preacher I ever heard."

"Faro has a remarkably clarifying effect on the brain. It enables a man to gain a good perspective on living. The cards are stacked against the bettor. That's taken for granted. And the poor players naturally can't buck the tiger. They see the odds and back down, or else continue playing with reckless desperation, which never gains them anything either. The good gambler knows the odds, takes plenty of chances, but takes them philosophically. He knows he might not win, and he's ready to take his losses. And because he's ready for anything, he's already on a par with the dealer, meeting him face to face. You can't beat a good player. You may take his money sometimes but you never really beat him because he has it all figured out ahead of time. He's prepared for anything. He knows his limits but he knows his potentialities too. That's what puzzles me about you, Steve."

"What?" Steve drank the second whisky and set the glass down.

"Well, you're better than average at faro, but—"

"Let's leave it right there."

"Why? I thought this was the room with no hiding places."

Steve grinned and Sloane continued.

"You're good at faro, at any kind of gambling. But when it comes to your personal life you play like a twenty-year-old with a pocketful of dust and hardly a fuzz on his chin. You go in all directions at once trying to beat circumstances. And when it doesn't come off as you planned you grab up whatever's left on the board and run as though Satan was breathing down your neck. Only with you it doesn't take the form of actual running away. It becomes a fine saloon with thick carpets and all the women you can comfortably manage, something you can flaunt at the rest of the world. 'See, I don't care. I've got all of this.'"

Steve stirred uneasily in his chair. "That strikes very close to my conscience. Because today I gave somebody hell for wanting to run away. Does that come under the heading of examining the beam in my own eye?"

"Maybe. Why were you so upset that she wanted to run away?"

"It hurt my pride."

"You're showing progress. I don't think you would have admitted that five minutes ago."

"Well, you seem to know a lot of things I wasn't aware of. You probably would have figured that one out too. Oh, hell, no use lying about it. The only thing is—" He paused and thought hard for a second. "With women it's different. A man can go off and be self-sufficient any time he wants to. But a woman has to stick with a man. She has to go where he goes. That's something you take for granted. And if you want a woman, you want her all the way. You don't like the idea that she just wants love from you and respectability from someone else."

"Did she say she wanted both?"

"No, but she said she wanted to run away."

"Didn't you ever run away from anything?"

There was a long pause. "Yes. I ran away. Maybe that's why I couldn't be rational about it this afternoon. Because I saw something in her that I'd seen in myself."

"An honest answer. But I don't suppose you told her that this afternoon."

"No."

"It might have helped a great deal."

"Maybe." Steve tipped his head back, closed his eyes and ran a hand through his short dark hair. For a moment he stayed that way. Then he crossed his legs on the desk, opened his eyes and sat slightly forward once more. His hair was mussed, giving him the fogged look of a recent sleeper. "I'll be damned if I know. I don't even know why I want her. In one way I know—the way I wanted her this afternoon. You want anything you can't get. But I keep thinking that there must be something else, something that kept me remembering her all these years." He looked up thoughtfully at Sloane. "You know, the first time I saw her she was on her honeymoon. I got her husband in a game of cards just for the hell of it and because I didn't particularly like his looks. But then all of a sudden I saw her sitting there and she looked like the loneliest person I'd ever seen. All drawn up inside herself, not knowing what she wanted, but knowing damned good and well it wasn't that lout sitting across from her. And for some reason I knew how she felt. Because I'd felt that way once myself. One day in New Orleans when my mother died. Only with me it was easier. I could strike out for myself, go any place I wanted to. There were a million new outlets for me. Maybe it was running away, as you say."

"Running away isn't always bad. Sometimes it's essential. It depends on what you're running from."

"And I thought to myself, she feels exactly what I felt. But it's not the end of something for her. It's the start of it. And instead of running away she'll have to stick with it and live with it and make it her life. I had a sudden attack of conscience. Oh, I'm not bragging. It was brief enough. But it was there just the same. The kind of feeling you might get walking off and leaving somebody to drown. And I remembered her. Does that seem strange?"

"I think it would have been stranger if you hadn't."

Steve frowned. "And there are other things. Different things that sort of bring me up with a jolt. The way she talks sometimes. Things she said about California and the West. They twist me around and get me mixed up. It wouldn't be easy for her to leave Sacramento. This place means something to her that it never meant to me."

"And what you mean is that you may have misjudged her. Perhaps she was making a greater sacrifice than you realized, offering to go away with you."

"Yes." Steve touched his mustache thoughtfully.

Sloane put his hands in his pockets and stretched his long legs out in front of him. "I think you were right about that part of it. I only think you were wrong in not explaining to her just how you felt. If you had shown her some of your own weaknesses, for example—"

"Human vanity."

"Yes. The insurmountable. And so what will you do now?"

"Have another drink and go upstairs to bed. Sophie's waiting for me."

Sloane smiled and shook his head. "And after that?"

Steve shrugged.

"Last cards coming up," Sloane said quietly. "Who'll call the turn?"

CHAPTER VI

FIVE DAYS LATER Treese paid a visit to Elizabeth. She had called on her cousin seldom since Elizabeth's marriage to Andy, not so much because of her own new preoccupations as because of certain subtle changes in Elizabeth that made Treese confused and almost ill at ease. In place of the old gaiety that had characterized Elizabeth, there was now an unnatural quietness, a serenity that had no peace behind it. Often Treese would find herself rattling away at inconsequential gossip only to turn to Elizabeth and see an expression of complete preoccupation as though she heard not a word, and try as she might Treese could not seem to shake the mood of lethargy from her. She wondered whether Elizabeth might be aware of her friendship with Annette and be resentful of it, but when

Elizabeth did speak she gave no sign of it. She was as affectionate as always with Treese, and the subject was never brought up between them.

A few times Treese had met Andy on the street. There was no perceptible change in him except that a few more lines had appeared around his eyes, and his mouth had a tired look. He shaved regularly and dressed neatly now, and his office no longer bore signs of seediness and neglect.

He had built Elizabeth the most talked-of home in Sacramento. It was situated only a few blocks away from Agnes's home, and in every respect its construction had been a quiet, supercilious, though perhaps unintentional blow at Agnes's prestige. Elizabeth had made no attempt to outdo Agnes, but the very house was a statement of quiet, contemptuous superiority. It was easily the loveliest house in the city. Yet even the acquisition of the house had produced no change in Elizabeth. She moved through it with a kind of quiet disembodiment, her physical being complementing it fittingly, but some part of her spirit never quite at ease there.

Treese was conscious of this strange detachment again as they sat before the fire in the pleasant living room talking. She watched Elizabeth's pale hands move restlessly with the satin tassel of her blue velvet dressing gown. Neither of them had spoken for the past five minutes, and before that the conversation had been in platitudes, mostly on Treese's part. She had tried to give her bits of gossip an undue importance and they had come out sounding heavy and a little ridiculous. Elizabeth's answers had been laconic and disinterested.

Treese tried another tack, striking boldly into a subject that she knew would awaken a response.

"I suppose you've heard about the trouble at the mines."

Elizabeth looked at her for the first time with something that approached real interest, but behind the interest seemed to lie a restless fear.

"Andy told me about it. Keith's up there."

"Yes. We're waiting for word every day."

"Andy's keeping close watch. He's going to let me know when there's any news. They won't hurt Keith, will they?"

"I hope not." Treese hesitated, wondering how much she should leave unsaid. "Keith has a daughter now, you know. A baby girl."

Elizabeth's blue eyes grew wide and strangely vacant. She seemed to be looking nowhere in particular. "I didn't know." Her voice was almost a whisper now.

"When you know Annette you can't resent her any more. You can't help loving her. I know it sounds hard, but you must realize it, Elizabeth. She's good for Keith. And none of it was her fault."

"It was her fault," Elizabeth said with quiet finality. "She wanted him, and she never gave up until she got him."

"No, that wasn't it. She might have wanted him, but she didn't try to take him away from you. She has a great deal of pride. She wouldn't have done that. It was Keith who did the pursuing. You should realize that, Elizabeth, even if it hurts, because you mustn't go on misjudging her."

"I know perfectly well that what you say might be true, but I can't believe it. If I believed it I think I'd die."

"Perhaps it's only that it's too soon for you to believe it. One day you'll be able to, and it won't hurt any more. It isn't a thing that can be rushed. But try not to form prejudices that only hurt yourself."

"You're so—I don't know—so adequate, Treese. I wish you'd come to see me oftener. Perhaps I haven't made you feel welcome. I know I haven't been good company. But I do want you to come."

"I'll come, Elizabeth."

Elizabeth sat back in her chair and closed her eyes. "She has Keith's baby now," she mused. "I wonder if she knows how lucky she really is."

"Of course she knows."

Elizabeth's eyes flew open. "I mean—just having the baby, that's nothing. But loving a man and knowing that it's his, that's everything."

Treese shook her head slowly and then moved to stir the ebbing fire. "I don't think it is, Elizabeth. I think that's a foolish romantic notion. The baby is important, yes, but as soon as he's born he's an individual himself, someone to be considered and lived for. You're not being fair to him if you judge him by your own set of circumstances and attachments."

"That's easy enough to say!" Elizabeth's voice rose agitatedly and she jumped up from the chair. She strode across the room to the windows, then back to the fire. Her hands were tight together in front of her and her face was pale, older by years than Treese remembered it. "But I'm going to have a baby, and I'd sooner be dead!"

"Elizabeth!"

"I don't care how it sounds. It's what I feel. Before this I was free, in a way. At least there was a part of me that was mine, that didn't belong to anybody. Now my whole body, everything that I am, is going into creating this baby. I won't belong to myself any more. I'll belong to Andy because it's his child. Treese, I don't know how I can stand it!"

"Elizabeth, there's nothing you can tell me about that that will be new to me, because I went through it myself. You know perfectly well that I never loved Charles. And when I found out I was going to have a child, I was more alone than you've ever been. You've never been that alone, have you? In a strange country with only strangers around you, with no one you can talk to at breakfast when you get up or at dinner when you begin to feel homesick?" She saw an interruption coming and waved it away. "Oh, no, Elizabeth, you've never known that. Andy's a good, kind friend whom you've known and respected for years. You've never been alone in all your life as I was alone that year. But I made plans for my baby anyhow. I made up my mind that whatever happened I'd bring him back to California as soon as I could. And, more than that, I made up my mind that he'd never mean any less to me because he was Charles's. But I needn't have even thought of that, because as soon as he was born he was just himself, and I wouldn't have cared if his father had been that bandit Tom Bell, I'd have loved him just the same. And you're going to love your child the same way."

For a moment, Elizabeth stared at her cousin, more surprised at the vigor of her outburst than at what she had actually said. Then her hands began to clasp and unclasp and her eyes took on the look of distance and distraction.

"I don't know," she said softly.

Treese watched her, observing the play of firelight against the pale skin and hair, noticing how even in stress Elizabeth never quite lost the appearance of energy beneath the surface.

"Poor Treese. I wish I'd known—all those other years—how lonely you were. But no, I did sense it. It was simply that there seemed no place of meeting for us. Lots of affection, lots of real love, but little understanding. Do you think that's possible, Treese?"

"I don't know. I think sometimes understanding is instinctive. It's there whether you realize it or not."

"And do you understand me?"

Treese hesitated. "Yes, I think I do."

It was nearly nine when Andy came in. He looked worried and drawn, but he managed a smile when he saw Treese.

"Hello, Treese." He took off his hat and coat and threw them over a chair. He moved over to stand near the fire, reaching out and touching the top of Elizabeth's head as he did so. She looked up at him, studying his face.

"You found out something," she said tonelessly.

Treese felt her own heart beat faster. "Did you, Andy?"

"Well, yes." Andy kept his tone easy, trying not to let any urgency creep in. "Treese, if I were you I'd go over to Keith's. I had the carriage wait outside. Are you afraid, this time of night? Would you like me to go with you?"

"Andy!" It was Elizabeth's voice, harsh and breathless. "What is it?"

"Well, they brought Keith home. He's shot up pretty bad. I think maybe you could give them a hand, Treese."

Treese was already starting for the hall. She threw her wrap around her and tied her bonnet with unsteady fingers. Elizabeth was still staring at Andy.

"Will he die? Will he die, Andy?" She looked ready to crumple in a heap, but somehow she remained upright in the chair. He looked down at her tenderly. "Don't worry about it. Try not to worry. We don't really know much about it yet."

Watching from the doorway, Treese could see the play of emotion across his scholarly face. Worry over Keith and the men for what he knew and had left unspoken, anxiety for Elizabeth, and through it all a kind of confused hurt that was hardest of all to see. She pulled her wrap tight around her and hurried out without saying anything more.

Across the emptiness of the parlor Andy and Elizabeth stared at each other.

Midnight came in various guises to Sacramento. Along J Street, where the gambling houses were beginning to roll up their sleeves for the night's take, she wore a necklace of plate-glass windows, gaslit and flickering, and dropped her cloak with the casual abandon of a harlot. On the rise of Sutter's Fort, where the grass grew taller and the wind sighed confidentially, she stepped softly, self-effacingly, mindful of the dream of empire that lay broken and dead within those precincts. Along the residential streets she walked carefully, picking her skirts above the knee-deep mud but bearing herself with a certain imperiousness that caused late-sitting householders to glance up with surprise and, out of respect for her, march obediently off to bed. Around the little one-story frame house of Keith Delaney on the outskirts of town she lingered for a moment, then scurried off in a huff, for there the lights still burned and she went unnoticed. At the graceful new gray-stone home of Andy Hart she hesitated restlessly, walked back and forth, and sighed once or twice at the windows.

From the spare bedroom, where he lay in a half-sleep, Andy heard her and turned over on his back. He lifted his head slightly from the pillow as though straining to make out something and then let it drop back. He was sleepy, but behind the desire for sleep was a restlessness. It would have been better if he had gone to Elizabeth. Foolish to think that he would have disturbed her. It would have been only a body in bed beside her—a nonentity. Which was why he had not gone, of course. A man clung to his pride. Still, it would have been better, for there would have been warmth and the nearness of another person. Sometimes these small physical things had a very demanding way about them. She had wanted to go to Keith tonight. That was natural. And was he so bound and strictured by a ridiculous moral code that he had forbidden it? No, that was not the way it had been at all. He was beginning to dream now, instead of think. He had forbidden nothing, for she had not asked. She had not said a word. She had sat in the chair there by the fire, looking across the space of a few feet at him and accusing him. Accusing him of what? He turned again in bed and cursed wordlessly at the night that had filled itself with provocations and arguments. It was natural that she should want to go to Keith, if she loved him. But where did love end and the desire for possession start? And if she only desired to possess Keith because he was lost to her, then how would it all end and what would come of it? Would there be no peace for them now or as long as they lived?

Then quite suddenly he slept.

He did not know how long he slept but he knew what had awakened him. It was Elizabeth, and she was in the room. He did not know how he knew, he only knew that it was so. And because he was sure he spoke her name, not questioningly, but with a chiding certainty. Then he saw her. She was standing in the doorway with the faint light of the hall behind her. He could see the little haze of gold around her head and the vague outline of her body through the white nightdress. She started to walk toward him, taking slow, hesitant steps. He was wide awake now and something was making his heartbeat quicken. She came over to the bed and sat down on the edge of it. The light trailed in through the door and showed her features faintly. They were quite pale but there was nothing out of the ordinary about their expression. There was almost a lack of expression there, a calmness that surprised him.

"Andy?" She seemed not quite certain whom she would find in the bed.

"Yes."

"I've been thinking."

"You should have tried to sleep."

"When I'd thought it all out I decided to come in and tell you."

What was there about her voice that chilled him? What was this feeling of panic that sprang inside of him at the sound of rational, quiet-spoken words?

"What did you want to tell me, Elizabeth?"

"I hope Keith dies." She said it conversationally. I hope it doesn't rain tomorrow, she might have said.

"Elizabeth, you don't hope that."

Now, quite without warning, she wheeled on him furiously.

"What do you know about it?" she screamed. "I hope he dies! I hope he dies! Then she won't have him! I hope he dies tonight. I hope he's dead now!" Her voice drifted off into a wail and she slid to the floor in a heap, sobbing hard.

Andy slid out of bed, grabbed her by the shoulders and pulled her up. She struggled and fought in his grasp and he slapped her hard twice. She showed no surprise but she grew suddenly quiet. He lifted her and put her on the bed, then drew the covers over her. He remained standing by the bed, looking down at her.

"Light a lamp, Andy." Her voice was almost normal again.

He struck a light and put it to the lamp on the little table near the bed. It flared up and he turned it down low. He could see the extreme paleness of her face now, the deep hollows where the lamp made shadows of her cheekbones. He reached for his robe and put it on, then stepped into his slippers. He went to a little cabinet across the room and came back with a bottle of whisky and two glasses. He poured some and held it out to her.

"I guess you need this."

She raised herself on one elbow and drank it, then sank back. Andy poured himself a drink and tossed it down. He thought about it for a minute, then had another.

"You didn't mean that, of course," he said.

"No, I didn't mean it." She was lying on her back, staring up at nothing. Her fingernails, where they clutched the edge of the sheet, were bluish.

"Are you cold?"

She nodded. He pulled back the covers and got in beside her.

"Take this off," she said, touching the robe.

He took it off and threw it on the floor. She came to him, holding herself so close against him that he could feel the warmth of her skin through the material of his nightshirt. He held her tight until she had stopped trembling.

"Andy, what am I going to do?"

"I don't know. What do you want to do?"

"I want to do what's right. But I want to be happy. I can't help it."

"You speak as if the two things contradict each other. Don't you know that whatever you do to be happy is right?"

"No, not if you hurt someone."

"Yes, even if you hurt someone. But with you it's not that easy."

"Why isn't it?"

"Because you don't have any choice. What would you like to do—go to Keith and offer yourself to him? He'd be a little confused, I think. And embarrassed. He wouldn't know quite what to tell you. He has what he wants, Elizabeth. What more could you give him?"

"That isn't what I want."

"Then what do you want? To suffer? I'm beginning to think that's it."

"Andy, why do you talk like that? You never did before."

"Then I never spoke the truth before. But I hardly think anything less than the truth would be adequate tonight."

"I never meant to deceive you."

"Deceit isn't a word that should come between us. We never deceived each other."

"Andy, I don't know how to say what I feel. It has something to do with being young and yet feeling life creep up on you. Wanting to hold onto the years and knowing that no matter what you do you can't slow them up. I won't be young always, and there are so many things I want. I'm selfish. I don't want to miss any part of living."

"What part are you missing?"

"I don't know."

"Then shall I tell you? You're missing something that never existed, something you manufactured out of whole cloth and endowed with a great many pleasant aspects it never would have possessed. Do you think if you had married Keith that there wouldn't have been nights when you'd have been left alone to wonder where he was and what woman he was with? Making possession legal doesn't make it complete. Do you think he would have always been pleased with you—or you with him? A man cast in the wrong mold or married to the wrong woman loses potentialities he might otherwise have had. If the thing is right, then the man becomes everything that's inside him. Anything he wants to do is open to him and all things are possible. Keith would have been less of a man with you, Elizabeth, through no fault of your own. And I, perhaps, could be more of a man if you would let me."

There was faint anger behind her eyes. "Are you blaming me for inadequacies of your own?"

Andy smiled a little sardonically. "There was a night when you came to me—I felt tall enough and strong enough to reach out and touch the moon. I made you feel it too. But neither of us has ever felt it since. Why is that, do you suppose?"

"You'd make me believe it's all my fault."

"Isn't this all a little ridiculous anyway, at this point? Recriminations don't help much. I only want you to see things for what they are. Do you see, Elizabeth?"

"I see it in my mind, but inside me it still hurts."

"I know that. And there is no remedy for what you feel."

"You mean it will be like this always?"

"In some measure, yes. Since there is nothing to be done about it, you must keep your hurt and live with it and learn to forget it for moments at a time, and then for hours, perhaps eventually for days."

"But it will always be there?"

"I suppose it will be, to a greater or less degree. There are worse things than that, Elizabeth."

"I don't see how there could be anything worse."

"You will know many things worse. We all will. You will say someday that of all you lived through this was the least. Because that's how life is—full of challenges and pitfalls and surprises. Most of them unpleasant. There are good things all around you that could help fill the void for you, things you haven't let yourself see because you were too taken with your misery."

"I know, Andy." She was lying a little apart from him now. She put one hand on his chest affectionately. "You're one of the good things. You're the best of all of them."

"Not the best, probably. But we could be happy, I think."

"We've always been good friends."

"Being good friends was not exactly what I had in mind," Andy said dryly. "I don't like being classed along with friendly old ladies that you bring jelly to. I'm a man, you know."

She looked troubled and somehow conscience-stricken.

"I never meant to deny you, Andy."

"That wasn't what I meant either. I don't expect dutiful submission. I want you the way you could be—the way you were the first night you came to me."

"You're asking for a great deal."

"Maybe. I don't think so."

She turned on the pillow so that she faced him and he almost imagined that something coquettish lingered in the slight swoop of her eyelashes.

"Do you love me that much, Andy?"

He eyed her warily. "I want you that much. It's not quite the same."

She seemed disappointed. "Isn't it rather hateful to think of your own wife that way?"

"Now you're being coy. That's a lot of drivel and you don't believe it any more than I do."

"No." She smiled.

There, he thought to himself. For a whole minute she has already forgotten it, but if I were to say so she would deny it. She's having the time of her life playing woman's oldest game, flirtation. Making herself desirable, holding something out and then snatching it away. But this is important. This moment means a great deal to both of us.

"Andy, I'm going to have a baby."

So that was it. That was the concealed weapon, the rabbit in the hat. Slowly, now.

"How long have you known?"

"A little while. Not long."

"And how do you feel about it?"

"That's not important. How do you feel? Does it please you?" Womanly again. Offering the fruit and labor of her body on altar of masculine vanity.

"Of course it pleases me."

She snuggled close to him again, her small hand a soft fist against his chest, her blonde hair cloudy over her shoulders.

"Will you take good care of me, Andy? Will you help me to forget?" He felt a little tremor through her body. It was there, the pain underneath the triviality, the hurt through all the coquetry. He felt a moment's passionate tenderness for her.

"I'll take good care of you, of course."

"And you'll help me?"

"No. You'll have to help yourself, Elizabeth."

He could feel her stiffen in his arms and he knew he had added one more hurt. He tried not to think of it. She pulled away from him and looked into his face. It was a puzzled, disbelieving look, a look of unhappiness and of lost illusions. Then, so gradually that he was not aware of its beginning, something in the look changed, grew firmer, less bewildered. Beyond that he could not read it.

"I never had whisky before tonight," she said.

"No? High time."

"But if it's all right with you I think I'll have another one."

"Fine. I'll have one with you." He sat up and poured two from the bottle, then handed one to her.

She held it for a minute and looked at it hard, then lifted it and drank it in one gulp. He could follow the passage of it down her throat. She shivered a little and closed her eyes.

"Feel better?"

She nodded and sank back on the pillow.

"I'll be leaving you then."

Her eyes flew open. "Where are you going?"

"Downstairs. I'm not sleepy any more. Here, I'll tuck you in."

He smoothed the covers around her. She watched, a little puzzled, more than a little annoyed at being so easily dismissed. She remained still for several minutes after the door had closed behind him.

Downstairs Andy poked once or twice at the dead fire, and observing no results set about rebuilding it. Then he sat back, watching small, diffident flames assert themselves until they became large, noisy ones. What he had told Elizabeth upstairs was true. About learning to live with the thing that hurt her, to acccept it. There was no getting around that. But as far as his own part in it was concerned, that was all over. Tomorrow, or the next day, or as soon as she could pack, he'd send her back to San Francisco and close this house. He'd managed very well living in the back of his office before—he could do it again.

He found that there was no relief in his new resolution, no sense of satisfaction in deciding what must be done. He leaned back in the chair and tried to doze off, but he found himself wakeful. He heard the clock chime once. Later he must have slept lightly, for he sat up with the startled awareness of a sleeper when he heard footsteps in the hall. And then it was several seconds before he could be sure whether he was waking or dreaming. For there was something strange and bizarre about the figure in the doorway. It was attired in voluminous bottle-green trousers, topped with a brown bodice and half skirt. Andy stared, and the memory of a distant afternoon stirred within him. The figure stood quite still, almost in an attitude of supplication; hesitant, wistful, yet suddenly so comical that Andy could not keep from laughing.

The wistfulness in Elizabeth's face gradually faded, and her eyes began to take on a sparkle that made her whole face younger, more gaminlike. She crossed the floor with quick steps and threw herself down in his lap, putting her arms around his neck and holding him tight.

His voice was muffled against her. "Where did you ever find that old thing?" He was still chuckling.

"In a chest in my room. With a lot of other old things. Andy—" Her voice faltered, with something that could have been laughter or a sob. "Andy, there were so many things in the chest, things that I used to love—things I'd forgotten about—"

He drew away so that he could look at her, and now he could see the tears standing in her eyes. He reached up and pulled her head down close to his, brushing her lips with his at first, then holding her close until the kiss became a thing that filled the whole night and almost unexplainably their whole lives.

CHAPTER VII

CHARLES REACHED toward the middle of the dining-room table, straining slightly, and pulled the dish of boiled potatoes toward him. The first moist freshness of them had evaporated, leaving them lukewarm and slightly crusted. He selected one, put it on his plate, and proceeded to mash it methodically with his fork.

"Mr. Codie preached a lovely sermon, I thought," Agnes commented aimlessly. She had taken only one small potato and was eating it sparingly, dabbing at it with her fork but leaving most of it. Agnes had been watching her weight lately.

"See where Leamers have taken one of the front pews," Charles observed through a mouthful.

"Well, they're inclined to be showy."

Across from Agnes, Richard ate with a kind of methodical doggedness, not looking up from his plate. He ate as he did everything else lately, Treese thought. As though it was something to be finished in the shortest possible time but with no reckless haste.

"I'd like to know," Charles said irrelevantly, "who's behind the *Dispatch* now."

"You can't tell. It might be anyone." Agnes adjusted her wide skirts that spilled over on either side of her chair and fell to the carpet in masses of flounces and ruffles. With each pound she put on she seemed to add another touch of ornateness to her gowns until it had become a mad race between the weight and the furbelows. And as though they had ascertained the futility of victory, they seemed now to have joined in a conspiracy that brought out the worst features of both. "But if I were you I'd stay out of it." She picked up her knife and cut a sliver-thin piece of roast beef.

Charles stopped his chewing suddenly and his mouth stiffened. The subject of the Protectors was the cause of constant irritation between them, seldom aired but always present, running its annoying course just beneath the surface.

During recent months it had become apparent that Charles, if he was not to be permitted the role of man-about-town, was at least determined to aspire to something better than a mere drudge in the employ of a determined mother-in-law and her young husband. Time had mitigated the shock of going to work. He had now managed to regulate that part of his existence so that it was no more than a minor irritation. And in some ways he fancied it gave him a dashing air to be forever running off to the mines in miner's boots and a wide felt hat. To add to the prestige which he felt had somehow been whittled into by Richard's joining the family, he was also becoming civic-minded. If he could not become a power in the town by virtue of his idleness, he was determined to become so by feverish activity. And so, although it cut across the grain of everything inherent in him, he threw himself zealously into the growth of Sacramento. He learned to mingle with men in a way which was perhaps not entirely fraternal, but which at least lacked his former cold superciliousness. He placed his shoulder foursquare behind a Boost Sacramento Committee which aimed at attractive real estate offers and inducements to desirable settlers. He had been initiated into the Masons. He was one of those most active in the movement for the formation of a Committee of Vigilance in Sacramento and he had already made appreciable steps in that direction by allowing the idea to take hold in the Sacramento Civic Protective Association, which he headed. As a power in the town, Charles had definitely arrived. That there was little similarity in purpose between the

Protectors and their straightforward, hard-hitting prototype, the
Vigilantes, did not occur to him, and if it had it is doubtful whether
he would have been deterred. The Protectors, after disposing tidily
of the claim-jumping attempt which threatened Delaney property,
had in semisecrecy ransacked and burned the office of the Sacramento *Morning Dispatch*. The *Dispatch* had been an ardent Broderick supporter all during the campaign early that year which had
at last placed Broderick in Washington. Its fiery editor, Frank
McCabe, had lived to fire further broadsides in the cause of aboli-
tion and the northern Democrats only by having placed himself
propitiously at the moment of the attack at the bar of the Red Tent
saloon, where he was tucking away several straight whiskies in the
company of Keith Delaney, not knowing of the violence being done
to his property. Thereafter he and Keith were often seen together,
and a kind of camaraderie seemed to spring up between them, both
as a result of their similar viewpoints and because each had suffered materially from what Keith called "my brother-in-law's social
ambitiousness." It was rumored that some of the heated front-page
editorials that appeared in the *Dispatch* as soon as it was once more
in print were written by Keith. The paper's overnight recovery was
still a source of irritation to Charles, who prided himself on having
done a thorough job. Moreover, in the course of his meteoric path
upward he had run afoul of Agnes, who had made no secret of her
displeasure after Keith was wounded and John Trask killed at the
mine, and who had opposed him forcefully and humiliatingly after
the affair of the *Dispatch*.

"I was thinking," Agnes announced, closing the entire subject
before it was opened, "that we might go for a drive in the country
this afternoon. What would you think, Richard?"

Richard swallowed unhurriedly before answering.

"Whatever you like, my dear."

"Treese? I think it might be fine for the baby, don't you? Summer won't last forever, you know."

"Well, I'd thought—I don't much care, Mother. Whatever you
like. I was rather planning on taking a walk over to the new house."

"Oh, ridiculous. You're over there every day. I don't know what
they could possibly have done since last time."

"I just like to look at it. The flooring's in now, and some of the
partitions. And it's a nice walk over.

"It's much too hot for walking."

"I don't mind it."

"Well, do as you like. Charles, what do you say?"

"I'm going to take a nap," he replied peevishly.

"Well, then, Richard, why don't you and I take the baby and go for a bit of a drive up past the Fort?"

Richard took a gulp of coffee, washed it around his mouth and swallowed. "Suits me."

Agnes hid the pleasure that she felt secretly. She and Richard alone would look like a young couple out with their own baby. She would wear the pink silk shawl. With Treese along one had to be cautious about colors. There was something strange and vivid about her lately—or was she only beginning to notice it? Something about her hair and the darkly flamboyant colors she had taken to wearing.

"Treese, I don't much care for your hair arranged up on top like that. Gives you too much height."

"Really, Mother?" There was neither defiance nor submission in the way Treese answered, merely a total lack of interest.

Treese had not been telling the exact truth when she said she liked to look at the new house that was being built for her and Charles, the house into which they and the baby would move in the fall. She did not like to look at it. But she liked to be there, which was something of a different matter. It was the only place she knew of where she could be completely alone. In its incompleted state the house was without a past, without identification. There was nothing in it to remind her of anything. There was only the smell of new lumber and sawdust, the sight of the paneless windows opening into the vacant lot, the empty rooms, many of them unseparated by partitions. It was the emptiness, she thought, that was most comforting.

The house had been her idea. Charles had made no objections. He seemed to consider a house of his own as the next logical tribute due him now that his standing in the city was assured. Agnes had been less pliable. It was a ridiculous notion, she fumed. Anyone with a beautiful home such as Treese had was foolish to build another one which would not be half so nice. There were a great many girls—she could name them right off—who would be overjoyed even to see the inside of a place like the Delaney mansion.

Treese listened to Agnes's tirade without answering. She stood there, not speaking but not giving an inch. And then Agnes looked at her, sized up the strength of her determination, and said in a quiet voice that if it was what Treese had made her mind up to, she might as well go ahead with it. She had not even brought up the argument Treese had anticipated, that if they were counting on her money to finance the arrangement they could just think again.

So the house had been designed and construction started. It was on a little rise of ground about a fifteen-minute walk from the big brick house. From the top floor a slice of the river was visible, and during the hot summer months there was a breath of breeze there while the rest of the city sweltered. It would be a simple two-story brick house. Treese had not even wanted brick, but it was a sensible protection against fire, and she had given in. Beyond that there was nothing to distinguish it from dozens of other houses in the city.

She caught sight of it now as she started up the slope toward it, the new red bricks brassy and flaunting against the motionless summer sky. She was perspiring a little. In spite of what she had said at the dinner table, it was too warm a day for walking, and she knew it, but she wanted to go and be alone in the house for a few minutes. She had left Charles stretched out with extravagant abandon on the bed, his shirt removed, the soft white of his flesh outlined against the darker counterpane.

She quickened her steps in spite of the heat as she approached the house. She entered and stood in the vestibule, letting the whispering emptiness close in around her. It was no quieter here than outside; it only seemed so. The vestibule was cool and dim, the new wood seeming to breathe a faint moisture.

Now, gradually, she felt it stealing over her; the peace that was the only peace she had known in months, the complete quiet that contained no comfort, that was devoid, rather, of either comfort or conflict. The complete emptiness, she thought. It offered no solution, but it was there—like a friendly person sitting across the room when one felt depressed—not chattering, simply sitting there.

She walked from the vestibule to the parlor, from parlor to dining room, from dining room to kitchen. She retraced her steps and mounted the backless stairs to the second floor. Here it was warmer but there was relief in the faint breeze that stirred through the window spaces. She walked down the corridor and looked into each of the bedrooms, but she did not enter them. She returned to the head of the stairs and stood there looking out the hall window. A carriage was passing by in the road. She heard the clop of hoofs, the turning of the wheels, then a high shrill laugh as though someone was being tickled. She sank to the floor and put her arms along the window sill, resting her chin on them and staring out. The carriage disappeared from view. After a few minutes two lovers walked by, their arms around each other, their heads close together.

Treese watched them unblinkingly. When they were gone she closed her eyes and let her head sink lower so that her cheek was against her arm. The small breeze whiffed through the hair close about her temples and ears, whispering a tuneless little melody that grew fainter and fainter and at last could no longer be heard.

She awoke with a start, conscious all in the same instant of the cramped sensation in her legs, the feeling that half her face was numb, and the length of the shadows outside. The sun had grown redder and was sinking down close to the horizon.

She stood up quickly but both her legs felt numb and she had to lean against the wall for support.

"I thought you were going to sleep there all night. I was preparing to dig in."

She wheeled around, grasping the unpainted stair railing and peering down into the shadows at the foot of the steps. He was smiling up at her.

"I thought of waking you, but I liked it down here by myself. This feeling of desertion has a tonic effect."

She did not move.

"Are you coming down or shall I come up?"

"I'll—come down." She descended slowly, hanging to the railing, for her legs still felt unsteady. Steve was standing at the foot of the stairs, leaning against the wall, his hands in his pockets. "What made you come here?"

"I was passing by. Curiosity."

"Did you know it was—"

"Of course. Why else do you think I'd be curious?"

"Oh." She became aware that she was still gripping her skirts tight around her and she let them fall. "I come up here sometimes. I like it the way it is now. Half done, empty."

"And when it's done and lived in—will you like it then?"

She did not answer. She walked to the parlor archway and looked in. "There are some planks and things here. We could sit down if you're staying."

"I won't stay long." He followed her and they sat on a pile of boards in one corner. The room had grown dimmer now that the sun had shifted so far to the other side of the house. Treese wondered whether she was yet quite awake. A feeling of opaqueness persisted inside her head, and she seemed to be observing things through a mist.

He nodded toward the empty fireplace with its half-finished facing of bricks. "Comfortable place to spend a winter evening.

To spend any evening, in fact. Three hundred and sixty-five of them. Multiplied by fifty—"

"Steve, don't."

He looked at her. The pile of boards was low and her knees were drawn up in front of her, her skirt billowing around her.

"You look very young."

"Yes?"

"Very young but very determined. When you make up your mind you don't waste any time, do you?" She did not answer. He looked around him and whistled softly. "What does all this accomplish?"

"I'm not sure. But I think it will be better."

"Building four walls to house it, nurture it, keep it warm."

"What?"

"Whatever it is you're afraid of."

"There's no use talking about it again, Steve."

"I don't recall that we ever talked about it at all. Not sensibly. I went off on something of a tangent last time."

"You had a right to."

"No, my pride was hurt. I fancied myself a little more irresistible than I turned out to be. But this house—this little monument to self-assertion—it's quite impressive." He glanced around again.

"I didn't intend it to be that. I felt that it would be a solution, in a way."

"What kind of solution?"

She looked at him. "There isn't any other, Steve."

"I offered you one."

"It's all settled. Do you only want to make it hard for me?" Her tone was almost resentful.

"I could draw you a very graphic picture of the next fifty years."

"Never mind. I've drawn that picture myself."

"And you still take it, in preference to—"

"In preference to what?" she demanded. "I told you before it was impossible. I have a baby to think of."

He raised one eyebrow speculatively. "You know what I think? I think that baby is your mental whipping post. I don't think that's your reason at all. You're just afraid." He was speaking thoughtfully, but his tone changed abruptly. "However, that's neither here nor there, since I have no intention of going over the whole thing again. I merely wanted to explain something to you."

"About me?"

"No, about me. Something I wanted you to know."

"What?"

"Suppose we reconstruct this thing. Thwarted lover, hard-hearted woman—"

"That's silly."

"Oh, let me embellish it a little for the sake of dramatics. He spends several months mulling over his heartbreak and then he comes to her. The answer is still no. The plot is at an impasse. Now, it may take one of two turns. Either they can carry on a clandestine affair—we reject that immediately, too unsatisfying—or he can announce with offstage fanfare that he's leaving, going away and never coming back."

"Steve—" Her voice was a dry whisper. "Steve, you're not going away!"

"No. That's why our little tableau takes on highly original aspects. I am not going away. And I want you to know why." All the bantering was gone now. The shadows were deepening around them so that she could no longer see his facial expressions distinctly, but she could sense the change in his manner of speaking. "I am staying here because you have taught me a very valuable lesson. You have taught me that there is nothing so futile as escape, nothing that is less escape, really, than running away from something. It was a lesson I was a long time learning. For essentially I was very like you, Treese. I sidestepped issues, I equivocated. I avoided making any decisions that were vital to me—inside, I mean. I drifted—physically and mentally. I considered myself emotionally satiated, which was just my way of considering myself worldly. Well, that part of it was knocked to pieces when I met you. I found that, far from having experienced the entire range of emotions as I had thought, I had actually known very little of any of them. Very little happiness, very little loneliness, very little love. I had them all thrust at me at once. And it wasn't easy, since I'd spent a lifetime avoiding them. For a time they became the most important part of my life. I lived with them every day, slept with them at night. Until one day I decided to take stock of myself. And the result was a minor shock. I found a person quite useless to anyone, least of all to himself."

"If you're trying to point a moral—"

"No, indeed." Now he had become quite earnest. "No moral at all. This applies only to me. Each of us has to examine himself. It doesn't do to pass judgment on others. But right then, when the truth about myself came home to me, I made a decision. I decided that I would stay here—oh, yes, there was a moment or two when I'd thought of leaving—that I'd stay here and do something I've never done before—quit sitting on the fence."

She frowned slightly. "I'm not sure what you mean."

"It's something you did for me. And now, staying here, facing things, it's all become very important to me."

"What have you to face?" She tried not to sound bitter.

"Any number of interesting things." He seemed almost to be smiling to himself in the dimness. "I imagine your husband will tell you about it as soon as he finds out himself."

"Steve—" Now she felt a real physical fear, a cold pervasive thing that was like another presence in the room between them.

"Do you know about the *Dispatch?*"

"Yes."

"Well, that doesn't matter. It's just that it gives me a little pardonable pride. Like an amateur farmer harvesting his first crop of wormy potatoes and scraggly wheat. I don't know why it should, but it does. But here's what I wanted to tell you. When I came here today, I thought maybe—well, I guess I had some leftover illusions about being able to talk you into something. I know now that that's all they were. I know you've made up your mind and that this is it." He made a little gesture that took in the bare house. His voice grew quiet. "But I hope you find what I found. Somehow."

When he left, his hands were thrust into his pockets again and he was whistling the fragment of a melody. *Hangtown gals are sweet and rosy*— She stood in the doorway and watched him as he made his way down the slope. The whistle was bright and had a lilt until just before he disappeared from view. Then suddenly—was it real or only something imagined out of the gathering blue of the new night?—it took on a mournful note. Was the sadness in him or in her? she wondered.

The bells that awakened her late that night were wild and insistent. She thought for a moment they were unreal, part of a noisy, disordered nightmare. They crashed about the house and shook at the windowpanes, forming themselves into a dissonant cacophony. She sat up in bed and stared around her, trying to remember what the dream had been and why the sound remained. Then she looked at the bed and saw that she was alone. The imprint of Charles's head was still upon the pillow, but his nightshirt had been thrown upon the chair beside it and his clothes were gone. Now the dream became reality; the veil between sleeping and waking vanished.

She threw back the covers and seized her clothes. She fumbled with hooks and buttons, shoved her bare feet into shoes and tied her shawl around her shoulders. She did not bother to do up her hair. She did not even go to the window. She could have seen it from the window, but she did not have to. She knew without seeing. She hurried into the upstairs hall. There were sounds of sleepy mumbling from Agnes's room. Then her mother's voice raised: "Treese?"

Treese hesitated, her hand on the stair railing. She did not answer.

"Treese, what's going on?"

There was the padding of slippered feet behind the closed door. Treese picked up her skirts and fled down the stairs. The front door stuck heavily and she had to wrench it open. She did not bother to close it behind her.

Out in the street the bells were louder and there were people running. It was a familiar scene, one she had witnessed dozens of times since she had come west. The man buttoning his pants as he ran, the woman with a cloak thrown over her nightdress, her hair streaming around her shoulders, the tardy fireman throwing on his uniform, his Philadelphia fire helmet sitting crazily athwart his sleep-rumpled hair. There were the dogs, running between legs and being cursed at, the adolescent boys who had slid down drainpipes. She felt herself being pushed and jostled as she neared J Street and the crowd grew thicker. Now everyone was running in the direction of the Embarcadero. She ran with them, her long hair bouncing and tossing with every step. At Fourth Street the crowd grew so dense that she could hardly push on. She stopped for a moment, caught her breath and looked up.

The whole sky was red with flames. The heat was searing and intense, the noise altered now so that the clang of the fire engines was all but obliterated by the crackling roar of the fire itself.

"Can they save it?" she asked.

The man next to her was observing the scene with relish, tipping back on his heels. He had thrown trousers on over his nightshirt, and it bloused out over the top of them. "They ain't even tryin' to. All they want to do is save the buildin's next door. I guess they got it under control now. They'll just let it burn itself out."

Treese turned on him in sudden fury, but she did not answer. Instead she pushed on through the crowd, heedless of the curses that followed her. She beat against backs and chests, struggled and inched her way until she was as far forward as spectators were permitted. Then she saw Steve.

He was standing a little apart from the struggling firemen on the outer rim of spectators and at first glance she knew there was something about him incongruous with the tumult of the night and the excited watchers. Far from being disheveled or distraught, he looked immaculate. His white shirt was spotless, his black cravat neat and crisp. He was smoking a cheroot and standing with his hands in his pockets, looking up toward the sky where the flames had just begun to shoot with red spurts through the roof of the blazing Red Tent.

She tried to shout his name but her voice was lost in the roar around her. She pushed forward again, this time breaking through the restraining line of firemen and running toward him.

"Steve! Steve, I was afraid I wouldn't find you!" It was harder to breathe now, and every breath seemed to be full of choking fumes that seared the insides of her lungs and throat. She could feel her clothing sticking to her and her hair was plastered against the back of her neck.

He turned to her.

"Treese?" He was frowning with surprise. "What are you doing here?"

Her hands were in tight fists. She pressed them against his chest. "Steve, I had to find you. The minute I heard the fire bells I knew what it was. I don't know how, but I knew. And the only thing I could think of—Steve, I didn't tell him. I didn't!" She was sobbing now, not so much from agitation as from sheer exhaustion and because she seemed no longer able to breathe.

"I was afraid you'd think I told him. On account of this afternoon. I didn't—I didn't!"

"Tell him what?"

"About you—about the *Dispatch*. Steve, I wouldn't have told him!"

He took her by the shoulders and held her up, for she seemed to be weakening. He looked at her face, dirty and stained with perspiration, at the flame-lit red of her hair, now seeming to be almost alive with color.

"I never thought you did. I never even gave it a thought."

She lifted her head and looked at him. And she knew that it was true. He was not thinking of her. Even as he looked at her, he did not see her. She could see the reflection of the burning building in his eyes, and beyond the reflection something else. His hands were still tight on her shoulders but she realized suddenly that he did not know it. He had already forgotten she was there. She moved slightly and twisted out of his grasp. He did not even turn to watch her go.

The lights were all on when she reached home. As she walked up the front steps she felt an irritating pain and looked at her hands. All the nails were broken or split and the hands themselves seemed swollen and hot. How had she broken her nails? She could not remember. She pushed the front door open and stepped inside. Charles and Agnes were alone in the parlor, Agnes with her robe over her nightdress, Charles in his Sunday broadcloth suit, looking quite unruffled. There were several lamps lit so that the room was as bright as for a party. She saw immediately that they were both in a pleasant frame of mind, and this surprised her. Mother should be angry, she thought. She hates Charles and she hates the Protectors. This should all be different.

Agnes's voice called to her pleasantly. "Goodness, Treese, but you had us worried. I never knew you to run out after a fire before. Look at you! You'd better come in here and sit down. You look ready to collapse. I really should give you a good scolding!"

Treese stood in the parlor archway. "I'm all right." She looked past Agnes to Charles. "Where have you been, Charles?"

Charles smiled and twisted the chain that spanned his vest. "Nothing to worry about, dear. There was a little meeting—"

"Something you had to get out of bed for?"

"We have to keep our little gatherings secret—it's ridiculous of course, but the men think it gives the lodge something of an air."

Treese stood quite still in the center of the archway, feeling exhaustion and weakness in every bone and muscle but exerting her last strength to remain erect. She would have to hold out until she could understand it. It was all here in this scene, if she could only figure it out. Charles must have known who was behind the *Dispatch*, that was apparent now. His little act at the dinner table was only part of his usual affectation. He had known, yes. So far it was right. And he and the Protectors had set fire to the Red Tent tonight. Then he had come home, perhaps opened the door softly. He had not wanted to run into Agnes. But the bells had awakened her earlier and she was already up. He had been defensive, perhaps, blustering. He had tried to cover up. But he had not needed to. For some reason this was all right. This was something Agnes was going to permit. There was pleasure in every motion of her plump hands at the waist of her robe, in the affectionate smile she was directing at Treese. And then, just as she had known in a single instant of realization what the bells meant earlier, Treese knew what this meant. She looked from Agnes to Charles, then back to Agnes. And on Agnes her eyes remained for a long instant.

"I see," she said quietly.

Charles took his watch from his pocket and consulted it. "Too much excitement for one night." He began to wind it as he walked past Treese and started up the stairs. "Coming, Treese?" His footsteps padded up the stair carpeting and grew faint.

Treese's eyes were on her mother. Agnes's smile of affection was still there but it had hardened at the corners, grown incongruous with the sudden coldness in her eyes. The two had not moved since Treese entered the room.

"I never knew you to be so interested in a fire before, Treese." Agnes's tone was light but curiously direct. "Or was it just this particular fire?"

CHAPTER VIII

"I suppose—" Agnes looked around her at the small dingy newspaper office with its jumbled piles of type, its ink-smeared piles of paper—"I suppose this is only temporary for you, Mr. Mallott."

"As headquarters, yes."

"Headquarters! That has a very official ring." Agnes moved uneasily in the straight chair where she sat and gathered her skirts close about her, looking apprehensively at the untidy floor.

"Frank McCabe was kind enough to offer it to me when I was so abruptly thrown upon the mercy of the community."

"Really," Agnes murmured. She looked across the table at him. He was seated there negligently, with a touch of insolence in his pose as though she were a visitor of no great importance. She did not feel irked. That was a natural defensive gesture. When one is not in a position to make terms, one shows bravado. "But it was really hardly generosity on the part of Mr. McCabe, since he is indebted to you for the existence of his paper. Isn't that so, Mr. Mallott?"

"I'm not in the habit of asking a favor in return for one. What I do I do because I want to. No one is my debtor for it."

"Really. How admirable. And may I ask how you like being in the newspaper business?"

Steve picked up a small lead slug that weighed down a pile of papers on the desk and held it thoughtfully for a moment. Then he quickly looked up at her again.

"I find it exciting. And how do you like my being in it?"

Agnes shrugged. "It's quite unimportant to me, Mr. Mallott."

"On the contrary, Mrs. Miles, I think you'll have to admit to quite an active interest in it. Otherwise you wouldn't have come here today."

Agnes laughed lightly. "Very well put, sir. Doesn't it seem odd to you that we two have never met, even though we've lived in Sacramento long enough to have run into each other a hundred times?"

"Perhaps."

"It gave me quite a turn of conscience when I thought of it. That was why I came here as soon as possible. I think we business people should stick together."

"You flatter me. I didn't realize you considered saloonkeeping a business."

"Everyone to his own trade."

Steve looked at her speculatively.

"Mr. Mallott, there's something I would like to get straightened out with you before I say anything more. I know the talk that's been going on in some quarters about the recent unfortunate—well—"

"The fire, I suppose you mean."

"Yes, the fire. I daresay there's been all kinds of gossip."

"To the effect that the Protectors started the fire?"

"Yes."

"Deplorable how gossip gets started." He shook his head sadly.

She watched him closely for another moment, then proceeded cautiously. "Well, what I wanted to talk with you about is business." She paused, then plunged ahead. "Mr. Mallott, I should like to offer you a price for your property at J and Second streets where the Red Tent stood."

He showed no surprise. "How much are you offering?"

"Whatever the property is worth according to current appraisal. I'm prepared to pay. I'm not hunting bargains."

"Why do you want it?"

She showed signs of irritation. "Isn't it perfectly obvious? It's one of the best locations in the city. Property is always a good investment. I certainly don't see where motives enter into the transaction."

"Quite right, Mrs. Miles. Only curiosity on my part. And how about the *Dispatch*? Are you making me an offer for that too?"

Agnes looked completely puzzled for a moment. "The paper? Why on earth should I want a newspaper?"

Steve chuckled. "That's all I wanted to know. I was curious about whether this was a personal grudge or whether ethics entered into it."

"I haven't the vaguest idea what you mean," she retorted coldly. "But your tone is most insulting, Mr. Mallott."

"Please overlook it. I believe in speaking frankly."

"Then be so good as to oblige me with a frank answer. Will you consider selling the property?"

He tipped back in his chair until it scraped against the wall. The sun coming through the dirty window made a vague pattern across the desk, which he observed idly. He could sense the impatience in the woman opposite him and it gave him a certain satisfaction.

"No," he said.

She flushed angrily. Then he could see her take hold of herself and compose her features haughtily.

"May I ask why not?"

"You've answered that yourself. It's a valuable piece of property. Why shouldn't I want to hang onto it?"

"You'll forgive me if I seem quarrelsome, Mr. Mallott. But I do not believe that is the reason."

He smiled. "Aren't you giving yourself away?"

Her mouth tightened and she stared straight ahead, not looking at him.

He tipped the chair forward again and crossed his arms on the desk, leaning on them. "Suppose I tell you why you want it. It's a good business investment, yes. I'll grant that much. But that alone wouldn't bring you to such a disreputable place as the *Dispatch* office dressed in your best tea gown." He observed the effect of his words, a little heightened color in her cheeks, a little stiffer attitude in the straight chair. "You want it for quite another reason. You think I'm pretty well licked financially, don't you? Well, I am. A newspaper, even such a one as this, costs money. A going concern like the Red Tent takes money to operate. Profits are good but there's continual reinvestment. You're right, Mrs. Miles. I am in very precarious financial shape. Not exactly down and out, but far from affluent. Buying my property would represent quite a triumph for you, wouldn't it? For more than one reason. It would demonstrate the superiority of the right class of people over an upstart gambler. That's number one. And number two, it's the only thing you can think of that might hurt Annette. Because she's in the same class I'm in, as far as you're concerned. You've never got over Keith's marrying her. It would show who's important in the town, who holds the power."

Agnes's voice had turned cold as stone. "I don't care to discuss motives. May I inquire to what possible use you'll put the property? Since you admit you're all but insolvent, I suppose you will sell to someone else. It's purely a personal grudge that's keeping you from selling to me then. Is that correct?"

"Not at all. I'm keeping it for another reason entirely. I'm going to rebuild the Red Tent."

"Rebuild it!" Agnes was genuinely surprised.

"Does that seem so strange to you?"

"It seems highly impractical. With what, may I ask?"

"With credit. I intend to borrow from anyone and everyone, if need be."

Agnes stared across the table at him for a long time. Then she spoke slowly. "I just don't understand it. I think it's the most ridiculous thing I've ever heard. If there was any good reason—"

"There is a good reason," Steve answered quietly.

"Well, it certainly isn't financial. You'll run yourself into the ground doing it."

"Yes, very likely. The reason is not financial."

"Well, then, what—" She broke off, perplexed.

Steve smiled slowly. "It's not a thing I'd expect you to understand, Mrs. Miles."

CHAPTER IX

TREESE LIFTED HER SKIRTS so they would not brush the board sidewalk and picked her way carefully down J Street toward the business section. The autumn dusk was already blue across the river at the end of the street and falling darkly over the town. They would be sitting down to dinner soon at home, commenting on her absence, wondering why she had taken such an unearthly hour for a stroll. It would have been wiser, of course, not to have come at all, but that was useless speculation, for she knew that sooner or later she would have to. Curiosity alone would have dictated it, and there were more things involved than curiosity.

She reached the corner of Second Street and stood there, diagonally across from the new building, looking up at it. Outwardly it resembled the first Red Tent, which she had also viewed in a stage nearing completion—raw timbers thrust against the outline of the town, a big formless building that was typical of the architecture of the West. The big double doors that would open diagonally upon the corner stood ajar and as she watched she saw what she judged to be the last of the day's crew of workmen leaving for home, throwing their short homespun coats over their shoulders, laughing and talking to each other in rough tones which the new night seemed to muffle and subdue so that they reached her almost as disembodied sounds. At the same time she saw a lamp being lighted on the top floor.

She drew her shawl closer around her and with the other hand lifted her skirts once more, as though to prove to herself that her errand was finished, that now she was really going to start for home. If she hurried, she might yet be in time for dinner. But still she hesitated.

The light on the third floor grew stronger, flickered and then steadied itself. She thought it odd that there were draperies at the window. Then it must be in a further stage of completion than she had realized, and the workmen must now be concerning themselves only with the finishing touches. He had really been racing with time. Time meant money, of course, in wages and in lost business. Naturally he would hurry.

Somewhere along the street a piano began to tinkle, and she thought with an odd catch of remembrance that there was always a piano on J Street. This one was not being played for the evening crowd, however. Someone was sitting alone at it, she guessed, in an empty saloon. The melody that came out was plaintive and touching, a personal thing, so that Treese, listening to it, felt a little like an eavesdropper. She hesitated for another moment, then crossed the street the long way, from corner to corner through the intersection. She stood at the open doors of the Red Tent and looked inside.

It was a long building with a compact row of pillars supporting its ornate ceiling and dividing it in half. To the left of the pillars was a gleaming mahogany bar. A covering had been thrown across the top to protect it, and some carpenters' tools had been left there. To the right of the pillars were the gaming tables, all with protective covers thrown over them, with only here and there a corner of new green baize showing itself. In back of the bar the wall was solid with mirrors, so that in reflection the room was doubled. The other walls were covered with pictures which in the dimness Treese could not make out. Far to the rear she could see a small stage with a green velvet curtain.

She stood in the open doorway for several minutes. Then slowly, tentatively, she stepped inside. Directly opposite the bar, dividing the row of gambling tables, rose a stairway which led to a balcony. Several doors opened off this balcony, the private dining rooms which might be hired for an evening. The doors were closed and dark, all but one at the far end of the balcony which stood open and disclosed a streak of dim light. Treese went to the stairway and started up, holding her skirt high so that she would not trip in the unfamiliar dimness.

She was out of breath when she reached the top of the stairs. She stopped for a moment, then began to tiptoe toward the open door. When she reached it she saw that it led to a small enclosed stairway and that the light was coming from a room at the top of it. She hesitated again, but not for long. Quietly she mounted the steps.

He was sitting in his shirtsleeves with his back to her, at a desk which was covered with lists and rough sketches. The room was a bed-sitting room, large and elaborately furnished, apparently quite finished. A walnut bed stood against one wall. Several deep upholstered chairs in dark red and green, matching the carpet were about the room and there were glossy walnut and rosewood tables everywhere, some with burnished cigar boxes, others with carafes and hand painted lamps. The windows were hung with damask. Her eyes traveled over it curiously, then returned to the figure at the desk.

"This is very elegant." Her voice sounded soft and shy in the strange room.

He stood up and turned all in one motion, so rapidly that the chair tottered precariously before it righted itself. His face was lined with weariness and his hair was uncombed. There was a shadow of beard where he had not shaven. His eyes gleamed darkly with disbelief.

"I was looking at it from the outside," she stammered, a little self-conscious at her own forwardness. "I'm afraid I was curious—"

His eyes did not move from her face. "Sit down." There was a lack of warmth in the invitation, she noted with a sinking heart, almost a wariness. She moved to a chair near the desk and sat down. He sank back onto the straight chair.

"How do you like it?" Now the wariness was not so noticeable, but the almost deliberate casualness made her feel like a stranger, an interloper here in the green and walnut room.

"It's very impressive." She folded her hands tightly in her lap to still their sudden inexplicable trembling. "Much more elegant than mine was when you came to call on me. And much more comfortable. I think I made you sit on a pile of boards, didn't I?"

He dug in his pockets and pulled out the stub of a cheroot. He lighted it before he spoke again.

"And how is your house? Finished?"

"Oh yes. For quite some time."

"You haven't moved in?"

"No."

He did not question her further or even speak. She tried to swallow and found her throat was dry.

"I suppose it was a little foolish, my coming here. But I wanted so to see this place."

"Why?" There was a harsh edge to his voice. It might have been only tiredness. She was not sure. It was hard to continue with him watching her like that, impersonally, without acknowledgement.

"Oh—for many reasons. I'd heard a great deal about it, of course. But I wanted to see it for myself. To see if you'd really done it."

"Didn't you think I would?"

"Yes; I don't know. I knew how much you would want to. But I knew how much it would take. Courage—"

"And money?"

"Well, yes, money."

"People were very obliging on that score. I found a great many friends I didn't know I had. Or perhaps I knew they were friends but never suspected how much friendship can mean sometimes. It was a funny thing. I didn't ask anybody for a cent. They all came to me. Some of them might surprise you. Some of them had plenty of money, others only a bittle bit, like Adam Sloane, my faro dealer, and Frank McCabe, and Keith and Annette. Andy and his wife gave me some. Andy instigated the whole thing. The biggest chunk of it came from somebody I'd almost forgotten about. A Greek I knew a long time ago in San Francisco. For some reason it was very important to all of them that I rebuild this place. Can you understand why?"

She nodded quickly. "Yes, I can understand that."

"And now it's more important than ever that I make a go of it. I owe something to all those people that has nothing to do with the money. I've found that it's better that way—not standing by yourself."

She looked down at her hands in her lap, away from the accusation she could hear in his tone, even though he had not voiced it. Now suddenly she wanted with all her heart to tell him the thing she had kept to herself through the long weary summer.

"I was with you too, Steve," she whispered.

He got up from his chair and walked away from her impatiently.

"That's all over," he said in a flat voice. "We finished it that afternoon in your new house. Let's not rake it up again." He had walked to the window and was holding the drapery aside, looking out over the street.

"This is something else," she went on rapidly. "Something that happened the night they burned your place down."

He turned toward her. His eyes had narrowed a little.

"When I got home I found Mother and Charles up. And when I saw them there like that, the two of them—and knowing they were responsible—something happened inside me. I don't know how to explain it except that all of a sudden I knew what I was going to do and there wasn't any choice any more. It was as if my mind had been made up right then almost without my realizing it. It was something I had to do, and I knew that nothing on earth could stop me."

He was still watching her closely. "Well?"

"I'm going to divorce Charles."

He let his breath out in a sardonic chuckle. "Is that the big news?"

"Don't you believe it?"

He shrugged. "I don't see that it concerns me much. That was three months ago. I was really down and out then. News like that would have meant a lot to me. Now it looks suspiciously like bandwagon-jumping. The Red Tent is built again. Quite a number of people have shown confidence in me. I'm almost a going concern. Why should I get excited about it? Especially since I find it a little hard to believe. Have you taken any actual steps toward the divorce?"

"Not yet—"

He nodded. "That's what I thought." He turned back to the window.

Treese raised her head and now the reticence in her look had changed, had hardened into a quiet anger that was strange and foreign to her gray eyes.

"You can believe it or not as you like," she said coldly. She got up and walked over to him, standing beside the window and looking up at him. "There were reasons why I couldn't tell you this three months ago, why I couldn't start divorce proceedings then. Mother had guessed about us."

"Your mother—"

"That same night—the night of the fire, she said something to me—nothing definite, just an insinuation. I knew she was feeling around in the dark, but all the same she had begun to suspect. The only thing that kept her from believing it completely was her own opinion of me." She laughed shortly. "She'd never think me capable of an affair, and of course that was on my side. I knew there wasn't any danger as long as I didn't show anything or let her realize what was really in my mind. So I kept my decision to myself. Do you think if I'd told them about it either Mother or the Protectors would have let you finish building this place?"

He was staring at her now with something close to amazement. Her cheeks had grown flushed and her eyes were darting with anger.

"And I'm still not going to tell them," she hurried on. "Not for a while. Not until you're a 'going concern' as you put it. You're still going to have a fight on your hands, but you knew that when you rebuilt this place. At least now you won't be alone. You won't be helpless as you were the last time. You'll have friends behind you, and prestige. Oh, you might not realize it yet, but what you've done has raised your stock in Sacramento considerably."

She turned and started away from him. He caught her arm and pulled her back.

"Treese, I'm sorry. It was hard to believe at first—"

"Well, now you know it's true. I must go. They'll be wondering where I am." She started to pull her shawl around her. Still he held her back.

"What will you do later—afterward?"

She looked away from him and her voice grew almost inaudible. "I don't know—"

He seized her by the shoulders and pulled her toward him, shaking her as though to punctuate his own intensity.

"Treese, tell them now. Tell them and be done with it. There's nothing to worry about any more. I'm not alone now, you said so yourself. Treese, go through with it now and marry me." He had bent his head so that his lips were against her hair.

She drew away from him and looked at him. He leaned over and kissed her slowly. They clung together for an instant, parted, and he kissed her again. And now, she realized, it was different from the other times. The insistence, the unspoken demand were there, the urgency, the sense of immediateness, the focus of a lifetime upon one instant. And yet now there was an inevitability with it, flowing through it, giving it importance. This was how it was going to be. She could feel the roughness of his beard, the slight movement of his lips against hers. Where her hands pressed against his back she could feel the warmth of him, and where he held her there was a returning warmth, deep and alive and growing.

"Treese—"

"Yes."

"Don't go for a little while."

"No."

"This is how you want it, isn't it?"

She nodded, close against him, suddenly unable to speak.

She had no way of knowing what time it was that she awoke but she realized instantly that he was awake beside her.

"It must be late," she whispered. "You should have wakened me."

He leaned over and touched her lips with his. "It doesn't matter much any more, does it? I liked to watch you sleeping."

"How can you see me in the dark?"

"Your eyes become used to it. I can see you quite well."

She felt herself blushing and pulled the covers up tight around her neck. She heard him laugh softly as he drew close and warm against her.

"This doesn't seem much like Treese Delaney, does it?" he asked.

"Why not?"

"Keeping a rendezvous over a saloon—and with a gambler."

"I think it seems more real than anything Treese Delaney's ever done."

He kissed her again as he let her out of the carriage in front of her house, but neither of them spoke again. Strange, she thought, as she gathered her skirts about her and hurried up the steps, how words are sometimes not needed at all to bind an agreement. She pushed the front door open and stepped into the hallway.

Agnes's sharp voice slashed through the stillness of her thoughts. "You had an escort home, Treese?"

Something cold and paralyzing crept over Treese, something almost chemical in its immediate bodily reaction. Not fear; she had been sure tonight in the Red Tent that it was no longer fear. Dread? Of what, then? What could Agnes or anyone else do now?

"Yes, a friend was kind enough to bring me home."

"I'll spare you the humiliation of explaining what you were being brought home from."

Even through the coldness that surrounded her, Treese noticed that Agnes had said "what" instead of "where." Her mother's voice went on.

"Do you know, Treese, that you are very much like your father? Same stubborn streak."

"You've always told me so—as an insult. I find I'm rather glad now."

"I should have expected that, of course. Insolence and effrontery."

"Is Charles at home, Mother? I want to discuss something with him."

"I can well imagine. No, he is not at home."

"I'd like to see him as soon as he comes in."

Later, when she was in bed, the conversation repeated itself in her mind and she found herself puzzling over it. The insulting tone had been in keeping with Agnes. But she had asked few questions, and although she had been angry there had been a surprising absence of real concern in her manner; more as though her pride had been hurt, or some scheme of hers set awry. It made Treese vaguely uneasy and she found herself unable to sleep.

When the front door downstairs opened again, Agnes was sitting in the parlor with a lamp burning dimly on the table beside her.

"Charles?" Her voice was low and urgent. He came to the parlor door and peered in.

"Something wrong?" His face was flushed with the drinks he had had, and he steadied himself rather more than was necessary in order to appear perfectly in command of his faculties.

"Come in and sit down."

"Isn't it a little late for talking, Agnes? Couldn't we—in the morning—" He parried in the doorway, straightening himself with dignity.

Agnes's voice was acid. "Since that drinking you were doing tonight was on my money, I think the least you might do would be to listen to what I have to say."

"Oh, very well—" He entered the room and took a chair near her, his legs sprawling untidily in front of him.

"Did you know that Steve Mallott is reopening his saloon next week?" she inquired abruptly.

Charles brought his eyes to focus on her with some difficulty. "Certainly I knew it."

"And what do you plan to do about it?"

He spread his hands in bewilderment. "I don't see what all this—"

She cut in sharply, "You'd better listen to what I'm saying, because it's important. Are you planning some action on the part of the Protectors?"

At the mention of the lodge, Charles straightened and began to take notice. "Why, we've discussed it, yes. Just what I told you. You said yourself it hardly seemed politic to burn it down again. Mallott isn't exactly alone now. We thought if a few of us were to go there week after week, and cause disturbances, perhaps some minor damage—make it hard for him to keep afloat—"

"Is that all?"

"Well—" He looked perplexed. "Say, what is all this?"

Agnes settled back in her chair with finality. "Minor disturbances won't be enough, I'm afraid."

"But you said yourself just a day or two ago—"

"What I said then has no bearing on now. You must do something far more definite."

"Such as what?"

She leaned forward and spoke rapidly, outlining her plans.

The flush that had mottled Charles's face disappeared suddenly into a white mask of fear and disbelief.

"You mean—to—"

"Yes, of course," she snapped.

"I?" He was incredulous, floundering.

"You have ample political protection. You know that. And besides, no man has ever been convicted in the West for protecting his wife's honor."

"Wife! *My* wife? Agnes, I don't like this whole idea. I don't want to—" He started to rise from the chair, white and trembling.

"Sit down, Charles," Agnes interrupted tersely. "There are several things I want to explain to you."

Charles sank back in the chair and the dim flickering light made hollows in his sagging face as he stared in disbelief at the woman opposite him. Agnes pulled her robe together and sat erect, leaning toward him slightly.

"Here's what has happened—" she began.

CHAPTER X

ADAM SLOANE looked up from the faro board, glanced over the crowd and let his eyes linger for a moment in fascination over the effortless ease with which the bartenders poured whisky and collected gold, all in one motion. His long thin fingers tapped out a little rhythm on the top of the dealer's box in front of him. Then abruptly he returned his attention to the game.

"Two hundred dollar limit, gents. Two hundred is the limit. All bets in."

The faro dealer was seated directly beneath a life-size painted tiger on the wall that advertised the presence of a game beneath it. The faro board was on a wide table in front of him. His quick eyes, dark and deep-set in his thin face, saw every card at once and the derringer at his elbow served tacit warning on would-be sharpers. At one side was Charlie the case-keeper, smaller and more rotund but with the same darting eyes which moved back and forth from the board to the small wooden box whose buttons and rods he manipulated to keep track of the progress of the game. At the other side was the assistant who paid and collected the bets. Thirteen cards, all spades, were pasted on the board and piles of gold were scattered on it.

"Keep your eye on the turn of the card, gents. Every corner squared." The Reverend's wrist in its somber black coat flicked easily and brought out a card. There were exclamations from the players and another card was dealt.

"And jack wins the turn. The winner is jack—"

Smoke spiralled up, then hovered in a bluish haze just over the tops of heads. Voices were mingled into a monotone that was punctuated only occasionally by a high-pitched laugh or a shout from an unexpected winner. It would be noisier in an hour or two. There would be a few who would be thrown out. But the gambling tables and card games would grow quieter. This was the first enthusiasm of the evening, the after-theater crowd. Men were still greeting each other and starting up new games, placing bets with pockets still full. Later voices would become terser, more monosyllabic, faces would be paler in the smoky light, eyes would be more sharply riveted on cards or on the turn of the wheel, the spin of the dice cage. The whole place would acquire a subdued feeling but there would be no relaxation in it, only tense undercurrents and sharp-eyed watchfulness.

A voice, professionally smooth and enticing, lifted from the direction of the roulette table. "Look at the wheel. The wheel spins. Bets are in and now the wheel spins. Has to be red or black—"

The new Red Tent had opened its doors that night, unobtrusively, almost as if business had never been interrupted. Fifteen bartenders, sartorially elegant in black with crisply laundered aprons that reached to the floor, stood behind the long bar and dealt out drinks with easy efficiency. Near the bar were small tables where groups of two and four sat, drinking or enjoying the company of the Red Tent's girls. All the space to the right of the pillars was given over to gambling, and tables for faro, roulette, and a variety of other "chances" currently popular ranged from front to back. Some had elegantly gowned young women for croupieres. Others were served by taciturn gamblers, dressed like Sloane in somber black.

The place was lighted by glittering chandeliers and the dazzle of the lights glanced off handsomely frescoed walls whose every square inch was covered with "art work," consisting chiefly of representations of young women in various stages of enticing abandon. In back of the bar the tall mirrors rose grandly. A small crowd had already started clustering around the stage at the rear in anticipation of the first show of the evening. At a small table near the bar sat a blonde young woman selling coffee and confections. Her dark dress was prim and high about her neck and covered her arms to the wrists. She greeted the men decorously as they passed by but her eyes, looking up into theirs, held a note of suggestion and intrigue.

From his seat at the faro table Adam Sloane looked up again and again, his eyes continually moving over the crowd, watchful and alert, his hand moving with the regularity of long habit to the dealer's box, flicking the cards out easily and calling the game. At last his eyes came to rest in the direction of the bar and hesitated there for a moment, narrow and speculative. He got up easily from the table without looking at it.

"Finish out the game, Charlie," he ordered.

He slipped his hands in his pockets and began moving through the crowd, edging through groups of bettors and dodging between tables. At the foot of the center stairway he paused and glanced around once more, then took hold of the railing, swung himself around lightly and started up. Sounds mingled and grew less distinguishable, while the smoke seemed to thicken and rise with him. He did not look around when he reached the top, but continued down the balcony to the private stairway at the end.

Steve was just coming into the bedroom from the small adjoining dressing room when Sloane opened the door. He was barefooted, clad only in his trousers, and his hair was damp and uncombed. He waved a towel in welcome.

"Have a seat. Everything all right below?"

Sloane nodded and dropped into a chair near the door. "Fire certainly didn't hurt business any."

"Any of the stockholders present?" Steve went to the wardrobe, selected a shirt and put it on. He stood in front of the mirror buttoning it. His bare feet were apart, sunk into the deep pile of the green rug.

"I saw Keith earlier in the evening with some friends. Frank McCabe's down there. Andy's not around. Probably home. He'll be a father any minute."

"That's right. I'd forgotten."

"You're fixing up mighty elegant. I suppose that's for the purpose of making a grand entrance." Sloane turned his head a little and observed the fresh ruffled shirt. Steve finished tucking it in his trousers and selected a cravat, winding it carefully.

"Something like that. The crowd expects a certain amount of dramatics. Good business."

"Well, you're not under any illusions about it, anyway. Some of them take it seriously." Adam Sloane slid down in the chair and stretched his long legs out in front of him. "However, if I were you—" He stopped, not sure how to continue. As though sensing the uncertainty in his voice, Steve turned to him, his forehead drawn slightly in a frown.

"You'd what?"

Sloane took a deep breath. "Well, if I were you I wouldn't go down there tonight."

Charles Wickham stood with his back to the bar and leaned against it with both elbows, steadying the glass of whisky he held in one hand and looking up toward the balcony. When Adam Sloane emerged from the door at the end and started downstairs Charles's eyes followed his progress, watching him as he crossed the floor and returned to his place behind the faro table almost directly across from where Charles stood. Charles shifted his feet nervously.

"He's taking the devil's own time showing himself tonight."

At his elbow, George Stanley moved so that he too faced the balcony. "He never comes downstairs before twelve-thirty, they say."

Charles bolted his whisky and signalled to a man who was drinking a few feet away from them at the bar. William P. Leamer come over to them, his shiny head gleaming under the lights.

"Where are the rest of the men?" Charles asked.

Leamer jerked his head toward the lower end of the bar near the door. "Some of 'em are there. Ed and Harry went over to the faro table."

"I don't like them scattered around like that. Get them together over here and keep an eye on them." Leamer nodded and hurried off.

The blonde young woman at the table of coffee and confections a few feet away from him looked up and caught his eye, dipping her head provocatively and smiling. Damned stock-in-trade smile, he thought irritably. He looked back at the balcony.

Where had it all started, he wondered in a moment of sudden desperation and panic? How was he involved? He knew an instant of detachment from his present life. Treese, Agnes, the house on Eighth Street, he had no connection with any of them. He felt alone, swept along by a force that should have meant nothing to him but that was all at once shaping the course of his life. He had accepted Agnes's word about Treese having an affair with Mallott. Yet even in accepting it, he knew he did not believe it. It was quite inconceivable. His mind rejected it without a moment's hesitation. And now the only important thing was that he was here with the Protectors, that they knew of his errand and that they were expecting it of him and that whether he wanted to or not he must go through with it or lose everything he had gained in leadership and prestige. But even that loss—would it really matter? Would it be worth the risk? But there wasn't any risk. He repeated it to himself. He had fifteen armed men with him and those fifteen men represented several score more, and together they personified the political power of California. That was hardly a risky proposition. His thoughts whirled confusingly. Except that there was always the personal element—the fundamental thing that was between two men when they faced each other and that had nothing to do with politics or power; the intimate thing that was the individual core of each man. He had felt that tremendously personal conflict once before with Steve Mallott. Once in a smoky room on shipboard, a room loud with noise and laughter. A game of twenty-one and his wedding night. What had there been that night between them— what silent enmity that had lingered, far beneath the surface even when there was no outward provocation for it? The thought of Treese came to him again, and again he rejected it. But this time it stuck in his consciousness and he could not entirely forget it.

The call of the roulette wheel came to him dimly. "The bets are made—watch the turn of the wheel—" At his elbow George Stanley gave a start, then nudged him violently. Charles's eyes shot to the balcony.

He was never quite sure whether the room did quiet down in that instant or whether it was his own imagination, the magnifying of his heartbeat that seemed to throw the rest of the noise into still- ness. But it seemed to him that a hush came over the crowd so that the whir of the roulette wheel and the spin of the dice cage seemed to float in space, unconnected with their surroundings. Voices be- came a low monotone, and there was no laughter. He bolted his whisky quickly, spilling some on his chin. He reached up and wiped it away with his sleeve.

Steve was standing on the top step looking down, his hand on the railing, one leg relaxed as though halted in motion, ready to make the next step. He was standing quite erect, his shoulders squared. His shoulders were broad for the rest of him, Charles thought. The black of Steve's fitted frock coat was sharp against the white ruffles of his shirt. His face above them was pale with the lack of color that comes from long hours indoors and from seldom seeing the daylight. His eyes were black and alive with watchful- ness. The fingers of the hand that rested against the railing were slender, but there was something strong and alert in them, as though even to his fingertips he remained poised and ready. His eyes traveled over the crowd, sizing up the house. They showed nothing out of the ordinary. He started matter-of-factly down the stairs.

Charles glanced around the room. The games seemed to be going on as usual. He could hear the click of the ivory ball in the wheel, the rattle of the metal buttons, the snap of the cards. There was even a murmur of voices. There was movement around him; someone jostled against him. He heard the bartender behind him put a glass on the bar and fill it. Why then could he not rid himself of this strange feeling of suspension, of time caught and held upon the pivot of one moment? He watched as Steve reached the bottom of the stairs and began to edge his way through the crowd, greeting the customers, shaking hands here and there, smiling a small taciturn smile.

Steve did not walk directly toward him. Rather he crossed the room to the bar several feet away from Charles where the Protectors were ranged threateningly. He greeted the first man cordially.

"Hello, John. Have a drink." He continued down the line, eyeing each of them sharply but keeping his greetings casual. "Hello, Harry. What do you think of the new place? Hello, Ed. Can't get better whisky than that in San Francisco, can you? Glad to see you, George."

He stopped in front of Charles and for a moment Charles could feel the pounding of his heart filling his throat and making a dull ache in the back of his head.

"Hello, Wickham."

Charles could feel the eyes of the Protectors. He did not speak, but his head moved in what he judged was a slight nod.

"Enjoying yourself? What are you drinking? Tom, pour Mr. Wickham a drink. No, not that—some of the best. That's right." Steve took the glass himself and held it out to Charles. Charles did not trust the trembling of his hand and waited a long time before taking it. Then he drank it in one gulp, to have it over with. The whisky seemed to be taking no effect on him but it seared his throat and made the ache in his head increase. He did not want it. He half turned to put the glass down and then straightened himself, putting his right hand in the pocket of his coat and closing it around his gun. The metal, warm from his body, was comforting. He held it tightly.

Steve followed the motion with his eyes. He had opened his coat and stuck both hands in his pockets. He smiled chidingly and nodded toward the pocket where Charles's hand held the gun.

"Wish you boys wouldn't bring those things in here. Makes the place look like a saloon."

From somewhere behind Steve there was the sound of a woman's giggle. Charles reddened with anger, but still he did not move.

Steve nodded to include the whole building. "Pretty nice job on such short notice, don't you think? Not so easy to get lumber these days either. Prices are high." He shifted his weight to one leg in an attitude of casualness. "I'd hate to have any more accidents. Hell of an expense, rebuilding every three months."

Slowly Charles began to be aware of the thing he had dreaded, the personal conflict, the core of one man exposed and tangible facing the core of another man, the lines of combat clearly drawn. As always when he was faced with fundamentals Charles felt confused and inadequate. He watched the ease with which Steve stood before him and turned his own eyes aside before the curious directness that was in the other man's. He should have come here alone tonight, he thought rapidly. It was having the others here that was doing this to him. Knowing they were watching his every move, waiting for him to—

He felt a sudden impact as Steve's hand shot out and closed over the ruffles of his shirtfront, pulling him up short and holding him helpless.

"Take your men and get out of here." Steve's voice was still low but he spoke rapidly and with something close to passion. "You and your friends think you run Sacramento, don't you? Look around."

Now the silence was not imagined, but real, filling the blue-hazed room and hanging with a quiet threat over the bar where they stood. Across the room men were standing silent beside the gambling tables watching the scene at the bar. At the faro table Adam Sloane's thin hand closed firmly over the derringer. Behind the bar Charles could sense the stoppage of activity as the fifteen bartenders stopped serving whisky and drew suddenly to attention. Panic rose in him. The hand that clenched the gun was slippery with sweat. He wet his lips and started to speak, but at that moment Steve loosened his hold and walked away without another word. Charles felt himself go limp as though he had been held up bodily by the other man. He sagged heavily against the bar. And at that moment he heard William Leamer's voice, soft yet sneering.

"Great work, Charles."

He roused himself with effort. They were still watching, taking it all in, seeing his defeat. After this there would be nothing for him in Sacramento. He would be finished after tonight. And what else would there ever be for him? What would he do and where could he go? He saw Steve's figure retreating through the crowd toward the stairway, saw him seize the railing and swing easily up the first step. In desperation he drew the gun from his pocket.

He had a moment's odd premonition of what was coming, even before the shot rang out from the faro table. And all he could think of before the blinding pain that made him crumple and slip into blackness was that it hadn't mattered at all to him. None of this had mattered to him, and here he was getting killed over it.

Across the room, beneath the great yellow tiger, the Reverend

Adam Sloane put the derringer back on the table and riffled through a discarded deck of cards. His hands trembled slightly but his voice was smooth and professional as he called out a new game.

"Fresh deal starting here, gents. Place your bets, first turn coming up. Nothing but square corners in the Red Tent."

From the first step on the stairway Steve looked back and his eyes met Sloane's. For an instant he hesitated, his hand still on the railing. Then as though making an abrupt decision, he wheeled around and pushed through the crowd and out of the double doors at the front. Once in the night air he stood quite still, watching the reflection of lights along the row of plate glass windows, listening to the muted sounds of the night. He reached in his pocket, took out a cheroot and broke it. Then, lighting it, he walked to the street and hailed a passing hackney. The horse moved impatiently as he got in, then started up at the pressure of the reins. The hackney gathered speed as it moved away from the saloon and little whirls of dust rose around the wheels a moment later as it turned off sharply on Eighth Street.